Dedication	3
One	4
Two	23
Three	32
Four	49
Five	67
Six	72
Seven	91
Eight	107
Nine	134
Ten	140
Eleven	147
Twelve	154
Thirteen	168
Fourteen	191
Fifteen	206
Sixteen	214
Seventeen	226
Eighteen	250
Nineteen	287
Twenty	303
Twenty-One	324
Twenty-Two	334
About The Author	339
Copyright	340

TO WHOM IT MAY CONCERN
The Book of Letters

By

Lou Conboye-Taylor

To Whom It May Concern – *The Book of Letters*

Dedication

For Mark, Andrew & Matthew
Thank you for being you
X

To Whom It May Concern – *The Book of Letters*

One

MATTIE is standing on the pavement, having just left the post office, and for a moment stops to let the traffic breeze by, along with the thought of the recent turn of events. She'd not expected to find it. After all, it was such a long time ago. But she did find it. Worst of all were the emotions that came rushing back when she opened it up, flicked through its contents, and was drawn back into a past that had been left behind. Or at least she thought she had.

If only I wasn't so eager to please my husband, she recalls, thinking of her willingness to organise and tidy his office – a trait she considers herself highly adept with, but not when it comes to paperwork. Her mind springs unwittingly to high volumes of post that hits her doorstep on a daily basis – or letters from school – or her children's copious amounts of artwork on cheap school paper that the paint flakes from.

She shakes away the image along with the reminders it brings of her adolescence and her peculiar experience of working in an office. Then she's not long wondering how she'd even let her mind momentarily take her on that particular journey when she'd only popped out to post a letter and do a spot of shopping because she'd ran out of certain ingredients.

For a few moments longer, she stares blankly along the main road, unable to stop contemplating what she found and what it means to her.

A parent from school strolls past and bids Mattie a good morning. She returns a faint smile and just about manages a slight wave in acknowledgement of the man's good nature while still

To Whom It May Concern – *The Book of Letters*

daydreaming. Then another neighbour strides up.

"I'm so glad I've bumped into you. Oh, you look lovely by the way."

Mattie Barton's over-exuberant neighbour Christine appears out of nowhere and starts to prattle on about her son Henry's birthday party. He's about to turn six, and is Mattie's son Nathan's best friend. They are inseparable at school, both very giddy – to the dismay of their teacher, often landing the little boys into trouble.

"Very rustic looking," Christine adds subtly. "You carry it off so well. Anyway, I was going to pop over to your place later and chat about Henry's birthday party..." and she gives another of her pathetic sighs, as if her rich country life-style is such a struggle. "Brian is actually home this evening, which makes a change instead of jetting off around the world on so called business meetings."

Mattie looks down at her muddy boots and worn jeans with a bemused expression. Rather than ponder on the comment, she listens but struggles to get a word in edgeways, unable to even wish her neighbour good morning because she's so engrossed in her son's birthday demands.

"He wants the stickiest of chocolate cakes and you know how demanding a six year old can be. He even wants to help make it. Can you imagine the mess? The chaos?"

Mattie watches Christine fluster about the party but she's not paying that much attention because of what is on her mind. She adjusts her grip on a wicker basket, which contains baking ingredients, and they are heavy. It was left in her house by the previous owner, so she decided to make good use of it. Plus it was just like the one her grandmother used to have.

Her focus is now drawn to the deadening and numbing of her

To Whom It May Concern – *The Book of Letters*

fingers wrapped around the woven handle bearing the heavy load of purchases. They ache, but she pushes away the pain and is trying her best to engage in the conversation although it's dominated by the neighbour. Then the dozen eggs sitting at the top of the load start to slide sideways, distracting Mattie from Christine's saga. She just about manages to catch them by putting the basket on the pavement, and is relieved when the blood supply flows back to her extremities. Now standing up again, she gives Christine her full attention, aware that where Christine is concerned, it isn't going to be a quick conversation.

Knowing she's most likely going to be asked, Mattie offers, "Perhaps I can help." But the offer goes unheard, and she silently wishes that her friend would get to the point, because apart from making scones today she's planned a number of other things to deal with - even though they are far less exciting tasks than baking.

Five minutes pass and Christine has somehow bypassed the birthday cake question, now talking about her recent problems with the plumber, who she categorically states came highly recommended. "I'll never use him again! What a waste of time. And he's cost me a small fortune!"

Mattie offers a second time to bake the birthday cake, but she is cut off yet again by ongoing rants about tradesmen and upholsterers.

"...and it means I'll have to get new curtains. Again! Seeing as they too are water damaged. It's a fiasco. Can you imagine having a child's birthday party while this is going on? I have visions of sticky chocolate hand prints across my kitchen cupboards." The more Christine goes on, the more flustered she becomes and remains oblivious to Mattie's offer. "Did I mention that he wants a piñata? Do you know what one is?"

To Whom It May Concern – *The Book of Letters*

Mattie shakes her head.

"A multi-coloured donkey that they beat with a stick and sweets go flying all over the place? My house is hardly child-friendly, and with the decorators moving in soon to fix the mess the plumber has made, I don't know how I'll cope." The back of her hand comes to rest on her forehead as she heaves a huge sigh at the prospect of redecorating and having a dozen little boys charge uncontrollably around her house.

Mattie simply nods. At least Christine's incessant chatter is stopping her from dwelling on that thing she found by accident in her loft but when Christine's rant goes on too long Mattie can bear it no more. "Christine!" she shouts, stopping her friend mid-sentence. "How about I come over to your place and we bake a cake together? I've got the perfect recipe." Christine's shoulders visibly relax as she finally registers the offer – something she's been working up to asking for all along. "Henry and Nathan can sit in the corner and play with some dough if they want to. It'll be less messy."

"Thank you, Mattie," Christine says and embraces her. "You're an angel. See you Thursday. Let's have dinner, the four of us. I'll check Brian's diary." With that she waves then shoots off.

"I'll phone you later," Mattie manages to shout after her now less stressed friend, who disappears around the corner as quickly as she appeared.

Once again, standing alone outside the post office, Mattie feels like a small hurricane has swept through her and the small village, exhausted from the conversation. And her day has only just begun. Picking up the heavy basket once more and repositioning her fingers to spread the weight, she heads home laughing with mild hysteria at devilish thoughts of Christine's

To Whom It May Concern – *The Book of Letters*

ultra-modern and sleek white gloss units being smeared with chocolate and also considering whether to buy Henry a Piñata for his birthday.

After contemplating how Christine would truly cope with two six-year-old boys in her new glossy kitchen, Mattie admits it would be less traumatic for all concerned if they came over to her house. It's not as if her friendly neighbour's expensive granite worktops are child-friendly, and Mattie is certain Christine has yet to fathom how to use the new fancy built-in multiple cookers. Neither was she in any mood for socialising. She makes a mental note to phone Christine later.

She arrives home and places the basket on the front step, again narrowly catching the dozen eggs as they teeter for the second time on the verge of falling to the ground, then sighs again as the blood circulates to her fingertips. She puts the key in the door and nudges it with her shoulder, while clutching a loaf of bread. The door hits a pile of post delivered that morning, making it hard to open. *More rubbish, arrgh!* And cussing at the unwanted circulars, she dumps them unceremoniously on top of yesterday's post, which she's walked past and ignored countless times in the last twenty-four hours.

"Remember what you promised?"

A welcoming voice startles her. "Oh, I thought you'd left." Mattie turns away from her husband Jake so that he doesn't see the embarrassing look on her face – a look that suggests she's committed a crime.

"You just walked past my car, Mattie," and before he leaves the house, he wraps his arms around his wife for a quick kiss and grope of her backside.

Less than a week ago they discussed the 'state' of the office, the fact that it was 'mildly untidy' – Mattie's choice of words.

To Whom It May Concern – *The Book of Letters*

Her husband wanted to say it was a mess, an utter shambles, but instead he'd rolled his eyes, seeing as *he* wasn't the one who did the filing. She eventually gave in and agreed that she'd been dumping it for far too long. A compromise was reached and a promise made to deal with the post on the day it arrived at the house – not days or sometimes weeks later.

Presently, *only* two days' post sits waiting to be attended to.

Sitting at the bottom of the stairs staring at the pile of unopened letters, Mattie debates whether to bake the scones for the Church Choir Committee now, or actually tackle the paperwork as intended. *It reminds me of my old job*, Mattie protests a little more about the filing, making great attempts at ignoring the stack of unwanted papers.

Plus, a large stack of boxes in the kitchen are the main cause of her absent-mindedness – and the red book that sits at the top. Along with other rubbish she pulled from the loft only a few days ago.

Only when she looks out of the corner of her eye is she distracted, in fact frozen to her spot – there's a spider on the wall. She curses, telling it that on this occasion it's got away lightly, as it scurries back to the hole it came from. However, the distraction from the dreaded thoughts she's been having recently has worked, and a few minutes later, she's unloading the shopping basket, putting the kettle on, and retrieving the necessary scales and mixing bowls from the cupboard.

Now that she's made the conscious decision to bake rather than file, very quickly flour is measured and butter is weighed then diced, waiting to be rubbed in. It's not long before a tray of cherry scones is taken out of the oven and left to cool on a rack. The smell is gorgeous and sweet and Mattie is tempted to eat one of the allotted scones, but she knows how much Mr Honeywell,

To Whom It May Concern – *The Book of Letters*

the Chairman of the Church Choir Committee, loves them – *and* he has ordered a full batch, so Mattie refrains. When he placed his order for a dozen scones only the other day, the charming elderly chairman even told her they were the most delightful scones he'd ever tasted and more delicious than his wife's. "Your secret is safe with me, Mr Honeywell," she replied, and the elderly gentleman confirmed that with a wink of the eye.

As the hot, sweet aroma lingers in the air, Mattie muses at the fact that it has indeed taken the choir this long to put in an order, seeing as every other village committee has been eating out of her cupboards for years.

Mattie finally relaxes with a well-deserved cup of tea. The radio plays quietly in the background as she flicks through the pages of a glossy magazine. She tries her best at singing along with the song from the eighties, and even though she doesn't know many of the lyrics she makes them up as she goes along, trying at the same time to absorb an article on the latest dermabrasion techniques – distractedly contemplating the post all the while. She dog-ears the corner of that page as a reminder to show this to Christine when she comes over, knowing how her neighbour likes to spend a small fortune trying out the latest beauty treatments.

The post can wait. I did enough sorting out the other day! She tells herself and cranes her neck to glance at the post in the hallway before moving onto reading about twist-up lipsticks. But before she realises, she's back weighing up the pros and cons of filing and of the promise she made to Jake of keeping the office tidy. Plus the book she unexpectedly discovered is sitting nearby. Mattie keeps glancing at it, tempted once more to flick through its pages. But she would get that chance soon – having made the conscious decision to deal with it.

To Whom It May Concern – *The Book of Letters*

It's no good. A promise is a promise. Not wanting to look at the book anymore, she marches out of the kitchen, grabs the post, and goes upstairs to the office.

Up until a recently, the office filing system consisted of three plastic boxes in addition to what had been shoved in the loft since they moved in. One box was allocated for the children's things, one for house bills, etc., and the third for anything else that a home couldn't be found for. Then Mattie became the proud owner of a filing cabinet, after Jake dragged her around an enormous stationery store and subtly hinted and pointed to a wooden two-drawer cabinet that would complement the desk. Later that day, she set herself the task of writing on little white pieces of card that would be used as labels for several suspension files. It was a tedious task, and although she now wonders how long it will take before this too becomes unorganised, she gets on with opening the post.

Dropping into Jake's plush leather office chair, Mattie swivels in it a few times like the children do, then stops to admire how tidy the office still is a few days on since her initial sort-out. She admits to herself that she's impressed at the absence of piles of paper lying around and realises how much easier it actually is to deal with them on a daily basis and so much simpler to find important documents when necessary. She swiftly opens the envelopes she's clutching.

That one's car insurance... rubbish... give to Jake... more rubbish... there... done. Surprised at how little time it takes to open a handful of envelopes and take out the free circulars about artificial turf and block paving before deciding what's important and what's not, Mattie leaves two opened letters from the bank on Jake's desk and drops one of the letters into the car insurance folder. Filing never has been her forte. It reminds her of when she

To Whom It May Concern – *The Book of Letters*

worked for a marketing company – and in that moment, that most unscrupulous of persons is back in her head. *Go away, Guy!*

After taking a few more turns in the swivel chair, the joy of doing this simple task is washed away when she recalls the biggest problem of all – her recent discovery. She swivels in the chair, sighing and rubbing her temples, trying to push *him* away, but along with many others, he is back in her mind, filling her with worry and mixed emotions.

Why did I go into the loft! Mattie emits a heavy sigh – then resting her head on the back of the leather chair she takes a moment to think about the discovery just a few days ago.

It only took a day out of her normal schedule to clear out the loft – the second promise she'd made to her husband of recent. She'd muttered behind his back that particular morning before he left for work when he past a remark about this second promise. Without further procrastination, she marched down the hallway, tugged the lock to release the steps that slid down slowly, and then ventured into that part of the house that was rarely visited.

Mattie popped her head into the vast space above. Nine years had passed since they moved into the house, and her eyes scanned across nine years of goodness-knows-what stacked into boxes - and a number of bin liners too! The only boxes immediately recognisable were the ones clearly marked *Christmas Decorations*. They were strategically placed close to the access, and although those boxes were brought down once every year, she'd been shoving junk around them since the day they moved in.

Mattie recalled the mad panic of moving in two months before her daughter Amy was born. It had been a crazy eighteen months for a number of reasons. She'd fallen in love – she'd left her job

To Whom It May Concern – *The Book of Letters*

under traumatic and dramatic circumstances – and she'd fallen pregnant quicker than planned. Christmas was practically at their doorstep, and when she should've been hanging tinsel and mistletoe and baking mince pies, she was heavily pregnant instead and frantically packing their belongings as they made that very untimely last-minute move.

The house they were moving to had been owned by a dear sweet old little lady, Mrs Watson. Mattie had met her a few times before she died and thought how sprightly and independent she was for her years. She was saddened when her mother-in-law Gail told of Mrs Watson's death. Mattie was amazed at how the octogenarian had kept the house in such good condition, considering she'd been widowed and living alone for the last twenty years of her life. When Gail said the property was up for sale, Jake jumped at the chance of buying a house in the village he grew up in.

It was the kitchen Mattie had fallen in love with, especially the range cooker, although initially it proved a testing time baking cakes in the unconventional oven. Countless times sponges failed to rise, leaving a big dip in the middle, or cakes hardened and burned because the timing was wrong. But she got there in the end, and there didn't seem to be any complaints in the years that followed from the various committee groups – only praise for her delicious cakes.

Their new home was idyllic. She and her husband had this grand idea that Christmas would be spent around the new large oak dining table they had bought for the big farmhouse-style kitchen along with visions of ample amounts of home cooking and Christmas decorations strewn about the house. Mattie wanted to have a Christmas that she'd never experienced before. So as soon as the offer on the property was accepted, they bought

To Whom It May Concern – *The Book of Letters*

furniture and even managed to get some new curtains made - but then the months dragged on because Mrs Watson's greedy beneficiaries wanted more money. Panic ensued and stress levels increased, as furniture went into storage and belongings were packed hurriedly.

Mattie peeped inside one of the boxes marked Christmas Decorations and felt rather excited that in a few weeks, she would put them up. Then she chortled at how Jake and his father Ted had ventured out on Christmas Eve to buy their first real tree the day they moved in. It was late in the day, but Jake was determined to buy one, no matter the size. How on earth they managed to get the ten foot spruce – the last tree available – onto the top of Ted's car was beyond her imagination. It was nearly as wide as it was tall, the top had to be lobbed off so it wouldn't hit the ceiling, and its girth filled an entire corner of the lounge.

"You two can decorate it also," said Mattie as she pushed a box of decorations towards them with her foot. She was slumped into a chair feeling very uncomfortable from an expanding waistline.

"It looks beautiful," Mattie's mother-in-law told her husband and son when to her surprise they'd done an excellent job at hanging and draping the red and gold baubles and decorations. She turned to her husband, "maybe from now on Ted I should let you decorate our tree."

He coughed at the suggestion. "I think decorating one this big is enough for many Christmases to come."

Still balanced on the loft ladder, Mattie shone the torch over the contents and noticed that some of the boxes were indeed from when they'd moved in all those years ago, yet remained unpacked. The enormity of it weighed heavy on her and she let out a sigh. *Not only is the garage full of junk, the loft is full of it*

To Whom It May Concern – *The Book of Letters*

too, she cussed. The feeling was overwhelming, and as the light beamed into the recesses of the loft, she wished she'd never made that promise and ventured up there. It was unknown territory as far as she was concerned, it was just a space to put things in and hide stuff that she didn't want to tackle. It was easy to put box after box into the loft. However, she'd recently been drawn to the loft for some unknown reason, feeling compelled to tackle the hoards of rubbish. Plus she was not about to renege on a promise.

She lifted herself into the only available free space, perched on her knees, and pulled a box towards herself. *Here goes!*

There were boxes of varying sizes along with bags filled with old clothes and unwanted bedding from when she lived in a flat she shared with Claire, her dearest friend. Amongst the nine years of rubbish and other effects she'd shoved into any available space, Mattie also eyed the numerous boxes of paperwork that she'd failed to deal with and had simply hidden them out of sight to avoid them. She spied unwanted and flattened cardboard boxes – one that housed the flat screen TV plus two empty laptop boxes. *Why on earth has Jake kept these? We don't even own those laptops anymore!* Another heavy sigh was heaved at having ignored the problem, but she continued rummaging through boxes, one of which contained old household appliances. A handheld blender without a plug was tossed to one side – not that she understood why the plug was missing in the first place – and the empty box was dropped through the loft access onto the landing below. Continuing to assess what to keep and what to throw away, Mattie cursed and swore through the entire process, but she couldn't decide whether she was more disgruntled at Jake for storing empty boxes or at herself for storing boxes full of junk and paper.

To Whom It May Concern – *The Book of Letters*

So that's where the sandwich maker went. The torch light identified a box of wedding presents, which she presumed had gone missing in transit the day they moved in. But not wanting to dwell on that, Mattie set to finally unwrapping the wedding presents, reading the tags even though the ink had faded. She then split the contents into two piles deciding what would be useful and should be kept.

It took her the best part of the afternoon to bring out any unwanted items and decide what to do with things that she'd forgotten they owned, and as she climbed the loft ladders yet again, the ache in her calves reminded her of the hard work and how she desperately wanted a shower to wash away the dust and dirt that had settled in her hair.

The tedious task neared its end when Mattie sat down, hopefully for the last time, stretching out her legs in the free space to ease the onset of a cramp. It was a large and useful space, she pondered, and within seconds, she imagined a child's playroom with fitted cupboards along one wall. With some careful planning and restructuring of some roof beams, an adult would be able to stand up straight in this space.

The house had remained quiet that afternoon, other than the noise Mattie made as she casually discarded unwanted items onto the landing below.

"Mattie, I'm home! Whoa! Watch out, honey," Jake shouted as a plastic travel iron narrowly missed him. A dirty face appeared with an apologetic look. He climbed a few steps of the ladder and placed a kiss on the bridge of her nose.

"Finally doing this I see?"

"Don't ask. I'm tired, hot, and sweaty. Anyway, why are you home early?"

"Meeting cancelled so I thought I'd work from home. I'd just

To Whom It May Concern – *The Book of Letters*

pulled into the car park when my secretary called, so I dropped by for ten minutes, had a quick chat with Jackson, and decided to spend the rest of the day at home. I thought I'd pick the kids up from school." He retreated down the ladder as Mattie went on to explain that Nathan was going to Christine's while Amy was also going to a friend's house for tea.

There were just a few more items to move, and while directing the torch light towards the far end of the loft just to make sure she'd accounted for everything, she caught sight of a particular cardboard box. It was tucked away in the eaves. With the last bit of energy she had, Mattie crawled towards it. In the dimness of the light, the bold black letters she'd written on the side were still clearly visible. MUM'S THINGS. Mattie dragged the box towards the light beaming up from the hallway.

"I can't believe it. Jake!" she shouted, "Jake, come quickly, you'll never guess what I've found."

The brown tape that had been used to keep the lid firmly closed was dry and brittle and came off easily. She opened up the old cardboard box and peered inside.

The first items Mattie came across were her Grandfather Barton's military service medals, and she wondered why she'd ever kept them, for they still meant nothing to her. Then she cast her eyes upon her Grandmother Barton's handwritten book of cake recipes. The binder was practically threadbare, and with a gentle hand, Mattie opened the front cover. A few loose leaves of paper dropped out from having been turned over so many times. She picked them up and took a quick glance at a recipe for a Madeira cake and the handwritten notes in the margins where the recipe had been amended and perfected. And while she scanned through other random recipes which she knew by heart, she was suddenly filled with joy and fond memories at the many hours

To Whom It May Concern – *The Book of Letters*

she had spent baking during her childhood in her grandmother's kitchen. The book was old and tattered, but feeling overwhelmed to have it back in her possession, she called out to her husband again, wanting him to see the discovery.

There were some photo albums, and underneath them, a few large photo frames that once sat on a sideboard in her grandparent's dining room. Below them was a brown envelope. Even though she took a look inside as if she didn't know what it contained, the pain she had felt upon her mother's death hit hard when she peered in and saw a stack of birth and death certificates. She told herself to get a grip, and when she heard Jake shout back asking what she wanted, it pulled her up sharp and stopped the tears from flowing.

Mattie knew what sat at the bottom of the cardboard box. She remembered exactly in what order she had packed it. She could even remember the striped towel she'd used to wrap around the item to stop it from getting knocked around during the move from the city to the country even though that item was secure at the bottom of the cardboard box. And while it was of no specific financial value, it was the only item that had belonged to her mother Josie Barton and it meant the world to Mattie. There was no holding back. The tears sprung to her eyes at thoughts of the many times she had sat and played with this little treasure chest as a child. With a careful hand, she lifted her mother's wooden jewellery box out of the cardboard box.

Thinking she would never see the wooden jellery box again, she'd decided many years ago to stop thinking about it because it brought back too many memories, especially the death of her mother. In a flash, the overwhelming memories of her childhood came flooding back. She'd cursed at her husband for losing the box of items when they'd moved out of London, having given

To Whom It May Concern – *The Book of Letters*

him strict instructions to take *this* particular one in the car. Then when he said he thought it went in the removal van, and it didn't appear, she'd cursed again at the removal company. The depot manager had given his reassurances that the van was empty when it returned to the depot. She had even called weeks later, but there was still no sign of the box.

She sat there quietly with the jewellery box resting on her lap trying to recall happy thoughts of her mother, even though they were tinged with such sadness. Then Jake finally popped his head into the loft space. When he saw it, he realised instantly what the shouting was about. His wife looked back at him with tears pricking her eyes, about ready to trickle down her face.

"Don't say a single word about it being here all the time and if I'd looked properly I would've found it" she stammered, as the fight to hold back the tears tightened her throat.

He smiled, said nothing, then reached up, gave her another kiss on her lips, and smudged away some of the tears that escaped and she was trying to smile through. As he made his way back down the hallway, he muttered something about owing him big time because he'd always maintained his innocence in the loss of this particular box, to which she responded light-heartedly, "Maybe later."

Mattie's impatience got the better of her. Eager to see it and its ornate detail in the light of her bedroom, she hurried there, quickly wiped her hands and face with a cold, damp flannel, and then sat crossed-legged on the floor with the heavy wooden jewellery box by her feet.

Time had passed, but she recalled her mother's words, telling her as a little girl to be careful and not to trap her fingers in the jewellery box when she'd asked permission to play with it. "Don't tell your grandparents. Remember, it's our little secret,"

To Whom It May Concern – *The Book of Letters*

her mother would say – for a fleeting moment, Mattie was transported back to her childhood and the happy times she had had with her mother, wishing she could have them back.

She carefully lifted the lid and the delicate ballerina sprung into her dance. A few seconds remained in her winder before the dancing and music stopped. She was quickly wound up and continued spiralling around, and although some paint on her dress appeared flaky, she still shimmered against the inlaid glass. *She's as pretty as I remember*, reminisced Mattie.

The box contained a few dull pieces of jewellery, but long gone were the cheap bangles she used to play with while prancing around her mother's bedroom, pretending to be the ballerina, and drifting off into her own fantasy world. She hadn't held on to that dream for long. The reality of her life had somehow quashed it. She looked through the various handcrafted drawers, unique in their style and handmade just for her mother. Nestled in one small compartment was a cameo brooch and gold hat pin that Grandmother Barton used to wear every Sunday when she went to church, plus her thin gold wedding band covered in tiny little scratches from the many years she wore it. It never left her hand even when she baked bread and made pastry, although bits of dough would stick underneath it, much to Mattie's amusement. Then, she pulled open another drawer and came across a gold ring containing a small diamond set into tiny gold claws. She put it on, twiddled with it, held up her hand, and saw a faint glimmer. Next to the ring was a gold locket. It was newer than the other pieces of jewellery. Without hesitation, Mattie put it around her neck and grasped it, holding it close to her chest, thankful to be wearing it once again. The ring was in need of a good cleaning along with the other small pieces, but as she admired it on her finger, happy to have it back in her possession, she remembered the undesirable circumstances that tainted the gifting of this to her mother – so she put it back.

The mixed emotions were strong and unexpected. She certainly never thought she'd find the jewellery box again, never mind the other items.

Losing the jewellery box had been too much to bear at the time because of what it contained. A few gold trinkets would have meant nothing to anyone else – they were of little value – but as far as Mattie was concerned, the sentiment they carried was invaluable. A tear fell on the box, which she quickly wiped away.

Still sitting cross-legged on the carpet, going through a few other items that were worthless, more images of her life back then flashed by unexpectedly. Thoughts of her controlling grandfather and how he treated Mattie's mother came to the forefront, and with them, a surge of intense feelings of hatred for him. She thought of the lonely existence her mother led after being forced to bear shame for getting pregnant out of wedlock. Unable to control the memories of her mother's untimely death and of the anxiety and anguish she'd held on to for far too long, Mattie gulped back the tears and closed the lid on the past.

She gave the box a final wipe to clear away any residue of dust and dirt, and as she was about to lower it into the bottom of her own wardrobe – just like her mother used to do when Mattie was little – her fingers touched upon two small brass buttons on either side the box. *I'd almost forgotten about this.* Pressing the two buttons, the secret drawer she had forgotten about sprung open, and when she saw a red leather book sat snugly in the compartment, Mattie froze in disbelief.

The smooth leather-bound book remained untouched. Unable to read the truthful words she had once written, she snapped the compartment shut, put the box away, and closed the wardrobe

To Whom It May Concern – *The Book of Letters*

door so it was out of sight from others, just as her mother did when it belonged to her. This beautiful box was their little secret as was the red leather book her secret.

To Whom It May Concern – *The Book of Letters*

Two

IT'S Saturday morning. The stack of boxes containing unwanted papers from the loft, one in fact full of receipts still leans precariously against the kitchen wall, waiting to be taken outside. They'd been there for a week while Mattie decided the quickest way to destroy the papers – some of which were confidential. Never mind the matter of the red leather-bound book.

A decision made that morning in haste that the only way to get rid of the rubbish quickly is to burn it was made - and she is preparing to spend Saturday evening doing just that. The red book sits on top of the pile. It was hard enough for her to take it out of the jewellery box after having vowed not to read the contents. Now, she glances at it each time she passes it and feels the temptation to have a peek again at what she wrote.

A tray of cherry scones was delivered to Mr Honeywell, Tuesday evening. Christine also breezed in and out with Henry as planned after school on Thursday, and as predicted, along with Nathan, the two little boys were content playing with some dough for a short while. 'No mess!' her friend had ordered, wondering how Mattie managed to have such control in the kitchen while two little boys squished the dough between their tiny little fingers. Meanwhile, Christine calmly sipped white wine and read snippets from a magazine, at the same time, recounting the water damage story again. In addition to that, various trips were made over the last few days to the local tip and charity shops to get rid of unwanted items. Yet the book and its contents remain in the back of her mind, constantly nagging her but Mattie still resists

To Whom It May Concern – *The Book of Letters*

the urge to take a look when she again walks past it, exiting the kitchen to go upstairs.

Mattie hears Amy playing with a new set of beaded jewellery in her room, while Nathan is helping his dad to clear out the chimenea and chop up some firewood for tonight. In the privacy of her bedroom, Mattie takes the opportunity to have a proper look at the old photo albums, plus debate what to do with her grandfather's war memorabilia. Again saying to herself, *I've spent far too many years trying to come to terms with the way he treated me and my mother.*

She opens one of the small albums, and a black and white picture of a group of young teenagers falls out. It's rough around the edges from being thumbed too many times. Creases cut through the image, distorting some of the faces. However, she instinctively recognises her mother sitting next to a young boy on a beach. Behind them, two other young men are kicking a football, unaware that a photo is being taken. Mattie spends a few moments looking down at the faces of the young group, as she had done many times before they were *misplaced*, wondering what the boy sitting next to her mother now looks like, and feeling sorry for her Uncle Patrick – one of the boys playing football.

She looks at photos of her grandparents standing upright, looking starched with their arms at their sides – expressionless faces in the monochrome photographs, also true of the other people they were pictured with. Not that she knew them. *Did no one ever smile in those days?* She wonders. Then, she turns to another handful of photos of her grandparents, when they were young. Some were taken outside a church and others in places she doesn't recognise. On close inspection, she notices that her grandfather is wearing the same suit he wore on most important

To Whom It May Concern – *The Book of Letters*

occasions and he's standing tall and proud. The suit was just like the ones she saw not long after his death when she helped her grandmother empty his wardrobe and at that time she thought how few clothes he actually owned. Amongst other bare essentials there were three suits, all very similar at a glance. She helped pack them in to plastic bags and as she neatly folded the clothes she again probed her grandmother for more information to help her comprehend the man that he was. But all Mattie got considering she'd had a heart-to-heart chat with Grandmother Barton only a few days before was, "You know how he was." Her thoughts linger on Grandfather Barton a while longer until she realises that negativity has invaded her. It makes her cross. She slams the photo album shut and curses for losing the control she thought she had once obtained.

"Mummy, who are those people?" Amy catches her off guard.

"Just some old photos, sweetheart."

Her daughter's blue eyes beam, and in that moment, it's as if Mattie's mother is looking back at her. Mattie instinctively opens up the album and finds a photograph of her mother when she was a young girl, and the similarity dawns upon her for the first time. The loss of her mother is intensified as she looks into her daughters eyes, but the regret she has felt over the years – that her mother never got to see her grandchildren – is pushed back so that Amy cannot she her mother's sadness. She takes a moment, pats the carpet and invites Amy to sit next to her. The child does and copies her mother's cross-legged pose.

"This is a photo of my mother," Mattie says and points to a black and white one.

"Why don't you talk about her?"

Mattie raises her eyebrows in amazement, not expecting her little daughter to ask her this question. She forces back the tears.

To Whom It May Concern – *The Book of Letters*

It's because they are all dead, Mattie wants to say, but she holds herself back, knowing that it is pointless. She wants to tell her little girl the truth. She wants to tell her about her own unhappy childhood. Instead, she strokes her daughter's long, blonde, silky hair, and replies, "Well, now that I've found these photos, I can tell you all about them."

"And who's that boy?" Amy asks pointing to another photo.

"That young man is my Uncle Patrick." She gulps then in a low whisper adds, "Unfortunately, he died when he was young."

The remark does not deter the young girl, and she points to another, eager to know who they are. "Who's that?"

Mattie almost chokes, and before she can say, "That's my father," Amy has spotted the jewellery box in the wardrobe and is soon looking on in awe at the twirling ballerina.

Jake, along with his little helper, starts taking the precariously stacked boxes outside. Mattie, who is busily making lunch, observes him pick up the red leather book from one of the opened boxes, hold it for a few seconds perhaps pondering what it is before placing it on the kitchen work surface. She wonders what he's up to and cusses again. *Whatever possessed me to hide it in the first place?* She wishes she'd got rid of it years ago, as she had intended, and cusses again at her own stupidity.

"I'm burning that first," she attempts to mumble discreetly, hoping Jake doesn't hear her as the door closes behind him. She marches out of the kitchen and down the hallway, putting distance between herself and the book. So far, she has refrained from reading much in detail, just a quick flick through when she found it which was enough to send her heart racing just over a week ago, but a deep desire has been burning inside of her to pick it up. Mattie stops part way down the hall. *Don't go there, Mattie.*

To Whom It May Concern – *The Book of Letters*

Don't pick it up. Her inner voice tells her that the passing of time has healed her wounds, and that it no longer matters. *You dealt with that part of your life a long time ago. You spent a fortune on therapy for Heaven's sake. Surely you'll be okay if you simply take a peep.* The devil in her head pushes her to read it. *What harm can you come to? It's only a bunch of words! You know you want to read it? Go on, read it!* Rooted to the spot, she begins to fear how opening that book and reading its contents will make her feel. However, regardless of the mind games, she turns around and goes in the only direction her legs will take her - into the kitchen.

She grabs it and briskly flicks through pages, not stopping on any particular one, although she glances at the odd name and snippets of sentences. Mattie's heart is sent racing once more as she catches glimpses of the inked pages, but unable to take any of it in, she slams it back on the kitchen surface and paces the room, cursing the damn book and herself for keeping it.

Amy still plays upstairs while Nathan happily helps his father outside, stacking the kindling for the fire. Temptation soars, pushing Mattie to take another look. *You know you want to.* The devil in her head convinces her, and with little hesitation, she picks it up again and randomly opens it. Her eyes fall upon bits of handwritten letters, capturing sentences from one, then from another – words and sentences are jumping off the pages in front of her. Each part she reads makes her swell inside with feelings that she once put to rest, or at least she thought she had. Now her own Pandora's Box is open, and the hurt contained in the letters hurtles back at Mattie at an incomparable speed.

"Hey honey, how's it going?" Jake stands in the doorway taking off his wellington boots, now that he has taken all the boxes outside, while Nathan sits on the floor near him, trying in

To Whom It May Concern – *The Book of Letters*

vain to pull his blue Thomas the Tank Engine boots off. Mattie does not expect the sudden interruption and quickly sniffles away her tears. She calms down and kneels to help her little boy, beaming at his cute face. "Let Mummy do that," she offers and pulls his boots off, taking his socks with them. He giggles as his feet are tickled and his damp sweaty socks are waved in front of his nose. It's the same infectious laugh her husband has.

Then she watches her husband dump his dirty socks next to his boots and walk barefoot across the cold tiled kitchen floor to grab a beer from the fridge. Jake flicks the top off the beer bottle and takes a long gulp. "It's going to be a cold night, Mattie. I'm not quite sure why you insist on burning this lot tonight. You know, the rubbish can be burnt any day of the week, or it can be taken to the recycling centre." Jake walks over to her. A lump has formed in Mattie's throat, making it difficult to reply. She knows that if he asks her if everything is all right, she will probably burst into tears. He observes his wife's silence, puts down the beer, and cocks his head to one side giving her *that* look – the one that says, 'Talk to me'.

"Here Nathan, take this and one for your sister and go and play in your room." Mattie hands her son two double chocolate chip cookies, then calls after him to put on some clean socks too, as he bounces up the stairs.

"Remember when I met you I was seeing a therapist called Dr Banbury?" Moving around the kitchen, she fills the kettle to make coffee in an attempt to act like nothing is wrong, all the while trying her best to avoid eye contact with her husband.

"Yes, her name was Joan, wasn't it?"

"Yes. Lovely lady. Well, you remember how she got me to write letters addressed to people about how they made me feel?"

"Yeah, you wrote plenty to Guy. And what about that school

To Whom It May Concern – *The Book of Letters*

bully you told me about?"

Sadie!

The book has brought back plenty of unwanted memories about her grandfather and Guy, and all the other people who made her life miserable. Since finding it, Mattie has struggled to get those thoughts out of her head. She fetches the milk from the fridge and takes a cup from the cupboard.

"I've found the book of letters." She says it casually, trying not to let Jake hear the break in her voice as she tries to maintain her composure while pouring the steaming hot water into the cup.

"Oh," he simply comments.

The mere mention of the book makes her hands tremble and milk spills onto the work surface. "Damn it!"

Jake takes the bottle from her hands. "I didn't realise I still had it. It was hidden in the jewellery box and I started to flick through the pages and..." Mattie says.

Her husband eyes the red book and walks over to pick it up. "This is it? You know, you never did show me the letters."

"But I told you everything." Mattie instinctively feels the urge to snatch it from his hands in case he looks through it, afraid of what he'll think of her. But she hesitates, letting her husband hold on to the book as she tries to look on nonchalantly. "Well, so much was going on then. And to be honest, I didn't think it mattered anymore."

When Mattie started dating Jake, she was already in therapy and had opened up to him, bared her soul, and talked about the emotional baggage she was carrying. He in return had listened, was empathetic, he gave her a shoulder to cry on and she'd let go. Or so she thought.

"Do you want to read them?"

She wants him to say 'no', because she can't see the point in

To Whom It May Concern – *The Book of Letters*

Jake seeing the words she had churned out, and thinks it pointless to let him read about the pain she endured in the past. It was from a decade ago, after all, and it was bad enough that she dared to flick through the book and read the reality of her younger years herself. Mattie hesitates, awaiting his reply, in case he says 'yes', then casually saunters past him, slipping the book from his hands.

Jake moves in close from behind and envelopes her waist with his strong arms, and begins kissing her gently on the neck. Feeling safe in his arms, Mattie relaxes back into him and sighs. "I thought I'd gotten rid of it, but seeing it has reminded me about all those sad events in my life I wrote about."

"Do you want to talk about it?" Jake asks concerned.

Mattie did nothing but talk about it when they first met. Along with the many valuable therapy sessions that had helped immensely coupled with the love Jake showed towards her - somehow it melted away the anguish she was holding on to. She didn't want to talk about it again. The thought of dredging up the past was harmful, let alone what actually happened and tells Jake nothing can be gained from talking about it.

Even though he's been working outside, Mattie can still smell the fresh Italian cologne that lingers on Jake's skin. She inhales his scent, savouring every moment of their closeness, as he plants delicate kisses down the nape of her neck. "Seeing some of the things that I wrote about is making me feel..." The distraction has her tingling all over and she struggles to complete the sentence. "...hmmm, that's nice," and he continues with the string of delicate kisses. "I don't feel as anxious anymore."

Jake turns her around to face him. "Anxious?" Pulling her closer, his lips meet hers, and Mattie is drawn into a long kiss. He pushes his hips into hers against the kitchen cupboard and whispers, "I can take your anxiety away."

To Whom It May Concern – *The Book of Letters*

Jake reaches for the buttons on her thick cotton shirt. The top two are undone within seconds, exposing more of the nape of her neck and collar bone for him to run his soft lips over. She wants him to take her there and then. His hand slips under her blouse, and she winces at his cool touch on her warm back.

"The children," she pants heavily and pulls away.

To Whom It May Concern – *The Book of Letters*

Three

THE afternoon passes quickly, and while Amy and Nathan are settling down for the evening, Mattie starts preparing the chimenea by throwing in some dried branches and homemade firelighters, which her father-in-law once showed her how to make from newspaper.

It was the day they moved into this house and it was bitterly cold, and while his wife supplied them with regular hot drinks and turkey sandwiches, Ted set himself to making a fire. This was all new to Mattie, because she'd only ever been used to a gas fire at her grandparent's home with the exception of her husband's London apartment, which had a combined heating and air-conditioning unit.

While Jake gave out instructions to the removal people about what went where, Mattie, albeit heavily pregnant, knelt on the floor next to Ted in front of the large stone hearth and learnt how to build a real fire for the first time.

Now, just like that first time, she sits outside, about to light the chimenea with her own homemade firelighters. Foolishly, she's chosen to sit on a small wooden stool that is high enough for her to perch on without feeling like her long legs and knees are tucked under her chin, but after sitting for only five minutes, she regrets her choice of seat. Then before she starts to burn a single piece of paper, she hears a disagreement coming from the house about a DVD, after Amy and Nathan had already chosen to watch Toy Story 3. Mattie wants to go back in and sort it out as the sound of Nathan's voice builds up into one of his tantrums. But she has a task at hand, and so, she reluctantly stays in her seat and

To Whom It May Concern – *The Book of Letters*

allows their father to deal with it. Thankfully, the disagreement turns into giggles, and Mattie is relieved at that little traumatic incident ending quickly, very well aware of what Nathan can be like when he wants his own way. She hears Jake doing what sounds like his monster impressions, and from the high-pitched squeals, it appears daddy has caught his little boy.

She moves around trying to get comfortable on the stool, but her bulky boots won't allow her feet to tuck under. *I really haven't thought this through properly. I should've taken up Jake's offer to get me one of the garden chairs from the garage. Maybe later*, she thinks. To ease the discomfort, Mattie reaches for the cushion she grabbed from one of the kitchen chairs on her way out and shoves it under her bottom.

She places three intricate folded and twisted firelighters on a pile of kindling and sets alight a piece of cardboard. Soon, the inside of the wood burner is engulfed in flames. There's already a nip in the air. She tucks her blonde hair into her jacket, turns up its quilted collar, and pulls the zip right to the top to keep her neck warm.

The warmth from the fire is instantaneous, but thinking about tonight and the decision she came to earlier after willingly talking it over with Jake, a chill runs down her spine. To ease the discomfort, she clenches the silly pink woolly hat stuffed in a pocket that her children insisted she bring outside. "Mummy looks silly in piggy ears," she said to Nathan, but when his bottom lip quivered on the verge of tears, Mattie had no choice but to promise to wear it should it get cold – along with the equally silly matching gloves.

The task ahead appears to be daunting. The euphoric bubble she's been living in these past ten years or so has popped, and once again, she feels at an emotional low knowing that to delve in

To Whom It May Concern – *The Book of Letters*

to her harrowing past will bring with it a wave of emotions. She squeezes the woolly hat harder, trying to get as much comfort as possible before facing the contents of the red leather book.

There's only one place to start – the beginning. She drags the first box forward, containing receipts. She grabs a handful of the small bits of paper and throws them into the heart of the chimenea. The thin synthetic papers quickly catch fire, and with a whoosh, are soon incinerated. Another handful is chucked in, then another. She watches them shrivel in the flames. One falls to the floor –she quickly grabs it, taking a look at the purchase. *Ah, the costly Ugg boots.* The ones she bought when Christine dragged her into a new boutique shop and insisted Mattie tried on, the same ones she's enjoying how comfortable and cosy they are at doing their job by keeping her feet warm on this chilly night. *It's a good thing Jake doesn't know how much these cost*, she muses, then decides that if Jake was to say something about them, she'd merely reply, 'Oh these old things? I've had them for ages,' in the hope he'd be fooled. At this, an ember spits out of the fire landing near her feet, making her quickly shuffle the stool back not wanting to get the newly acquired item burnt or dirty just yet.

But Jake finding out how much these boots cost is the least of her worries tonight. *Did they really cost me two hundred pounds? Ouch! He knows I'm worth it, though.* And when she thinks how she'll show her gratitude if he discovers their price, a broad smile lights up her face.

"Honey, would you like a hot drink?" Jake shouts from the kitchen doorstep. His offer hastens her process of burning the receipts from other miscellaneous purchases.

"Yes, darling, that'd be lovely." *Phew!* The panic recedes as she watches them reduce to ash within seconds.

To Whom It May Concern – *The Book of Letters*

The temperature is rapidly falling as the sun retreats below a line of trees that border the bottom end of the garden. Mattie considers how long she will last before donning the piggy hat and gloves. Autumn has arrived early this year, bringing with it cool, crisp mornings, but high winds. The trees are practically stripped of their leaves, and while it's barely the middle of October, a blanket of brown and golden leaves keeps snaking from one side of the garden to the other when the wind picks up. Jake keeps telling her that getting the leaf blower out and at least blow them in the direction of the compost heap is on 'tomorrow's to-do list'. But she knows she'll probably end up doing it herself, seeing as he's so busy with work. Mattie makes a mental note to add it below the entry to make a sticky toffee pudding for the school head teacher on her own endless to-do list.

Earlier in the week, a welcoming weather front swept across the south of England, adding a last-minute blast of warmth before winter sets in with its long, dark nights - such as today. The day started off relatively mild, and the sun glistened and provided a few hours of autumnal heat. But Mattie knows that with this clear sky above her, it's going to be a chilly evening, just as Jake predicted. As the sky begins to darken, the stars become more noticeable.

More receipts are scrunched and tossed into the blazing fire, keeping the flames roaring and giving Mattie the much-needed warmth. It is fun seeing the whoosh of flames as the fire engulfs the small pieces of shiny paper – to see them shrivel and burn, and to listen to the kindling crackle under the intense heat. It doesn't take long for the fire to build up, and there's plenty of small dried, broken branches and bits of wood to keep this fire going into the early hours of the morning if need be.

Mattie looks at her watch and realises that only an hour has

To Whom It May Concern – *The Book of Letters*

passed. She is pleased with the progress so far, as she has worked through two boxes of mostly old receipts and one containing very old utility bills, but a sideways glance at the remaining stack of boxes drop her spirits, when she sees the amount still to work through. She sighs heavily at the thankless task and chastises herself out loud for the millionth time this week, promising to never let it get this bad ever again.

Mattie drags the boxes closer. Not only did she stuff every nook and cranny of the loft, she knew that the garage was equally filled with junk and unwanted or useless items. Mattie makes another mental note to hire a skip and attend to *that* thankless task next. Until earlier this week, she considered herself as being organised – it was the way Mattie was brought up or was 'told to be'. It was drummed into her from an early age to put things back where they came from. She recollects her grandfather's words, 'Everything has a place and everything should be in its place,' or 'Martha! Stop leaving your school bag at the foot of the stairs,' and 'Martha, put your shoes away,' amongst other things. She shakes her head to stop the words from her past and the tone of voice he used from ringing in her ears. But just thinking about him makes her shudder.

Clearing out the loft and being surrounded by the stacks of paper makes her realise why she has ignored dealing with it for so long. As much as she has convinced Jake and promised that she will deal with the post when it arrives rather than weeks later, or sometimes never, she realises that she still has an intense dislike towards it and admits that this dislike is never going to change – regardless of how many two-drawer filing cabinets he buys. Then Mattie has a flashback to a neat pile of school books on a shelf in her dull and dreary bedroom, stacked just as grandfather insisted - a desk at work with a stack of glossy reports - printing, copying,

To Whom It May Concern – *The Book of Letters*

filing, shredding - endless and mindless weekly tasks she came to detest, along with her boss.

Another box is slid towards the wood burner, the contents of which are soon burnt, all-the-while Mattie is going through this motion she glances at the red leather book, knowing full well that she will soon be dealing with it.

Realising that the offer of her hot drink has still not materialised, Mattie reaches for the glass of red wine she brought out after dinner and takes a sip. The taste is now sharp from the cool air and regardless of the fact that it has lost all trace of the blend of oak and berries, she's not prepared to let it go to waste. This time, she takes a much bigger gulp to quell the rising trepidation. It's still there – the red leather book – resting on the wrought iron table next to her. Seeing it sends another chill through her bones. She drinks more wine, which causes a slight buzz in her head and dulls her senses. She's grateful for this small mercy as she gets closer to tonight's real task.

Finally, the last box containing a mix of old insurance and policy documents and old Christmas and birthday cards is hastily burnt, and while she tears the pages in half and scrunches them so that they burn quicker, she can hear muted voices of her children coming from the house. Then that last cardboard box is finally emptied, and with a few hard tugs to tear the cardboard, that too is thrown into the chimenea. Drinking the wine dregs, she glances at the book and says, "It's your turn next!"

It's time to deal with the past – her past. Mattie begrudgingly picks up the book, holds it in her hands, and for a moment, ponders over whether she should simply throw it in the fire now. *It would be easier after all. Why go back to the past? What purpose does it serve?* Plus Mattie acknowledges that if her friend Claire knew what she was up to, she'd rip it from her

To Whom It May Concern – *The Book of Letters*

hands and destroy it in an instant. Jake had also asked his wife to consider doing the same but they'd discussed it as Mattie convinced her husband that this was the right thing to do. Now doubt was setting in.

Thinking about the last few days and how she has come to be sitting outside burning paper on a cold night – when she could be inside her warm home, snuggled on the sofa with her husband and children – she is still flummoxed about *why* she decided to venture into the loft. It certainly wasn't the thought of retrieving the Christmas decorations, because she has at least another month before that. Mattie shakes her head, trying hard to recall why she had the impulse to delve into that part of the house other than making a glib promise to Jake one day. Whatever compelled her she is beginning to regret, but when she flicked through the pages and saw what she'd written and how the past came hurtling back, Mattie knew that regardless of how long it would take, how hurtful it would be, she had to take that journey through her life. A daunting and possibly haunting task lay ahead.

It's time, she thinks.

"Coffee for Madame," offers Jake.

"At last! I thought you'd forgotten." She takes the mug and wraps her cold hands around it while listening to Jake explain why Nathan was ticking off earlier.

"Will you be okay?"

"To be honest, I'm not sure how I'm going to feel. I only know that I've got to read them."

"You know you don't have to do this. If you want when the kids are in bed I can come outside and help you."

"No!" She answers firmly. *I want to do this alone.* "It's fine Jake. I'd rather you were in the house with the children." *I just can't let you read the letters.*

To Whom It May Concern – *The Book of Letters*

"Promise me one thing – if it gets too much, you will please come back inside. I can think of other ways to spend a Saturday night."

Jake gives her that come-to-bed smile and is promptly rebuffed, so he settles for a kiss. While he saunters back to the house after being reassured that she'll be fine, Mattie smiles at the look in his eyes and remembers how she fell in love with him the day they met. Earlier, they chatted about the consequences of reading the book and how it would probably make her feel. This reminds her of the day she opened up her heart to him and blubbered over a cup of coffee. The charming man sat patiently, listening to her every word, and when she ran out of tears, along with asking her out on a date, he also said he liked her honesty and told her to never stop being honest about her feelings no matter what, adding that they were better out than in.

It is time once again to be honest. With this thought, Mattie opens the red leather-bound book.

Inside the front cover, her name is written in big bold and underlined letters – <u>MATTIE BARTON</u> – like a child at school who'd do the same in their workbook in case it was lost. She sees that she has also written her address, which she now thinks to be foolish. She instantly recalls one of her first therapy sessions with the lovely Joan, and how they discussed anchoring feelings. Seeing her name in block capital letters, Mattie realises she has done exactly that with the book. 'No more!' With a sharp tug, she pulls the paper from the binder and throws it into the fire. With this simple action of letting go, a sense of relief prevails when she watches that first page burn.

The letters Mattie wrote so long ago are in chronological order. As recommended by Joan, Mattie took to pen to paper to

To Whom It May Concern – *The Book of Letters*

write about events that made her unhappy. She wrote a series of letters starting with her earliest unhappy childhood memory. And once she started writing, there was no stopping her. Hour after hour, night after night, Mattie spewed up all the wrongdoings of the people in her life did towards her, writing letters to them about each event that she thought had done her harm. She emptied her heart and soul of the emotional turmoil she'd been hanging on to – from her childhood through to adulthood – on to paper.

The first one stares back at her in defiance. Neatly written, unlike some of the others. Mattie starts to read it.

~~**~~

Dear Miss Grant,

I am writing this letter to tell you how sad and upset you made me feel when you punished me in front of the entire infant school. You accused me of leaving the school premises without permission, and as a result you saw it fit to make an example of me. To this day I still stand firm in the knowledge that I did not do what you accused me of.

I was probably about four or five years of age at the time. The memory is vivid. I was playing in the school yard and I saw Father Doyle leave church to come into the school through the common entrance. I liked Father Doyle a lot, he always made me laugh. As he made his way I opened the gate and took hold of his hand to lead him into the school. I did not go near the

To Whom It May Concern – *The Book of Letters*

footpath or near the main road. I did not go out of the school boundaries.

I remember walking through the school yard holding his hand. Next I recall you sharply pulling my hand away from his and pulling me into the hall then you started to shout at me. I was so afraid as I had no idea what I had done wrong.

When the bell rang for the end of play you paraded me in front of the entire school as you chastised me more, then you slapped the backs of my legs really hard. I was made to stand with my back to the children at the front of the school hall and I remember the tears that rolled down my face. All I could do was wipe them from my eyes and the snot that ran down my face I wiped on my cardigan sleeve.

I have never forgotten the feeling of the sting on the back of my legs as you slapped me hard. It seemed like forever standing there. My skin was still stinging when I was eventually allowed to return to class and sit down. I remember the pain. I was further ridiculed and embarrassed with jibes and taunts from some of the boys and more tears ran down my face and all I could do was look down at the floor in shame.

When my mother collected me from school that afternoon she was called into your office and I had to wait outside. The voices were muted, but even though I was a young child I knew you were telling her that I

To Whom It May Concern – *The Book of Letters*

had been naughty. When my mother came out she said nothing to me. I cried all the way home and although I tried to tell her what happened, she did not listen. She was only interested in hearing what the headmistress of the Catholic school had to say. My words meant nothing.

I was too young to understand why you treated me like that when all I wanted to do was hold the hand of a person I looked up to. It has taken until now, as an adult, to realise the anger I have been harbouring over this incident. From that day I could not look Father Doyle in the eye, and I resented not only you but him because he too did nothing to protect me. You were the first person that made me stop liking my church and made me stop believing in my faith. Did you know that?

Children need to be listened to, understood, and most of all cherished. You did not listen to me on that day, you did not try and understand what I was doing and you certainly did not cherish me or the children that were under your protection. Not then. Not ever!

For so many years I thought it was my fault. I believed I had been naughty, because that is what you told me. Therefore I had to be punished. All I wanted to do was hold his hand.

Now I realise that I did not do wrong and because of that I can now let go of this negative thought that I have carried for so long.

To Whom It May Concern – *The Book of Letters*

Yours truly,
Mattie Barton
Once a happy little girl

~~**~~

She tears the letter addressed to Miss Grant from the book and throws it into the fire without feeling or regret for the infant school headmistress. It was one from a string of unhappy memories that made her dislike and distrust a person she had previously looked up to. Mattie would see the lovely old lady each Sunday at church along with other teachers she would eventually get to know. She recalls vividly how polite Miss Grant used to be to her grandparents. But after that reprimand, even though Mattie was very young at the time, she knew the teacher was wrong to have punished her that way, and could no longer bring herself to look at her in the same loving manner she once did. On one occasion when the teacher came over to talk to her grandparents, Mattie hid behind her grandmother's legs.

Mattie takes a moment to revisit that very old memory of being accused of opening the school gate to hold Father Doyle's hand. She can see the incident clearly, as if it was yesterday, and now as a mother of two, Mattie still stands firm in her belief that she didn't do anything wrong. The punishment had been long-lasting in her memory, and it wasn't until she underwent therapy did she realise the damage it had caused. She lingers on the incident, and while she didn't care for nor agree to that type of punishment, Mattie decides that Miss Grant had otherwise been a good headmistress.

To Whom It May Concern – *The Book of Letters*

Watching the letter burn, she lets out a mock laugh for allowing this event to take hold of her emotions, and also at the words she wrote in a childish manner. It was as if Mattie became that little girl when she wrote it. As the feelings dissipate and the letter burns, she notes something specific she wrote and reads it out loud. "You were the first person that made me stop liking my church and made me stop believing in my faith."

Mattie suddenly realises that she has not been able to separate her feelings for Miss Grant as a teacher and as a representative of the church. *I thought I'd dealt with this. Obviously not!* It has been ten years since she had therapy, and she is surprised at the rise in her heartbeat, which still indicates that the mixed feelings about school and the church are still deep-rooted.

Joan and those first therapy sessions are also vivid in her thoughts. She flicks through the pages, astounded at how many letters she wrote. *Was I so screwed up back then?* She recalls the impulse to write this letter and the many others. *If it hadn't been for Claire I don't know how I would've coped.* And the day that Claire flung a telephone directory at her and told her to get a life comes back to her clearly. She stood over Mattie and watched her make that first call to Dr Joan Banbury, adamant that she should seek professional help.

The volume of letters to be read is daunting, and glancing at parts of them, Mattie is flooded with unexpected negative memories about horrible teachers, school bullies, and the employer who made her life a living hell –and how on that day in her early twenties she walked into Dr Banbury's therapy room and was offered a seat – and how she put her head in her hands and cried and sobbed her heart out. It was as if she'd never cried prior to that even though she'd done nothing but cry on an off for years, and in the process, had pushed her friendship with Claire to

To Whom It May Concern – *The Book of Letters*

extreme boundaries.

The recollection of using up an entire box of tissues in that first therapy session is almost comical. Mattie knows that she's come a long way since then, and if Joan Banbury was here, she'd be saying the same thing.

It had only taken half a dozen or so one-hour sessions with, the fifty-something-year-old woman, to get Mattie to unlock her thoughts and help her towards rebuilding her inner confidence. She was amazed how quickly Joan was able to chip away at the emotional brick wall she'd unintentionally built. It had been there for so long, for more years than she cared to admit that it was a part of her life.

The first letter is reduced to ash and sits at the bottom of the chimenea, adding to the pile of burnt receipts and Christmas cards. She has barely opened the book, and like taking the lid off Pandora's Box, she feels she's unleashed a torrent of negativity. It's thick with handwritten letters, and even though the evening is still young enough to read each letter in detail, it would be emotionally exhausting and time-consuming. She has no intention of being seated here when the sun begins to rise. She briefly reads the next one.

~~**~~

…. and it was very cruel of you to pull me to the ground that day by my hair. It hurt ….

~~**~~

Ah, Jimmy Cartwright, nicknamed Little Jimmy because he

To Whom It May Concern – *The Book of Letters*

was the smallest boy in the class. If memory serves her right – which it does because she's written about it – he used to run past the girls pulling their hair and making them cry. Mattie continues to scan various sentences on the page.

~~**~~

Why did you kick me that time when ...

~~**~~

Another childish letter makes her laugh at the pettiness of it and writing about such trivial events. She hastily tears it from its binder and throws it into the fire. Then, taking a letter written to Jacob, a school boy who used to taunt her for reasons that she can now no longer remember nor is inclined to read about and think of the harm or ill words he threw in her direction, as the memories are from long ago and have been distorted by life itself, she crumples it in her hands before burning it. Mattie carries on turning page after page, reading through some and pulling others straight from the book without even a mere glance, to watch them burn. Another letter addressed to another forgotten child is thrown into the flames. As she swigs the lukewarm milky coffee, she watches them glow in the chimenea, enjoying the warmth and the fact that she's actually letting go of inconsequential events. She questions why they've had such an impact on her – squeezing her eyes shut to bring up an image of Jacob and other children's faces proves too difficult, so as each letter burns, Mattie lets go of the memory and the associated feelings.

The night is drawing in, and even though she's only gone through a handful of letters, she's underestimated how doing this

To Whom It May Concern – *The Book of Letters*

would make her feel. Soon, Mattie is drawn back to her childhood with flashbacks of big old schools, playgrounds, and teachers. The images flood back in waves of an infant school called St.Margaret's. *I'm not entirely sure if it's still standing anymore*, she wonders. *It was such an old building.* She vaguely recollects a nativity play in which she played an angel. Memories of what seemed like a large classroom with wood panelling on the walls and big old oil-filled radiators come back to her. During winter, the wind used to howl through the gaps in the window frames. How cold those rooms were!

Think happy thoughts, Mattie. Think! She closes her eyes, thinks hard about anything positive about St.Margaret's, and a smile spreads across her face when she recalls the rare occasions they were served ice cream instead of the normally served semolina pudding at lunch time along with the little bottles of milk. It makes her giggle. And the memory of making paper chain Christmas decorations brings her some pleasure.

It was such a long time ago. Mattie is disappointed that she can recall only a few happy thoughts other than the negative actions of Miss Grant slapping her across the back of the legs. *Stop holding on!* Mattie further chastises herself – then hearing her children's laughter from the house as they get ready for bed, she's pulled away from Miss Grant and decides to pop inside and kiss them goodnight.

Five minutes later, they're in their beds, and before heading back to the garden and the hard stool, she takes the opportunity to get a warm and comforting hug from Jake.

"How's it going, honey?"

"Well, at least all the boxes are empty."

"I mean the book."

I know you do. "Let's say... it's going to be interesting."

To Whom It May Concern – *The Book of Letters*

"Once Nathan settles down I'll come and join you," Jake offers. "You know how he plays up when I put him to bed," he says rolling his eyes, and this tells her all she needs to know about how difficult their son can be at bedtime, a trait that has become more prominent of late. Last night he climbed out of bed at least a dozen times, and Mattie lay wide awake listening to her husband's gentle snoring while thinking about the red book in between putting Nathan back to bed.

Uncertain whether to accept Jake's offer, she tells him she will be fine. Jake strides towards her before she leaves the house, cups her face in his hands and profoundly adds, "You're not that person anymore, Mattie. Look at you now. You are strong, independent, and full of life."

"Hey, I'm fine," she lies, "It's just a book." But deep down, the fear of what is contained in the letters that she has yet to read once again begins to consume her with dread. Taking that much-needed hug, she heads back to the chimenea.

A half hour passes, and glancing back towards the house, Mattie sees various lights being turned on and off. She hopes Amy and Nathan are asleep, and in the darkness, she catches the outline of Jake through the kitchen window walking towards the stairs and switching the light off behind him. Sitting alone in the darkness other than for the glow of the fire, and taking a swig of the now ghastly cold coffee, she turns back to the book. *It would be far simpler if I threw it into the fire and a damn sight quicker.* But holding it in her hands makes her more determined to carry on reading.

To Whom It May Concern – *The Book of Letters*

Four

THE next letter that Mattie starts reading is long, and she soon feels the resentment she once held for this particular teacher. It makes her realise how the slap on the back of the legs from Miss Grant was nothing in comparison to what this teacher did. Plus she questions whether it was fate or simply bad luck that she came across such horrible people?

~~**~~

Dear Mrs Williams,

When I went to Sacred Heart you were my first year junior teacher. I clearly remember being in the school hall with all the children and then each class in turn being led to their new classroom, filing out of the hall in alphabetical order. I felt important because I was near the front of the queue because my surname begins with the letter B. It was an exciting day.

The first few weeks passed quickly. I remember you teaching us how to make paper ~~mashe~~ mache plates. I painted a yellow daffodil on mine and gave it to my mother. She fixed it to the kitchen wall...

~~**~~

She pauses momentarily. *How could I have forgotten about*

To Whom It May Concern – *The Book of Letters*

that plate? The memory fills her with sadness when she recalls how her grandfather made her throw it away, and she asked as she did a million times before as to why he did that. But rather than dwell on him now, she dismisses that thought and turns back to the letter.

~~**~~

Then I remember you not being at school for a while and we had a different teacher. She was small with blonde wavy hair. She was also very bubbly and full of energy and we liked her just as much as we liked you. She enjoyed showing us how to paint and make things as you did. Lucy and I were always quick to assist her in getting the art supplies out of the cupboard seeing as we sat close to it.

~~**~~

 Resting the red book on her lap, Mattie relaxes into the sweet memories of her then best friend, Lucy Anderson and those early days at Sacred Heart.
 Mattie was seven years old, a happy-go-lucky girl. Even though the end of summer was near and the cooler, dewy mornings had arrived, she was still made to wear white ankle socks with black buckled shoes. On that first day at school, she'd been told by her mother how beautiful she looked in her new uniform, while Mattie twirled around the small kitchen of the flat the two of them shared. She was too excited to eat breakfast, keen to go to the new school and see who her new teacher would be - maybe it would be someone she knew from church?

To Whom It May Concern – *The Book of Letters*

They arrived at school in time to hear the big brass bell being rung, and before her mother kissed her goodbye, she gave Mattie a piece of paper and reminded her daughter to give it to the teacher. Mattie tucked the yellow piece of paper into her pocket, hugged her mother, and skipped through the playground. All the children were ordered into groups by class year. Mattie searched the school hall for anyone she recognised and noticed the teacher with the long, thin face with half-rimmed spectacles that sat perched on the bridge of her nose. Soon, she along with other children was being shepherded by the teacher who wore a green tweed skirt and flat brown shoes into a classroom.

"Good morning, children! My name is Mrs Williams." Without prompting, the children replied in unison, "Good morning, Mrs Williams".

"All those with a yellow slip please put up your hand."

It was then that Mattie came to meet and befriend the lovely Lucy Anderson. Lucy was sitting next to her and whispered, "Do you know what it's for?" Mattie shook her head. "Free milk and free lunches. Is your dad dead too?"

"I don't know who my father is," replied Mattie, to which Lucy simply said, "Oh!" And on that first day, Mattie learnt what a widow is and that Lucy's father had died unexpectedly when she was a baby.

Oh, poor Lucy, Mattie thinks. Suddenly conscious of the time and number of letters to get through, she picks up the book and carries on reading the letter to Mrs Williams.

~~**~~

The new teacher helped us rehearse for the Xmas play, but all I can recall is wearing gold tinsel on my head

To Whom It May Concern – *The Book of Letters*

as we sat at the front of the stage while older children acted out the nativity. Christmas came and went quickly, as did the next half term, and when we returned to school at the end of February you were back and the new teacher had gone. But you were different. You had stopped smiling, the tone of your voice was sterner and your attitude towards us was harsher. Even when I saw you at church you kept your head down although I kept on hoping I would get that smile from you I once got.

~~Then one day I heard my grandparents gossiping,~~ Then One Sunday I heard my grandmother talking to another teacher about you but I did not understand what they were saying. I was only a child.

As the weeks went by you began to shout at the slightest thing. Snapping with a vicious tongue and making children cry, including me. One particular instance stands out when I didn't do some work to the standard you expected so you tore the work up in front of my face and threw it at me. You bellowed at me in front of the entire class and called me 'stupid'. Then you made me stand in the corner of the room with a tall hat on my head that had the letter 'D' on it. I didn't under-stand what this meant until later that day when I was taunted about it in the playground. Then you gave me a dismal report at the end of the year and again there were more tears when I tried to explain it to my mother.

I watched how you ridiculed other children in the class

To Whom It May Concern – *The Book of Letters*

and I only felt some recompense when Timothy Fallon who had enjoyed making fun of me was also reduced to tears and spent nearly a full day standing in the corner wearing that same stupid hat. But you would not even let him go to the toilet when he so desperately needed it and eventually he wet his pants. Then you shouted at him even more. I can remember feeling very afraid as your voice rose in anger, louder than I had ever heard anyone shout, except for my grandfather and the class were speechless seeing Timothy huddled in the corner crying with a damp patch on his shorts.

I was so glad by the time the summer term arrived knowing that when I came back to school in September I would have a different teacher.

The remaining junior years that followed without you directly teaching me were happier than that first year and then came the news that you were leaving. The entire school had to go to mass to celebrate your service to the school and community, but as we sang the hymn we silently rejoiced in the fact that you were leaving and we would no longer have to tolerate the punishment you so freely gave.

It was only years later when I was in my late teens and old enough to understand that I overheard a conversation between my mother and grandmother. For the first time I plucked up the courage to tell them what I thought about you and how you treated us all. At first they did not believe me. My Grandmother in fact

To Whom It May Concern – *The Book of Letters*

told me that I was deluded and didn't want to listen to my tales. But when I stated all the things that you had done to me and to others, they knew that I was telling the truth. So she told me that your husband had died of a sudden heart attack during that Christmas of my first year and then I realised that it was from that moment your life changed and knowing that made me feel a certain degree of sympathy for your loss.

~~But~~ However, you chose to deal with your grief by punishing others and that was unacceptable and unforgivable. During my junior school years you imposed such a heavy form of discipline on young children, punishing them for the slightest of things when at times no wrong was done. You literally put the fear of God into us. But it wasn't until I started having therapy that I realised I had held on to the physical hurt and emotional pain you caused me and how this in turn affected my confidence when growing up.

I don't know whether you are alive or dead. All I hope for is that your conscience has made you question your actions and that you can deal with the consequences of your own behaviour.

Yours truly,

Mattie Barton
A very disappointed Sacred Heart pupil

~~**~~

To Whom It May Concern – *The Book of Letters*

She gasps at the sadness she has expressed in the letter. The pain and memories that she thought to be long gone are back in full force as she pictures the deputy head teacher waving and pointing her long, spindly fingers in her face. Before burning it, Mattie casts her eyes once again over some of the words, and soon recollections of her days at Sacred Heart Catholic Junior School come flooding back.

It was the same school that her mother attended when she was a child. It was walking distance to her grandparent's house, who they'd visit often at the end of a school day. The school was another big old red brick building and, like the infant school, was also cold in winter, so Mattie's mother used to make her wear a vest under the white polyester blouse. In extreme bouts of bitter cold, Mattie's legs would be mottled and red around the knee caps. The best she could do to ease the sting from the cold air was pull the socks as high as possible above the knees while they hurried home.

The school was a few minutes' walk from the church of the same name – the church that Mattie attended every Sunday with her grandparents - but without her mother. Mattie knew the school well enough even before attending because her grandmother often baked cakes for the summer and Christmas fêtes. It was through this that Mattie came to know of and recognise many teachers.

Mattie smiles at the memory of the cakes – which she can almost smell now. And of helping her grandmother to sell them. The smile continues at the fond memories of the games she played with Lucy and other children in the playground – skipping and the game of elastics and who could do the highest scissor kick. *I was rather good at that*, she reminisces, feeling happy about how high she could get her legs in those days. Then

To Whom It May Concern – *The Book of Letters*

laughing out loud, she visualises hopscotch and the rough game of British Bulldog they sometimes got away with playing when a teacher was not on yard duty.

But with these sweet memories of the school are also attached the unhappy ones. The distressing thoughts of Mrs Williams are back, and Mattie is swiftly drawn back to the first year of junior school when she noticed the unprecedented change in her teacher.

Mattie wondered what had happened. Why did Mrs Williams now keep her head bowed in silence at church? Then again, she was just like the rest of the cloned congregation in their long dark coats, kneeling in prayer. But the child knew something was wrong.

I only wanted a smile and a little bit of acknowledgement from her, she recalls. *Was that too much to ask?*

When Mrs Williams returned to work, she made discipline her raison d'être, and to this day, Mattie is aghast that she got away with it in the years that followed. Mrs Williams would make the children line up along the corridor outside the classroom before they were allowed to enter for registration – the boys down one side, the girls on the other. The corridor was long and seemed to go on forever, with doors leading to the numerous classrooms and lines of children waiting in silence to enter theirs, only once their teacher was satisfied that they were quiet and standing straight. A loud hum of voices would emanate after break time, but at the blow of a whistle, silence would descend. While Mrs Williams walked past her pupils listening for a crack in the silence, daring anyone to speak as she glared over her half-rimmed spectacles, and correcting any person's posture, shouting at them, 'Shoulders back,' she'd slap the long wooden ruler in her hand. Mattie quivers at that once forgotten memory - of that ruler, and instinctively sits up straight to correct her posture, pulling back

To Whom It May Concern – *The Book of Letters*

her shoulders as Mrs Williams would have expected. And as Mattie sits upright, she feels the dull ache between her shoulder blades from slouching on the hard, uncomfortable stool.

The tall teacher looked intimidating when she towered over the small children, looking into their apprehensive eyes, wondering if they'd been good, and whether they should be punished that day. Mattie lost count of how often Mrs Williams would brandish a hard slap with the ruler across the palm of any child who spoke without permission or slouched or indeed did something that was considered to be wrong or disobedient in the eyes of Mrs Williams. She would bend their fingers back, making the skin taut, so that the slap stung even more and left red marks on the little hands.

Mattie balls up her hands and winces at the ghost pain in her palms from the unjustified punishment, the anger towards Mrs Williams slowly simmering again inside her. While doing so, she recalls a conversation she had as a teenager with her grandmother, when Mattie eventually learnt that Mrs Williams' husband had died.

"You know, Grandma, she was appointed to her level of incompetence."

"What do you mean by that?"

Mattie had read this particular phrase in a book and thought it rather smart to pass this comment about Mrs William's promotion to deputy head. "It means that she was promoted to a position that she was not capable of doing."

Grandmother Barton looked at her aghast, while Mattie's mother sipped her tea, not wanting to engage in the awkward conversation. "How can you say that? You are still a child. What would you know?"

"I know plenty," she dared answer back without being in

To Whom It May Concern – *The Book of Letters*

earshot of her grandfather.

"Do not talk to your grandmother like that, Martha. Anyway, since when did you start using such big words?" her mother asked sternly. "What on earth are they teaching you at school these days?"

If only you knew, Mother, Mattie thought, but contained the comment and said, "Are you aware of what she did to us – what she did to me? She was a vile teacher who took pleasure in hurting children because it suited her to do so."

"Mrs Williams? Surely not. I know her only to be a kind and gentle woman."

Mattie apologised to her grandmother when she said she didn't wish to discuss the subject anymore. However, Mattie wanted to talk incessantly about Mrs Williams as they had now brought up the subject. But she could see that her words were wasted, and if she pushed the point too far, then Grandfather Barton would be drawn into the argument for sure. Her mother's glare became stronger, indicating that Mattie should be silent if she knew what was best for her.

A few minutes passed by. Mattie finished eating the piece of shortbread freshly made that day, and while she could hear her grandfather pottering about in the garden, she took the opportunity to continue. It was about time they knew and listened, and she told them everything about the harsh treatment most children received at the hands of Mrs Williams.

"Come to think of it dear, I do recall Mrs Jacobs one day mentioning something about her grandson Edward. If what you say is true, then I apologise. But her being strict didn't do you any harm, did it dear?"

For a moment, Mattie thought she'd achieved something, that she'd been listened to and understood. But for all that was said

To Whom It May Concern – *The Book of Letters*

about the sinewy teacher, Mattie knew her grandmother didn't really want to accept the teachers' cruelty. Plus her mother was prepared to say very little in support.

Mattie simply said, "No."

The letter to Mrs Williams reminds Mattie of how she stripped the happiness from her and other children entrusted to her care. The impact she had on Mattie during that first year of junior school had been immense, but she thought she had got over it, until now. Even writing the letter to her hasn't truly ridden Mattie of those feelings, and she sets her eyes upon it, seeing how it is riddled with errors – mistakes made, then corrected, thoughts expressed with determination, then amended as she tried to stick to the facts when writing.

Once she started writing, it was like a tap turned on with the words of frustration and anger flowing out onto paper. It didn't matter whom she was writing to or what she wrote about. Whatever it was that made Mattie unhappy and angry, she sought to get out of her system and let go. And if writing letters was the tool, then it was used to great effect.

Until a few days ago, life without the red book was blissful, but with her daughter seeing the old photos and the flashbacks to a previous life has made her face her past. However, Mattie knows that life will continue to be blissful once she truly lets go of this harrowing past, even though she thought she did that effectively through her many therapy sessions. But for as much as Joan was kind, helpful, and there when Mattie needed someone most to listen to her, she realises that the simple act of opening the front cover of the book has unleashed the past.

Mattie gazes into the darkness across the garden. She is surrounded by the scent of earth, and nocturnal animals start to

To Whom It May Concern – *The Book of Letters*

make an appearance, making various noises. Though she hasn't read many letters, and the more hurtful ones are to come, she's flooded with mixed emotions, various images of good and bad times, glimpses of people she no longer knows, those who are no longer here, and a life that ended many years ago.

Then he's back with her – her grandfather taking control and turning the happy memories of her mother and grandmother sour. It doesn't take much to take her mind back to Sunday mass, a stiff navy blue dress and its prickly collar, the heavy overcoat that made her skin itch, which she'd feel sick from wearing if the weather was warm. If she wriggled around on the pews, she'd receive a stern tap on the shoulder from her grandfather to stand up straight, face forward, and hold her hands together in prayer. To recite the prayers correctly, to bow her head in silence, to sing out loud, to... to... to....

She cannot bear the bitterness of these overwhelming memories, and to turn away from him, Mattie promptly starts glancing over the next letter addressed to the same teacher, Mrs Williams. It's about the May Procession. *I dreamt about being the May Queen for so long*, Mattie sighs. It was the highlight of the year and the topic of chatter amongst the girls in the playground closer to springtime. Who would be chosen? What would the dress look like? *I so wanted it to be me!* Mattie marvels at the beautiful hymns they sang compared to the regular Sunday ones that were endless verses of high notes and poorly attempted singing that competed with the heavy sounds of the church organ. One missed or bum note from the organist, and the congregation were lost. She sighs again at the once forgotten memory, only to be reminded because of this particular letter.

Her negative thoughts float between her grandfather, Mrs Williams and the church, at which she reminds herself not to be

To Whom It May Concern – *The Book of Letters*

cruel. But every Sunday was the same. The elderly choir's ageing vocal cords could no longer belt out at soprano level, leaving pregnant pauses passing through the church. Then left to hold the notes were a few male baritones and the voice of the odd lady who held her ground at alto to carry on the hymn alone. The congregation were no better, thinks Mattie. She lets out a few more sniggers at how they tried to reach those long high notes, with the guarantee of only a warbled voice to drown out the half-hearted attempts at singing.

Then in that moment, Mattie realises why, when Mattie was a small child, her Grandmother stopped singing part way through a hymn followed by a small cough before singing again. She too couldn't reach those high notes.

And come to think of it, I don't think Grandfather Barton ever sang. Hypocrite! Once again, the feelings of contempt for this man rush back at her. As quickly as she has a happy thought about her mother or grandmother, it is squashed with the memories of the anger she held for him – she's astounded at the way she is feeling tonight, and that those feelings of anger are just as strong. She has an image of a man standing tall, looking forward, without emotion. He says his prayers, bows his head when he has to, kneels when instructed, and takes Holy Communion each Sunday and on every other available Holy Day as he had been conditioned to do. *And for what?* Mattie wonders. *Did it help him with his own suffering?*

She squeezes her eyes shut, and in that forced vision, tries to see him singing a hymn. But she sees nothing there. Instead, she hears a voice clear in her ear like it was yesterday, telling her to collect three hymn books as they enter the church.

And she's that young girl back at church...

To Whom It May Concern – *The Book of Letters*

"Martha, go and get the hymn books," and she did as Grandfather Barton instructed every Sunday morning. She walked ahead of them, picked up three books from the shelf at the back, and then quickly got back in line as they made their way to the front of the church. Once she'd climbed into the pew after her grandmother and sat on the cold wooden bench, *he* told her to kneel. Again, she did as he instructed, but eager to see which hymns they were going to sing, Mattie kept hold of the book until she was reminded to put it down and pray.

"In the name of the Father..." began her prayers, asking for God's forgiveness even though only a week had passed since she was last asking the same. At the tender age of ten, Mattie wondered what she'd done that was so bad in only a week that she needed to repent for, apart from pulling her tongue out at a boy who'd pushed her over. In her mind, that was fair enough. However, the teacher had caught her doing this and made her stand outside the classroom, insisting that she apologise to the slimy boy. Mattie kept her head bowed, and rather than repent for what she considered a minor sin, she said a Hail Mary for her mother instead, wishing she would come to church someday.

A little peek, she thought, seeing her grandparents were engrossed in their silent prayers. Then she said "Amen" loud enough for Grandfather Barton to hear, turned around, and sat down on the bench to look up at the numbers on the small wooden plaque ahead. *Number 162* – she flicked through the pages to that hymn. *I hate that one*, she thought, but unwittingly said it out loud.

"Be silent, child!" came the reprimand, and she looked up into the angry eyes of her grandfather, who then told her to stand up as the organ struck its first chords of *Morning has Broken*, and the mass began. Sandwiched between her grandparents, the child

To Whom It May Concern – *The Book of Letters*

appeared trapped, and when two other parishioners arriving late squeezed in at the end of their allotted pew, she was compressed further between her elderly grandparents, which made her uncomfortable.

The usual view that Mattie was presented with at mass was the backs of the heads from the row in front, some of which were bald and shiny, along with the heavy dark overcoats and the tiny white speckles of dandruff on the shoulders of Mr Andrews who owned the local paper shop and who always seemed to be in front of her regardless of where they sat. She stood on tiptoe, craned her neck, and tried to see which school friends were at mass, then leaned closer to Mr Andrews and gave a gentle blow at the white specks, hoping they would move, but they didn't. While the congregation hammered out the dull and dreary hymn, she mouthed the words in unison but refused to sing along to the one she disliked so much.

After having searched the hymn book and hoping they'd sing one of the modern ones they had been learning at school, it was another disappointing mass. As Mattie grew older, she came to look upon Sundays as an overall disappointing day. She was tired of listening to an ageing priest lecture about virtues from the pulpit, when all she wanted was to be at home with her mother. Even if her mother had come to church, it would have made the experience less painful.

Grandfather Barton is at the forefront of her mind, with the resentment she held for him and the Catholic faith because of the way he and the church treated her mother. She says out loud, "I hope you are listening, you stubborn man!"

The pain her mother must have felt having a baby out of wedlock hits her hard. Mattie shakes her head at the incomprehensibility of her Grandfather's actions and behaviour.

To Whom It May Concern – *The Book of Letters*

Knowing that many penned letters to her grandfather are to come and trying not to linger on the painful memories she has of him, she draws her attention back to the letter about the May Queen procession and catches snippets of sentences from the past.

~~**~~

Dear Mrs Williams,

When I was in the second year of junior school, you asked the class if anyone wanted to be the May Queen.

~~**~~

She eagerly starts reading the details of how the girls had to form an orderly line, write their names on a slip of paper, and place it in a box that Mrs Williams had promised she would randomly choose a name from.

~~**~~

You told us that the chosen girl would be informed the following day. We all waited patiently and the following day came and went without any notification of who had been chosen.

~~**~~

Mattie's grandmother had promised to make her a dress from her own silk wedding gown, seeing as it had never been used by her own daughter, Mattie's mother and it was unlikely that it

To Whom It May Concern – *The Book of Letters*

would now be. The old dress was still immaculate in its original box. Her mother said she would make her a crown from fresh flowers if she was chosen. Plus, she made a solemn promise to go to church that day if Mattie was picked. Mattie crossed her fingers, hoped her name was pulled from the box, and prayed hard that night.

This event from long ago is no more of importance. Not bothering to read it fully, Mattie tears the pages from the book and watches the letter burn. Mrs Williams had not been true to her word and never pulled a random name from the box. Jane Smith was chosen to be the May Queen because her mother was a school governor. All the other girls in the class were upset, including Mattie. Later that day, Mrs Williams pulled Mattie to one side and told her she was too tall to be the May Queen. As for the smaller, cute Jane Smith, she had to stand on a box to crown the statue of the Virgin Mary. When she stepped down, her shoe caught in the hem of her dress, and she fell backwards, taking the statue with her. A quick-thinking teacher caught the Virgin Mary before it toppled to the ground and swiftly placed the lopsided crown of flowers back in its original position.

The small memory of this event that had at one time caused Mattie anguish, enough anguish that she felt the need to write about now brings her much laughter – the same hysterical laughter that spread throughout the rows of children at church on that day when their parents gasped in disbelief at the toppling statue. "That was so funny," she laughs out loud. The more she thinks about how hers and her classmates' shoulders bobbed up and down in church as they tried to hold back the sniggers along with the sight of Mrs Williams face turning puce, the more it adds to the amusement of it all. All Mattie could think through the hysterics is that she still would've made a great May Queen.

To Whom It May Concern – *The Book of Letters*

She wipes away the tears of laughter and takes a moment to reflect on the range of emotions she's experienced so far this evening, having read such few letters. Before turning to the next one, still eager to burn them all, she wonders whether Mrs Williams is still alive. And if so, is she as lonely as she looked the last time she was seen, which was at Mattie's Grandmother's funeral? Deciding that the teacher is not important and that it's not worth hanging on to and getting upset anymore about these old distorted memories, she turns back to the book.

To Whom It May Concern – *The Book of Letters*

Five

CONSCIOUS that the red book is resting on her knee with plenty more letters to read through, and realising she has already dwelled for far too long on insignificant events, Mattie sits up straight to carry on. But before she can continue, she takes some time to reflect on the events that instigated her to write the letters, and while she feels some are trivial, she's still thankful to the person she turned to, who set her on the path of ridding herself of the pain.

The first few therapy sessions Mattie had with Joan Banbury were in the main spent crying, blubbering into handfuls of tissues with her head bowed in shame, and blurting out random crap that was in her head and heart, followed by an equal number of apologies Mattie thought necessary. Joan listened intently, making notes and saying very little. Mattie ranted incessantly about anything and everything that had or was pissing her off – even if she thought the journey to Joan's home had been unbearable that particular day, she raged over it. It was the way Mattie was then. It was the way she felt. Even the insignificant things in life added to her anger and sorrow, let alone what Guy was doing to her at that time. As for Sadie – Mattie shudders at the thought of the letters she's getting close to – *she* was such a bitch.

She thinks about Joan Banbury, the wonderful woman, the therapist who Mattie credits for getting her life straight. This takes her back to the large comfy single armchair she sat in weekly, enveloping her with its big fluffy cushions.

To Whom It May Concern – *The Book of Letters*

"Close your eyes, Mattie, and relax," Joan asked of her.

Mattie let her head sink back into the puffy backrest. The crying, although subsided, had fatigued her, and all she wanted to do was fall asleep and drift away into a world of make-believe, where only she, and perhaps Mr Blond, existed. It had been another one of those bad days at work and she was glad to be in the comfortable surroundings of Joan's therapy room, where she felt safe.

"I want you to describe how you feel. If it helps, tell me what pictures or colours you imagine."

"I feel angry, sad."

"Good, but if you describe those feelings, or what they mean to you it would be more helpful."

A picture came to Mattie's mind. "I feel like a mouse on one of those wheels trapped in a cage. I'm running on it continuously and I can't seem to get off it. The more I run the faster it goes and it's exhausting." She breathed a heavy sigh as if she was enduring the experience. "...and the people on the outside are looking in and laughing at me..." Mattie stopped as the tears came back. Joan handed her a tissue again.

"Carry on, Mattie. You're doing well."

"They laugh at me because I can't get off this stupid wheel. I'm trapped. They're like giants standing over me, just pointing their fingers at me and laughing. I'm surrounded by them."

"Can you see their faces?"

Mattie keeps her eyes closed, and when the images of the people staring at her come into focus, she scrunches up her face and squeezes her eyelids even tighter to force the image away. "Sadie is one of them, and some of the girls from school. Guy is there too."

"Okay, now describe your pain."

To Whom It May Concern – *The Book of Letters*

Mattie's hands immediately came to rest on her chest. "I have this pain right here," and she jabbed a finger just below the breastbone, "it feels like a vortex spinning inside. At times it hurts and I want to grip it to make it go away and then my breathing gets faster and faster." Her heartbeat quickened with the description. "Then my head begins to throb until I feel sick."

"Well done, Mattie. Now take a deep breath. You've described your anxiety, and I would like to explore ways you can gain control of your feelings because at the moment, your emotions are controlling you."

Mattie looked at Joan quizzically.

"Over the next few sessions, we are going to look back at your life and identify the moments and situations that you consider to have had a negative impact on you."

I've plenty of them, Mattie wished to admit.

"You may be surprised at some of the negative thoughts you are holding on to and you may also be surprised at how far back in your life you will have to look. Often we are unaware of situations we're holding on to that are detrimental to our well-being. A negative event in your early childhood could still be affecting you emotionally and I'd like to explore that with you. If that is okay?"

"Yeah sure, whatever helps," Mattie said then continued listening to what Joan had to say.

Joan explained it clearly, and even though Mattie's head ached from the crying and built-up tension, she also deduced from the conversation that the negative events she apparently hadn't let go of were being exhibited through her behaviour. She'd allowed herself to be on the receiving end of ill treatment rather than take control and give it back. That was about to change now.

That evening, Mattie stopped off at the local newsagent to buy

To Whom It May Concern – *The Book of Letters*

a book so she could write letters to people who tormented her, just as Doctor Banbury had suggested. The book was bound in red leather, smooth to the touch. That night she stayed up through to the early hours of the morning writing letters, putting into words anything that she wanted without the fear of incrimination or rebut. She felt free in expressing her feelings in words, with the knowledge that no one would judge or criticise her. Although mistakes were made, lines crossed through sentences, and entire paragraphs erased as she attempted to extricate the thoughts from her mind, Mattie felt relieved that no one but her would see them. Not even Joan, unless Mattie thought it would help.

Night after night, letters were churned out as Mattie began to let go of the past and the negative feelings that were destroying her from the inside. All of them had one thing in common. Control. Each letter depicted a person and event that had some form of control over her. They had been fundamental in the way her life had been moulded until now, and Mattie, with Joan's help, was desperately trying to undo it all and shape a new life, a brighter future.

A continuous cycle of thoughts ran through her mind, reliving the feelings that her behaviour reflected. The behaviour then exacerbated the feelings, filled her head with negative thoughts, and once again, she became that mouse trapped on the wheel going round and around. Mattie underestimated the extent of the emotional turmoil she was holding on to. It was as if she wore it with pride, like a heavy chain around her neck for everyone to see, and the only person who was blind to this was Mattie herself. For so long, she had swept all her problems under the carpet, in the hope that everything would be fine.

I didn't realise I'd written so many letters! She thumbs the

To Whom It May Concern – *The Book of Letters*

edges of the many pages, capturing Sadie's and Guy's names appearing multiple times. She finds it hard to believe that she allowed the behaviour and actions of other people to influence her feelings so much. The therapy and letter writing made her acutely aware of her own behaviour and how it affected those around her.

Mattie is still grateful for the person who, for the first time in her life, truly listened to her and helped her see and think with a clear conscience. Joan's words of advice come back to her.

"You cannot put good on top of bad as the bad will eventually seep through and destroy the good."

Joan was right.

The more Mattie thinks about the letters, the events, and the therapy sessions, the more she realises that she hasn't completely let go. She captured her deepest feelings in words, trapped them in a red book just to be hidden away in a wooden box, and that box too was locked away in another cardboard box, although by accident, as if it the book never existed. Mattie feels a pang of anger for doing this, finding comfort only in remembering Joan's words of wisdom all those years ago. Thinking of Joan's advice, Mattie knows it is exactly what she needs to get her through this night.

I have to let go, once and for all. Unleashed and expelled from my life forever!

And she turns the page to the next letter.

To Whom It May Concern – *The Book of Letters*

Six

APART from the small amount of light that comes from the upstairs hallway of the house and what emanates from the chimenea, Mattie sits in almost darkness contemplating the next letter. It feels rather eerie that all that can be heard is the crackling of the flames and the occasional wildlife, which snoops around the garden investigating this night-time disturbance, if only to remind her she's not entirely alone. But the tormenting voices in her head are enough to keep her company. She argues with them as images rush by, trying her best to keep back the worst ones, because she's not quite ready yet to completely open up her mind. Not until she gets to those letters at least.

Mattie shifts her buttocks on the wooden stool to release the numbing pain that is now distracting and drawing her thoughts away from what she cares not to think of just yet. Some blood rushes back – not quite what she was expecting to soothe the numbness. She remains steadfast, sitting on the silly wooden stool she should never have brought outside in the first place. She looks down towards the book.

The name on the next letter practically jumps off the page and slaps her across the face, and the anger she thought she'd let go of for this person comes hurtling back quicker than Mattie is prepared for. *Bitch!* She hisses under her breath. Her backside is now experiencing a crescendo of overwhelming pain that she can't stand anymore. Leaping from the stool, she slams the book face down onto the wrought iron table and heads in the direction of the garage.

With a few long strides across the patio and a good few rubs of

To Whom It May Concern – *The Book of Letters*

her knuckles over her thighs in a poor attempt to enable blood circulation, she sees an upstairs light on and shouts out to Jake, wanting him to get her a more comfortable chair from the garage as he promised. There's no response, much what she expected, assuming he's in his office taking advantage of time on his own to do some extra work for his important meeting first thing Monday morning. *Pah! Corporate slavery!*

Jake was right about tonight, it IS cold. Mattie looks up at the cloudless sky, pure black and speckled with stars. The only thing visible is her breath. "I've never noticed how beautiful the sky is at night, I must sit outside more often," she whispers. Mattie takes a few twirls in the darkness, enjoying the solitude and again in a gentle whisper she says thank you to Jake for being a wonderful person, not that he can see or hear her.

A few minutes later, she's back, seated in front of the chimenea with a travel blanket wrapped over her legs for extra warmth. She's even succumbed to wearing the hat with the piggy ears.

She ventured into that other place – the garage – she usually refuses to go into. Not because it is untidy, but because it is a home for spiders and other creepy crawlies. One winter, Mattie moved a box full of polystyrene to discover numerous holes in it along with a mass of shredded manmade material, and she jumped back in surprise when a mouse shot out of one side, landing on her foot and running away. And as she reached over a pile of things to get the sun chair she is now sitting on, a few strands of a spider web brushed her face. That would normally have bothered her. But tonight of all nights, she is past caring about what is lingering in the corners of the garage. She merely brushed the cobwebs away.

"I've come a long way since I wrote these letters," she firmly

To Whom It May Concern – *The Book of Letters*

says, not wanting to keep the thought purely in her head. "I'm no longer that screwed up young adult. I am Mattie, a wonderful wife, a fantastic mother, and an amazing cook. Apart from other things," she then giggles.

The mantra seems to help, preparing her for Sadie. She waits a few moments, enjoys the warmth from the fire, and looks at the down-facing book, debating what harm it could do to read at least one letter addressed to her. Eventually, she admits the answer is 'nothing'. Then accepting that she was bound to arrive at these letters sooner or later, and now that the bitch is once again renting free space in her brain, she decides it is time to get rid of her. Once and for all.

Mattie stops fighting back the horrid thoughts and emotions and picks up the book to read on.

It all started when she moved to a new school, much to her dismay.

Mattie had happily stepped up from Sacred Heart to All Hallows Catholic Senior School along with her best friend Lucy. She remembers being kitted out with the full school uniform, a cost her mother could ill afford, seeing as she was a single mother. However, she still managed to buy everything that was on the lengthy school list of items by putting in extra hours at work, adamant that Mattie looked smart and didn't stand out from the crowd and risk the stigma attached to being a bastard.

The first day was great – Mattie felt very grown up and confident. She met Lucy at the bus stop to catch the school bus. There was the hustle and bustle from all the children cramming into the bus with the older ones taking pride of place on the back seats, both upstairs and down.

All the school buses that came from different directions

To Whom It May Concern – *The Book of Letters*

arrived at school at the same time, and the children were herded off like cattle. They were directed towards the assembly hall on that first day – another hall of another new school. Each time, the halls and schools were bigger and noisier. Once again, they were at the bottom of the food chain, and even though Mattie's height was above average for her age, she still felt small amongst the other year groups and fearful of the outcome of looking one of the older students in the eye.

The assembly hall buzzed with excitement, filled with the chatter of children who had not seen each other for the best part of two months, eager to catch up on what happened, where they'd been, and any other interesting facts that school children saw fit to discuss.

Mattie and Lucy stuck together like glue, waiting patiently for the class call. They crossed their fingers and would have crossed their toes, if at all possible, for more luck in being called for the same class. Then the headmaster's voice bellowed across everyone's heads.

"Good morning children. Welcome to All Hallows Catholic Senior School." It silenced the children instantly and all eyes fixed upon him as he introduced himself to the new students and welcomed back existing ones. The anticipation sent their hearts racing, as each form teacher stepped forward and made a roll call.

"Lucy Anderson?" Lucy made her way towards the stage, climbed the few steps and stood in line next to the four other children whose surnames were at the start of the alphabet.

"Martha Barton?" Mattie's hand shot in the air and she let out an audible squeal when she was called to be in the same class as her best friend.

They got what they wanted, and the finger crossing they firmly believed in seemed to have worked.

To Whom It May Concern – *The Book of Letters*

It took only a few days to get used to what appeared to be an enormous place – going from one classroom to the other and navigating various staircases, long corridors, and across long halls to separate buildings. In that first week, only once had they ended up in the wrong place when the maths group had an unexpected room change. That aside, Mattie quickly picked up where to go and the quickest way of getting there with so little time between lesson changes. She was enthralled with the array of subjects – cooking in particular – and was keen to show the teacher how much she already knew about baking cakes because of the many hours she'd spent in her Grandmother's kitchen. When the teacher, Mrs McClusky, who knew her Grandmother very well, selected her to assist with the first cooking demonstration, Mattie felt pleased to show the teacher her skills. And it pleased her when the teacher said she was a natural cook, which she was quick to relay to her mother at the end of the day.

On occasion, after school, Mattie and her mother would visit her grandparents. On this particular school day, a few weeks into the first term, Mattie had baked a batch of scones at school. She'd substituted the raisins and sultanas for cherries, preferring the overall taste and thinking that something red and glistening made for far better presentation than a lump of dough with black bits stuck inside. Atop each scone was a beautiful glazed cherry for added sweetness. She was eager to present them to her grandmother, and while she knew her grandfather to be less inclined at handing out compliments, she was still keen to present them and receive his praise.

Mattie's grandmother rewarded her with a hug. "Put them on the table dear." She took them through to the dining room along with the jam and clotted cream her mother had purchased on the way, and placed them closest to Grandfather Barton's place

To Whom It May Concern – *The Book of Letters*

setting.

The man whom Mattie considered to look older than his years, ate his dinner in silence, and when he finished, he asked Mattie, "How was school today Martha, are you doing your best?"

"Yes grandfather. I love it there..."

Before she could finish the sentence he rebuked her for using the word 'love'. Mattie gave it some thought and corrected her words.

"Yes grandfather, I am very happy at All Hallows School and I enjoy every subject." She smiled through the little white lie she had told him when in fact her least favourite subject was Religious Studies.

Keen to please her grandfather even more, she offered up the plate of scones. She'd even positioned the largest scone closest to him, hoping he would pick it. He had first choice.

"Not at the moment Martha, I am far too full to eat anything else," he dismissively passed them over and the joy fell from his grand-daughter's face.

Grandmother Barton noticed Mattie's smile drop. "Never mind dear, I'm sure your grandfather will have one for supper. The scones are wonderful. Well done, Martha!"

Mattie looked on as he got up to leave the table, waiting for a nod of approval, but when he said 'maybe', it did nothing to abate her feelings. The eleven-year-old girl put on a brave smile, but the rejection weighed on her and her face told a different story. She cared not that he was full but only that he ate one of the cherry scones and told her how scrumptious they were, how proud he was of her efforts.

With the turn of events, the clotted cream may as well have been sour. Mattie was growing up fast, and whereas previously she would not have been bothered by his reactions or comments,

To Whom It May Concern – *The Book of Letters*

she was now becoming more observant of the way her grandfather treated her. It didn't seem to matter when she was a little girl – after all, he was her grandfather, whom she loved as much as her mother and grandmother. The love was never questioned. But as time went on, Mattie became more aware of his behaviour.

Her first end-of-term school report was excellent and was rewarded with an embrace of adoration from her proud mother. Then, when it was handed to Grandfather Barton, who insisted that he read each school report, he told her that she'd achieved what he expected of her. Mattie didn't quite understand the remark he passed with only the hint of a smile, and her mother stepped in to reassure the child whose expression was one of confusion.

Time seemed to pass by quickly. With every passing day, Mattie's confidence at school grew, but home life was different. Soon they were approaching the end of the second term and breaking up for the Easter holidays.

Then it all changed in a moment, and without warning.

The final decision was made on Easter Sunday. They ate the usual roast dinner at her grandparents', but for the first time ever, her mother bought Mattie a very large Easter egg. She'd gone against her father's incessant jibes about it being a waste of money and his orders that she wasn't to spoil *the child*. But Mattie had convinced herself that it must be because she was working so hard at school and getting good grades.

It was wrapped in shiny red paper with a gold bow tied around the middle, and it sat in its display box on the dining table, screaming to be opened and eaten. Mattie wasn't allowed to touch it until she finished eating her dinner. All of it. So she had to make do with staring at it through every mouthful of food,

To Whom It May Concern – *The Book of Letters*

even eating the peas she detested, which had been mashed in with the creamy potato and gravy to disguise their foul taste. Every mouthful.

After forcing down the last of the potato with some water, she put down her knife and fork and looked up at her mother with a huge smile.

"Martha, can you please leave the room for five minutes and let the adults have a conversation in private?"

The tone of her mother's voice had become serious, but being a typical child, Mattie was more bothered about being asked to leave while the adults talked. Again! Plus it meant waiting longer to get her hands on the Easter egg. At first she refused to budge, but then her grandfather gave her one of his glares she knew best not to challenge. She left the room quickly, huffing on her way and shutting the door firmly in defiance of the unsolicited request.

Having a desire to listen because they must have been talking about her, Mattie pressed her ear against the door, but the voices were low and muffled. *Speak up, I can't hear you.* Lucy Anderson had once said that she always listened in on her mother's conversations. So Mattie, deciding to take the same action, tiptoed to the kitchen, grabbed a glass, and pressed it against the door. She was breaking all the rules about listening in on private conversations and respecting an adult's privacy. Doing this in her grandparents' house was surely going to send her to hell, but Mattie needed to know what they were saying. She held the glass firmly, careful to not make any noise and arouse suspicion. A lump rose in her throat, knowing that if Grandfather Barton caught her doing this, she'd also be grounded for the rest of her life. But she was prepared to take that chance. It didn't deter Mattie from listening through the base of the glass even though she'd missed part of their conversation.

"The decision is final!"

"But father, you know how happy she is at this school and she's settled in so well. She has her friends and..."

"Enough!" Mattie's grandfather raised his voice and silenced his daughter. "You need our help and this seems the best solution. If you'd never gotten pregnant so young then perhaps you wouldn't be in this predicament..." then he held his tongue when his wife gave him a disdainful look. In a quieter tone he turned back to his daughter, adding, "I have given it much thought and it is in both your best interests we do this."

"I accept that the new school has a wonderful reputation but so has All Hallows. Wouldn't it be in her interest not to disrupt her in her first year at senior school?"

"I think your father is right," added Josie's mother. "We have discussed this at great length and Martha will soon find new friends. She'll settle in well and will get over it sooner than you think. Mattie is a strong girl and will be fine at the new school."

"And the other thing we discussed? How am I supposed to tell her about that?"

Josie was still young herself, she'd yet to reach the age of thirty and while having had a child at such a young age and been forced to grow up quickly, she still lacked the maturity to hold a reasoned argument with her father.

Mattie could hear her mother's voice. It was clear and precise, and with each passing word, her mother became agitated and her voice rose in defiance, but to no avail.

"The child will start at the new school straight after the Easter holidays and that's final!"

Mattie screamed and let the glass fall to the floor. Its heavy base thudded on the carpet and rolled to a rest against the skirting

To Whom It May Concern – *The Book of Letters*

board.

"No!" Flinging the doors open, she barged into the room. "Please tell me it's not true!" She looked towards her mother for confirmation.

Mattie's mother dropped her head in silence, ashamed to look her daughter in the eye. Then with her head still lowered, she spoke.

"Martha, I've lost my job." Mattie could tell through the stuttered words that her mother was crying.

"But, you'll get another one."

"It's for the best Martha," interrupted Grandmother Barton, taking hold of her hand and forcing her to sit back at the table. "We were going to tell you sooner but we didn't want to spoil your day."

"Grandma," she said with tears streaming from her eyes, "I don't want to leave All Hallows. I love it there. And what about Lucy?" Her Grandmother squeezed her hand tightly, but Mattie yanked it back and folded her arms in defiance. "You can't do this to me!" The inconsolable girl again looked towards her mother for an answer. *Please say something, Mum.* She pleaded with her eyes. But the tears and words made no impression, and her mother kept her head lowered.

Grandfather Barton stood up from the table. The giant of a man with his overwhelming presence looked down at Mattie and banged his fist hard on the table. The crockery rattled. "You will do as you are told, child. There will be no more discussion about this! Is that clear?" Then he left the room.

Still feeling solemn, her mother decided to take Mattie on a shopping trip the following day. It was out of the ordinary, and Mattie assumed it was a way to cheer her up, so she eagerly put on her shoes and grabbed her coat, ready to leave.

To Whom It May Concern – *The Book of Letters*

Her mother bought Mattie a skirt of her own choice with a matching top. Then the two of them went to a café, where she was told that she could order whatever she wanted. The offer was accepted innocently. Mattie didn't even question the generosity of the shopping spree that she wasn't accustomed to and promptly ordered a chocolate milkshake.

"I need you to understand why we've made these changes." Her mother's tone turned serious again.

Mattie had recently turned twelve years old, and as she listened to her mother's explanations, the recent clothing purchases and the milkshake she was sipping through a straw was a temporary distraction from the fact she was being made to move schools.

"You do realise that because I've lost my job I can't afford to pay the rent on the flat?" The child nodded and took another drag on the straw, pulling up the thick milky drink. "I already owe the landlord a few months' rent. The money I earn..." she stumbled on her own words, "The money I *used* to earn was never enough. Your grandparents have always given me some money to get by."

Even though she was twelve years old, Mattie understood enough to realise that her mother was talking about something entirely different and asked why rent had anything to do with changing schools.

"It isn't as simple as that. Your Grandfather feels that he can provide a better lifestyle for you."

"What's a lifestyle?"

Mattie's mother hesitated and looked at her daughter's forlorn face. "Well I guess it means the way we live, how we live," Josie said, then cocked her head to one side to see if Mattie understood what she was trying to tell her.

She wasn't even a teenager, and at that age, she didn't want to hear the excuses and explanations no matter how good a picture her mother painted of her own elderly parents. They sat in silence a few more minutes, but sensing her mother's unease, Mattie asked what was wrong.

It was said rather matter-of-factly – a verbal bomb dropped into the conversation, which further shattered Mattie's life that Easter, the buzzing in her ears drowning out her mother's words as she tried to make sense of it all. Mattie put her hands over her ears to block out what she was being told. *No, this cannot be true!* More tears rolled down her face and her shoulders shook while she sobbed.

"We'll be much better off when we move in with your grandparents. After all they've been very generous over the years..."

Mattie cut her short. "How can you do this to me? I like where we live," she stammered through the sobs. "It's just the two of us and..." the heaving prevented her from giving her justifications.

She was too young to understand, and a part of her didn't want to. Josie put a comforting arm around her daughter, but the child pulled away. All she knew was that her mother had done her best to keep them together, but in Mattie's eyes that wasn't enough. "Why can't you get another job?" she demanded to know.

"Life isn't as simple as that Mattie and I know you do not truly understand how difficult it has been raising you on my own."

Mattie remained angry.

They made the short bus ride home in utter silence, other than the sound of Mattie's tears, which she continued to shed regardless of what her mother did or said. There were no more discussions about it, there were no choices. The gifts had been given to soften the blow of the bad news. It didn't matter how big the Easter egg was or how nice the new clothes looked – they

To Whom It May Concern – *The Book of Letters*

couldn't compensate for the fact that Mattie was going to be taken away from her best friend, Lucy Anderson.

Her mother's words, "I've come to a compromise with your grandfather," was another statement that Mattie didn't comprehend. That day at the shopping mall, Mattie was told that they would be moving in with her grandparents within the week.

It took a few days to pack everything and move out of the small flat Mattie shared with her mother. The few possessions they were allowed to take were placed in the boot of her Grandfather's Volvo Estate. At any available opportunity, Mattie pleaded with her mother not to move in to her parent's home, but the pleas were rebuffed. She was told yet again that she was too young to understand, and that she didn't know what she was talking about.

When they arrived at the house, Mattie needed no one to show her which room was hers. She knew exactly where to put her belongings. As she stood in the doorway of the small pale blue room that previously she hadn't been allowed to enter, her heart felt heavy, and sad. The rare occasion that she caught a glimpse of its empty interior was when she'd used the upstairs bathroom and Grandmother Barton had accidentally left the door open. The few pictures and mementos that Mattie had once seen in the room had since been removed. The room felt cold when she stepped in, but her mother promised it would be decorated very soon and that it would look much prettier after a fresh coat of paint and the addition of a few pretty and decorative items.

She put down the box of books she just brought in and walked over to the window, resting her head against the cold pane of glass to look down at the garden with a heavy sigh. The clusters of daffodils and tulips swayed in the breeze, but the pretty view was no compromise for the small blue cell she now inhabited, and

To Whom It May Concern – *The Book of Letters*

no matter what her mother said she would do to the room, it would not take away the sadness she was feeling at that moment.

The house was a moderately-sized three bed built partially with red brick. Apart from her soon-to-be-decorated blue room, all other walls in the house were washed over with magnolia. Woodchip paper clung to these walls under layers of the ghastly bland paint, slathered on over the years because it seemed to be the only thing you could do to hide that horrendous wallpaper. A dull green carpet ran throughout the rooms, including the stairs and landing. It was never-ending and lifeless and clashed with the blueness of her bedroom walls. *How drab! And now I'm living here*, she whined, still pressing her head against the glass, forcing a headache from the coldness. The only rooms that didn't have the green carpet were the kitchen, bathroom, and toilet. Instead, those floors were covered in grey linoleum. *Equally as drab*, thought Mattie, looking down at her grandparent's perfectly manicured garden.

The house was hardly fashionable. It was as if time had stood still. Various matching pieces of dark wooden furniture filled the lounge and dining room, and a Grandfather clock that was wound daily by her grandfather stood in the hallway – all impeccably clean. It was a house Mattie had partly grown up in, visiting almost every Sunday and often during the week, but now that she'd moved in, she viewed it differently. She noticed things she'd never bothered with previously. It was cold, without colour and without soul. She pleaded with her mother every day for the best part of the first month to move back to the flat, but it was of no use. No one wanted to listen to what the child had to say.

The few ornaments on the mantelpiece were nothing much to look at. A silver candelabrum that was only ever used at Christmas and Easter took centre-stage on the sideboard that

To Whom It May Concern – *The Book of Letters*

matched the dining table. For the rest of the year, it was an item to be dusted, but something for Mattie to pick the hardened wax off, mainly out of boredom when her elderly grandparents weren't looking. Placed either side of the candelabrum were matching picture frames, one containing a photo of Mattie's mother when she was a young child that looked like it had been taken professionally. The other monochrome photo was of her grandparents on their wedding day. She took a good long look at the photos, studying the features, the smile on their faces at the joyous occasion, and for a tiny moment, she wondered what on earth had happened since that day to make her grandfather so grumpy.

The day they moved in, she noticed a third photo – that of a young boy. She'd asked about it, and without explanation, it was removed that same day, and Mattie was told kindly by her mother not to mention it again. There was a new set of house rules to abide by. No longer would Mattie be able to get cosy on the sofa with her mother while they watched the television, even though it was a black and white one Josie had been given by a dust-bin man. Conversations between just the two of them would most likely stop, and there would be no privacy and no time for just her with her mum.

The few books and toys that she was allowed to bring to her grandparents' house brought little change to the freshly painted magnolia bedroom walls. For an entire week, Mattie could still smell the acrid paint, even though a large onion cut in half was placed on the windowsill in a vain attempt to absorb the smell. But the contrasting odours still cut sharply into her nostrils, and trying to sleep in that room surrounded by that smell was a nightmare. Each morning, she whined about the small room, the

To Whom It May Concern – *The Book of Letters*

horrible smell, and how she wanted to go home, until she was reprimanded and politely told to stop. So she took to staying in her room. Even though the smell was revolting, it soon became the best place to be in within that house – out of everyone's way and lost in her own thoughts, lying on the bed, wishing the years to pass quickly and get to the day she could leave.

The Easter holidays were nearing the end and Mattie, afraid she may never see her best friend again, was eager to tell Lucy what was happening.

There came a gentle knock on the door. "Yes Mum, come in," Mattie said and sat up, sliding her legs over the edge of the bed.

"Your grandfather wants to know if you've finished reading your book." Her mother didn't respond when Mattie rolled her eyes and told her it was the most boring book she'd ever read. Instead, her mother followed Mattie's gaze to see the book closed and kept at the foot of the bed.

"It doesn't seem that long ago since I read that book." To appease her own father, Josie gave Mattie a quick synopsis of the story, telling her not to bother reading it. "Your grandfather will have no idea that you've not finished it. I thought it was boring too but let's keep that to ourselves, shall we?"

"Why do you put up with it mum?"

It was a question Josie could ill afford to answer. For her it was a matter of survival, something she'd been doing since the day she announced her pregnancy when she was only sixteen years old. For as much as she hated to admit it, she needed her parents support and hoped that Mattie would eventually come to understand that.

Mattie lay back on the bed once her mother left the room, putting her feet on the covers while still wearing her shoes, another act of defiance. It made her smile to know this would infuriate the adults if they were to see her do that. Then she had a sudden thought. She put on her coat and crept down the stairs. She could hear her mother and grandmother in the kitchen, while grandfather was reading a newspaper in the lounge. No one heard the large heavy wooden front door creak as she pulled it closed as gently as possible. It was still light outside, and apart from an elderly lady living opposite them, who was peering through her curtains, there was not a single person on their road that evening.

Within minutes, Mattie was making her way towards Lucy's house having used the loose change left over from her shopping trip. The bus was cold and she felt vulnerable sitting upstairs, with a few older boys sitting at the back smoking and mucking around. Mattie rested her head on the steamed up window, closed her eyes, and wished for the next twenty minutes of the journey to pass as quickly as possible and without hassle from the boys at the back.

As she walked the final steps towards Lucy's front door, her friend caught sight of Mattie from her dining room window. Lucy was eating dinner with her new family – her mother had recently remarried – and as soon as she saw Mattie, she darted from the table towards the front door. By the time the door opened, Mattie was already crying, as she had been since she got off the bus.

"Mattie, whatever's the matter?" asked Mrs Davenport, as she was now known. She then put a comforting arm around the sobbing child, pulling her into the warmth of their home.

"They're taking me away," Mattie blubbered.

"What are you talking about, child? Here, sit down and tell me."

She was ushered into the lounge, and while Lucy sat cross-legged on the floor, staring at her best friend with disbelief, Mrs Davenport held Mattie's hand. Mattie told them through streaks of tears that she was moving school and that she and her mother had also moved in with her grandparents. Lucy began to cry too, telling her mother it wasn't fair, and asked what she was going to do about it.

"So I've run away," Mattie blubbered into another tissue. Mrs Davenport gave her a sympathetic hug then left the room. "I don't want to go to a new school, Lucy. I'll miss you."

Lucy Anderson made a promise that they would visit each other on weekends and write letters often. The idea brought a glimmer of hope for a sad Mattie, and while the two girls talked about how they would remain friends, Mrs Davenport phoned Mattie's grandparents.

They never considered my feelings back then! Mattie mutters reluctantly under her breath, realising that those feelings she'd once thought buried still sit strong within her.

With the book resting on her lap and thoughts of Sadie still lingering in the background, she takes a few more moments to think of Lucy Anderson, *that* particular Easter, and of her controlling grandfather. It was her one and only experience of running away, even though there'd been plenty of occasions when she thought about doing it again.

"Sorry Mum for putting you through that. I never thought it would hurt your feelings and make you sick with worry," Mattie whispers while looking up to the sky. "How stupid of me!" Again chastising herself for the times she'd caused her own mother stress from trying to stand up to her own beliefs. But anything to get out of that house, she reflected. Anything for some sanity.

The last time she saw Lucy was on that day. They promised to be friends forever and that they would always write to each other and see each other as much as possible. They did write a letter or

To Whom It May Concern – *The Book of Letters*

two in the weeks that followed and tried to make arrangements to see each other, but as far as Mattie was concerned, she may as well have been shipped to the other side of the world. Eventually, the letters and arrangements stopped.

Mattie had made it clear to her mother and grandparents that she didn't want to move house or school, but it wasn't until she was older that she began to understand that her mother had no choice. She had lost her part-time job five weeks before Easter, when the business she worked for was sold and the new owners brought in their own family to run it. Mattie only lost her best friend Lucy, but her mother lost her dignity and independence.

A few tears prick her eyes for her mother. She quickly wipes them away, thinking how difficult it must have been for her. Now as a mother herself, she acknowledges the sacrifices that were made. But Mattie still begs the question – did they really have to move in with her grandparents? Could her mother not have found another job?

Looking back and piecing the memories together like a jigsaw, Mattie realises that changing schools must have been planned for some time and that she was being blackmailed with an enormous chocolate egg and new clothes. Mattie momentarily giggles away the resentment and the memories of what she did back then. She picked up the weighty chocolate egg, took it into the kitchen, and in anger, smashed it on the work surface. Then she threw the broken pieces into the bin. Her mother was upset and her Grandfather was furious at the waste of money, never mind her bad behaviour. As she throws some more kindling into the fire, she still hears his voice bellowing at her.

To Whom It May Concern – *The Book of Letters*

Seven

THE fire burns strong, and the blocks of hardwood that Mattie has added to it crack and hiss under the intense heat. It doesn't take much thinking to bring Sadie to the forefront, as her thoughts turn to those horrendous first few weeks at St.Benedict's Private Catholic School. The years that followed weren't that fantastic either. *How could some people be so horrible?* Unable to understand the behaviour of others, she can, however, remember throwing herself onto her bed when she returned home from school each night of that first week, sobbing into the pillow, refusing to come out of her room, and refusing to let anyone see how upset she was. She knew that no matter how much she cried, her grandfather wasn't going to let her go back to All Hallows, back to Lucy and her other friends.

She takes hold of the book and again looks at the letter that she's been putting off reading. *Oh Sadie, Sadie, Sadie! What a horrible, horrible person you were, you were, you are!*

~~**~~

DEAR MOST HORRIBLE PERSON IN THE WORLD!!!!!!!!!

I've hated you for so long!
I HATE YOU. I HATE YOU. I HATE YOU!

The mere mention of the name 'SADIE' or anything

To Whom It May Concern – *The Book of Letters*

remotely similar makes my skin crawl because it reminds me of you and of what a bitch you were to me. Thank god your name is not common so that I don't have to fucking think about you often!

Some people think it's fortunate to attend a private school but I had no choice in the matter. For reasons beyond my control I was whipped out of a very good school, taken away from friends I had known for years, then thrust into an environment with people who had little respect for one another. I soon learnt that no matter how rich you or the others were, you didn't have any respect for each other. Who gave you the right to treat people like shit????? <u>WHO?</u>

~~**~~

The bitterness in the penned words makes her wince, and she stops just for a moment to question what there is to gain from reading this particular letter. After all, she hated the bitch! She still does. It isn't exactly a nice trip down memory lane, but with stubborn determination, Mattie carries on...

~~**~~

...The school was miles away from where I lived with my grandparents and it used to take me ~~ages~~ an hour travelling each way. On my first day I was shown the lockers, the location of the toilets and my form class. As for the rest, I had to follow along and get on with it. I felt lost and so alone and it didn't take long for you to

To Whom It May Concern – *The Book of Letters*

pick up on how vulnerable I must have looked, being the new kid at school.

It was a daunting experience. My mother didn't even have the time to buy me the correct uniform because it was the Easter holidays. I recall for the first week having to wear my grey pleated kilt from my other school, and it made me stand out from everyone. You and some other girls took great delight in taunting me about this amongst other things. That was the start of things to come and of the cruelty you inflicted upon me throughout my senior school years. YOU made my life a fucking misery for five years.

FOR FIVE FUCKING YEARS!!!

~~**~~

Mattie takes a moment to breathe deeply and calm her nerves because seeing the heavy written words, the exclamations she used to replace expletives she so wanted to write instead have made her breathing racy. She recalls an image of the form tutor's classroom and the way the tables were positioned – in the shape of a horseshoe, with children sitting on both sides, so some students had their backs to the teacher. The only available seat was facing a row of small girls. Mattie thought this room layout slightly bizarre, as she'd just left a school where all the classrooms had uniform rows of tables and chairs that faced the front of the class. It was what she was used to.

She returns to the letter-

To Whom It May Concern – *The Book of Letters*

~~**~~

I can remember that first day at school as if it was yesterday, sitting opposite you and your friends all eager to ask me questions. Well at least three of them seemed interested in me. I suppose new people are always the topic of conversation, I understand that concept. But you didn't like the other girls talking to me, asking me my name, where I lived, did I have any brothers and sisters etc. Your questions were more devious. You told the other girls to shut up and on that first day I knew that you were the leader in that group and that the others did what you told them. You wanted to know why I had changed schools part way through a year. Had I been expelled? Had my parents divorced, and a multitude of other questions you threw at me.

I was naive and unprepared for the barrage of questions, and while I tried to hold back on giving out too much information about my family, the moment you discovered I lived with my grandparents and that I had no father, you took that information and used it as a weapon against me in the years that followed. Even my name gave you much amusement when you took it upon yourself to nickname me 'Tatty Mattie' because in those days I wore my hair in pigtails. It wasn't my fault that I was named after my great-grandmother. That nickname stuck with me for five years! Have you any idea how you made me feel? Who am I kidding, the answer is NO because you're not a

To Whom It May Concern – *The Book of Letters*

nice person and you don't give a shit about anyone!

Then you decided that the other girls were talking to me too much on that first day and you started kicking at my legs. I ignored it, I ignored you and when you did not get a response you kicked harder to see what reaction you got. ~~I said why.~~ *I asked you why you did it and told you to stop. I can still hear your response clearly, 'because I want to, because I can.' I went home with bruises up and down my legs and I was too afraid to tell my mother because I knew she could not do anything about it.*

~~**~~

Mattie momentarily stops to rub her shins, as if the pain and bruises are still there. She wishes she had more wine in the glass to numb her senses while reading her letter to Sadie.

~~**~~

After a few days I thought your bad behaviour would wear off. But you just carried on and I had to put up with your continual bullying and harassment.

Not only did you enjoy provoking me when we were in the same lesson, by either making fun of my name or 'accidentally' knocking my work to the floor, you took any opportunity to shove or push me in the corridor, to hide my games kit and make me late for PE. Or you would steal my school tie and leave it hanging from a

To Whom It May Concern – *The Book of Letters*

tree with a nasty message attached. You always found a way to intimidate me. I could go on but writing this letter is making me feel bad even though my therapist told me it would help.

Your behaviour worsened as we moved through the school years. You were cunning, sly and always seemed to manage to provoke me or inflict something upon me away from the prying eyes of the teachers. The pulling of my hair, the spitting at me on the school bus and the abusive language that came out of your mouth. What foul language!

I dreaded getting on the same bus as you but I had no choice. It was the only way I could get to and from school. I complained to the teachers but they didn't do anything. I was kindly told that the best way to deal with this was to ignore you and that eventually it would stop. How naive of me to think this would work because it didn't!

I never understood why you behaved so badly. Then a few years after leaving school I bumped into one of your friends - Denise Carlisle. We ended up sharing a coffee while she offloaded unwanted information about you. Did you ever realise that she never liked you but she knew that the best way to deal with you was to become your friend? The better the enemy you know than the enemy you don't know she told me. That's how she survived. Looking back, I think I would still prefer to be your enemy than to pretend to be your friend and

To Whom It May Concern – *The Book of Letters*

behave the way you or your friends did. You are despicable!
Denise said you behaved badly because you were starved of affection at home. She told me that your father worked abroad most of the time while your mother went from one affair to another. I believe your mother caught you in bed with the gardener but she was more outraged - not because you were under-aged but because she too was sleeping with him along with her tennis coach from what I was told. And your father wanted to throw you out of the house when he found out.

You didn't care about anyone but yourself. You didn't and probably still don't have a kind bone in your body and were only nice when you were jumping into bed with the next willing boy. Did you never wonder what they used to say about you behind your back? 'Slapper Sadie' amongst other things.

WHO gave you the right to behave so badly towards me? WHO gave you the right to abuse me emotionally and physically? Did you enjoy treating me and other people like that? Did it give you some sort of fulfilment? A bit of a thrill?????

Because of this I am so, so bitter towards you. I despise you with a passion. You are an evil, **EVIL FUCKING BITCH** who deserves nothing good in life. You reap what you sow you oxymoron. And for your information, Claire and I enjoyed calling you that.

To Whom It May Concern – *The Book of Letters*

My glimmer of hope is that I write this letter in an attempt to let go of anger towards you that I have held on to for far too long. My therapist was right. I have enjoyed writing this letter. I feel better already. I have let these negative thoughts control my life. I may not have been in control of your kicking or the shoving and pushing, but I am in control of my feelings and behaviour. And guess what bitch? You don't control me anymore. So FUCK OFF and have an unhappy life!

'Mattie' to her friends and that's NOT YOU!

~~**~~

Surprised at the venomous hatred in this letter, Mattie rips the pages from the binder and throws them into the flames, relieved she has managed to get to the end remaining relatively calm. The deep breathing earlier seemed to work. The words she wrote came from the heart – it was the truth as she knew it – and at that time, she had to get it out of her system because it was eating away at her.

Mattie closes her eyes and takes a few more deep breaths, thankful that she has passed this part of her life, when a welcoming interruption from her vibrating mobile phone. She removes the piggy gloves and reaches into her pocket. It's a text message from Claire. She hits a few buttons to read her friend's poor attempt at telling a joke. A second message is fired through then a third in quick succession, Mattie soon reads about Claire's latest trip to Italy and the renovations she's doing on her villa.

'Funny ha ha,' she quickly replies, adding a smiley face, then follows it with another text. 'Drinking wine and snuggling on the sofa with my favourite man. Xxx'

The few moments of distraction are enjoyable, but she refrains from texting the truth about her evening activity because she knows all too well that Claire will immediately hit the dial button and demand that Mattie tells her everything and that she's to get in touch with Joan again.

The phone vibrates. Another message! And this time it's about Claire's son falling over the day they arrived in Italy and breaking his arm. She sends a reply showing concern, adding to give little Marco a big kiss from his Aunt Mattie – sure to make him cringe. Then she slips the phone back into her pocket.

For the time being the distraction has cleared her mind of Sadie and Mattie acknowledges that she and Claire have come a long way since they met during those first days at *that* private Catholic school, noting that if it wasn't for her friend's kindness and ability to make her laugh like she has done this precise moment, she probably would have gone insane at St.Benedict's. But she's since been able to return the favour of emotional support many times, such as when she and her Italian boyfriend, Frankie, now her husband, were having commitment issues with Claire citing she needed to get some perspective...

"I thought you said he'd proposed to you?"

Claire flopped on to the bed in the spare room. She threw her coat on to a nearby chair and huffed when Mattie mentioned marriage. "Sure. He's always asking me. But not properly, not the way I want him to. Did I ever mention that he proposed within a week of dating but look at us, five years on and no sign of a ring!" She pouted, holding up her left hand.

"You know he loves you, right?"

To Whom It May Concern – *The Book of Letters*

Claire pouted a little more.

"I've never known anyone to outwardly demonstrate so much love as Frankie does to you," Mattie continued, giving her friend a comforting hug. "You'll be back with him in a few days, wait and see." And as predicted Frankie turned up with a bunch of red roses and a diamond ring. He got down on one knee in the driveway and shouted up to the window. Claire leant out, taking only seconds to say yes to the proposal and she moved back into their shared apartment that same day. Six months later they were married.

Another time, the two friends went skiing and Claire broke her ankle and had to spend a few days in an Austrian hospital. Frankie couldn't be with her as he was in the process of opening a new family restaurant, so upon the girls' return, Claire moved in with Mattie and Jake until she got used to hopping around on one leg.

The best thing Mattie walked away with from St.Benedict's was her friendship with Claire. The first week at school was traumatic, and Claire stepped in and protected Mattie from Sadie, offering comfort in the new strict and austere surroundings. It was a relief. While witnessing the harassment and bullying, Claire sometimes too used to be at the receiving end of Sadie's bitchy ways, but where possible, Claire shielded Mattie from the school bully's cruelty. Somehow, she had an inner strength that Mattie struggled to find within herself – to be able to stand up to people like Sadie and, most of all, not let the girl's wicked ways get to her emotionally.

They lived in opposite directions from school, and because Claire's mother worked from home, she had the luxury of being driven to and from school along with her brothers. Mattie would watch her friend from the school bus, climbing into the front of her mother's Land Rover, because she refused to sit in the back with her squabbling siblings. Mattie would laugh at their daily routine – her eldest brother Dominic trying to climb into the front seat and Claire yanking him out by the strap of his school bag. Much to Mattie's amusement, Dominic once admitted to her that he used to do it just to wind up his little sister. Deep down, Mattie wished it was she who was climbing into that huge, plush car and driving back to their house instead of her own. She would've been happy to sit in the back with the boys regardless of what they were arguing about. Eating dinner at Claire's dining table surrounded by noise, fun, and laughter or listening to them argue was still more exciting than the quietness that prevailed at Mattie's grandparent's house. Plus she thought Dominic was absolutely gorgeous. Instead, Mattie endured the gruelling bus journey home along with Sadie and some of her equally horrible school friends, aware that the bitch was going to make her journey a misery.

Mattie pictures her friend's bubbly face pushing her way through Sadie and her entourage of bullies when they surrounded Mattie in the playground the week she joined the school. All the other students in that first year of senior school had had months to settle in and make friends, just as Mattie had done at All Hallows, until the security was whipped away from her. Alone, she met with a barrage of questions from the group.

"The new girl says she's not a virgin," mocked Sadie.

"Piss off oxymoron, before I get Dominic."

"Slag," retaliated Sadie.

Then Claire pushed her to one side.

"Don't listen to that cow. She's as thick as two short planks." The humour instantaneously made Mattie smile. Then Claire

To Whom It May Concern – *The Book of Letters*

further mentioned rather indifferently, "Sadie asks all the girls that. Tries to trick them, then they feel stupid when they say no. You did tell her you are one?"

Mattie looked at Claire rather befuddled.

"You know, what she asked - a virgin?" The bubbly girl stood with her hands on her hips. "I'm Claire Fielding. My mother says I should always introduce myself to new people and to treat them the way I... blah, I can't remember exactly but basically she tells me I should always be nice. I think you're in the same set as me?"

Although still unsure as to what a virgin was Mattie smiled back. She was slightly stunned at Claire's brusque yet friendly manner but at the same time she was questioning her own mind why she was always being told to be silent by her grandparents when introduced to someone. "What's an oxymoron?" Mattie asked.

"Not sure, but my mum says I'll know one day, and when I do I'll laugh about it. It sounds good, doesn't it? Plus *she's* no idea and it makes her angry," she added looking over her shoulder towards Sadie.

Mattie agreed, seeing as it had worked.

Claire's outgoing personality was in contrast with Mattie's reserved nature, but they soon became the best of friends. She stuck by Mattie's side and showed her the *dos* and *don'ts* of St.Benedict's. She explained all the legitimate school rules that teachers expected them to abide by. And then there were the unwritten rules that past students had created, those deemed as being the most important – God forbid if you broke them...

They shared the same interests, liked the same music, and laughed at the same stupid jokes, mostly told by Claire. She was the laugh-a-minute type of girl, always one for acting the fool and standing out in a crowd. Over time, her confidence rubbed off on Mattie, but more so when the two were together. Away from her friend, Mattie reverted to being shy and introverted, even though she wanted to be more like Claire. She admired her inner strength, her robust personality, and her adaptability to any situation, and in those first few months, Claire helped Mattie come to terms with her new life at this school. Over time, the loss of Mattie's friendship with Lucy Anderson hurt less and was soon forgotten.

To a certain degree, the two of them looked similar, both with long blonde hair and equally as tall as each other – and for the first time, Mattie had a friend she didn't have to look down at.

During those years in senior school, she spent as much time as possible at Claire's house, often staying over for full weekends. Mattie's own house had too many restrictions, in addition to not making noise because her grandfather didn't like it. 'He's getting old,' Mattie's mother would say, at which Mattie would roll her eyes each time she heard the word "no" followed by a tut. So she revelled in the less-constrained surroundings defined by Claire's parents. They were permitted to stay up late and listen to loud music, and Mattie even kept a secret stash of make-up at her friend's house. In return, Mattie helped out at Claire's as if she was one of the family. One day, she helped her new best friend's mother bake a Victoria sponge cake for Dominic's birthday. And when he kissed her on the cheek to say thank you, she blushed with embarrassment. But on the occasions she couldn't stay at Claire's, they simply hung out at the local shopping centre or went to the cinema. Anything to stay out of her own house for as long as possible.

Claire had her own ideas about her future clearly mapped out and was determined about what she wanted to do with her life.

To Whom It May Concern – *The Book of Letters*

No one was going to get in the way of Claire Fielding. Her parents backed her whole-heartedly, and when Claire's mother once asked Mattie what she wanted to do when she left school, she told her that she had ambitions to bake cakes for a living. Mrs Fielding thought it was a great idea. Claire's parents treated Mattie in many ways as one of their own, but Mattie still had to go back to the house she shared with her mother and grandparents, a place she struggled to refer to as 'home'.

I had ambitions too, back then! But not wanting to dwell on that particular issue, she looks down at the book. *It's going to hurt, I know that but I've got to get her out of my system.* And Mattie starts to read the first few words of another letter to Sadie, thinking she could have filled a book full of letters just to this one person, when she's drawn to the time the bitch and the group of girls she hung around with pinned Mattie against the wall in the school changing room.

About a year or so had passed at St Benedict's, and Mattie had become wise to Sadie's antics. But one day, she left herself wide open to further ill treatment at her hands. Mattie was the last to leave the gymnasium changing room – a mistake she learnt not to repeat.
"Hey bitch," Sadie shouted, grabbing Mattie's tie at the throat and slamming her against the wall. Sadie's long, black hair was tied back in a ponytail, revealing her sharp features, her dark brown eyes enveloped in heavy layers of eyeliner and black gloop mascara.
Mattie screamed back, "Get your hands off," and pushed her away. But the words fell on deaf ears as the other girls circled her.

To Whom It May Concern – *The Book of Letters*

"Don't struggle bitch," Sadie hissed in Mattie's face. "If you don't want to get hurt, you'll know what's good for you." Her friends stood close laughing and sneering, but it was Sadie who did all the shouting and talking.

It was anyone's guess as to what Sadie would do, and fearful of what she was capable of, Mattie did as she was told and stood still. The voice in her head shouted, *PUSH HER AWAY*, while her body froze and remained motionless, petrified of the repercussions.

Sadie's hand tightened around Mattie's throat.

"Jackie, search her bag!" she bellowed at one of the girls. Without hesitation, Jackie ransacked Mattie's bag, throwing her belongings onto the damp floor. When a door banged open nearby, it made Sadie instantly let go, and before Mattie could catch her breath, the girls scattered like rats, leaving her alone to collect her sodden belongings. Mattie rubbed her sore neck, aware that Sadie had left her mark on it. When an older student came into the changing room and looked around at the mess, neither of them spoke – the student perhaps knowing what had gone on, and Mattie too afraid to tell.

Later that day, Claire threatened to set Dominic on to Sadie, but the threat did not deter her for long. It amazed Mattie how Sadie got away with such bad behaviour, how she and her equally horrid friends were rarely caught, and when they were, how they went unpunished. There were many petty incidents, such as when the group of bullies would rest their feet on the backs of other students' chairs, making their clothes dirty. If Mattie or Claire were in the same class, they made sure not to sit in front of Sadie. Instead, they watched other girls slap at Sadie's legs to put them down, but they would still walk out of the classroom with dusty footprints on their clothes.

To Whom It May Concern – *The Book of Letters*

Mattie presses her hands to the side of her head and massages her temples, thinking of the sly teenager with the vicious tongue who was cruel to so many – how she hurt Mattie emotionally as well as physically, and sometimes, all it took was a glare in the wrong direction to grab Sadie's attention. She rubs her temples harder, trying to get Sadie out of her head, for she's back there, sending her emotions running wild at the memories of those horrible school years. Then she glances at the letter – one written with ferocity and such intensity that in places she's pressed the pen down enough that it has gone through the paper. Her hands tremble, but trying not to fight back the bad thoughts and to finally let go of the negativity, she lets the images of Sadie flash by in her mind like pictures on a cine slideshow. She takes a few deep breaths, letting the feelings swamp her until they eventually dissipate, and her breaths become deeper and more controlled.

The stress of it all and reliving those hurtful years at school have heightened Mattie's feelings. It takes a few more deep breaths to steady her nerves, but the sudden intake of cold air hits her lungs, making her chest burn with pain. "You cannot hurt me anymore, Sadie!" Mattie splutters. Scrunching up the torn letter tightly in her hands, she throws it into the belly of the fire.

To Whom It May Concern – *The Book of Letters*

Eight

FATIGUE is taking over Mattie. She yawns, and another deep breath of cold air adds to the ache in her chest. She stretches out her arms to ease the pain before moving on to the next letter addressed to Grandfather Barton. Thoughts of the tall and dominant man sadden her, as all she can remember is his dominant demeanour.

There was so much about him she grew to dislike, and throughout the therapy sessions with Joan, Mattie came to the conclusion that those feelings were primarily moulded because of a lack of communication within the home. *I wish you'd shared your feelings, grandfather. It could've been so different. Maybe I would think differently about you!*

Finding his few belongings in the box has brought back the contempt she held for him, and it shocks her to realise that so long after his death, she still feels the same way. Not even the therapy sessions have abated her feelings for the man who dominated her life, and soon she's thinking about the many times she couldn't forgive him for all of his selfish acts, especially the one that occurred when she was in senior school.

It was spring time, and being in the middle of senior school, Mattie was to make a decision about what optional subjects to study in her final two years at school. She'd hardly slept a wink that night, worrying about how to approach her grandfather on the matter that she wanted to be a professional cake maker. It had been discussed at great lengths behind closed doors with her mother, who'd eventually came round to the idea that if that was

To Whom It May Concern – *The Book of Letters*

what Mattie wanted and she knew she would be excellent at it, then she should have that opportunity.

"You know you'll have to learn to speak up for yourself," her mother had said. "Reason with him. Tell him about the qualifications you'll get and the career path you want to take. You need to convince your grandfather by showing him what the potential is and what you can achieve. Don't just make it sound like you want to work in a cake shop, you'll know what he will say if that happens."

"But Mum, you know how unreasonable he gets," she whined.

"Yes I know." Josie rolled her eyes, "but you need to show him how strong and determined you are about this. He would admire that in you. You know you're so much like him in many ways," her mother said, and she lifted her daughter's chin to remind her to be strong and smile no matter what.

Mattie didn't quite understand what her mother meant when she said Mattie was just like her grandfather, only that she had to do this on her own. If she didn't ask, then the answer would always be 'no', her mother had told her, whereas she was used to Grandfather Barton saying 'those who ask do not get'. Neither choice bode well with Mattie, and no matter what the outcome, it was going to be tough talking to him. But as her mother had said, she had to be strong and determined and show him what a confident young woman she was growing up to be.

At dinner, Mattie pushed the food around her plate, having eaten very little. The nerves in her stomach were somersaulting into a mass of knots, leaving her with a sickly sensation. The more she looked at the food on her plate, the more she felt like throwing up. Her hunger had disappeared as soon as they sat down to eat, and even though under normal circumstances she would've eaten the grilled pork chop, green beans, and boiled

To Whom It May Concern – *The Book of Letters*

potatoes, she sat looking at them, wondering how to swallow the food when her throat was tight with tension.

"It's a sin to waste food," barked Grandfather Barton, "Think of all those starving children in Africa."

She rolled her eyes, which he caught sight of and quickly handed out another scolding. It only made matters worse, as the nerves gripped her stomach, twisting her insides. *This is going to be so hard*, she thought then looked towards her mother for support. She pleaded with her eyes for her mother to speak on her behalf, to say something positive and lead her into the question at hand. But her mother sat at the table eating her dinner and remained silent, in spite of knowing how difficult this was for Mattie.

Josie spoke eventually. "Try eating more, dear."

Is that the best you can say? She thought, before shoving another spoonful of bland food into her mouth. The potato had gone cold – it was dry and clumpy, making Mattie want to gag on it. She took a large swig of water to push it down. Again, she looked towards her mother for moral support, but all that her mother returned was a faint smile and nodded for her to speak.

Grandfather placed his knife and fork on his empty plate. It was now or never. As the adrenalin kicked in and rushed through her veins, she prepared herself to ask the dreaded question.

"Grandfather," He looked up at his granddaughter with a thoughtful look, making her cheeks redden. "Can I talk to you about school?"

Gesturing for her to continue, her grandmother and mother got up to clear the table, leaving the two of them alone. It had been a while since she'd been left alone with him and she didn't welcome the awkwardness of it all, but with a gulp of confidence, she spoke up. "In a few days, we are choosing our final year options, and I want to choose Home Economics as one of them."

There, I've done it. I've actually asked him to his face. Now all she needed was his approval.

He stared at her for a few seconds, then took his napkin from his lap, wiped his mouth, folded it neatly, and placed it on the table. You'd never have known it had even been used – so precise and exact in his ways. He sat still for a few moments longer, pondering the question.

It was difficult to know what the man was thinking, which way he would turn. The room remained silent, and apart from the odd clank of dishes from the kitchen, the only other sound that seemed to echo around the house was the ticking of the Grandfather clock in the hallway. The ticking sounded in line with the beat of Mattie's heart, two sounds resonated in her ears while she looked on in earnest at Grandfather Barton. *Please say something, just speak!*

"Martha," he spoke her name calmly and softly. "I am not paying for an expensive private education so that you can become *a cook.*"

"I don't want to be just *a cook.*"

But he put up his hand to silence the teenager before anything else could be said. Tears pricked her eyes at his short, sharp response. She swallowed hard to hold them back in defiance, which only made her throat ache all the more. She clenched her fists in frustration under the table, determined to act grown up while she looked him straight in the eye, and not cry like a child.

He continued, "You can already bake cakes and very good ones at that. You do not need a certificate to prove that. It is a waste of a qualification." His manner was firm yet calm. "There are far more important subjects to choose, and you would be wiser to choose those that will give you a broader choice of

To Whom It May Concern – *The Book of Letters*

careers."

She kept her eyes wide open, trying her best to hold back the glistening tears collecting in her eyes.

"There are a host of professions out there that will earn you far more money than catering. Take management for instance."

"But I'll learn about management as part of the..."

Again he silenced her by holding up his hand.

"My dear child, the only thing the Home Economics course is going to teach you about management is how to sell fairy cakes on a market stall. Is that what you want to do for the rest of your life? Sell cakes on a stall?"

The tears that she was fighting so hard to keep back trickled down her face slowly, while she listened to his adult reasoning. She didn't dare blink, knowing that once she did, the tears would flow uncontrollably for sure.

"The way forward is to get proper qualifications – ones which are transferable," he added, completely unaware how his stern manner was affecting his only granddaughter. Plus half of what he said went over her head in a total blur. He was talking gibberish as far as she was concerned.

It was too late. She snivelled, and a sob forced its way up, catching her breath as she tried to swallow it back.

"And if you are going to cry about it rather than be sensible and listen to what I have to say, then go to your room."

Fourteen-year-old Mattie remained seated. Determined not to run to her bedroom and wail because he'd once again refused what she considered a simple request, neither did she want to give him the satisfaction of his triumph. She remained in her seat and blinked a few times to let the captured tears finally fall and disappear along with her dreams.

The conversation was short, ending as swiftly as it had begun.

To Whom It May Concern – *The Book of Letters*

"Everything all right, darling?" Mattie's mother asked, entering the room with two bowls of steaming hot apple pie and custard. Mattie couldn't look at her. If she did and saw a sympathetic look, then the tears that gripped the back of her throat would come flooding out.

Later that evening, her mother came into her bedroom, and Mattie pleaded with her to talk to her grandfather. Josie gave her some reassurance and said she would try her best, but a few days later, Mattie was told kindly not to question his authority again. She could not understand the behaviour of her ageing grandfather, who seemed to be without emotion – the older he got the worse he became.

For the time being, Mattie had to remain content with baking cakes on a Sunday afternoon with her mother and grandmother. Hours were seamlessly spent as butter was rubbed into flour, icing sugar was sprinkled, and creams were whisked. It was their little ritual, and it was the one day she was happy to be in that house, but even that had been soured by the disagreement. It was the relief she needed from living in the place Mattie struggled to call home because it was lacking in affection. There was a big void in Grandfather Barton's heart that no one wanted to talk about and no amount of creamed scones or fluffy sponge cakes could fill it for him or get him to change his mind. As the weeks and months rolled on, Mattie had to accept what life had dealt her until she was old enough to change it herself.

Her grandfather was tall, had a thick mop of white hair, and was stern in appearance. Her mother often told Mattie that she'd inherited his intelligence and long legs. Each time Mattie heard that remark, she would reply under her breath, 'Thank God that's all!' His austere personality was as strong as his stern presence. With his stature, he made heads turn when he walked into a room,

To Whom It May Concern – *The Book of Letters*

even in his ailing years when he began to stoop slightly. He knew his own mind and everyone else knew that of him too, and when his deep voice resonated around the house, Mattie knew too well to keep out of his way, for it made her quiver in her shoes and his disapproving glance would cut through her.

She could not dispute that the man who always looked old to her, was clever and hardworking and had spent forty years working as a civil engineer.

A few years after his retirement, a sudden heart attack ended his life. Then it was too late to get the approval she yearned for. It had started off as a normal school day for Mattie not long after starting her final year at school, except that she noticed Sadie was not on the bus, and for the first time in a long time, the journey to and from school had been peaceful without Sadie's normal melodrama. Perhaps it was because of this she remembered the day well.

When she arrived home, Mattie walked through the front door. Seeing the local priest sitting at the table, drinking tea with her mother and grandmother, followed by a sudden hush of voices, she knew something was wrong. She dropped her bag at the bottom of the stairs, and ignored the fact that Grandfather Barton would disapprove as she'd been told countless times that bags scuff skirting boards.

Her mother was holding Grandmother Barton's hand, and the three turned to look at Mattie when she walked into the room. "What's the matter?" she asked looking at her grandmother's bloodshot eyes.

"Here child," Father McNamara said in a kind voice, "Sit down with us."

She did what he asked, taking the chair between the two women, and listened to Father McNamara inform her that her

To Whom It May Concern – *The Book of Letters*

grandfather had died earlier that day. The priest's gravel yet gentle voice was soothing in the situation – every word spoken was carefully chosen, providing her grandmother with maximum comfort in her hours of need.

"You need to be strong for them both. It's been a terrible shock. Your grandmother will need a great deal of looking after. Now there's no man in the house," the Irish gravel-voiced priest told her.

Mattie nodded, turned to her grandmother, and gave her a big hug. It was all she could offer at that time, in her teenage years, not knowing what else to give, what words to say, or understand how she could help her grieving grandmother other than be there and do whatever was asked of her.

Her grandfather was buried within the week. His funeral was solemn, and apart from a handful of old work colleagues, there were few people at the church to celebrate the life of this man. Mattie looked down to read the order of service while the small congregation put in their best efforts at singing *Morning has broken*, apparently his favourite hymn.

"Born 12 December 1920." Quick to do the sums in her head she realised he was only sixty six years old. Not as old as she'd always thought. "And his first name was Joseph, not Norman?" Mattie said silently in surprise, wondering why this was so.

While the mourners sang, she carried on reading the information, realising how little she knew about her own family. Mattie closed her eyes tightly to block out the depressing hymn and focus on her grandfather. She couldn't remember hearing him swear, although he often raised his voice. She could not remember him telling tales of his own childhood. The more she squeezed her eyes, the more she found it difficult to remember the things she thought she should've known about him. The not

To Whom It May Concern – *The Book of Letters*

knowing saddened her, and she was suddenly filled with questions to ask him. But it was too late.

Within a few hours, they were back at the house. Mattie decided to spend some time in her bedroom while her mother and grandmother made small talk with the elderly mourners that came back with them. She lay on the bed, looking up at the stark white ceiling as she'd come accustomed to doing when she wanted to think things through. She hadn't cried at his funeral service, but now permitted a few tears to run down her cheeks onto the pillow, in recognition that no matter what type of man he was, he was after all her grandfather. To make herself feel better, she told herself that he did love her, regardless of whether he showed it or not.

Mattie must have drifted off to sleep. She later awoke to the sound of her grandmother sobbing. Tiptoeing into the hallway so as not to alert her, she noticed the door to her bedroom was ajar and caught sight of her sitting on the edge of the double bed. Gently pushing the door, Mattie decided to walk in. It was the first time since she'd moved into the house that she'd set foot in their bedroom. She looked around, taking in the staid decor and the few personal items on the dressing table, and then noticed a pair of striped pyjamas neatly folded and placed on top of a pillow. Upon seeing them, she realised how much her grandmother was missing her beloved husband. Mattie moved forward and put her arms around the crying elderly woman.

"Thank you dear." She dabbed her eyes with a white embroidered handkerchief. "I suppose things will be different from now on."

Mattie wasn't sure how to respond without upsetting her more, but ever since Father McNamara had pointed out that it was just the three of them, it was not difficult to imagine that things were certainly going to change within the house. It was obvious that her grandmother missed him dearly, but she was right. The atmosphere would now be more relaxed, and Mattie had to admit that that was a good thing.

Since the funeral, many questions burned in Mattie's head, but one in particular. Plucking up the courage, she asked, "Grandma, did Grandpa love me?"

The woman turned and stared at her granddaughter. *I've been too insensitive*, Mattie thought, seeing Grandmother Barton's reddened eyes. Then her grandmother smiled as more tears flowed.

"Sorry Grandma," Mattie apologised, hugging her tightly again. "I didn't mean to upset you."

"You haven't dear." Her eyes were slightly puffed and reddened from the crying, but they were filled with happiness as she began to talk about the day she met Joseph Norman Barton.

"You know, I was only sixteen when I met your grandfather. He was older than me but he was the most dashing man I'd ever seen in a uniform. It was during the second world way and we met at a dance at the local church hall and because he was so tall he stood out from all the other men."

Mattie listened quietly.

"I was determined to go to the dance." Her grandmother's soft voice emanated contentment. "Being so young my parents told me I couldn't go, so I sneaked out of the bedroom window and went with my cousin Daisy. She only lived a few doors away from where I lived. We got into such trouble when we got back." She laughed as she told Mattie how she would shimmy down the drainpipe holding her best shoes, then carefully stand on the dustbin to get over the back wall each time the young women wanted to sneak out of their respective houses. They would walk the half mile to the church hall while Daisy would light up a cigarette she'd stolen from her own father's packet that they would share. "I felt so grown up back then."

Mattie listened with gusto, keen to hear about her grandparent's youth and their lives. For the first time, an adult member of her family, not that there were many, had opened up and talked about their past. Within a few minutes, Mattie had learnt more about them than she had ever known.

Grandmother Barton even laughed when relating how his and her parents didn't approve of the relationship because of the age difference, grandfather being six years older. Then she told how when he returned to the war she wrote him letters and waited impatiently for his safe return.

"The war couldn't end soon enough for me. We were married within a month of his return."

"So quick?"

"Well in those days, dear, there was no need to wait, and it wasn't as if we could live together unmarried," she said, giving her granddaughter a disapproving look.

Mattie blushed, "Of course."

"We had to live with his parents for the first two years of our marriage. That was a difficult time. Plus he'd recently left the navy and was training for his new job." She stopped for a minute and took a deep breath to compose herself for what she was about to tell Mattie. Dabbing away the tears that were lingering in the corners of her eyes, Grandmother Barton carried on.

"It was years before we had children. I thought we'd never have any because the doctors told me I couldn't." When she said that, the restrained tears flowed freely.

Did she just say children, as in more than one child? Mattie was intrigued by the comment. She desired all this information,

To Whom It May Concern – *The Book of Letters*

and the more her grandmother talked, the more she wanted to know, especially about the other child. She had always known her mother to be the only one.

Her sad grandmother tried hard to fight back the tears. "Every year we used to take a week's holiday in Tenby, South Wales..."

Mattie sat perched on the edge of the bed, soaking in every word about their lives, which was now being given in rambling snippets that she tried her best to unscramble and make sense of. One moment she was talking about dances, the next she was talking about holidays, and then back to when her husband was in the Navy.

"Your mother loved it there. We stopped going when she was sixteen and..." she trailed off again before adding, "We had such happy times."

Don't stop, Grandma, don't stop. Mattie looked at her, pleading for her to go on. *Tell me about the other child.*

As if sensing Mattie's request, Grandmother Barton got up from the edge of the bed, walked over to her bedside cabinet, opened the drawer slowly, and retrieved a picture of a teenage boy. "He was our miracle baby. Such a loving child, it broke my heart when..."

"I've seen this picture before," said Mattie.

"The accident happened so quickly. Norman..." She corrected herself, "Your grandfather didn't want him to buy the motorbike. In fact he forbade him, but Patrick was so stubborn, just like his father. I can still hear your grandfather shout at Patrick when he came home the day he bought it to show it off, and your grandfather told him, 'As long as you live under our roof you will never own a motorbike.' Patrick had saved up for a few months without us knowing. He was working, you see, and could afford it..."

To Whom It May Concern – *The Book of Letters*

She trailed off again, the words bringing a lump to her throat. She clutched the picture to her chest. "I loved him so much, your mother too," she added to reassure Mattie. "He was such a sweet little boy. He looked so much like his father at the time of his..." and again, her grandmother struggled to say the words. "The loss was too much for your grandfather. That is why he was the way he was." She let the tears flow freely, and they rolled down her cheeks, gathering at her chin, falling on her chest and onto the picture frame. She swallowed hard and still found the courage to carry on talking.

"He couldn't bear talking about him after his death and..." she lifted her head and turned to look at Mattie. "Dear child, he only wanted the best for you. He didn't want you to make the same mistakes as Patrick."

"I've no intention of getting a motorbike!"

"It wasn't just about the motorbike. It was that Patrick didn't listen to his father's advice. He punished himself for that thinking he should have been stricter, and your grandfather didn't want you to make any mistakes that you would later regret."

"Is that why he was so hard on me?" Mattie asked.

Before her grandmother had time to answer, they heard the front door closing as the last of the mourners left, followed closely by Josie's footsteps coming up the stairs. It snapped Grandmother Barton out of her sorrow. She quickly wiped her eyes, blew her nose, and put the photo of her beloved son back in the drawer. She then took *his* pair of pyjamas and placed them in another drawer.

"Mattie, oh there you are," Josie said, surprised at seeing her daughter in her own mother's bedroom. "Why don't you come downstairs and help me clear up?"

It was a rarity that her mother called her Mattie, especially as

To Whom It May Concern – *The Book of Letters*

she knew Mattie preferred it. Changes were already happening, as her grandfather was not around to correct the use of her name to Martha or correct anything else for that matter.

"Thank you," Mattie whispered, giving Grandmother Barton another big hug. "I love you, Grandma." As the bedroom door closed behind her, Mattie heard a surge of sobs.

There was little to clear away – a few plates and some cups and saucers. Mattie's mother had awoken earlier than usual that morning so she could prepare sandwiches and a batch of scones for after the service. The smell of sweet pastry still lingered in the air and crumbs littered the dining table. Someone had carelessly dropped a dollop of jam on the crisp white linen tablecloth, and Mattie knew her mother would spend time later vigorously scrubbing out the red sticky substance to get it back to its pristine appearance.

Mattie washed while her mother dried the plates, taking great care with the china tea service that had been in the family for over forty years and only made appearances on high days and holy days. Today was neither, as far as Mattie was concerned. However, her grandmother was insistent that they be used today. But as only months had passed since the old china tea service had last been used, it all had to be washed again before use.

"Martha, I want to talk to you about your grandfather." *Oh, another story*, Mattie considered. *And why aren't you calling me Mattie? He's not here anymore!*

She kept her hands in the hot soapy water but turned to give her mother a sideways glance. "I know all about him."

"Who?" She asked while stacking saucers neatly on top of one another.

"Grandma told me, about the accident and everything."

It took Josie by surprise. She sat down at the small kitchen

To Whom It May Concern – *The Book of Letters*

table and gave her daughter who was growing up too fast a sorrowful look. "It was a long time ago, Mattie. I was only sixteen years old when he died." She settled back to her preferred name and her voice once again softened. "You would've liked Patrick. He would have been a good uncle, so full of life and good humour. Not like me. Anyway, that's not what I want to talk about," and as if discussing her deceased brother was still a taboo subject, she got back up and continued putting the crockery away. "Do you remember my jewellery box?"

"Of course I do. I was always playing with it when I was little but I've not seen it for a long time. I know you still have it. Is it still our little secret?"

Josie smiled at the comment. "Not anymore. I told your grandmother everything a long time ago. And the funny thing was, she knew."

Mattie dried her hands and looked her mother straight in the eye. "Promise me one thing, Mum?" Her mother nodded. Mattie continued, "That we will talk more often. Having watched you and Grandma over the years not being able to speak your mind has been horrible. Plus I've had to keep my mouth shut when on some many occasions I've wanted to..."

Her mother stroked her hair. "Don't upset yourself, Mattie. He's gone, and from now on things will be different. My daughter is more grown up than I thought. It seems only five minutes ago that you were that little girl playing with the jewellery box."

"It's been hard you know, and now hearing about Patrick and the accident I feel like I'm about to burst inside," Mattie expressed. "I don't know how you've gone all these years without telling me you had a brother. Are there any more secrets?"

To Whom It May Concern – *The Book of Letters*

Josie struggled to answer the direct question, when in fact she'd made the decision to tell Mattie about her father. Somehow, it didn't seem like the right moment, and instead, they remained in the kitchen talking mainly about her grandfather, but also about the uncle she never met.

Mattie awakens from the sad memories. Still feeling frustrated at what she learnt on that day, she rocks back and forth for her grandparents' loss, and the tears fall on her lap. The book falls, hitting the opening of the chimenea, and a flame jumps out and catches its edge. She instinctively grabs hold of it then thwacks it hard on the floor to put out the flame that has singed the corners of a few pages and turned them black. The fiasco brings her back to the letter she wrote all those years ago to her grandfather. Flicking off the charred pieces, she begins reading the long letter.

~~**~~

~~Dear Grandfather~~
~~Dear Grandfather Barton~~
Dear Sir

I don't know what to say. There's so much in my head that I don't even know where to begin.

Dear Grandpa

My earliest memories are of sitting on the floor by your feet, most likely playing with a toy but I wanted your attention. You would be reading the newspaper, like

To Whom It May Concern – *The Book of Letters*

you did most days. I would pull at your trousers and you would fold back your newspaper, look down then continue to read. Occasionally you smiled back, but if memory serves me right, you would call for my mother to come and move me. It's a vague image but I know it to be true.

From such a young age, you and Grandma would take me to mass. I can visualise holding your firm hand as we walked into church and I would smile at everyone. I don't recall getting many smiles back, not that it bothered me at the time. I was none the wiser because I was a little girl. All that I knew was that I felt safe and secure in your presence.

Every Sunday up until I was about eleven years old we had the same routine. We came to your house and from there we'd walk to church while my mother stayed at your house preparing the vegetables for the dinner later that afternoon. Week in week out, year after year we went through the same process, but as I grew older and I began to notice the behaviour of others towards us at church and I soon learnt that it was because my mother wasn't married.

But you held your head high and looked beyond the prying eyes of those who thought themselves to be better than us. You let pride lead you through the mass and past the aisles of gossiping old parishioners who had nothing better to talk about than me being illegitimate. Silly old sods! I admire you for that if

To Whom It May Concern – *The Book of Letters*

nothing else.

Then, without discussion my life changed when we came to live with you and from then on I started to notice more your strange behaviour, in particularly towards me. I recall packing up my favourite toys to take to your house. You made it clear that we could not bring everything as you did not want your own house filled with clutter. Mum had to throw away a lot of possessions plus items that belonged to me that I wanted to keep. Still to this day I can see the paper-mache plate I made at school sat on top of a box of items to be thrown out. How I cried and was quickly reprimanded when I said I wanted to keep it. It felt like my love was being thrown in the trash along with our possessions. Did you ever stop to think what these items meant to us? To me? Probably not.

Neither were there any discussions about my schooling other than when I had to present you with a weekly rundown of what I had done and achieved. I suppose this was your way of checking that the school fees you paid was money well spent. It was your way of keeping me in line and checking that I didn't make any silly mistakes along the way, like Patrick did!

Having to deal with the restrictions you imposed pushed me away from you even more. Not only did I experience difficulties at school and was too afraid to tell you or my mother, I felt that you expected me to achieve too much. Perpetually driving me to do better, to achieve

To Whom It May Concern – *The Book of Letters*

more and get the best results. Always saying that I had to get a grade A in every subject and that lower than that was worthless. Always telling me that I needed to focus my career towards management. Always telling me what I could and could not do. Even when I got those high grades it never felt like it was good enough.

Did you realise how heartbroken I was when you said I could not take up cooking as a career? And when I achieved the fantastic results that you so desired of me I got little praise in return. I never truly knew if you were pleased with my achievements because you rarely showed it. I often wondered what it was all for and if the hard work I put in was worthwhile. No matter what others told me I never felt that you cared for or valued me for who I was, your granddaughter! **YOUR only grandchild!**

I worked hard at school. Partly driven by the thought of having to please you and justify my existence but mostly driven by the desire to leave home as soon as I was old enough. I wanted to get out of that house, your home. It was a house devoid of affection when you were around. My only reprieve was the time I spent in the kitchen with my mother and grandmother baking. And I was ecstatic when you bought me a portable television for my bedroom. Even though it was second-hand it meant so much to me because I could stay in my room even longer and not have to sit downstairs with you!

You probably didn't realise how much Grandma used to

To Whom It May Concern – *The Book of Letters*

bake and give away to friends and people within the community. Hours and hours were spent in the kitchen baking rather than being in the sitting room with you. She was constantly popping out to take cakes somewhere. I think the only times I can picture you and grandma together was at meal times and going to church. How sad is that?

Countless hours were spent sat around the dinner table with very little conversation. Having to sit and eat in silence was boring, and if I spoke you would promptly remind me that I had to refrain from talking until everyone had finished their meal. But the atmosphere was often so tense that nobody wanted to speak after dinner anyway.

You have no idea how much I wanted to climb on your knee as a little girl and give you a big hug or to receive a smile at church or some form of acknowledgement that you cared for me. I wanted to hear you say 'Well done Mattie' when I returned home with an excellent school report. All I wanted was a little accolade, a few words that would have shown me that you were proud and loved me would have been nice. Would it have really been that hard to say something nice? Instead all I got was 'don't do this, don't do that.'

~~I felt like I was starved of affection~~ I WAS starved of affection but when I asked grandmother she reassured me of your love and even of your love for her and my mother. 'It is the way he is,' she would say but I didn't

To Whom It May Concern – *The Book of Letters*

understand because nobody bloody wanted to talk about what was really going on!

Then you died and Grandma told me about the loss of your only son, Patrick, my mother's older brother whose zest for life and adventure led him to his own death at the wheels of a motorbike when he was in his late teens.

I felt so sad that my grandmother had bottled up the memories of her only son in order to keep peace within the house. She and my mother were never allowed to talk about Patrick because of your own heart ache. Their hearts were broken too! Did you ever stop to think about that? NO. Probably not! You even emptied Patrick's room of all of his belongings except for that one picture, so that you didn't have to be reminded of him every time you walked past his room. Did you know that my grandmother kept a few photos and mementos of her son hidden away in a shoe box out of your sight? She used to look at the picture every time she went into her bedroom. She would talk to the photo and when she lit a candle at church after mass it was always done with Patrick in mind and the hope that you would open up about your loss. You never knew that did you? If you'd asked you would've known these things!

It also took your death for my grandmother to feel free to visit her son's grave. You actually used to stop her from going to the cemetery! I can't believe you would do that, it's unthinkable.

To Whom It May Concern – *The Book of Letters*

Grandma told me that you forbade Patrick to buy the motorbike. Your words being, 'over my dead body.' And it was over his dead body. That was the price he paid for speeding around a bend. I believe it was then that you shut down your emotions to everyone. To those you had shown love and affection to and who loved you dearly in return. Emotions cut off and kept within because it suited you to do so rather than talk about them. Or talk about Patrick.

*You did not cry or grieve for him the way I did for my mother when she died, instead you punished yourself and those closest to you because you were too afraid to talk about Patrick and give in to your emotions. Some people may call you proud, but I want to tell you that you were **STUBBORN, SELFISH & FOOLISH**. Too foolish and stupid to admit that you loved your son and that it hurt. I don't think your wife or daughter would have thought any the less of you had you chosen to show your grief. Grief is not a sign of weakness!*

~~**~~

Although it was a long rant and a release of pent up anger, Mattie finds the letter all too sad. She struggles hard not to cry, but the tears eventually fall catching the burnt edges making them crumble. More tears soak the paper and the black ink spreads blurring some of the words. Still unable to comprehend her grandfather, she reaches for another tissue before continuing.

~~**~~

To Whom It May Concern – *The Book of Letters*

~~When my mother said she was~~ Then my mother told you she was pregnant. She told me how scared she was at telling you and how angry you got. She was just sixteen, young and immature, and you never forgave her for what she did. 'Tarnished my reputation,' I was told were the words you said to her along with, "You are a disgrace, a disappointment!" For God's sake Grandpa, did you have to be so bloody cruel?

I learnt about all of this after you had died because Grandma and Mother were then free to talk about you and the past. I was sad for your loss but so angry at the way you treated my mother for her one and only indiscretion in life. She never forgot and I don't think she ever forgave you.

I finally began to understand why you behaved the way you did. Why people continually stared at us when we went to church like we were lepers. You had already suffered a great deal of pain and you chose to close yourself off to love and affection so that you would not get hurt again. The strict control you enforced on me was your way of trying to make sure that nothing bad happened. Unfortunately, it had the adverse effect, but because you had closed yourself off to all emotions, you could not see the damage you were causing. I used to think it was my fault for being ~~a bastard~~ illegitimate.

~~**~~

Mattie notices how she's scribbled out the word 'bastard' – a word Sadie freely used when she was being vicious. The stigma hits her hard and the pain she once suffered at the hands of that despicable girl resurfaces momentarily, but for her own sanity she continues reading the lengthy letter to her grandfather.

~~**~~

I needed a father, someone to care for me and tell me that they loved me. It is too difficult to handle the fact that you stopped my mother from telling the person who had got her pregnant that he was going to be a father, the young man that wanted to marry her who I'm sure would have looked after her and me if given the chance.

Somewhere out there I have a dad and I cannot find him because I don't know anything about him. You took away my rights of having a father, you took away my mother's rights to happiness. And for that I still cannot forgive you even though you are dead.
You are my grandfather, that is a fact, and perhaps one day I will find the strength to stop being angry with you for what you did.

Martha Barton
Your illegitimate Granddaughter

~~**~~

The final few sentences are harsh, and she feels bad for the bitterness she has shown and how she has held him responsible

To Whom It May Concern – *The Book of Letters*

on so many levels. *I just wish you'd talked, Grandfather*, she wishes out loud. *Just maybe you would've been happier.* But Mattie cannot ignore the fact that he stopped her from having a father regardless of the death of his only son.

After her grandfather died, she made a promise to not turn out like her family and repeat their mistakes. She couldn't comprehend the way they chose to live in the belief that problems should be brushed under the carpet and forgotten about. *How could a person spend a lifetime hiding their true feelings and shutting down in self-preservation? It's too damn hard!* She was certain she would not live a life like that, spending hour after hour, day after day not having the freedom to speak, to ask questions, and to resolve issues. But that was then, and now years later, she realises that to a certain degree she had done exactly that. She'd had the therapy, gained more confidence, and learnt to deal with emotions. But then she trapped them in a book and locked the book away.

The memories and realisation of what she's done make her want to scream out loud in the dark open air in frustration at her own stupidity, but she clenches her fists and holds back from the outburst.

She takes the letter, rips it into tiny pieces, and finally screams at that stubborn and stupid man. The sound is intrusive, and something nearby flutters away while this sad and bitter letter goes up in flames. Mattie is still angry with him, but to further make sense, she goes back to that time in her life.

The atmosphere in the house softened in the weeks that followed her grandfather's death. Grandmother Barton relaxed a little, too. However, most of the time she put on a brave smile. No matter how her husband had displayed his affections, she was

To Whom It May Concern – *The Book of Letters*

lost without him and it was clear in the loneliness she suffered.

On one occasion not long following his funeral, Grandmother Barton prepared for church as she did on every Sunday. Still confused about her feelings towards her grandfather after being told about Patrick and then not twenty four hours later to be told how he treated her mother when she announced her pregnancy, Mattie took his death as an opportunity to reject the church who she felt had played its part in her unhappiness - that of her grandfather's too. She knew how they'd been silently punished by other church-goers for her mother's indiscretion, and having learnt a few more such truths; she was less inclined to go. But when Mattie watched her grandmother put on her best coat and get ready to leave the house for mass, she thought otherwise and decided to go with her.

It was the least she could do for her – remembering the priest's words on the day her grandfather died. She knew that her grandmother needed her more now than ever. Mattie grabbed her coat, and as they were about to leave the house, her mother called back. The two turned around to watch Josie walk down the stairs, smartly dressed, telling them to wait while she put on her coat too. Josie decided it was time she went to mass. Other than her father's recent funeral, Mattie's mother hadn't attended church since Mattie had made her First Holy Communion several years earlier, and even that had been difficult for her, where she tried hard to avoid stares from the hypocritical elders who knew nothing about their lives.

The three stood proud side by side in the front pew without a care in the world of what the congregation were thinking.

For the last few years of her grandfather's life, Mattie started shutting down to the Catholic faith. Spending most of her time with eyes closed and in her own silent prayers, wishing her mother to break free and take her with her. She simply didn't want to go to church for she'd lost faith in faith. But sitting with her mother and grandmother, she prayed for Grandfather Barton's soul. She prayed that somehow he find peace in heaven, now that he was with his son Patrick, but she also gave thanks that the burden he'd placed on himself had died along with him and no longer hung like a dark cloud over the Barton house and the people who lived there.

The house was beginning to feel more like home and at least a place she was content to return to after a day at school. Some rooms were redecorated over time by adding a touch of colour here and there. Even the occasional vase of fresh flowers made an appearance. They bought a new sofa and Grandmother Barton even had a new colour television installed in the lounge. It didn't take long for her to get hooked to the mid-afternoon quiz programmes, and in the evenings Mattie would sit with them to watch the occasional soap opera.

Mattie was allowed to revamp her bedroom, within reason. The woodchip paper had to stay, but it received a fresh coat of a soft yellow tone and new curtains replaced the dull beige ones that had actually been hanging since Patrick occupied the room almost fifteen years earlier. For the first time, she was allowed to put up pictures, and soon the walls became adorned with a plethora of colourful accessories and wall hangings. Even Claire was invited to stay over, although Mattie had been hesitant when asking her mother. The changes perked up life in addition to making the bus journey home with the horrible Sadie less insufferable.

To Whom It May Concern – *The Book of Letters*

Nine

SADIE is quickly in Mattie's thoughts again, but Mattie is willing to go back there just one more time, to think how she dealt with the *bitch*. The image of that spectacular day at school brings a smug smile to her face...

It was the final day at St.Benedict's Catholic School. Mattie had studied hard for the final exams because she still craved the independence it would give her if she got excellent results. Her confidence had grown because she was no longer surrounded by the restrictions at home since the death of her grandfather ten months earlier, and the feeling of being unloved had finally dissipated.

"Pens down," the invigilator announced.

It was precisely three o'clock, signalling the end of the last exam. Mattie put down her pen and sat back in her chair in relief. She'd written page after page of information she was sure would get her an excellent grade. And in a few months, the wait would be over. She'd already decided which college she would attend. One that was as far away as possible from St.Benedict's, without any association to that school and its students –past or present.

The single desks were set out in uniformed rows in the sports hall. Mattie spotted Sadie from the corner of her eye, three rows across to the right. *As long as I stay clear of her I'll be okay!* That would be the last time Mattie would ever see or clash with her.

"Thank God that's all over." Mattie stood behind Claire queuing to hand the paper in. "I can't wait to get out of this goddamn place and away from the oxymoron."

To Whom It May Concern – *The Book of Letters*

Claire sniggered at their little joke that they'd found highly amusing for the past five years. Sadie still didn't know what it meant. "Are you coming back to my house?"

"That's the plan. My mum knows I'm staying at your place tonight."

The two were a few feet away from the desk when Mattie was shoved hard sending her forward rapidly. Sadie's rancid breath gave her away when she leaned in too close to dish out another of her verbal warnings.

"Hey, Tatty Mattie! Wait 'til we get outside," she said, resembling a pig and snorting nasally, as she often did when displaying her anger.

A couple of her mates, Hazel, Jacqui and Denise were standing nearby, and they started goading Sadie even more.

Claire could see the rising anger in Mattie's face.

"Don't let her get to you. Five more minutes and we'll be out of here." Claire tried to encourage her friend to ignore the jibes.

They handed in the exam papers but the pushing and shoving persisted until Mattie could tolerate no more. She'd put up with it for five years, and this private school had ignored the likes of Sadie bullying and harassing her and other girls all this while. It had to stop! Mattie turned on Sadie in a fit of rage.

"You bitch! You fucking bitch!" she hissed and grabbed Sadie by her shirt, pulling her forward. Through clenched teeth, a seething Mattie vented a few choice words at her for the first time, holding onto her shirt tightly and watching her go puce in the face at the sudden outburst. "Don't you ever, EVER, fucking touch me or even speak to me again. You stupid fucking bitch!"

Sadie stood motionless finally receiving the backlash that she surely must have known was on its way. After all, she'd dished out enough dirt in Mattie's direction since she'd joined the

To Whom It May Concern – *The Book of Letters*

school. It was only divine retribution that she got some of it back.

"I've put up with your shit for five years - but no more!" Mattie had had enough of Sadie's verbal diarrhoea and now seized the opportunity to get back at the snorting school bully. Mattie's blood rose quickly. At a loss of words, she blurted out, "You. Are. A. Stupid. Fucking. Oxymoron!" enunciating every syllable, making clear her intentions.

"What?" Sadie spluttered. "What the fuck is that supposed to mean? You two keep calling me that!"

Claire giggled, and a ripple of laughter spread throughout the onlookers standing on tiptoe to get a good view of Mattie putting Sadie in her place. Even Denise, who'd been a part of Sadie's group sniggered. Nose to nose with Sadie, still maintaining a tight grip of her shirt, Mattie spoke with calming reassurance.

"You want to know? Let me use words you understand. You're a stupid pretty ugly fucking bitch! If you'd spent more time studying instead of bullying, you might have an idea!"

Then Mattie let go and stepped back to a round of applause from the rest of the crowd who had been blocking the invigilator's desk.

A few loud whistles and a number of "whoop whoop" drowned out Sadie's protests. Even her so-called friends seemed pleased that Mattie had finally stood up to her bullying jibes, but they quickly dispersed before they ended up on the receiving end of the now aggrieved Sadie.

"Wow, Mattie!" said Claire, "Have you any idea how many times you said 'fuck'? I'm impressed."

The anger soon dissipated when Mattie watched her best friend coil up laughing at the sudden outburst and noticed Sadie scurry out of the school hall on her own. The outburst lasted only a few seconds, but it felt good to tell her what she thought of her.

To Whom It May Concern – *The Book of Letters*

She just wished she'd done it five years earlier, and perhaps her senior school years would have been more bearable. However, the event was still significant – first, because she was finally leaving the school, and second and more importantly, because she finally found the courage to stand up to Sadie, even though it was because she'd been pushed to the brink. Too many times Mattie had tried to be nice to the girl. In the past, she'd asked her kindly to leave her alone, and other than call her an oxymoron and a few other choice expletives, she'd never truly retaliated - until now. It seemed the only way to deal with her.

With a smug grin still clearly spread across her face, Mattie savours the memory of that sweet act of revenge, seeing Sadie's face as she ran from the school hall, and feels genuinely thankful that she never saw the girl ever again. But she came close to it a few years later.

It took a while for Mattie to stop looking over her shoulder, just to make sure Sadie wasn't around, despite the fact she'd chosen along with Claire to attend a college that far away from St.Benedict's. Deep down, she still thought Sadie would someday appear and make her life a misery. Prepared for that day, Mattie carried on normally, eventually she stopped thinking about her altogether. Until she met Denise.

The red book still feels rather weighty – not surprising, as she wrote several letters to Sadie notwithstanding the reams of paper she scribbled on when venting about Guy. She pulls angrily, more expletive-riddled letters addressed to the school bully and throws them into the pit of the chimenea, and while watching them incinerate and shrivel, she casts her mind back to a particular therapy session with Joan.

To Whom It May Concern – *The Book of Letters*

Joan read the long letter Mattie had recently written, and as she often did Mattie walked impatiently around her room. Her body language displayed impatience at waiting for her therapist's comments about what she thought. Joan's opinion mattered more than anything.

"What do you think?"

Joan came to the end of the letter and handed the red book back to Mattie when she finally sat down in front of her.

"Your final statement about the fact that this person Sadie no longer has control over you is a positive step forward. Ultimately only you can change you. It is you who is in control of your emotional feelings, Mattie."

She's right. I've got to be the one to change. "It's me who's holding me back, isn't it?"

Joan nodded. "You are letting past events define who you are. I can give you guidance, advice, methods to help you control thoughts and feelings, but ultimately, only you can make those changes and take emotional control of your life."

"When I left school I clung on to the hatred even though I'd finally stood up to her and told her what I thought. I suppose I got to the stage whereby I didn't even realise I was doing it, and it has become a habit, a very bad one that's a part of me."

"What has gone on before in your life, Mattie, is in the past and cannot be undone. But moving forward, we can focus on dealing with the emotions and helping you to build a brighter future with you being the one in control. Regardless of how bad she treated you, you did finally voice your opinion. You found the inner strength to say 'no' to her therefore that was a positive action you took."

"I know that now. But there's so much going on in my life at the moment, and I'm finding it so hard to stand up for myself and think clearly." Mattie slumped back into the comfy chair with the intense worry that she was shouldering about her current job. "I've had a lifetime of being told what to do, when to do it, how to do it, and I find it difficult to question that authority. Now Guy is manipulating me and I don't know how to cope."

"This is not a quick fix or short-term process. There may be times throughout your whole life when you cannot say 'no', or feel emotionally weak for a number of reasons. But what you must learn is to take back that control as you are doing now. You are a strong woman, and now is the time to stop being the victim."

Mattie thought about the words 'control' and 'victim', and finally, it was all beginning to make sense. It had suited her to play the victim and complain to those around her about how sad and hurt she was but wasn't prepared to do anything about it. That is until she met Joan.

Death within the Barton family hung over Mattie like a dark shadow, her boss was proving to be an irrational bastard, and even her best friend was drifting away. Her therapist encouraged her to take a good look at herself emotionally. She wasn't wrapped in cotton wool or allowed to wallow in self-pity at every moment, although she cried plenty and went through a fair few boxes of tissues. Joan showed Mattie the strength she had within and how she could draw upon that emotional strength to get through life. But it had to be one day at a time – tiny steps towards building up emotional control and independence.

To Whom It May Concern – *The Book of Letters*

Ten

THE past is staying in the past, Mattie chants several times over, *and people like Grandfather Barton, Sadie, and Guy cannot hurt me anymore!* She repeats it a few more times, saying the affirmation over and over in her head just to keep the feelings of angst at bay, which have surfaced by reading the letters. *I'm fine. I'm more than fine.* Mattie further adds as proof of her positive attitude. *I'm blissfully happy.*

For the last ten years, Mattie has drifted along in a bubble of bliss – as a mother and an executive's wife, when required. But now it's all changed, and she knows that when the letters are all burnt and the next day dawns, life will be different. She'll be different, because she has ventured back to that part of her life she thought she had left behind and finally let go of the hatred and pain.

Feeling emotionally wrecked, she begins regretting finding the book in the first place. But with stubborn determination, she's prepared to see it through to the bitter end no matter how many tears she has to shed. She forces a smile to lighten the heavy emotional load that has fallen on her through her own doing, and to ease the effect it is having upon her, Mattie turns back to her sessions with Joan.

God, she'd have me locked up if she knew about this! Before long, Mattie is back sitting in the comfortable surroundings of Joan's office, hearing her soothing words.

"Write down ten things that you like about yourself."

Mattie gave Joan a bemused look and wondered where this

To Whom It May Concern – *The Book of Letters*

was heading.

"You have ten minutes."

Mattie clenched the pen hard as she struggled to think of anything that she liked about herself. She actually thought it was easier to write ten things she didn't like about herself, but she was not tasked with that. Five minutes passed, and she'd yet to write a single word. Joan walked slowly around the room. It made Mattie feel nervous, watching her movements, seeing her toying with the vase of flowers, moving them out of the direct sunlight.

Noticing that she hadn't written a single word, Joan commented, "Surely there must be something good you like about yourself." Then she changed the angle of the blinds as the minutes ticked away.

"I can think of ten good things about *you*, Joan. Would that be okay?"

A sweet smile full of gratitude passed over her face. "This is not about me, Mattie, it's about you."

Several minutes passed.

Life wasn't great at the moment. In fact, it was positively putrid as far as Mattie was concerned. She'd been dealt enough blows, and trying to think about what was good about herself was proving harder than imagined, she just wasn't used to this. Conscious that only three minutes remained, she scribbled on the paper, 'Nice hair'. It was the best thing she could think of, although recently, her hair too had fallen limp. Joan sat down opposite her, and while she tried her best not to look at her directly, Mattie knew Joan's eyes were upon her. For the few minutes that remained, Mattie was back in the classroom writing end-of-year exams and under intense pressure, trying to think of one more sentence to cram in before the invigilator told everyone to put their pens down. But in this instance, no matter how hard

To Whom It May Concern – *The Book of Letters*

she gave thought to the task, Mattie could not find anything nice to write at all.

The ten minutes seemed like eternity. Joan took the pen and paper from Mattie and looked at it.

"Nice hair," she read out raising an eyebrow. "Is that the best you can say? I can think of many kind things to say about you, Mattie, and I have only known you for a few weeks."

"I'm not used to praising myself." *Or being praised*, she thought.

Joan could see how apprehensive Mattie was. "The purpose of this exercise is not to upset you, but for you to start thinking in a positive manner, and the best place to start is with you. It's easy to praise other people, tell them they look nice or are clever, but what about you telling you? What do you say to yourself that makes you feel good?"

Mattie pondered the question. "But isn't that being conceited?"

"Says who?" Joan laughed back. "If you do not love yourself first and foremost then how can you give out love to others?"

"Well, says the Catholic church."

Joan held Mattie's hand and walked her to the oak cheval mirror standing in the corner of the room. "Mattie, you have so much to learn." She made her stand in front of it, took a step to one side, and asked, "What do you see, Mattie?"

"Me?" Came the rhetorical reply.

"Okay, describe you."

"I have blonde shoulder-length hair. I'm wearing a navy blue trouser suit and white blouse. Navy shoes too, but god are they uncomfortable..." and so she went on describing how she was dressed that day. It seemed a simple task to do.

"Good, but you're only describing what is on the surface. Now look deeper at the person you see. Look into her eyes and tell me about all the good things that are inside that person." Joan jabbed her finger at Mattie's reflection. "Tell me what she likes to do, her favourite things, what music she listens to – whatever comes to mind that makes that person you are looking right at feel good. She's right there, looking back at you. Go on, you know you can do it."

Mattie hesitated, looking back at Joan for reassurance and then back at her own reflection. She saw the hazel eyes of the frightened young woman staring back and knew that in there was Mattie Barton screaming to get out. Unaccustomed to such an activity, she took a hesitant step closer to the mirror and tucked her hair behind her ears. Then with a deep breath, she began.

"I am Martha Barton but I prefer to be called Mattie. I'm twenty-three years old and I like..." she glanced at Joan again, seeking reassurance. Joan nodded back. "I like cooking..." again Mattie hesitated, unable to just let out what was burning inside. With a further push from her therapist she took a deep and steady breath and began to talk. "In fact I love to cook, especially cakes. My grandmother taught me from a young age and we used to spend most Sunday afternoons baking in her kitchen..."

Further pushing Mattie to talk openly and be honest, Joan then stood back to watch.

"I like all types of music, especially Jazz. There's something seductive about it. My favourite film is High Society. Wouldn't you agree?"

Her therapist nodded in encouragement yet still willed her to go on.

Mattie had never done anything like this before, and even though it felt strange to talk about what she liked or what excited her, it was also liberating. She continued, "I liked art in school

To Whom It May Concern – *The Book of Letters*

and was very good at it. When I was about ten years old, I fancied George Michael and I had a poster of him on my bedroom wall. But when we moved into my grandparents' I wasn't allowed to take it amongst other things..." Realising she was about to sour the memory, she promptly pulled away from it and moved on swiftly to something that was happier.

Minutes later, Mattie stopped, unable to add more. But her breathing was racy and there was a glow in her cheeks.

"Well done, Mattie. Look how you are buzzing with enthusiasm. That was not so hard, was it? Now I want you to go back to what I asked you to do before and give me ten positive words to describe you."

She looked back at her image once more in the mirror and thought, if Claire was describing her, what would she say? But she wasn't Claire, and as advised by Joan, she had to allow her own thoughts and words to tumble out freely, not what she thought other people would say about her.

"Hardworking, focused, intelligent, generous, and amiable." Mattie stopped momentarily, surprised at how freely the words came out, then added "loving" followed by "kind, caring, and. ." Then with a final look at Joan, she added, "Beautiful and confident."

Joan stepped forward. "Excellent, Mattie! You have finally seen what I saw the day I met you, but you had to learn to see it with your own eyes."

"I'm not used to hearing those words, and when I was young, I was told it was vain to think like that."

Joan frowned, which stopped the negative and self-destructive comments. "You have to love yourself in order to love others. It's got nothing to do with being vain or conceited, and you most certainly should not feel bad for thinking that you are beautiful and intelligent. Because of your past, you have limiting beliefs, and that in turn is stopping you from moving forward in a positive manner."

Mattie looked at her for clarification and queried the last statement.

"You use words and phrases that put you down. You say things such as 'I can't do that'."

"Oh. That obvious, is it?"

"Who is telling you that you can't do whatever you want? You know you are hardworking and intelligent because you tell me often about the hours you put in at work and how good you are at your job. But do you believe in those words? Do you believe in you?"

Mattie turned back to the mirror and looked long and hard.

"For the next seven days, I want you to repeat this exercise."

Mattie questioned the purpose of repeating this.

"It's an affirmation, and the more you tell yourself, the more you use and hear those words, the more you will start believing in them. Eventually, they will form a habitual and natural part of your everyday life."

"You make it sound so simple." At this, Joan reminded Mattie not to belittle the technique.

"Life is not simple, Mattie. Believing in the words is just a part of the process. You have to live and experience them, too. I also want you to do an activity each day, if possible, which is purely for you, is about you, and is something that will make you happy."

"Such as walking barefoot in the park?"

"If that is what will make you happy then yes, walk barefoot in the park. Hug a tree."

"Bake a cake?"

To Whom It May Concern – *The Book of Letters*

That night Mattie stood in front of the bathroom mirror and thought of another ten words, each one filling her with good intention. Then she made a Victoria sponge cake.

"What are you doing?" Claire shouted from the lounge.

"Changing my life," she replied.

To Whom It May Concern – *The Book of Letters*

Eleven

AS the evening draws on, Mattie pulls away from those thoughts of Joan. Like all those years ago, the positive words still ringing in her head have quashed the angry feelings towards Sadie. She moves on to the next letter, looks down at it, and squeals with laughter at the event and what she did to Darren that time in the canteen. She allows a few more moments of indulgence about him – the adolescent she once thought to be her first true love. That was until she met Mr Blond. Thinking about that delicious yet untouchable man sends a dreamy hot flush through her body.

When the opportunity presented itself to finally sleep with Darren – whom she classed as her first real and serious boyfriend – Mattie leaped at the chance. It was soon into her second term at college that Mattie met him. They were in the same economics group. He was cute and a great kisser. And she loved the feeling of his silky black hair that he wore in a ponytail. It was something to grab hold of when Mattie snogged his face off. He was also the first boy she'd brought home and introduced to her micro family, even though when she did, he had mocked the staid decor and thought Mattie's bedroom was too pink, saying it needed to be 'Gothed up' to bring it into the twentieth century. She told him she'd think about it.

Mattie and Darren spent weeks kissing and fumbling, until the right moment presented itself. Claire's parents were away for a week, her brother Adam was at University, and her eldest brother Dominic, whom Mattie still had a crush on, was working in

To Whom It May Concern – *The Book of Letters*

America. It was late-January. They'd only been at college for five months and the two sixteen-year-olds were being given the run of the house for a whole seven days. Mattie gave her mother the excuse that she was keeping Claire company because Claire didn't like being alone, and moved in with her friend for that week. Mattie considered telling her mother the truth, or at least a version of it, but didn't suppose she'd be that understanding. Josie, however, had an inkling of what her daughter was up to and said that she had no desire to be a young grandmother, neither did she want Mattie to repeat her own mistakes. Josie could see her daughter growing and maturing fast, and while there were house rules to abide by as her grandmother was ageing and it had been impressed upon her how important her studies were, Mattie was given the freedom she desired, within reason – even to bring home boys – if that was what she really wanted.

On the first night the two took advantage of their freedom and feeling grown up, Mattie and Claire raided Claire's parents' drinks cabinet and got equally drunk on a variety of concoctions, including a cream liqueur. Mattie spent the rest of that night asleep in the toilet with her head resting on the hard white plastic seat. She vomited until she could be sick no more, vowing never to drink again, whereas Claire crashed out on the lounge floor, fully clothed. The following morning, the two looked deathly white and agreed that mixing drinks wasn't wise and mature after all. Even the smell of toast made the pair want to wrench more. It was mid-day before they felt well enough to venture outdoors to meet their respective boyfriends at the college campus.

That week flew by with Mattie and Claire just about managing to get to college on time. Then the night for their boyfriends to stay over arrived. Claire was dating Tom, a nice boy in the year above, and while Darren and Tom didn't mix in the same social groups, the two guys seemed to hit it off when they were all together.

The sexual experience had been planned out in Mattie's mind for some time. It was going to be right out of a Mills and Boon – stars and roses story – it was going to be simply thrilling and satisfying. Under Darren's grungy dark clothes was a sweet good-looking lad who showered Mattie with affection in a way she never previously knew. Through her rose-tinted glasses, she saw fireworks, shooting stars, and wolves howling in response to them making love. It was all mapped out in her head – just how she was going to lose her virginity – and a plan was put into action.

It was Saturday night, and while the heavy bass music reverberated around the house, Mattie, Darren, Claire, and Tom set to playing poker. Careful of not taking any more alcohol from Claire's parents' cabinet, as a few bottles had already been topped with water, they bought some cheap cider and snacked on crisps and peanuts.

"Well, I'm off to bed. Coming with me, Tom?" Tom looked up at Claire with a grin of the cat that had got the cream, and before he had the chance to reply, she grabbed his hand and the two hurried upstairs.

Mattie looked over to Darren, wishing him to do the same. The spare bed had been made up, she'd put roses in a vase by the side, and a few petals lay scattered across the pillow – all out of a book she'd read. She'd even sprayed some eau de parfum – purchased that morning – around the room, to further enhance a sexy ambience.

"Let me put these things away and we can go upstairs if you like."

Darren looked at Mattie with a growing intensity and longing

To Whom It May Concern – *The Book of Letters*

to have her.

"Come here," he said and took her hand, pulling her towards him on the floor. Mattie straddled his legs, pressing her hips into his groin, and when he pressed his lips hard against hers, she could feel him. He slipped his hand up the front of her jumper, squeezing her breasts with the same intensity. She grabbed the back of his hair – held it tight – and kissed him back equally as passionately. *Sod the rose petals and soft sheets*, she thought.

He flipped her over, sending poker chips scattering across the carpet, and the upturned bowl of crisps crunched under her back.

"We need to be careful," she gasped, releasing herself from his kiss.

In the short time since she and Claire had left St.Benedict's, Mattie's life had somersaulted forward, almost beyond recognition of how her senior school days used to be. She was still sixteen years old and had decided that sleeping with Darren was what she wanted.

Darren got up and pulled out a small packet from his pocket. "I come prepared," he said, and they laughed at his fair choice of words.

The visions she'd had of undressing each other seductively – each button undone provocatively, shoes slipped off tenderly, and clothes peeled off gently, lying naked next to each other while he ran his fingers tenderly over her skin just as she'd seen in the movies and read in books – vanished. Within seconds, Darren had unzipped his trousers and pulled them down to his knees, allowing his penis to lop out in front of her. She gasped in shock, not only at the size, but also at his candid attitude. Lying amongst broken crisps and dirty glasses and being told to take off her knickers was as seductive as Darren got.

He peeled back the foil wrapper and removed the condom.

To Whom It May Concern – *The Book of Letters*

"Do you want to put it on?"

She shook her head.

"Lie back. It won't hurt. I promise."

"But what if I'm no good at this?"

Ignoring her worry, he climbed on top, fumbled around, and tried to push inside.

"Relax, you're too tense." He kissed her hard on the mouth again with the sweat taste of cider still on his lips, and then slowly slipped in.

It was over within moments – a few hard thrusts, and Darren was finished and disappearing to the toilet. Mattie lay on the floor. She pulled up her trousers and waited for him to return.

"Look Mattie, I promised a mate I'd meet 'im for a drink. I'm gonna shoot!"

She wasn't expecting that! The experience wasn't wonderful, but she still hoped he'd lie by her side in bed. Maybe the next time they made love it would be something to remember. Instead, she told him it was okay to go, and he went.

~~**~~

Hi Darren,

Ha Ha Ha. I hope you enjoyed having the milkshake poured over your head.

~~**~~

Mattie pauses to consider the so-called myth that the first sexual experience is supposed to be special and momentous, going so far as to think it is meant to be earth-shattering. None of this happened. Well, at least not with Darren. But reading the letter about the uneventful experience and what followed next, she laughs out loud at being that stupid for believing so much in the words of soppy love books and the sweet nothings he whispered in her ear. The amusement continues when she pictures pouring the drink over his head.

A week passed without a word from him, and he failed to turn up to class. Then Mattie received a phone call from a girl whose name now escapes her, but who was quick to say that Darren slept with her friend at a party the same night she'd lost her virginity to him. Mattie felt dirty, cheap, and used, and realised that he had only wanted to get into her knickers.

~~**~~

How could I have been so naive to think that you loved me? IT WAS LUST, NOT LOVE! And even though your manhood is very big you have no idea on how to use it. I've had far better since.

~~**~~

She reads the letter with uncontrollable sniggers, thinking of that momentous occasion in the college canteen – Darren pleading with her to not tip the thick strawberry milkshake over him, begging for forgiveness, as it was poured down his face, with the sticky liquid clumping up his smooth hair. And when an unknown girl came over and slapped Darren across the face, sending a spray of milk across the table into the path of his mates, Mattie clapped with sarcastic joy.

The silly letter to Darren is scrunched up and more bouts of

To Whom It May Concern – *The Book of Letters*

laughter pour out at her stupidity. *How could I have been so naive?* She carries on giggling at her idiocy at some of the things she's written about, and to people who she can barely remember what they even looked like. And then she realises that tonight has not just been about letting go of bad memories, but also about taking a good look at what she was like and the things that happened and some of the silly moments in life.

Turning over more pages in the red book, Mattie merely takes a glance at some letters written about events which, upon reflection, are irrational and not even worth a second look. Skimming through the trivial and meaningless words, she hastily pulls pages from the book and burns them quickly, deciding at long last that after all it was such a long time ago, and that time is a great healer. When she detects movement in the house, she wonders what Jake is up to at this time of the night and giggles some more, glad that he's not sitting with her, having not joined her as he'd intended, as there are some things you simply don't tell your husband.

To Whom It May Concern – *The Book of Letters*

Twelve

MATTIE continues to laugh about her own behaviour during those two years at college and how intense the studying was at times, even though it was also a period when she met new people, had new experiences, and went to many parties. But the happiness subsides momentarily, when she considers her choice of A-level subjects and the reason behind this choice.

Grandfather Barton left Mattie financially secure. It was a complete surprise when the Will was read a few days after his funeral.

"...the sum of thirty thousand pounds is bequeathed to my only grand-child, Martha Barton..."

Mattie turned to her mother and grandmother in surprise. "But what about you two, surely he left you something because that's a large amount to leave to me and..." Her grandmother reached over, took her hand and told her not to worry. The solicitor continued.

By the time the solicitor had finished detailing the amount bequeathed to his daughter Josie, and other conditions of his last will and testament, Mattie was stomping around the office livid.

"How can he do that," she ranted. "He's dead and he's still dictating how I live my life!"

"Mattie dear, sit down and be rational. You know he only wants the best for you. It's a small caveat to do a management degree and consider how it will easily cover your college fees and should you go to university then those too." Josie begged her daughter to sit down.

To Whom It May Concern – *The Book of Letters*

"I'll give the money to a cat sanctuary!" Mattie pouted like a petulant child, still fuming. She saw the hurt in her grandmother's face and felt sorry for her. Was this the best way she could show her gratitude for the gift of money? Mattie thought long and hard. "Okay then, if that's what he wants but I'll never use it to cover my tuition fees. I'll do that myself."

Once again her grandfather was in control of Mattie's future, and now he was doing it from the grave but she finally acquiesced. It was a sizeable amount and would certainly fund her further education. So she accepted the money after some heavy persuasion from her grandmother. But the gift of money only made Mattie more determined to run her own life as she wanted to, even if it meant not dipping into the education fund. So when the opportunity presented itself during her A-level studies, she jumped at the chance of taking the part-time waitressing job at Luigi's Italian Restaurant.

Claire was jealous about Mattie's new job because her parents said she had to wait until she'd completed her A'level studies. One Friday night, to compensate, she settled for visiting Mattie after work and from there they would go out.

"Mattie," Claire called out to her inside a toilet cubicle. "Who's that hot guy behind the bar?"

"Which one?" Mattie knew exactly whom she was referring to – the boss's son.

"You know? The one with the small tight ass and dark sexy eyes. Has he worked here long? I've never seen him here before."

Mattie pulled open the toilet door after quickly changing out of the uniform – a black skirt and white blouse – into a pair of tight jeans and a red t-shirt. "That's Francisco". Then she slipped on her new high-heeled shoes, knowing that by the end of the evening, she'd have blisters on both heels to show for it. "I guess you could say he's worked here long."

"Has he got a girlfriend?"

Refusing to answer her friend, she touched up her lipstick, applied more mascara, then eventually turned to Claire and said that he'd recently broken up with his long-term girlfriend. That was as much as Mattie was prepared to tell about the lovely, adorable Francisco, who was best kept at arm's length where Claire was concerned, while he healed his broken heart.

"Well maybe I could make him feel better. You know, give him a shoulder to cry on."

"You've only just dumped David," Mattie said with a disapproving look. Claire got the message to drop the subject about the cute guy, with the small tight ass and dark sexy eyes.

Each Friday thereafter, Claire arrived at the restaurant ten minutes before Mattie's shift ended, hoping to get a glimpse of Frankie, as everyone called him. Mattie wasn't going to tell her friend yet that he was the owner's son and that he was there most weekends, generally working in the back. She was enjoying the job and could do without the added distraction.

David had been another in the long string of boyfriends Claire had dated and dumped quickly, justifying each breakup by saying that "they weren't the one". Mattie loved her friend's passion for life, but in her passion for men, Mattie tried her best not to get involved. Plus she wanted to keep the waitressing job. So the longer she kept Claire away from Frankie, the better.

Enrolment day for university fast approached, and the two of them moved into a student flat. It was too late to change career paths, Mattie decided, although she had once considered dropping out of her A' level studies and attending catering college. But the thought of going backwards didn't thrill her when all Mattie wanted to do was move forwards and get the degree, the one of her grandfather's choosing, out of the way.

She still refused to dip into the inheritance, adamant that she would get by like other students and pay her way through. The first two weeks at University went by in a blur as Claire and Mattie went from one fresher's party to another, turning up for long lectures with eyes half-closed from the late nights. In addition, Mattie chose to work most evenings at the restaurant.

One day, while they queued to get a coffee in the canteen, Mattie informed Claire, "I've put in a good word for you at Luigi's because one of the waitresses has resigned. She didn't give them any notice and they could do with the help sooner rather than later, if you're interested." Claire had been celibate for a few months now, and still eager to work at Luigi's. It was a matter of time before she and Frankie met and Mattie succumbed to their eventual liaison.

"Really? That'd be great, and maybe I might get to see that hot-looking guy again. I've not seen him for a while. Is he still single?" she enquired enthusiastically. "Oh my god!" Claire gave Mattie a firm nudge in the ribs. "Look! Over there, it's him." She spotted Frankie sitting at one of the tables with a group of other students. "Let's go over. You've got to introduce me, Mattie."

Armed with coffees and rather dry-looking cheese sandwiches, they made their way to the group of students.

"Hi Frankie!" greeted Mattie. The lovely Frankie looked up and beamed his big Italian white smile. "This is Claire. Remember me telling you about her?"

Claire nudged her again and muttered, "That makes me sound desperate."

"You are," Mattie whispered back. "Claire, this is Frankie, he

To Whom It May Concern – *The Book of Letters*

is the boss's son. Frankie, this is Claire, my *desperate* friend."

When Claire realised she'd been played all this time, she gave Mattie a sideways glance of disgust, but when the tall, good-looking, Italian stood up and gave her the same squeezing hug he gave Mattie upon meeting her for the first time, lifting her from her feet, the disapproval vanished.

"You start work at Luigi's tonight?" he asked her.

Claire was left speechless. The normal talkative person looked on in awe with reddened cheeks once Frankie put her back down, so Mattie filled in the missing words as Claire's mouth lay wide open and dormant, making it apparent that she was smitten with this good-looking guy. Within a week of their introduction, they were dating, and the one person who was adamant about not falling in love because she had a career to focus on had gone and done just that.

The trio had a ball working together at Luigi's, and Frankie's family were very welcoming of Claire, as they had been of Mattie. Those first few months in the shared apartment were a scream, an absolute riot. Frankie became a regular visitor, staying over most nights – not that it bothered Mattie, as she too started dating a lad called Josh.

How the two young women managed to stick to university assignment deadlines in that first year still remains a blur to Mattie. She got through it, Josh was dumped – for what reasons she wasn't exactly sure other than he wasn't the one. Then another winter and cold January arrived and brought with it a long chill, bringing towns and cities to a grinding halt under the extreme icy weather conditions.

A breeze whistles past Mattie, making the few remaining leaves clinging on to the trees in defiance of the oncoming winter

To Whom It May Concern – *The Book of Letters*

sound a disgruntled rustle. A chill cuts through her and down her spine like it did that winter when her grandmother died. Mattie tucks the blanket around her legs again, making sure there are no gaps for the cold air to seep through and throws on a few larger blocks of wood to replace those that have now broken down into smaller fragments, left smouldering at the bottom of the fire. They glow, and once again the fire roars.

It was her second year at university when Grandmother Barton slipped on some black ice in the driveway. The doctors assured Mattie and her mother that the elderly woman would make a recovery from the broken hip, but a few weeks after the accident, she was gone – pneumonia took her away.

Her sudden death rocked Josie's world.

Mattie awoke to the sound of her mother crying as she sat at the bottom of the stairs, visibly shaking from the news. The hospital had phoned in the middle of the night and said "she died peacefully in her sleep", but that didn't feel like a consolation.

Mattie shakes her head in disbelief at how a common cold could quickly turn into something so bad that it took the life of her loving grandmother. She'd never considered how long her grandmother would live without Grandfather Barton by her side, but she certainly never expected her to die like that. Five years had passed since his death, and though it took time for Grandmother Barton to mourn him, she readjusted well to life as a widow.

For Mattie, seeing her mother's heart break and weep for her own mother was a whole new experience. While she witnessed her mother express little grief upon the death of her father, the woman who'd suppressed her feelings for so long had broken down and wept uncontrollably when she lost her mother.

To Whom It May Concern – *The Book of Letters*

As Mattie held Josie's hand when they walked behind the coffin, leaving the church after the short and simple service, she caught sight of a woman sitting at the back of church wearing an unusual hat. How old-fashioned, thought Mattie of the round, charcoal grey hat with a big black feather protruding from the top. Like all the other mourners, she was dressed in black, but the woman sat alone, and when she looked up to give her condolences, Mattie recognised the elderly lady.

The teacher, Mrs Williams, whom she no longer cared for, took Josie's hand and said a few sympathetic words before moving on. But Mattie could not bring herself to look her in the eye and had no feelings other than contempt for the horrible teacher.

Mattie sat next to her mother in the funeral car as it made its way to the cemetery, wondering what she would now do with the rest of her life. It seemed inappropriate to ask, but her mother was finally free to live her life as she pleased. It had been a long week for her mother, making preparations for the funeral and dealing with solicitors. Her complexion was grey, and when Mattie squeezed her hand and smiled at her, a faint glow appeared in her cheeks. For a moment, Mattie knew there was hope after all.

The day of the funeral was damp and bitterly cold, and there were no signs of the harsh winter breaking. Mattie tucked the red cashmere scarf that her grandmother had gifted her that very Christmas securely around her neck to stop the wind whipping around her and making her colder than she already was. Then she laid a red rose – her grandmother's favourite flower – on the coffin, just before it was lowered into the grave to be laid to rest with her husband. She shed a tear and held onto her mother's arm, thinking about all the happy times they had spent baking. Her thoughts, however, were tinged with sadness when she

To Whom It May Concern – *The Book of Letters*

looked around at the mourners who'd turned out on the miserable day to pay their last respects. Surprised at the numbers who attended Grandmother Barton's funeral, considering their tongues had wagged inappropriately for such a long time about Mattie being illegitimate, Mattie wanted to tell them they were all hypocrites. But they stood side by side, as if nothing bad had been done, while Mattie struggled to make sense of it all.

With both of her grandparents now dead and a second inheritance that simply boosted the first – albeit with no conditions attached as to how and when she spent it – along with her mother rattling around in the house that was far too big, dull and dreary for her, life carried on.

A few weeks following the funeral, Mattie would've been at a lecture if it wasn't for the fact that the tutor was sick. Initially she decided to visit her mother in the free time and maybe they could grab something to eat – maybe even go out to lift the gloom that Josie was in. But instead, she decided to take advantage of the free time. Armed with books and folders, she queued patiently at the coffee shop, opting to work on a marketing assignment. All she had to do to complete the assignment was finish the conclusion – for which she thought five hundred words or so would do just fine – plus update the bibliography, and that would be another assignment completed. She'd visit her mother on another day, Mattie decided.

The barista handed Mattie the large cappuccino. She turned to make her way to a small table that had just become free, tucked away in the corner of the shop. *Perfect! Out of the way*, she thought.

"Martha? Martha Barton, it is you?"

Mattie turned to face the person who'd called out to her – a woman dressed brightly in red and fuchsia from head to toe.

To Whom It May Concern – *The Book of Letters*

Casually surveying the pink velour tracksuit and the vibrant shiny red wig of the woman who gleamed back at her with a big smile displaying extra-white veneered teeth as she ordered a large skinny mocha with extra cream and chocolate sprinkles, Mattie struggled to recognise who this woman was.

"It's me, Denise. Denise Carlisle from St.Benedict's."

The look on Mattie's face intensified. Who was she? The high-pitched voice was familiar, but she struggled to recall the face, most of it hidden under a pair of large dark sunglasses and a long, bright red fringe. "I'm sorry, I don't remember you. Were we in the same year?"

Denise removed the sunglasses, and it only took a split second for Mattie to connect the name to the petite face and high-pitched voice. A knot formed in her stomach. She was one of Sadie's friends.

Where's Sadie? She instinctively turned and scanned the coffee shop to find her.

Reluctantly, Mattie admitted to having a vague recollection of the woman in pink. "It is a few years ago, after all," she said. "You look – different?"

Denise smoothed her hand over her red, silky hair as if to ask whether Mattie liked her ensemble, but Mattie was more concerned about Sadie's whereabouts and was still peering over Denise's shoulder, eagerly watching the passers-by outside. She'd put up with five years of Sadie and her posse and figured that if Denise was here, then *that bitch* would be too. Mattie's hand began to sweat from the loose change she was holding tightly. She wanted to bolt out of the coffee shop as quickly as possible, but she was holding a large hot mug and a stack of books, which made her escape difficult. Denise pushed up the sunglasses, dragging back and pinning the red fringe to the top of her head and revealing large golden hoop earrings that swung about her neck.

"I'm a dancer," she said and gave a little twirl to demonstrate. But Mattie's eyes were only fixed on the diamanté logo that emblazoned the velour-covered buttocks.

Mattie politely smiled back, trying her best to say as little as possible. "Well, I've work to catch up on. You look great, nice to see you," she said and made her way to the still vacant corner table.

Denise collected her chocolate drink and followed her. "I'm sorry."

The words made Mattie look up from her marketing book, but she didn't want Denise's apology. It was far too late for that.

"I never did like Sadie, you know, and... and well, I feel really bad at the way she... what I'm trying to say is that I'm truly sorry for the way *we* treated you."

Mattie was taken aback by the honesty of the red-and-pink clad woman, and when she sat down next to Mattie without invitation, Mattie thought it rude not to let her speak her mind. It was about time she received an explanation, if nothing else.

"You haven't changed, you know."

Mattie touched the ends of her newly styled hair thinking she didn't look anything like she used to look at school – having been eager to shake off that image along with a lot of other things.

"I hated myself for a long time. I behaved so badly..." The door had opened for Denise, and for reasons unknown, she began to unburden herself, speaking about her troubles at school.

Mattie listened sympathetically to her tales of how she pleaded with her parents to send her to another school so she could get away from the bullying gang she had 'unwillingly' been dragged into. "...so I dropped out of college and took up dancing professionally. I'd had lessons from being a kid so it wasn't that hard to get back into it."

When she caught sight of Mattie hiding a smirk behind her coffee cup, she casually added, "I'm not a pole dancer, if that's what you're thinking."

"No, I never thought that for a moment," Mattie lied.

"I'm also taking acting lessons, and in fact, I've just been for an audition, and well..." she trailed off, "...I'm keeping everything crossed that I get the part. This is a wig, by the way. And I don't normally dress like this. It's just for the audition, you know. In fact, I rather like this outfit. Being incognito and watching people look at you through these sunglasses is amusing. I've actually had some funny looks today. Even you didn't recognise me," she enthused.

Denise continued recounting her life story since leaving school and briefly touched upon the subject of the 'other girls' who participated in bullying and harassing Mattie. Mattie lacked the energy to listen to the tiny details and was more interested in the little boy sitting nearby, who merrily crushed his biscuit into a blended mush on the table along with some milk, much to the dismay of his grandparents.

At first, Mattie didn't want to hear the tales, yet she nodded and even asked the odd question out of pure politeness, hoping secretly that Denise would leave.

An hour passed swiftly. The little boy had long gone and a young teenage boy sat in his place listening to music through his headphones and tapping his pen to the rhythm of the music on the table, looking like he too was studying.

Then eventually, Denise touched on the one subject Mattie knew she was leading to. *I don't want to be here and listen to this tripe!* But she managed a faint smile and said very little, trying

To Whom It May Concern – *The Book of Letters*

hard not to be forced into a conversation about Sadie. It was as if Denise had waited years to have this conversation and beseech Mattie's forgiveness. However, it would take more than a confession and admission of guilt for her to forget what they did.

"You know she got what she deserved. Little Miss Perfect now has a crap life," Denise laughed. "Do you remember that last day at school?"

Of course I do! Mattie let her carry on and said nothing.

"You know, after that exam when you got angry with Sadie, it really shook her up? It was the first time I'd seen someone stand up to her like that, and I thought 'good for you, Martha, for doing it'. It was then that I realised what a horrible person I'd become and I'd no intention of... well you can guess what I mean."

Denise went on to tell of Sadie's parents' divorce soon after they left St.Benedict's, and while she relayed information of that bitch, Mattie became more interested in what Denise had to say.

"You know, her mother ran off to Portugal with her tennis coach when Sadie was only fifteen, leaving her with her younger brother and father. Then not long after that her dad filed for bankruptcy and they lost their home. They lost everything. Can you imagine?"

"Poor Sadie," Mattie muttered sarcastically. She wanted to jump up and down with joy.

"Did you know she had an abortion while still at school?" Mattie shook her head in horror. "Then she turned up on my doorstep a year later with her first kid in tow. Pah! Looking for a place to stay, she was. My parents of course took pity, but she only stayed a week. Thank God! I didn't want her in my house. She'd not changed. I caught her stealing money from my mother's purse and there was no way I was going to start behaving badly again."

To Whom It May Concern – *The Book of Letters*

Mattie's head ached from listening about Sadie. She'd allowed herself to be dragged back into the world of a person that she'd tried so hard to forget, and the more Denise talked about Sadie's misfortune and how her life had turned out, the more Mattie's head throbbed from the overload of the girl's misfortune.

"...the last I knew she was living off benefits somewhere in Yorkshire and had three kids from three different men. Can you believe that – we've only been left school as many years?"

That afternoon, Denise walked away feeling a whole lot lighter, having offloaded her emotional garbage, and by the time she left, saying that she was going to be late for another appointment, Mattie was drained and felt sick to the stomach. Denise walked out of the coffee shop in the knowledge that she'd done a good turn by telling Mattie all of this and apologising for the part she played. However, Mattie remained seated at the table, completely drained and no longer having the energy to work on the assignment plus wishing she'd visited her mother.

It doesn't take much thinking to allow Sadie back in Mattie's thoughts, making her feel weary. When Mattie wrote the many letters to Sadie, she was smug in the knowledge that the school bully, who'd come from a wealthy upbringing, had her life turn upside down and was now living a crap life. But as much that she wanted to see her burn in hell for what she'd done, the reality was that the ill thoughts didn't actually make Mattie feel good inside. No matter what she wrote, the memories brought back the pain. The words tumbled out of her frantically. Feelings of utter contempt and hate poured from the deepest parts of her soul onto the paper. And she also knew that if it would have achieved a positive outcome, then maybe she would've considered confronting Sadie or post the actual letters to her.

To Whom It May Concern – *The Book of Letters*

"I wish I'd had her address. I would've marched up to her front door and thrust them into her hands. That would've wiped the smile from her face!"

But Mattie accepts that no matter how much she wanted Sadie to hear the truth about how evil she had been to her and others and to see her face seethe in anger because someone had dared to confront her, it also seemed a pointless task. If anyone had to change, Mattie knew it had to be her. And she did just that.

To Whom It May Concern – *The Book of Letters*

Thirteen

"DARLING, fancy another hot drink?" The sudden interruption from her husband snaps Mattie sharply from the depressing thoughts of death, funerals and school bullies, and as her senses spring to life, she's more aware of how bitterly cold it has now become.

"That would be great," she shouts back as a shiver runs through her, and she waits eagerly for Jake to bring out the coffee just so she can see his face.

Within minutes, he's placing the steaming hot mug of coffee on the table. He then sits on the stool still kept nearby. "You look rather cosy," he says and nods towards the blanket, adding with a grin, "That hat suits you too."

"A kiss will make me feel a whole lot cosier," Mattie says and leans in towards him, allowing him to plant a gentle kiss on her lips. "Thank you, I needed that."

"That bad, eh?" he asks and scans the remaining letters.

Thank goodness you can't see my blotchy face from all the crying.

"How's it going?" Jake blows into his hands in a poor attempt to warm them then decides to hold them in front of the fire. His breath is visible in the cold air. "It's coming up to eleven o'clock. How much longer do you intend to be outside because I know where I'd rather be. In bed with you." He leans in for another kiss.

Mattie shrugs her shoulders, indicating that it will take a lot longer than she's anticipated, and she glances at the book, knowing that she's yet to get past Guy. For as much as she wants

To Whom It May Concern – *The Book of Letters*

her husband to force her to throw the damn letters in the fire and drag her away from her self-inflicting torment to go back inside where she belongs, she insists that it won't take long to finish the few that remain. He gives her another kiss before dashing back to the house. Once again, the door closes and the lights downstairs turn off as Jake makes his way upstairs.

Mattie wraps her hands around the hot mug to extract as much heat as possible through the gloves and takes a few big well-deserved gulps. The milky coffee is hotter than she expected, but it slips down her throat easily and brings a sudden surge of heat against the cold air that she's been breathing in for the past few hours. The taste is pleasing and the warmth more so, and as always, it reminds her of that first coffee she properly shared with Jake, of that fortuitous meeting, and of the day that changed her life forever.

The book rests open on her lap but is somewhat lighter. She doesn't need to look down to see which letter follows, because the order in which she wrote them is clear in her mind. *It's all about you, Guy.* Mattie closes the book and sits back into the sun chair. Her muscles tense and a bitter taste forms in her mouth, not from the coffee, but from the churning in her stomach at thoughts of her ex-boss and that time of her life she considered to be the most hurtful and traumatic. She sees Guy's face laughing back at her, even though he's long gone. But for now, he's back in her mind, bringing with himself intense feelings of anxiety.

As part of the marketing degree course Mattie embarked on, Mattie had to do a placement in the third year. With the high grades she achieved, she was quickly picked up by a prominent marketing firm, Carter Gales. Claire was also nearby at a corporate bank, and whenever possible, they travelled to work

To Whom It May Concern – *The Book of Letters*

together and met up for lunch.

Mattie didn't know what to expect of the firm or what they expected of her. They had a suite of offices with a swanky reception area on the eighth floor of a high-rise building in London's Central Business District. The two-hour interview held before the end of term of that second year was nerve-racking to say the least. She had given her first formal interview – a completely new experience – sitting opposite a board of directors and executives, examined under the spotlight by highly intelligent people she'd never met before. She didn't have to go through such an elaborate process to work at Luigi's. All they expected from her was a huge smile for the customers, even for those that didn't deserve it, plus an excellent memory and the strength to stand for hours on end. She was sad to leave the family-run Italian restaurant for a desk job, and she would miss having aching feet at the end of a shift. But she was just as anxious about Carter Gales' expectations as she had been on her very first day working at the restaurant.

Her mother added to her anxiety, determined she look smart for the interview. Mattie was hustled to buy smart clothes because her university wardrobe of jeans, sweatshirts, and a few sparkly tops, didn't seem adequate for the interview.

Mattie sat on a black leather sofa in the reception area, waiting with anticipation and thinking about her mother's encouraging words on the phone moments before she left her apartment. "Don't forget to smile, say please and thank you, and ask lots of questions."

It was hot outside, and even though the building had air-conditioning, Mattie felt clammy and fidgety. Perched on the edge of the sofa to stop her legs from sticking to the leather fabric, she tugged at her short skirt wishing she'd worn stockings

To Whom It May Concern – *The Book of Letters*

or trousers. Perhaps a longer skirt would have been more appropriate. There was far too much leg on show, but when her mother told her how beautiful she looked the day they went shopping, Mattie decided to wear it. It was too late to regret her choice of clothing. She figured that had Grandfather Barton still been alive, he would've had something to say about the skirt and most likely insisted that she change it. But even he was no longer alive to voice his opinion, so she sat, nervously fiddling with her recently manicured nails, having made sure she looked groomed from head to toe. The feelings were like the first day of a new school again, especially St Benedict's. Wondering what to expect and the not knowing made it all seem much worse.

Mattie cussed silently at her stupid insecurities, saying she had to get a grip because if she didn't get this job, then she'd be sitting on another sofa in another reception area getting worked up all over again. But her hands were starting to sweat from the rising anticipation. *I was selected from over a hundred candidates!* She reminded herself, checking if that little accolade would make her feel any calmer.

"Miss Barton?" Mattie was broken away from the rising flush of insecurities by a young receptionist. The wait was over. The pretty young girl who could've barely been eighteen escorted her to a meeting room. *Here goes!* Mattie took a hesitant step into the room.

She was presented to a panel of four smartly dressed men, attired in crisp dark suits, white shirts, and an array of mid blue and grey striped ties – except for one. The two dark-haired men greeted Mattie as she sat down on the solitary seat positioned opposite the table at which they sat. One of them smiled and the other older gentleman kept his head down as he scanned through some papers. She put her bag on the floor, and as calmly as

To Whom It May Concern – *The Book of Letters*

possible, took a few sips from the glass of water that the pretty receptionist had offered. It just helped to cool and calm her nerves, even though unbeknown to them, she was shaking on the inside.

The older gentleman, grey-haired, slightly balding, then introduced himself and quickly launched into an outline of the business. Four sets of eyes stared at Mattie, and as she looked from one to the other when they spoke, she could not help but feel distracted by the rugged blond man – the one who smiled at her whose pink and yellow tie sat loose at the nape of his neck. He was less refined than the others, with the top button of his shirt undone, and he appeared the most relaxed. The others were neat and exact with their personal attire, and their mannerisms seemed to match too. Occasionally, she allowed herself a glance to study his face, and each time she did, he looked right back with intensity.

When she arrived home later that day, Mattie slumped exhaustedly into the sofa, still reeling from the rigorous interview. Question after question was thrown at her – each of which she was quick to respond to – and her mind was in a spin from the barrage as well as from meeting the blue-eyed blond executive. *I wonder whether I'd get to work with him if I get the job.*

She hardly had chance to relax and give the question much thought, when the phone rang.

"Well, darling, how was the interview?"

"Good. I think, Mum."

"Oh, you don't sound so certain."

"It's not that. They asked me so much and... Well I'm not sure if I'm what they are looking for." Mattie crossed her fingers, knowing there were other candidates to be interviewed over the coming days. "I was there a while though – almost two hours." That was the best she could offer her mother, still struggling to remember most of what they had asked because her thoughts were elsewhere, thinking about the blond, rugged executive.

"I'm sure if they spent that amount of time getting to know you then they must be interested." Mattie appreciated her mother's positivity, but it had been her first formal interview, and Mattie kept her expectations low.

"I know I was nervous, and the room, well... it was so damn hot. All I can really recall were four men looking at me and asking lots of things. Anyway, we're having lunch tomorrow, so by then I'll have probably remembered more."

They said their goodbyes, and Mattie walked towards her bedroom to start getting ready to go out with Claire and Frankie, but before she reached the bedroom door the phone rang again. She hurried back and grabbed the receiver. "Mum, I said I'd speak to you tomorrow."

"Can I speak with Martha Barton please?"

"Oh yes, sorry. This is Mattie, I mean Martha."

"Martha, I'm Janice Cooper from Carter Gales, their Human Resource Manager. I believe the directors were very pleased with your interview this morning and they would like to offer you the placement."

She was shocked at the quick decision. Whatever Mattie said during the interview must have impressed them. It all happened so quickly. One minute she was being interviewed, the next she was walking through the doors on her first day at work as a Junior Marketing Executive – not that she really understood what the title meant.

It was surreal. Within a few weeks of finishing university for the summer, she'd gone from wearing jeans and sweatshirts to

To Whom It May Concern – *The Book of Letters*

wearing black and navy suits. Her wardrobe was revamped with the uniform corporate clothing and matching leather court shoes so that she portrayed the right image, having noticed on the day of her interview what all the other people about the office were wearing. At first, Mattie wasn't overly keen on the formal dress code because it reminded her of all those years wearing a blazer at St Benedict's school and the restrictions she associated with it because of the austere regimen they imposed, amongst other things. However, she had to accept it was part of the job and she was part of a team representing – according to the company literature – the biggest marketing company in London.

The idea of baking cakes for a living was long gone, and on the occasions that she visited her mother, they didn't spend time in the kitchen up to their elbows in flour as she'd grown up doing. It was as if that dream too had died along with her grandmother. But she'd finally accepted her grandfather's wishes of his career choice for her, and now she was embarking on the next stage in her life.

On the first day of her new job, Mattie took a final look in the mirror before leaving for work to make sure she looked the part. She ensured that the hemline of the new skirt was respectably longer this time. She thought how smart and professional she appeared and hoped she'd be able to make a difference. Whatever that difference would be, she was sure as hell going to succeed at Carter Gales and show them her potential. Her mother had even bought her a new black leather satchel, but the only thing inside it apart from fresh air was a set of pens and a notepad. She felt like a fraud, carrying the big posh empty bag after having already observed so many businesspeople entering and leaving the building armed with bags bulging with work. Mattie thought them to be important but for the time being she was grateful that being in effect a student, she would not be put in that demanding position for a long time.

Mattie checked her watch. It was 8:50 AM. She pushed her way through the revolving doors with a mass of other people and headed for the ground floor reception.

"Welcome, Martha, to Carter Gales." A small attractive woman shook her hand vigorously. "I'm Janice Cooper. They said you were tall." She eyed Mattie from head to toe and back up again, just to clarify she was actually that tall.

"Pleased to meet you." *You are shorter than I imagined.* Mattie noted that she was at least a foot taller than the HR manager.

The fifty-something-year-old woman with cropped black hair – the grey strands that threaded it showing signs of ageing – greeted her with enthusiasm. Wearing a black pinstriped trouser suit and flat black shoes, the grey streaks and small black-rimmed glasses seemed to match her overall appearance, making her look distinguished.

"Here's a temporary ID card. You'll get a permanent one by the end of the week." Mattie slipped the plastic card into a pocket and followed Janice into the lift. "You have a meeting at 9 AM with Mr Carter, the Managing Director," Janice read from a clipboard. "It shouldn't take long. It's a quick chat about the company – he likes to do that. It helps the new employees to settle in quicker if they build up a relationship with the boss on the first day. It isn't always achievable though, because he's often away on business," she continued, looking down at the list while the lift worked its way up to the eighth floor. "So you're lucky he's in the office today. Sometimes weeks go by before new employees get *the corporate chat*." The lift stopped and they stepped out on the eighth floor, which Carter Gales' offices occupied. "I believe they rolled out the red-carpet for your interview?"

Mattie looked at her quizzically.

"All the directors are not normally present when interviewing for junior executive positions but it just happened that they were also interviewing for a more senior roll. So you got a thorough interview. Anyway, at 9.30 AM I will take you on a tour of the rest of the building."

The bubbly Janice reeled off information about the fire extinguishers rather matter-of-factly and pointed to emergency exits and first aid points as they walked past them. "It's important to know where the emergency exits are. Then after lunch you'll have to sit and watch a corporate health & safety DVD'," she continued, pointing in various directions as they made their way through the large expanse of office to an unoccupied desk. "Then you will have some forms to fill out, and after that you should be good to go."

Mattie nodded in understanding of all she was being told.

"Don't look so worried, Martha. By the end of the week you'll be settled in and today will be a distant memory."

Is the apprehension on my face that obvious? Mattie simply smiled back at the short, feisty woman.

Janice reminded Mattie of an air steward – except that she was not very tall – pointing her arms out to the left, then right, as she indicated who sat where and what they did. Heads turned each time they passed a desk. Some mouthed a 'Hello' while they chatted on the telephone, some even gave a faint smile and a slight nod to gesture 'Welcome to Carter Gales', while others were reluctant to make any acknowledgement at all. It really felt like that first day at St Benedict's – only this time there was no Sadie. Thank God for that.

To Whom It May Concern – *The Book of Letters*

"This is your desk," indicated Janice. "I hope you don't mind being right outside the boss's office. You must have impressed him during your interview, because he normally puts the students around the corner and out of his way. But you," she looked up at Mattie, "He seems to want to take you under his wing. How nice."

Mattie wasn't quite sure whether Janice was being a touch sarcastic. However, she said that she was fine to sit here, and with that, she gulped at the prospect of being on constant watch.

Sitting outside Bob Carter's office may have been deemed a privilege by the small HR manager, but for the moment, Mattie thought she had nothing to offer Carter Gales other than what she'd studied at university. She knew she would be scrutinised at every corner, and having to put what she'd learned into practice suddenly became a reality. A lump formed in her throat as she took her place at the spacious empty desk.

After Derek, the IT manager, was introduced to her, he showed her how to work the most important piece of office equipment – the vending machine – adding that although it was a little after nine, he was already on his fifth cup of coffee. He said the computer was set up and he'd be back soon to demonstrate how to log in to the company system. Then he proceeded to tell Mattie how he hadn't slept well that night because his five-year-old son had the chicken pox, before being called away to fix a jammed photocopier. Fifty pence for a coffee seemed a fair price, but the first taste confirmed why it was so cheap, and she wasn't sure if she could agree with Derek that she'd ever get used to it.

Carter Gales sold advertising in many forms that Mattie was still trying to wrap her head around, in spite of refreshing her memory that morning, while on the underground, by reading through the literature that Mr Carter had handed out at the interview. The London office was the head office, and from what she knew, it was an expanding business with offices in Paris and New York.

"We are planning to open offices in the Far East and Frankfurt in the next twelve months..." Bob relayed this information when she finally met him that day. It was a little after nine thirty. Mattie said very little, trying to absorb everything the managing director and founder of the company mentioned, giving him the occasional nod and making sure she smiled throughout, just as her mother kept reminding her to do. "Take this brochure," he said, passing her another glossy booklet. "It's more up to date than that one," he commented, glancing at the company brochure resting on Mattie's lap, which showed signs it had been read well and marked at certain sections from being dog eared. "It'll tell you more about the future plans for the business." With that, he stood up and shook her hand again, as Janice entered his office to take Mattie through the next part of the induction process.

By the time she arrived home at the end of the day, she was worn out, and all she could think about were red fire extinguishers and little white men on illuminated green signs in various poses. *How am I supposed to differentiate between a carbon dioxide and a water extinguisher when they are all painted red?* Yet even as she travelled home on the underground, that very day, she took it upon herself to take note of the emergency exit signs that she'd previously taken for granted.

Mattie dropped her new black satchel on the floor, kicked off her shoes to ease her already aching feet, and threw her suit jacket with disregard across the armrest of the sofa. Then she flopped into the soft cushions. It was day one of being pushed along with throngs of working people into the London underground, carrying similar bags to sit at similar desks and look out of the glass at the large expanse of the city below. She'd finally turned into what she never wanted to be. But as far as she was concerned, it was too late to go back and change careers.

"Hi Mattie!" Claire's enthusiasm knew no limits as she bounced through the doorway in her usual happy and chirpy mood not ten minutes after Mattie. Noticing her slumped on the sofa, she asked, "Oh, I guess by the look on your face you didn't like your first day?"

"It was as much as I anticipated. I'm not sure if I'm cut out for corporate business." Mattie refrained from saying that she secretly wished the blond-haired director had been there – maybe it would have been a more interesting day. "Anyway, how was your day?"

"Great," Claire replied. "It's only my second week there but I'm getting into the swing of things at the bank and, yes, I like it." She sat down next to Mattie, kicking off her own shoes and matching her slouched posture. "Well, I can't stay chatting too long, got to get ready. I'm off to the cinema with Frankie." Claire looked at her friend's miserable face. Did it really say so much? "Are you coming with us?"

"No thanks. I think I need a soak in the bath," Mattie replied.

"You know it's only for a year," said Claire, and then sauntered off to her bedroom.

Claire was right, of course. The job was a part of the degree course and only for a year, and whether Mattie liked it or not, she had to stick the year out. She was at the bottom of the corporate ladder, at the bottom of another food chain. It was a starting point for her career, and she had to knuckle down, accept it for what it was, and deal with it. After all, it wasn't forever.

Mattie reluctantly admitted that Carter Gales was the right place to spend her year out of university.

To Whom It May Concern – *The Book of Letters*

As for her best friend, Claire's career was moving in the exact direction she wanted. She would get a first class honours degree for certain, work in finance, and earn loads of money, thought Mattie, even though her friend had fallen in love with an Italian hunk. Not even that affected Claire's determination, as she remained focused and resolute of her destiny. Neither did she let any bullshit bring her down.

The first few months at Carter Gales passed by in a blur. Being the newest employee, Mattie was given the most boring tasks. At one stage, Mattie questioned what part of her degree course covered filing and shredding. Only the photocopier was challenging with its array of buttons to press, and one day she wasted a good twenty minutes trying to figure out how to print on both sides and in triplicate. Thankfully, the lovely Derek was on hand and came to her rescue. He hit a few buttons, and within seconds a set of documents materialised out the other side in orderly piles. Using the laminate machine was a totally different concept and learning experience altogether, and Mattie lost count of the number of documents that went through that machine and came out the other end in a hot crinkled mass, resulting in further printing to replace the damaged documents. Then she would fight with the thick bundles of paper on the ring binder - all of this was in aid of producing a glossy weekly report that had to be placed on the boardroom table by 10 AM each Monday morning or sooner if the boss said so. Mattie underestimated how tiring this particular task could be, and it took a few weeks to get in a routine and perfect the smooth operation.

Mattie came to the conclusion that if she was going to succeed in this mostly male-dominated environment, then she had to get her head down, keep quiet, and do whatever work was thrown her way – and on occasion, it literally was. She managed to convince

To Whom It May Concern – *The Book of Letters*

herself that she could handle these tasks even though the work was boring – monotonous most days, to say the least. She questioned how long she could keep up this act and do the crappy work that only served to relieve the secretaries so they could spend more time filing their precious long nails.

When Janice walked passed her desk one Friday afternoon, Mattie plucked up the courage to speak to her. "Janice, can I have a quick word please?" Mattie had begun to regret not taking the other job that she was offered at a much smaller organisation. Janice pulled close a chair. "In private, if that's okay?" asked Mattie.

They stepped into Bob's large open-spaced office, and with some trepidation, Mattie told her that she was thinking of leaving if putting reports together was the only experience she was going to gain in the next twelve months. "I've got a dissertation to do and I was hoping to do 'other' work that would help with this. I want to put into practice the marketing tools and strategies that I have spent two years studying."

"Very well, Mattie, I totally understand your predicament. I have to say that so far you've handled this work admirably. All students are given these tasks. We like to call it character-building."

"Are you saying this is some form of test?"

"I wouldn't necessarily use those words, but if that's how you'd like to refer to it, then yes. You've passed with flying colours. You've also lasted... let's say longer than the average student," she added with a wink.

The chat with Janice worked, and soon after, Mattie was given reports and statistics to analyse. It felt rewarding to finally start using her knowledge, being able to prove her worth to the boss and remind him via the HR Manager that she was prepared to tackle any type of work they put her way - even if it meant coming in earlier and staying late.

Meanwhile, Mattie had not forgotten about the blond-haired man who'd sat in on the interview, even though he'd done very little talking. She aptly referred to him as Mr Blond when mentioning him to Claire, and frequently her flatmate would ask if Mattie had seen him, watching for her instant blush at the question. His name appeared on printed reports, and occasionally, she sent brochures to him at the New York office. He seemed to be somewhat of an enigma. Not much was spoken about him in the office although he managed the one in America and made regular visits to London to see certain clients. His rugged features and blond, wavy hair were ingrained in her mind from that first meeting, and though she directed all her focus at work, she waited with bated breath for the day he would walk into Carter Gales' London office again.

A few weeks following their chat, Janice said to Mattie, "I've had a talk with Bob and he's very pleased with your progress, Mattie." She ticked a number of small boxes on a sheet clipped to a board. Three months had passed and it was time for Mattie's probationary review. The two sat at the small table in one of the spare meeting rooms, sipping on the bitter vending machine coffee and enjoying an iced doughnut that Amanda from accounts had brought because it was her birthday.

While Janice continued to check that she'd settled in well, Mattie only felt glum, as the day before she'd missed Mr Blonds' visit because of a dental appointment. Plus the month before when he'd arrived in the UK, he'd gone straight to a meeting somewhere north of London with Bob and never managed to make it to the office.

"You'll be pleased to know that the filing and shredding is

going back to the secretaries."

"Thank goodness for that. Sorry, I didn't mean that." At long last, Mattie felt comfortable with Janice, but realising she was still the newest recruit, she remained cautious of her words, careful not to speak ill of others or undermine their position. "What I mean is that..." Mattie continued, hesitating while thinking of an appropriate response, "...I've mastered the art of shredding and filing."

Janice stared over the rim of her glasses. Then a smile crept across her face, easing the discomfort Mattie had put herself in. "Good choice of words, Martha. I couldn't have put it better myself. The secretaries aren't happy about having to do it, but well, it's not as if they have a great deal to do."

Janice said that Bob was pleased with Mattie's analysis work and that she was to hold on tight a little longer as more interesting work would come her way. 'Persevere' was the exact word she used. Janice also told Mattie that if she needed help with the reports and brochures, she should ask the secretaries Julie and Amy because they'd been told to help.

Before the meeting finished, she said to Janice, "Is there any chance you could tell the directors to call me Mattie instead of Martha. I've never really liked the name - it's a little too formal."

"Okay, I'll let them know."

The review was over and Janice told Mattie her work so far was exemplary. They left the room, and as Mattie prepared to walk back to her desk, she noticed a smartly dressed man walking past reception and the obvious giggles from the office girls he walked by. He was heading her way.

"Let me properly introduce you to the New York Director, he's such a lovely man," Janice said, turning to Mr Blond, and shook his hand vigorously, as she did with everyone. "This is..."

"Janice," a loud voice boomed across the office. "I need you now!"

"Got to dash," she said hastily and scurried off in the direction of Bob's office, leaving Mattie in front of the gorgeous man who had sent her pulse soaring at the interview and with every thought thereafter.

"Martha, isn't it?"

He remembers me? "Yes, but please call me Mattie."

"Mattie it is. How are you liking it so far? Is Bob treating you well?"

"Yes." She was cordial, unsure of which question to answer first. He stood inches away with those beautiful blue eyes looking right at her, and the best she could think to ask him in return was whether he'd had a nice journey. But before he could answer, Bob came over.

"I need to speak with you urgently," said Bob. Then they were both gone.

Mattie returned to her desk, flopped into the chair, and buried her head in a report before anyone noticed the flushed cheeks, hoping that the New York director hadn't noticed the effect he had on her either. That afternoon, she tried to stay at her desk as much as possible, just to catch a glimpse of him in Bob's office. But for most of the time, he had his back to her. Mattie had to settle with admiring the back of his head, but even looking at the loose blond curls at the nape of his neck that gave him a slightly scruffy appearance gave her more than a pleasant tingle. When the men left together, they were in such a deep conversation that neither of them looked her way.

The following day, Mattie heard that he had taken an early flight out of Heathrow. But he left behind a young woman whose stomach was in knots, wondering when she would see him next.

To Whom It May Concern – *The Book of Letters*

Is this what love feels like? She dismissed the stupid notion and the feelings churning within.

Mattie's determination and commitment showed. Bob Carter had no complaints, and when he noticed her staying late to get through the work, he realised how hardworking she was. Eventually, this led to her contact with clients. It was minimal to begin with – sometimes taking his calls when he was out of the office and making appointments, which the secretaries normally did. On other occasions, she would be asked to sit in on short meetings taking notes or merely to observe and learn. Initially, Mattie felt like a glorified secretary. It was frustrating some days, but she understood it was all part of the learning process. What else could she expect as a university student? Some colleagues didn't view her as an employee at all because they expected her to leave at the end of her academic year, so they kept their distance. Others tried to offload their own tedious tasks onto Mattie for the same reason. She was at the bottom of this particular food chain, the minion at Carter Gales Marketing, which some colleagues took enjoyment in reminding her.

It was not long after her introduction to Mr Blond that Bob handed Mattie her first account to oversee. The client account was small and new to Carter Gales, but on Bob's advice, she was to give them the same attention that the multimillion-pound clients received from the key account managers. She listened intently with eagerness to learn, most of the time keeping a pen and notepad in her hand, in case she wanted to make a note of something important to remember. Whatever advice Bob or the other senior staff members had to offer, she took it all on board and made sure she could rise and meet the challenges that lay ahead.

The months passed quickly, and most of Mattie's time was

To Whom It May Concern – *The Book of Letters*

consumed with work, but she was content to do it, with the added incentive of seeing Mr Blond at Carter Gales every month. Other than know he was British, along with the fact that he ran the New York office and still handled some of the UK accounts, Mattie knew little else of him. She gave him the same cordial smile she gave to everyone else and spoke politely to him when the opportunity presented itself, though she yearned to say more. But at the sight of him, the butterflies in her stomach fluttered intensely, the words struggled to form, and the rare conversations between the two were stilted.

One Monday, Mattie arrived earlier than normal, as a meeting had been brought forward. Also, seeing a memo on Bob's desk a few days ago informed her that the man who sent her heart racing would be landing at the airport shortly before 6 AM that very day. Presuming he'd be able to traverse across London with ease, he would most likely arrive at Carter Gales two hours later. At that time in the morning, there were few members of staff, most of them arriving between 8.30 and 9 AM, apart from Jackson, the new young account manager keen to show his ability and determination.

Mattie was standing by the vending machine. She had a clear view of the reception area, and as predicted, Mr Blond stepped out of the lift at precisely 8 AM. For someone who'd spent the night on an aeroplane, she marvelled at how dashing a figure he still cut in a smart suit. First, he stopped at the reception desk, leaned over it and picked up a large envelope marked for his attention, and when doing so, he glanced in Mattie's direction. The machine spat out its blend of bitter coffee mixed with a blast of UHT milk into the plastic cup. She looked up from her coffee, giving him a smile.

Then her smile turned sour. *Where the hell did you come*

To Whom It May Concern – *The Book of Letters*

from?

From a nearby office, Cynthia, one of the more mature account managers, bounced towards Mr Blond, leaned in towards the reception counter to get close to him, and obscured Mattie's view. *I should've realised you'd come in early. Flouncing your large breasts!* Mattie cussed at Cynthia, who toyed with the lapel on his jacket. He took a tentative step back, looked around her, but by then Mattie no longer wanted to watch the sideshow and went back to her desk.

It wasn't long before Bob arrived along with other account managers, keen to start yet another lengthy meeting – each one happy to talk over a colleague and puff up their own feathers like a parading peacock in demonstration of who was the best. For the rest of the morning, they were locked in the boardroom, Cynthia included. When Mattie walked past the room, she heard bouts of laughter and Cynthia's voice ringing above her male counterparts.

Mr Blond made heads turn wherever he went, in particular of the secretaries, who made an extra effort to make sure he had everything he needed during his short visits. It was obvious all the women in the office fancied him, especially Cynthia. Her usual ploy was to take a report to him when he worked alone in one of the small meeting rooms, when she could've sent it by email. The staff and Mattie alike would observe her lean over the back of his chair while her extra-large breasts practically rested on his shoulder. The bank of offices and meeting rooms with their glassed walls and vertical blinds hid very little from the outside, but Cynthia had no scruples and didn't care what other people saw and certainly didn't care what they thought of her. Her behaviour was verging on obscene, but no one really bothered about it. With well-publicised opinions and the fact that she'd

To Whom It May Concern – *The Book of Letters*

been outspoken and specific on more than a few occasions about what she'd like to do with the New York director, the actions of the busty, mature woman disgusted Mattie, and also served to confirm Mattie's jealousy.

Shocked at her feelings growing stronger, Mattie strode in the direction of the Post room. *How can I feel like this, I don't even know him!* Mattie tried to get a grip of whatever was going on inside her head. Never-mind the summersaults in her stomach.

"Mattie!" Bob's voice boomed along the corridor. She looked back to see him waving some papers in his hand and beckoning her. She scurried over.

"Yes, Bob."

"Five copies please, and after lunch I want you to join us. Don't look so surprised, Mattie. I'm good on my word and I promised you more input."

There was no reason to doubt Bob's sincerity. As Janice had said, more involved work would come her way other than just filing and shredding. Mattie just hadn't expected it to be when the man she longed to get close to would be sitting at the same table.

Mattie lingered outside the boardroom with anticipation, waiting for them to finish the platter of triangular sandwiches. Then when she plucked up the courage to try and step into the room unnoticed, at the same time, a junior secretary brought in more fresh coffee, bringing about a pause in the various conversations as she sat in the empty seat next to Bob.

"Here to pour the coffee Mattie - one sugar in mine. Or are you taking minutes?" Cynthia piped up, noting the pen and pad in Mattie's hand. She ignored the dig and the few giggles of laughter from some of the other account managers. A welcoming smile from Mr Blond quickly put her at ease.

The few hours of listening to new market strategies and the

handling of some awkward accounts passed quickly. She scribbled many notes, keen to appear as important as the others. And when Bob asked her to talk about her own account, Bluefield Ltd, she did so confidently.

"Excellent Mattie, we'll make a fine executive out of you," her boss congratulated her along with promising comments from Mr Blond. However, Cynthia merely sucked in her cheeks at the kind gesture.

When the meeting finished and everyone filed back to their own desks, Mattie remained behind in the hope to be near *him*, under the pretence of asking Bob if he needed anything else.

Mr Blond gathered his papers, putting them into his briefcase.

"Did you have a nice weekend, Mattie?"

"Yes, what about you?"

"I went to a baseball game with some friends and we..."

"Oh, still here are you," Cynthia interrupted when she popped her head around the door, abruptly halting the rising butterflies in Mattie's stomach from the simple conversation she was enjoying with Mr Blond. "Sorry to interrupt you Mattie while you clear the cups away." She then turned to New York director. "Can I have a quick word before you go? I've got something important to discuss."

He rolled his eyes. "Ignore her," and zipped up his bag, and left. Mattie watched them in the corridor, Cynthia once again playing with his lapel and inching closer to him, flaunting herself at every available opportunity and looking back at Mattie with a smug grin, knowing she didn't like it.

Powerless to do anything and kicking herself for not telling the man who was making her feel wondrous on the inside about her weekend when he asked, Mattie headed back to her desk.

"Mattie, see you next time."

To Whom It May Concern – *The Book of Letters*

She turned to see him wave before exiting the offices and smiled back at him. A victory for her, she mused.

To Whom It May Concern – *The Book of Letters*

Fourteen

MATTIE is aroused from the dream she's long drifted into by the hoot of an owl in the distance. Squinting her eyes, she can just about see the hands on her watch, telling her another half hour has passed while she has been drifting in and out of the past. The pieces of wood she last threw into the chimenea have burnt quickly. Feeling the chill even more, partly due to tiredness, she hastily chucks some branches in and the last of the paper firelighters. It reignites and emits a blast of heat towards her legs, seeping through the thick woollen blanket and finally through the fabric of her trousers, until eventually reaching her cold legs. It feels good, and as she claps her hands firmly against each other, the warmth filters to the ends of her fingertips too, giving her the strength to hold the book.

The memories of going to work and finishing university are vivid as if it was only yesterday – she can recall every little detail. It doesn't take much thinking. Even the conversations remain fresh in her mind after all this time, especially the ones with her first love, Mr Blond. Keen to think about him more, to see his rugged face and intense blue eyes and hold on to those wonderful memories, Mattie snuggles back into the chair. With the fire now blazing, she drifts back to those dreamy thoughts. She sees his face again – not that it is hard to forget how handsome he was – but lurking in the background is Guy's with his lascivious, smug grin and she can't shake away his image no matter how hard she screws up her face. It's no use – she lets the images of Guy flash before her because to think of her first love she has to think of the other man, as the paths of their lives crossed over and some

To Whom It May Concern – *The Book of Letters*

memories cannot easily be separated for they've merged into one.

    Over the following months, Mr Blonds' visits were regular. Each month, he normally arrived on a Monday morning and left by the Wednesday of that same week. Most of the time he was trapped in meetings with Bob and other account managers, and when he was out of the office, he was visiting his key UK clients. If Mattie was lucky, she got to sit in on the meetings, and when Cynthia always sat next to him, laughing and giggling like a teenager, Mattie would sit across. She could look at him and admire him from afar and preferred it that way. Plus she got to see him roll his eyes at Cynthia's often stupid remarks, much to Mattie's amusement, as the forty-something woman had no idea.

    Mattie took pleasure in her brief conversations with Mr Blond, which often took place by the vending machine or on the periphery of Bob's office, mostly interrupted by someone needing him. Plus she'd become accustomed to Cynthia's advances on him which he always rebuffed. She was at least fifteen years his senior, with over-tanned skin resembling that of a cracked walnut. But that didn't deter her from what she wanted – him.

    The one-year placement scheme drew to an end all too quickly. In that time, Mattie had built up a good rapport with colleagues and clients and was handling five, albeit small, accounts. She held a great deal of respect for the slightly balding grey-haired Bob Carter who was approaching sixty years of age. He was keen to part information about the company provided the recipient was prepared to listen, so Mattie made it her objective each day, or at least when he was there, to ask him as many questions as possible. One day, he commented that he'd never employed anyone who asked as much as she did. She took it as a compliment.

While Mattie no longer had the desire or the time to bake cakes, the sense of achievement and the glowing report for the university from Bob gave her a buzz. Her thirst for knowledge and her determination to prove her worth in the world of marketing, knowing that she was good at the job, pushed her even more. Still lingering heavy in her heart was the caveat that came with the inheritance from her grandfather. But she had a stubborn streak, just like him, and was adamant to make it on her own.

Looming ahead was the fourth and final year at university, plus a twenty-thousand-word dissertation. Various work options had been discussed with Bob, and while he would have preferred her to stay working full time, he also valued the importance of a degree and agreed to employ Mattie on a permanent but three-day-a-week basis until she completed her studies. After that she'd be a full-time employee. "It will maintain continuity with the clients you look after. Plus they like you," he told her, "as do I but don't tell the others I said that, they will think I'm a push-over." He followed the remark with a wink.

How could she refuse? Especially after that compliment. Underneath the hard sales executive exterior, he was a fair and kind-hearted man. At times, some of the tasks assigned to her were overwhelming, but he only ever asked her to do what he thought she was capable of, and Mattie – although at times it proved difficult – soon learnt to balance out her time between work, university, Claire, and her mother.

That summer, before the start of the final academic year, Mattie took two weeks off work to do some research and plan her dissertation. She was alone in the apartment enjoying the blissful silence while Claire was sunning up in Italy with Frankie and meeting his extended family. Using every minute of the noise-free zone, Mattie ploughed into the dissertation to get ahead. Surrounded with books, often only surfacing to eat, drink, and grab some sleep. Even her mother didn't get to see her only daughter during those two weeks. Only occasionally did Mattie allow her mind to wander off to a certain person, although he hadn't visited recently.

The weeks of that summer passed quickly, and the mounting pressure of university and work began to make Mattie irritable. Life was fizzling into nothingness, as was her friendship with Claire, who along with Frankie breezed in and out of the apartment.

"I'm going back to work at Luigi's," Claire announced one day towards the end of August. She said that the bank had already offered her a full-time position once she completed her degree. "And to be honest, I can do without the added stress at the moment. What about you, Mattie?"

"Bob has reduced my hours."

"Oh. You're staying there then?"

"Yes," she replied bluntly. "Why shouldn't I?"

"I'm just saying." Claire held up both hands apologetically, realising that Carter Gales had long ago turned into a touchy subject. But she carried on light-heartedly in an attempt to persuade her friend to think otherwise. "It's going to be a tough year, and it's not as if you need to earn the money. Come back to Luigi's with me. We'll have a great time again."

Mattie turned away, holding her tongue so as not to offend Claire, even though she was in two minds to tell her that she knew very little of her life at Carter Gales as they hardly had many conversations these days. The cracks in their friendship were starting to show.

"There are other marketing companies in London," Claire

To Whom It May Concern – *The Book of Letters*

added with a smirk, "Or is it because you have the hots for *Mr Blond*, that you don't want to leave?"

Recently, Mattie had kept her feelings about him under lock and key. She snapped back, "Of course not! Anyway I haven't seen him for ages. For months, actually!" She negated the sharp tone with a quick apology then went on to justify her intentions. "I like where I work. Plus unlike you, I can't guarantee that a job will be available there in twelve months' time if I were to leave now. I cannot imagine my boss would be that accommodating."

Mattie knew her friend to be right about one thing – she was staying at Carter Gales in the hope of seeing her favourite person there, the New York director. But it also partly had something to do with proving to her dead grandfather that she could see the job through to the end of her degree course, then after that… well, she'd not thought that far ahead. But at least she'd be free to do as she wanted.

Claire ignored the bad mood that was lingering over Mattie and went on with her persuasive argument about why working at Luigi's would be all round better for her, that she should lighten up and have some fun. But after a few minutes of her efforts falling flat on their face, she changed tactics again to bring her friend out of the gloomy mood she'd put herself in.

"I wish you'd come out with me and Frankie tonight. It isn't healthy being cooped up in the flat all the time on your own. We're meeting up with Johnny and Abigail, plus Marcus will be there with a few others. You know Marcus likes you?"

The prospect of seeing one of their friends who she knew fancied her for a few months now but hadn't plucked up the courage to ask her on a date still did nothing to lift Mattie's spirits.

"I can't. I've got studying to do."

To Whom It May Concern – *The Book of Letters*

"Mattie, you are well ahead with the dissertation. You are probably the only person I know who has almost finished it, and we haven't even started the final year yet!"

Mattie thought about it for at least thirty seconds, then said she'd prefer to stay in and study, reminding Claire that she'd witnessed enough people drop from the course because they failed to get organised and plan ahead. What a waste of three years of studying, she said.

But Claire snapped back. "You need to get a life, Mattie. There is more to life than work and studying."

Biting back the urge to tell Claire a few truths about how she was feeling, she ignored the flippant remark and declined the invitation as politely as she could. "Thanks all the same but it's the last thing on my mind right now. I want to crack on with this marketing book, perhaps next weekend all being well?" Mattie held up the heavy text book purposely exhibiting her reasons for studying.

Working part time soon lapsed into being at work most days apart from when there was a lecture or tutor meeting, but even on those days, Mattie would return to the office and catch up on any missed work. By the time she caught the various underground trains to get home, she'd be walking into an empty flat as Claire had normally left to go to work at the restaurant. It was lonely and depressing, but it was part of the routine she'd fallen into. She never planned it. It just somehow seemed to happen, and all that Mattie could say to herself to keep cheerful was that it wouldn't be forever.

The Christmas of that fourth and final year at university hurtled towards her, and with each passing week, Mattie felt like she was being dragged down into an endless pit of work reports, sales targets, and university work. Deadlines loomed ahead that

To Whom It May Concern – *The Book of Letters*

she had to meet no matter what. She had to grin and bear it because she'd not come this far to start asking lecturers for any extensions, and neither was she prepared to let work down. As for Grandfather Barton, he remained a constant reminder of the goal he set for her, and she was determined to prove she could complete it.

To ease the pressure and to get a decent meal, Mattie moved back in with her mother for the festive season. Little had changed in the house Josie occupied since her parents' death, other than a lick of paint to brighten it up and some new furnishings. Mattie had wanted her mother to sell it and move to something smaller and more comfortable rather than rattle around in this one. The gigantic house with its beautiful brick facade was far too depressing, but despite her feelings for this place, she knew she could lock herself in her old bedroom, away from the world outside, and away from the lovely but noisy Claire, whose spare hours were spent mostly under the duvet with Frankie.

Mattie and her mother sat at the table surrounded by all the Christmas trimmings. Gold crackers and red silky napkins added a touch of luxurious colour to her grandparents' white bone china dinner set, which was in stark comparison to the sparse old decorations that had in a previous lifetime adorned the house. Not one for exchanging expensive presents, Mattie still found time to buy a beautiful gift for her mother, a gold chain and locket. She placed it on the table.

For all the hours involved in the preparation of the turkey dinner, the chipolata sausages, creamed sprouts, and extra-crispy roast potatoes, the sumptuous meal was eaten in a matter of minutes.

"That meal was amazing as always, Mum. I'm not sure if I've room for pudding right now." Mattie patted her full stomach, smiling at her mother but totally oblivious of how quiet she'd been and at how little she'd actually eaten. "And I think there's enough left over to feed you for the next week!"

She was eager for her to open the present and passed it to her. "Merry Christmas, Mum."

Josie gently removed the festive ribbon and lifted the lid of the jewellery box. "Oh Mattie, it's so beautiful. You shouldn't have." She took the gold locket from the box and opened it to reveal a photo of her and one of Mattie.

"Look at the back."

Her mother turned it over and read the inscription –

The Two of Us
Forever
xxx

"Oh, it's absolutely gorgeous! Here, put it on me."

Mattie placed the necklace around her mother's neck and fastened the clasp. "I knew it would look lovely on you the moment I saw it."

"Thank you, Mattie. It's a wonderful gift, but you shouldn't have. It must have cost a fortune!"

Sniffing away a few tears, Josie handed Mattie an envelope. "I hope you buy yourself something special."

"Mum, is everything alright?

"Of course, why shouldn't it be?"

"You look a bit pale, that's all. Plus you've been very quiet."

"I'm tired, darling, and my throat feels a little sore. That's all. Maybe I'm overdoing it with all the volunteer work. Pour me a sherry and after we've cleaned up we can relax on the sofa. Perhaps watch an old film like old times?" Josie's voice sounded

To Whom It May Concern – *The Book of Letters*

croaky, and she retreated into the kitchen before Mattie could probe anymore. When she followed, her mother was blowing her nose and sniffling back the tears. Hastily she said, "I think I've definitely got a cold coming on"

Once again, Mattie took on the role of plate washer while her mother dried the delicate bone china crockery. The sink was filled with soapy bubbles, and she passed the plates through hot water to rinse them before placing them one by one on the drainer. It was calm and peaceful, and in the background, Christmas songs could be heard on the radio. For some unknown reason, the atmosphere reminded Mattie of the day of Grandfather Barton's funeral, when they'd talked about her Uncle Patrick's terrible accident among other things. Quickly dispelling the thought and now rinsing the dessert bowls, Mattie continued to sing along to a Christmas jingle.

The precious dinner service was put away very calmly in the exacting standards her mother had followed so many times before, stacking them neatly in the cupboard where they would remain until another social event, most likely Easter. While Mattie continued to scrub the pans, the hard bits of caramelised turkey skin stuck to the side of the roasting dish proving extremely difficult to remove. "I'll let this one soak," Mattie said and filled it with steaming hot water, squirting an extra dash of dishwashing liquid into the dish before leaving it to rest on the drainer.

Mattie turned around to look at her mother and asked again. "Mum, are you sure you're okay? You don't seem yourself."

Again, she was told that everything was fine, but Mattie thought otherwise when her mother reached for some tablets, swallowing down two with a few sips of water.

Every care was taken at rinsing the heavy cut glass crystal

glasses. All the while Mattie hummed along to another favourite Christmas song after being assured by her mother that she was fine. But Josie decided she could not evade her daughter's questions anymore.

"I need to talk to you, Mattie."

"You're selling the house finally, that's it, isn't it? I knew there was something you wanted to tell me, you've been acting strange since I arrived." Ignorant of the sadness in her mother's voice and enjoying the sing-along, she carried on with the task at hand, swishing her hands in the soapy water in tempo with the music.

Just then her mother said. "I'm sick."

Mattie stopped. Her hands remained in the hot water and she looked out of the window down at the garden. She looked beyond the fence, and at the backs of the neighbouring houses, to the roof tops and then the skyline. She could tell by the tone of her mother's voice that there were implications attached to the short statement. She knew she wasn't just sick, and that it was more than that. Mattie pulled her hands out of the water and turned to face her mother. Her arms hung limply by her side, soapy suds and water dripping onto the floor. She took a good hard look at her mother and saw the grey pallor of her complexion. *Why did I not see this before?*

Josie calmly handed her a towel.

She scanned her mother's face for more information, and Josie said it again, "I'm very sick, Mattie."

Mattie froze on the spot.

Life had vanished from her mother's eyes, and the dark circles around them suddenly became apparent through the fine layers of makeup that had been applied smoothly. Mattie could see the lack of lustre in her mother's normally glossy hair, the overall frailty making her clothes hang loose. *How could I have been so blind not to see this?*

"How sick?" Mattie stammered. *Please don't tell me, please don't, Mum.* She closed her eyes to let the words float over her. The words slipped out and echoed past, whirling around her ears until they made sense. "How long?" She stammered and twisted her hands in the towel, preparing for the imminent devastating blow.

"Six months, maybe a year, if I have treatment."

A torrent of sobs began working their way up, clutching hard at Mattie's stomach, burning her throat as they rose until she could hold them back no more, and she buried her face in the towel and let the tears rack through, shaking her entire body.

"Why?" she asked earnestly.

Josie took her daughter in her arms as she cried into her mother's jumper, but she couldn't answer the young woman's question.

By the time Mattie stopped shaking, enough to look her mother in the eye, the two of them sat down to talk. Her mother spoke with little emotion, in the same way she'd done the day of her father's funeral, telling Mattie all she needed to know and nothing more. She kept the details of the cancer simple while Mattie incessantly apologised, through further bouts of crying, for being too engrossed in her own problems. And later that evening while Josie talked about her own funeral arrangements, Mattie realised her mother had accepted her own fate even before the treatment had started.

Why is this happening to her, why is this happening to me? Blame had to be apportioned and Mattie could only look in the direction of her dead grandparents for not allowing her mother to be who she wanted to be and let her make her own choices in life.

To Whom It May Concern – *The Book of Letters*

Now her life was about to be cut short by that dreadful disease and there was nothing she could do to stop it.

Mattie woke up early on Boxing Day, swamped with a feeling of helplessness, and went back to her apartment. Staying another night in *that* house was too much, as death once again came knocking on its door. She left a note for her mother on the kitchen table, telling her she'd call later that evening. But Mattie didn't make the call, and by the time she dragged herself out of bed, another day had passed and it was mid-afternoon. With a thumping headache from crying, lack of sleep, and drowning her sorrows in a bottle of red wine, it was evening before she plucked up the courage to visit her mother. Mattie promised not to cry in front of her and to be strong no matter what because her mother needed all the support she could get. So she swallowed hard and held her tears back.

The doctors informed Josie they would start treatment immediately, and it may give her six to twelve months, but the prognosis was not good. The quality of life she would lead was anyone's guess. So for now, her life was in God's hands and only a miracle could save her. As for Mattie, she had to simply accept her mother's illness and wishes.

The few days after that were spent huddled on the sofa, the two of them watching old films, ordering takeaway meals - and baking cakes for the first time in a long time, just as they often did years ago. Every moment was treasured as both had no idea if they would ever get to have those moments again, so they crammed in as much as possible in that short amount of time. And by the time Mattie was ready to leave on the morning of New Year's Eve, while a great sadness weighed heavily in her heart, she was thankful for her mother's insistence that she got on with living her own life and enjoying herself because neither of them knew what was waiting around the corner.

The dissertation, the work, and the cancer that had invaded her mother's body, were put to one side as she prepared for a long overdue night out. Before they made it out of the apartment, Frankie, Claire and Mattie shared a bottle of Chardonnay. Then they stopped at a number of pubs, drinking more and snacking on the various platters of free sandwiches, crisps and pork pies – within an hour, Mattie's head began to spin. Plus the stress of everything and her nerves working overtime had propelled the drink into her veins quicker than anticipated.

Mattie was feeling worse for wear, but they eventually arrived at Luigi's for a private New Year's Eve party. A huge voice bounded across the heads of the party-goers along with loud music the moment they entered. "Welcome!"

"Papa," shouted back Frankie, as the women were whisked off their feet and herded towards the bar. Glasses of Prosecco were thrust into their hands, and it took little encouragement for the two women to drink them as they were greeted with great big Italian hugs by more of Frankie's relatives.

The heat within the restaurant added to Mattie's already queasy feeling. "You don't look well, Mattie. You look like you're about to..." Claire quickly pulled her friend towards the toilets.

"That's better," Mattie managed to say after throwing up. Then more of the undigested pork pies mixed in with lager, vodka, and Prosecco came up.

"Here, drink this." Claire handed her a glass of cold water that she wasted no time in drinking. "Now sit on the loo while I sort you out. You look a mess." She powdered Mattie's face, did her best to conceal the smudged eyeliner with a touch of foundation, and applied some pink lip gloss as well as rubbing some into her

To Whom It May Concern – *The Book of Letters*

cheeks to make her glow.

"There ya go! You'd never know," said Claire, displaying one of her sweet smiles as if nothing had happened. "Now let's get back to the party," and she sashayed out of the toilets.

When Mattie tried to stand, her legs were still wobbly, but the hot, sickly feeling had for now subsided. After a few more minutes of composure, she was ready to continue with the New Year festivities at Luigi's.

The following morning, Mattie was rudely awoken by the sound of a door banging in the apartment above. Then another bang from somewhere, adding to the thumping already in her head along with the sound of her heartbeat that bounced from ear to ear while pressed into the pillow. She lay motionless, hoping that the sound would subside. Another door banged above. Mattie cursed the couple who lived there, wondering why they had to get up so early. "It's New Year's Day for crying out loud!" Mattie bellowed.

At that something next to her moved.

Mattie slowly turned over. "What the...!"

She slid out from under the duvet and grabbed a dressing gown, taking refuge on the floor. A naked man lay asleep in her bed. He stirred again, making the covers slip down, but allowing Mattie a glimpse of an exquisitely sculpted and toned body, moderately tanned too. The unknown man made a few more noises in his sleep, and then pulled the duvet up to cover his muscular bottom that she'd been momentarily admiring while wondering who he was and how he got there and why was she naked too!

Okay, so I danced on the table. That I remember. Then a man kissed me at midnight. That's acceptable on New Year's Day. Isn't it? Trying to remain convinced that her behaviour, although out of character, was still honourable, the questions ran around her throbbing head while she tried to justify why there was a naked man in her bed.

Shit! Mattie scrambled across the floor towards the bin then sat back in relief when she saw a used condom in it. He stirred again, but before he awoke she scuttled out of the bedroom.

She sat huddled on the sofa, holding a steaming mug of tea, when Frankie appeared shortly after and sat opposite.

"You okay?" His question was simple and his look of empathy spoke volumes. He was asking about her mother and nothing else, and in that moment, Mattie could understand why Claire had fallen so much in love with him. He was a keeper.

Mattie nodded and took a sip of the hot drink to hold back the tears. She'd cried enough already to last a lifetime. "So, who's the guy in my bed?" she asked, dropping her head in shame.

"Alexander. He's a cousin from Naples. You like?" Mattie laughed at the way Frankie spoke English and at how he made it sound so sexy and innocent. He'd lived in England long enough to speak like a native, but he preferred to drop the occasional pronoun, knowing it got the women drooling over him, much to the jealousy of Claire.

Needless to say, Alexander from Naples was never seen again, even though the handsome Italian had pleaded with Mattie at the door when he was kindly pushed out of the apartment, telling Mattie the sex was great and that she was a great lover. But she didn't need nor want romance right now. Having steamy hot sex to de-stress sounded like a good offer from Alexander from Naples, but with a head filled with worry for her mother and a degree course to finish, life was complicated enough. Plus it wasn't Alexander she wanted, it was someone else.

To Whom It May Concern – *The Book of Letters*

Fifteen

THE bitter winds of that February hit the mainland with a vengeance, sweeping across the Atlantic Ocean and bringing ice, sleet, and anything else the cloud and winds could carry. Josie was coping with the treatment, and on the surface, appeared to be responding well. Mattie, along with support from her tutors, kept ahead with her dissertation. There was hope after all, and maybe she would get that miracle she so desired for her mother. *Just a few more months to get through the work and I'll be able to spend more time with her*, she thought.

In the main, Mattie spent the weekends visiting her sick mother, and each time she left *that* house she began to despise more than ever, she would feel the pangs of guilt. Regardless of her mother's insistence that Mattie put university first, adamant that she finished what she'd put so much effort into these past four years, it didn't make the departure on a Sunday evening any easier. Mattie was always sick with worry that something bad would happen while she wasn't there. If she couldn't get to her mother in time then what? Her mother told her that she had to grasp all opportunities they got with both hands and somehow enjoy what little time they had together. But for Mattie, the strain of it all was too much, and she simply could not process the thought of her mother dying.

Mattie felt like a wound-up toy running permanently on low-energy batteries that one day would run out, bringing her to a grinding halt, and that prospect scared her. Bob was sympathetic of the times she had to leave work early to attend hospital appointments with her mother. Claire and Frankie were also

To Whom It May Concern – *The Book of Letters*

wonderful, providing bucket loads of emotional support, asking what could be done for her and trying to get her to go out with them to simply chill out. But Mattie pushed away the support that was at arm's length and became blind to her own actions and ignorant of the pressure that was slowly mounting up.

The weeks that followed seemed to be an endless stream of underground journeys – working – studying - visiting her mother, and returning to an empty, lonely flat because Claire had in some ways given up on Mattie, and therefore spent most of her time at Frankie's.

By the time spring was upon them, Josie said she felt much better and confident that she was through with the worst part of the treatment, and with that wonderful piece of news, Mattie was relieved that perhaps she was going to get that miracle after all. Sometimes, the two would venture out together, taking in the fresh air and sometimes doing a spot of shopping. On the day Josie decided it was time to shave off what little remained of her tufts of hair and buy a wig, her daughter took it in her stride, although she was shocked when she saw her mother with a completely bald head – what she saw was a pale and frail woman. But putting that aside, the two laughed together as Josie was transformed by the caring sales assistant into a redhead. Josie tried on a long blond, curly wig and paraded around the shop, then tried on other long and short ones, until she settled on what resembled how she used to look when she had hair. Mattie finally accepted that for now, it was a good day, and decided to take one day at a time.

Finally the twenty-thousand word dissertation was handed in, the degree course was over and Mattie was thankful for that small mercy.

Considering her mother had lost a lot of weight, she still

To Whom It May Concern – *The Book of Letters*

looked stunning in a pale pink suit at her only daughter's graduation ceremony, and the short, black bob wig that Josie chose to go with the outfit after trying on so many, suited her petite face. The celebration was low-key, just the two of them enjoying a sumptuous meal at Marcello's along the banks of the River Thames, a reservation that Mattie made a few months prior in the hope that her mother would be there. Mattie was eternally grateful for her mother's presence that day, and as they sat opposite each other chatting about the future, she watched every mouthful of food her mother took ensuring she kept up her strength. Regardless of how delicate the food was, Josie pushed it around her plate, eating tiny morsels at a time and only sipping on the white wine.

Mattie looked on, knowing that time was running short, so she decided to tread where she often feared her mother dared not go. She put down the knife and fork and asked once again, "Tell me about my father."

The uncomfortable look that this conversation always brought about returned on her mother's face. "We've been through this before."

"I need to know, Mum. What was he like? Did you love him? Anything?"

"What more can I tell you, Mattie, that I haven't told you before? I've told you everything."

"Really?"

Her mother gave a reluctant sigh at her daughter's request.

"Well you certainly get your looks from him," Josie said, acknowledging that it was now or never to talk about Charles Ushworth. "We'd known each other for a few years before..." she stopped because she couldn't say the word 'pregnant'. Mattie told her to carry on regardless. "As I've told you, we were two

To Whom It May Concern – *The Book of Letters*

families that used to holiday in the same town each year. Your grandparents became very good friends with his parents, and as children, we all played together."

Mattie listened intently to her mother talk about the happy holidays they all shared in Tenby. Images of Josie as a small child playing on the beach with her older brother Patrick along with Charles and his older brother sprung to mind, yet at the same time, it was hard to imagine they were at one time a happy family – something Mattie had never witnessed growing up.

"Your father, Charles was a year older than me but because his brother and my brother Patrick were that bit older, they often went off and left your father and I alone. We got used to playing and being together without them from a very young age. I suppose our love grew from that."

"He was your childhood sweetheart?"

"Yes," she replied, "You could call it that. He was serving his apprenticeship as a carpenter and was very good. The jewellery box – he made that and gave it to me on our last holiday." Josie took a handkerchief from her handbag and dabbed her eyes. It had been years in the waiting, but at last, Josie was giving Mattie the detail she'd yearned for. So Mattie sat back to engage in her mother's tales, lapping up all the previously untold information, even though it pained Josie to speak of them. "I'd just turned sixteen before that last holiday. Your father would do all sorts of jobs even though he worked so he could save up and buy me a ring. It was a second hand one which he could ill afford. I told him he was stupid when he asked me to marry him, that we were far too young. What would our parents say? Then when he got down on one knee I knew he was serious."

"He actually proposed?"

"Yes! When I look back on it we were far too young, but he

loved me so much, and I..." she dabbed her eyes again. "I loved him too. It was that night I gave in to my own desires and well... the rest you know."

"It sounds very romantic. Please tell me everything, Mum. I need to know."

This time her mother took a huge gulp of wine to steady her nerves. It was the most she'd drank during the meal. Mattie sat back and watched her speak openly about that time in her life and she didn't want her to stop. She needed to hear this as much as her mother actually needed to tell her, because neither knew if they would have this opportunity again.

Holding back the tears, her mother went on, "You can hardly call having sex on the beach romantic..." The comment made Mattie nearly spit out her wine. Josie continued, "I was so excited about getting engaged, but Charles swore me to secrecy and said he would write to me and make arrangements to visit. He wanted to ask my father's permission to marry me. We were young but he was honourable and a proper gentleman regardless of what we did, and so he wanted to do the right thing by me."

Josie started laughing as she told the story of how she smuggled the jewellery box into the car and then into the house with the help of Patrick, even though in return she was made to hand over four weeks of her pocket money just to stop him from telling their parents.

"Is that it?" Mattie asked pointing to the ring on her mother's right hand, wondering why she'd never seen it before and why her mother had kept it hidden all these years, especially as her own parents were now dead. She thought there were no secrets between them anymore.

Josie continued with sadness in her voice.

"Your Uncle Patrick was killed not long after that holiday.

To Whom It May Concern – *The Book of Letters*

Your grandparents were heartbroken, but your grandfather was also very angry. When he collected the motorbike after the accident, he smashed what was left of it into pieces. He literally pulled it apart with his bare hands – he was so mad at Patrick for not listening." The tears began to roll down her cheeks. Josie took another gulp of wine before she carried on, "I never knew he could get so angry. It frightened me. Then not long after the funeral, I discovered I was pregnant and I was too afraid to tell my parents." Her mother then chastised herself for being so naive to think she wouldn't get pregnant and put her head down in shame. "It was such a difficult time for us all."

The shame and hurt showed in her eyes, but it was just the two of them sitting at the table with no one else to judge what she still considered a shameful act. Neither did Mattie care about the couple sitting nearby, keen to listen to every word of their private conversation, so she urged her mother to carry on.

"I never got the chance to tell Charles that I was pregnant. Your grandfather wanted to throw me out of the house, but your grandmother screamed and begged him not to do it as he pushed me through the front door. She said *she* would leave him if he made me go."

The hurtful truth shocked Mattie and she muttered a few unpleasant words about Grandfather Barton, until her mother took her hand and told her to stop.

"There was a compromise, Mattie. If I was to stay at home and receive help looking after you until I got on my own two feet, then I was forbidden to tell Charles that he was going to be a father. He wrote to me, of course, but my mother intercepted the letters. She told me that just after your grandfather died. I guess Charles must have thought I'd changed my mind about marrying him."

To Whom It May Concern – *The Book of Letters*

"But what about when it was the two of us living in the flat. Did you try and find him, Mum?"

"I wrote him a very long letter telling him everything. I even enclosed a photo of you."

"And?"

With pain in her voice she said, "I never received a reply. I could only assume he'd moved away or was not interested in me and you. I broke his heart."

Mattie asked if her mother had any photos of Charles. She took a purse out of her handbag, opened it up, and pulled out a black and white photograph of a group of young people. "This is all I have. It was the last photo taken of us on *that* holiday. I managed to sneak it out of the pile before your grandfather threw the rest away. He couldn't cope with seeing pictures of Patrick, and neither did he want to see any of your father or his family. He severed ties with them completely. He just didn't want to have anything to do with them, so they never knew about the pregnancy."

"But why did he behave like that? Wouldn't it have been better if Charles had been allowed to marry you? At least I wouldn't have been born illegitimate and then maybe he wouldn't have felt so ashamed of me and you?"

Mattie's anger at her grandfather was evident in her rising voice, and other diners were starting to look at the pair who appeared to be arguing. Josie held on to her daughter's hand and asked her to calm down.

"He was never ashamed of you. You mustn't think that. I can only think that your grandfather thought he was acting in our best interests. Maybe he thought I was too young to marry, or that Charles wouldn't be able to provide for us. He was so sad when Patrick died, but I'll never quite understand because he refused to talk about it."

After all those years, Mattie finally got some of the information she wanted, and a photo too, albeit slightly out of focus, along with the name of a town where her father once lived. She had to be content with that for the time being, because after seeing the sadness weighing heavily on her mother, now was not the time to go searching for Charles Ushworth. But one thing was for certain. She was angrier than ever with her dead grandfather.

To Whom It May Concern – *The Book of Letters*

Sixteen

SOON after her graduation, Carter Gales Marketing offered Mattie a full-time position. It seemed at long last that at least some aspects of her life were falling into place and were becoming less stressful. Her mother was doing well, of that Mattie was certain, because she had told her so. Neither did she have assignments and university deadlines to adhere to, so she thought that maybe she should get her social life back on track.

Mattie was mostly ecstatic about the job offer, which proved she'd worked hard and that Bob had recognised her commitment to the company, even though deep down she often wondered how long she would cope in that hard-selling environment. It certainly didn't form part of any dreams she once had about making cakes, visualising her own little quaint shop painted a soft pink and full of the most delightful chocolate, iced, and cream-filled-fluffy and soft sponge cakes. However, when the main consolation apart from being rewarded for her efforts was the hope of seeing Mr Blond, she settled for the job offer in good faith and assured Bob of her continuing commitment.

Much to her dissatisfaction, however, Mr Blonds' visits had become less frequent since Christmas and Mattie could only assume this was due to the opening of a new office in Frankfurt, and any hopes for something more than a casual conversation by a vending machine were fast disappearing. So Mattie relied on her vivid imagination instead to keep her going when she was having a bad day.

It was mid-August, and accepting that nothing was ever going to happen between her and the elusive New York director, Mattie decided to get back on the dating scene. Claire also told her she was being ridiculous holding out for someone she didn't know much about and rarely saw. So she decided it was about time to sort out her love life, and with that, Claire fixed her up on a blind date.

Nice was the best way to describe Kevin, who was rather good-looking in a cute kind of way. Plus he was taller than Mattie, which was always a bonus with her height. He was kind and a good listener too. What more could she want? He was not a 'keeper' – as she would say to Claire of her Italian boyfriend – and she knew this the day she met Kevin. Meanwhile, she still had her fun with him in and out of the bedroom. It was all Mattie was prepared to commit to, and on the rare occasion that Mr Blond visited the London office, he still put her insides into turmoil and sent her heart racing.

A few weeks into September, she got the phone call.

"Everything all right, Mattie?" questioned Janice as Mattie whizzed by.

"Can't stop!" Mattie shouted back. Seconds later, she was in the lift making her way to the ground floor.

The twenty-minute taxi ride to the hospital seemed like eternity. Mattie fidgeted in the back seat, and every time the taxi came to a stop at a traffic light, she counted the seconds until the light changed to green, holding her breath during the time wasted in standing traffic.

"Where is she?" Mattie asked as soon as she reached the hospital. The young nurse took one look and knew whom she was referring to. "My mother, Josie Barton, how is she? Is she going to be okay?" Mattie probed, frantic with worry. The nurse smiled back politely and led her to a curtained cubicle.

"Your mother collapsed while out shopping," the nurse said.

To Whom It May Concern – *The Book of Letters*

Mattie noticed the bag of groceries by the side of a bed that was occupied by a frail-looking person who did not resemble her mother. She slumped into a nearby chair in despair and disbelief. The pale skin of the person wired up to various monitors and drips looked more fragile than ever. But for the time being Josie was asleep. "The consultant will be here soon."

The nurse's softly spoken words floated over Mattie as she looked on emotionless, wondering how they'd arrived at this point in her mother's life. It had only been a few weeks since they were last together. Mattie looked back at the nurse, seeing her lips move, but the only sound that rang in her ears was the bleep of the monitor to remind her that for the moment, her mother was still alive.

A few hours later, Josie awoke and gently squeezed Mattie's hand. It was dark outside, and Mattie had fallen asleep in the chair with her head resting by her mother's side. She helped her mother sip on some water. Her mouth was dry, her lips looked cracked, and it was a while before she could muster the energy to talk. Mattie looked on helplessly, seeing how her mother had aged a lifetime in a matter of weeks.

When the consultant finally came around later that evening with the test results, Mattie discovered the depth of her mother's illness. Josie had learnt how to wear makeup to disguise her sickly pallor, telling her daughter she was fine every time she asked about her health and check-ups, when in reality she was far from okay. Mattie's mother was dying before her eyes and there was nothing Mattie could do to stop it.

With the little strength she had left, her mother pleaded to be taken home, so Mattie set about turning the lounge into a bedroom, and to freshen up the surroundings, an endless supply of fresh flowers were brought in daily. They were as much for

To Whom It May Concern – *The Book of Letters*

Mattie's needs as for her mother's. It was something beautiful to focus on, in the knowledge that she was going to watch her mother die.

Mattie made up a bed on the sofa to be near Josie and only left the house when carers arrived so she could pick up work from Carter Gales and deal with urgent issues. Bob Carter showed great sympathy and eased her burden by allowing Mattie the time she needed, while Claire brought in food parcels and other essentials. All the while, Kevin was kept at arm's length.

Before her mother started slipping in and out of consciousness, she found the strength to talk about funeral arrangements that Mattie had previously refused to listen to. It was difficult to hear the requests, but determined to stay strong, Mattie held back the tears and promised her mother that she'd get the bouquet of white lilies and that there wouldn't be any wreaths or any sad hymns sung. Josie insisted Mattie mustn't cry. But that particular request Mattie could not promise she would fulfil.

The sleep Mattie grabbed during those last few days was little. Each staggered breath her mother took Mattie presumed was the last – too afraid to close her eyes in case she missed that last moment to be with her mother, to hold her hand and tell her how much she loved her, how much she'd miss her, and how she would not be able to cope without her.

It came and went so quickly. One minute Mattie was holding her mother's hand saying goodbye, the next she was being cremated. That was another wish written into her will, that she was not to be buried in the family grave along with her parents. There would be no head-stone - no mourning over a slab of concrete on birthdays and special occasions for the rest of Mattie's life, insisting that her daughter start living it to the full. The funeral, however, was held at the same church with readings and words of sympathy from the same priest who'd presided over her grandparents' funerals. But no amount of words could bring back her mother, and no amount of sympathy from the well-wishers that surrounded Mattie could make her feel better.

"Mattie, please come back with us tonight?" Claire pleaded after the service.

"I will tomorrow, I just need to be alone right now."

"But you hate that house."

Mattie nodded in agreement at her and Frankie, with Kevin standing firm by her side, an arm steady around her waist in support as he'd done throughout the service.

"I need one more night there, Claire. I've a few things to attend to."

Claire reached out to hug her best friend again. "Promise?"

"I promise. I'll be fine."

"You phone me if you want me to come over and keep you company. Okay?"

"Okay."

Kevin drove the few minutes it took to get back to the house, and once parked, they sat in silence.

"I need to be alone, Kevin. You do understand, don't you?"

"Of course! But I'm not happy about it. You shouldn't be alone tonight. Not after all of this. It's just not right." He leaned in to kiss Mattie on the lips, but she tilted her head to one side offering a cheek. He withdrew his arms from the embrace he'd tried to offer her, gave her a blank look, and from that, Mattie knew he didn't truly comprehend what she was going through.

She stepped into the house, closed the door, and dropping to the floor she screamed as loud as her lungs could scream until there was no breath left to scream anymore.

To Whom It May Concern – *The Book of Letters*

~~**~~

~~Dear Cancer,~~
~~Dear C~~ ~~Dear...~~

What do I write? I can't think straight but my head is so full of things I want to say. I want to scream and shout and scream and shout...

Dear Cancer

I CANNOT forgive you! I can't forgive you for taking my mother away from me. I am so angry with you.

DAMN YOU FOR DOING THIS! DAMN YOU.

You've no idea how much it hurts and how bad I feel!!! It was bad enough that she lived a lonely, miserable life, but I am so angry that you came along and took her just as she was given the chance to enjoy it and be free. She was too young to die!!!

You were unforgiving in the way you ravaged her body and life without a care in the world. You riddled it with blackness, like a thick tar that stuck to her organs and seeped through to her bones.

YOU do not suffer the consequences of your actions. YOU do not care about how you make people suffer. YOU

To Whom It May Concern – *The Book of Letters*

have no soul.

She'd never been given a chance to be the person she wanted to be and have a life filled with happiness. Why did you choose her? **WHY? WHY? WHY?** *You could have taken me instead!*

She was my mother and I want her here, by my side, to tell me that she loves me and so that I can tell her how much I love her too.

I have so much I want to say to her, questions about my life that remain unanswered, and now I can't, because you took her away.

I'll never forgive you for what you have done.

Mattie Barton
Daughter of one of your victims

~~**~~

Mattie awakens from the sad thoughts. She's clutching the red leather-bound book close to her chest with one hand while clutching the gold pendant around her neck with the other, and the tears are running freely down her face, dripping from her chin and dampening her neck to eventually rest under the collar of her coat. She coughs, trying to keep the tears back, but it's futile and she lets go of the pain as it racks through her body while the tears further sodden her face until her head pounds. When the crying

To Whom It May Concern – *The Book of Letters*

finally subsides, she reaches for the box of tissues that Jake brought out earlier and gives her cold nose a good blow until another torrent of tears for her mother is unleashed, making Mattie's throat ache even more from holding them back. The only way to stop the crying is to re-visit in her own head, Joan – her therapist.

It was months following the death of her mother when Mattie started having therapy, but the truthful words Joan spoke are ringing clearly in her pounding head. Joan asked about Mattie's letter to cancer, and especially why she had referred to it as a person.

Mattie shrugged her shoulders. "I'm not sure. I just wrote it that way. It wasn't a conscious decision. At least I don't think it was." She hesitated a moment longer, thinking about what she'd written, and more importantly how she'd written this letter. "Perhaps it's because it is the only way I can identify with it."

"Go on," Joan encouraged.

Mattie paced the room trying to explain her feelings for the illness that took her mother and her overall helplessness in it all. "It's like a human being that has inflicted excruciating pain upon me." She hesitated, reluctant to say what she was really thinking, until Joan looked at her again and told her to say what was on her mind regardless. "If... if I refer to cancer as a person, then I've someone to blame for the pain I'm feeling."

"What type of pain?"

How am I supposed to answer that? She fiddled with the flower arrangement, shrugged her shoulders again, and looked down at the floor – something she often did when she wanted to avoid answering one of Joan's deep probing questions.

"Mattie?"

To Whom It May Concern – *The Book of Letters*

"Right here," Mattie replied. Lifting her head she placed her hand on her chest, "I feel like I've been stabbed in the heart and the pain won't go away." More tears glazed her vision. "It's as if a part of me is missing. There's a big hole right here and I can't cope with it. It hurts so much."

Joan handed Mattie the box of tissues. "Do you think you could have changed anything?"

"I wish I'd been more observant, more conscientious. I could've done more for her. If I'd seen her looking ill I would've insisted she went to the doctor's and then just maybe the tumour would have been detected earlier. Instead I was too wrapped up in my own little world. I let work and studying get in the way. And look where that has gotten me." Mattie paced around Joan's office muttering expletives about her new boss Guy. "I know ultimately I couldn't save her. Nothing could be done, but I feel so guilty and I need someone or something to blame."

"Why are you so intent on punishing yourself and thinking that you are to blame?" Joan asked. "You didn't make her ill. From what you've said, your mother hid the true extent of her illness from you. She encouraged you to keep on studying because she wanted you to have the opportunities she didn't have. So why do you feel guilty?"

Mattie didn't answer. Her head pounded from the tears and from having to think about the probing questions, and the mascara that had run into her eyes made them sting. Mattie was a mess emotionally, and with everything that had been happening at work with Guy, she felt too fatigued to carry on with the session. Joan kept a watchful eye as she wandered around the room. Eventually, Mattie sat down and sank into the comfortable chair, looking up at her therapist with acceptance of the questions.

To Whom It May Concern – *The Book of Letters*

"Does it make you feel better to feel guilty?"

The brusque comment was swiftly negated. Mattie then added with a touch of sarcasm, "It's called being a Catholic." She didn't expect Joan to understand her faith and how they liked to use their religion as a big stick to beat them-selves up with. Upon reflection, Mattie apologised. "I shouldn't have said that."

"Mattie, while you are in here you can say whatever you want to say, I won't be offended. You need to be honest with your thoughts and feelings so that you can deal with them. If you keep stopping yourself from being truthful, you're stopping yourself from dealing with the issues, and it will not help with your recovery."

Mattie stood on the pavement. The weekly session had finished, leaving her drained of energy, and rather than use public transport and spend another exhausting hour navigating a revised route to get home, she hailed a taxi. Climbing into the back of the black cab, without giving a second thought she instructed the driver to drive to Sacred Heart church. She sat back and closed her eyes.

The church was almost empty apart from an old lady kneeling down at the front, praying the rosary. The fast mumbling of the Hail Mary and the intermittent click of the beads resonated around the old church. The old lady did not stop her prayers even when the large wooden door closed with a thud and Mattie's court shoes clanked noisily across the thoroughly polished parquet flooring.

Mattie quietly slipped into a bench at the back of the church, closed her eyes, and drifted into the serenity and peacefulness that the building encapsulated – something she'd failed to notice as a child. A few minutes later, a door from the nearby sacristy opened and the distraction interrupted Mattie's private conversation with God, where she was telling him that she wanted her mother back and that life wasn't fair. Eventually she opened her eyes and watched a young priest unbeknown to her, genuflect as he passed the altar, then walk down a side aisle towards a confessional box mid-way. He entered, and a yellow light turned on indicating the priest was ready to hear confessions. *What a waste of a young life*, she thought of the young priest.

Mattie looked around to see who was waiting to confess their sins. Apart from the old lady still clicking her rosary beads, she was the only other person in the church. She thought about it for a few moments then got up, walked up the aisle and entered the small wooden confessional box. She knelt down on the pew, and faced the wooden mesh in the wall that separated her from the priest. She could vaguely make out his outline.

It had been years since she'd last been to confession, always hating that her grandfather made her go during Lent to be absolved of any sins. However, she'd been programmed from a very young age, and so, Mattie began her repentance. "In the name of the Father, and of the Son, and of the Holy Ghost, Amen. It has been..." she paused to contemplate telling the truth but did not want to offend the young priest so she decided to say, "It has been a while since my last confession and I have so much to say but I don't know where to begin."

"Then start at the beginning," the priest answered.

It was as simple as that. So she did.

She could hear his rhythmic breathing while he sat in silence on the other side of the mesh window listening to her every word. Thirty minutes later she left the confessional box, feeling like her soul had been unburdened by the young man, and even though she still had a headache, her life somehow felt much brighter.

To Whom It May Concern – *The Book of Letters*

The priest let Mattie off lightly with two Hail Marys and one Our Father. It was a small price to pay for being absolved of her sins and dumping all of her shit on the priest, and for making an elderly gentleman wait his turn. As to how long he'd been sitting there she had no idea, but Mattie felt the need to say to him, "It's been a while." Then taking her turn on bended knee and bowing her head, she said her penance.

A few months had passed since Mattie's mother died of cancer. Dealing with the bereavement was just another incident stacked atop the stress she was trying to manage along with the bitterness she held towards her grandfather and other people who'd made her life difficult to date. Now Guy had stepped into the shoes once occupied by Sadie and was making her work life hell.

During the hours she spent at Joan's place, Mattie discussed her upbringing and faith, recalling how she was often chastised by Grandfather Barton with some form of threat connected to the Catholic Church if she did or said something that he didn't approve of, being told that her tongue would turn black if she told a lie, or that staying in bed past nine o'clock on a Saturday was considered to be a mortal sin, that she would go to hell if....

When Mattie finished her allotted penance, she sat back on the cold wooden bench. The old lady saying the rosary had since gone and another elderly man was now seated a few benches behind her deep in prayer. Taking a few moments to absorb the calmness the place embodied, she watched hypnotically the flickering flames from the tall candles stationed on the altar. It was peaceful and tranquil, and by the time she came out of the almost trance, Mattie decided that enough was enough for feeling guilty and blaming others for her own misfortune, and that it was time to let go of the turbulence in her head.

To Whom It May Concern – *The Book of Letters*

Seventeen

TAKING a deep breath and trying to shake off the morose thoughts of her mother's death, Mattie pulls the letter written to cancer from the book and throws it into the chimenea. It alights, and with a sudden whoosh, is incinerated like the ones before it. She takes more deep breaths to steady her nerves even though the bitter cold air hurts her lungs. But it doesn't last long, and the adrenalin pulses through her veins at the thought of what lies ahead. She sees his face clearly, as she has been seeing all evening. The smug grin he normally wore. That lascivious smile meant only for her. Mattie thinks of some of the sordid things he did, the time he cornered her in his office. A ghostly hint of his rank aftershave wafts by along with a host of jumbled up images of Mr Blond, bruises on her legs, Guy's comments, and Joan's help and advice.

Mattie defiantly shakes her head. *Why am I doing this? Am I not content enough with what I have?* She stands up, throwing the book to the ground in temper, and starts stomping around the lawn. It's late. Mattie knows this because the astrological position of the stars she'd taken note of some hours earlier has shifted so much that she no longer recognises the forms they make. She takes a moment to gaze upon them to clear her mind and get some perspective on what is actually happening here. But with increasing emotion, she realises the destructiveness of the book and shouts out loud that it has to stop right now!

Consumed with fatigue, and the rising cold damp steadily working its way through her furry boots up her legs, Mattie moves around the lawn to prevent the cold air from seeping

To Whom It May Concern – *The Book of Letters*

through to her skin. A light turns on in the house and she thinks Jake is about to come outside, but when it goes off again, she sighs heavily, wondering what he's up to assuming he'd long gone to bed. A part of her still wishes he'd come and sit with her to hold her hand and tell her that everything is fine but Mattie realises that that is not the answer.

Evident from the tears she's shed this cold autumn night, there are surprisingly many deep-rooted feelings sitting heavy in Mattie's heart. *I have to continue this last part of the journey no matter how difficult it is*, she wills herself while she takes a few more strides around the dark garden, if only to keep the blood flowing, never mind keeping a clear mind.

"You can't hurt me!" Mattie announces out loud, making something flutter away with the exclamation, and with a defiant stride, she goes back to the sun lounger and prepares for the next letter.

"I'm the one in control. I'm the one in control..." she chants over and over again, reaffirming Joan's advice. "The thoughts cannot hurt me. The thoughts cannot hurt me. The thoughts are not real, they cannot hurt me..." She continues to chant the positive mantras she once used to chant and thinks back to the stark advice given to her as she prepares to deal with Carter Gales. But as much as she chants her mantras, she can't block out the past, and the mixed emotions for Mr Blond and Guy charge back.

Soon after her mother's cremation, her grandparents' house, the house that gave her mostly sad memories was put up for sale. Kevin was gone too. Mattie decided that she'd rather have nothing than settle for *nice*. *Nice* was not enough and not what she wanted. The breakup shocked him, but she had no time for explanations about their relationship, even when Claire told her that it was rather callous, the way she unceremoniously dumped him. Regardless, Mattie had to do it, whether he liked it or not. It was not about him. It was about her.

The young woman was an emotional wreck reeling from her mother's death. Being in a relationship with a person she didn't love merely added to the complexities in her head, and it was time to get focused and get a grip on her messed up life. Apart from her friendship with Claire – and even that was fraught with tension – Mattie only had work to cling on to and take her mind off her bereavement. The only consolation was perhaps seeing Mr Blond again. It had been some time since that smile of his lit up her day, not that he knew the effect he had on her.

Bob welcomed Mattie back with open arms, and within a short time, she slipped back into her normal daily routine. It suited her to be busy as it stopped her from wallowing in self-pity. And she enjoyed working for Bob Carter.

One particular morning he signalled for her to enter his office as she walked past with her head slightly dropped as if she was looking at the floor. Recognising that this was how Mattie nowadays often looked he said, "Good morning Mattie, how are you today?"

"Fine!"

Bob also recognised her need to quickly defend herself so he offered, "If there is anything you need then you must ask."

She recognised her sharp tone and in a softer manner she thanked him.

"I've got something to tell you Mattie. I'm officially taking early retirement and I wanted you to be one of the first to know."

His retirement was no secret and had been talked about for months but now it was real and he told her that he was finally taking his wife on the world cruise she'd so desired – as long as there were golf courses he could visit along the way. But with everything else that had been going on, Mattie was surprised and upset at the announcement.

"I'll miss you. When do you finish?"

"You've got me for a few more months, my son Guy will be taking over the London office. I think you've met?"

Mattie nodded. She liked the kind-hearted Bob Carter but dreaded the thought of working for his son Guy, whose shocking reputation preceded him. There was little time left as far as she was concerned under Bob's supervision to learn as much as possible before he handed the business over to his supercilious son.

Guy had joined the London office while Mattie was absent and nursing her mother, but most of that time he spent visiting clients and planning a smooth handover of the business from father to son. She'd read a memo about it and saw him briefly in Bob's office one evening when she called in to pick up some work. At the time she wondered who the good-looking man sitting at Bob's desk was, but when he gave her a lewd look, Mattie knew instinctively it had to be Guy. Janice's description of him had been perfect – tall, dark, and handsome, likes women, but lacking in personality. That particular night Mattie had grabbed her work, given Bob a quick wave, and left before either of them had the chance to engage her in conversation. It was not the time for pleasantries when a funeral had to be arranged.

The days and weeks following her return rolled into each other. Summer was over – not that Mattie noticed the glorious days and the mini heat wave while nursing her dying mother. With weeks left until Bob's retirement, she consumed her every moment soaking up the knowledge he parted, as it had been

To Whom It May Concern – *The Book of Letters*

rumoured that Guy had no time for students or new employees, although she was neither anymore. As for the key account managers, they spared little time for her too, so she was on her own. However, Janice – even though it was not her area of expertise – gave advice where possible, and Mattie, through sheer hard work obtained all necessary information before Bob left.

The only reprieve from the monotonous days was the rare glimpse of Mr Blond, when he made an unplanned visit in October, and she took the opportunity to have a quick chat with him. But with the impending handover, he was subdued, and the conversations they held were very brief to say the least. A 'hello' from him was as much as she hoped for during his three-day trips. At times, that was all she got, and she was content with it. She'd have to wait another month to see him again, but at least it was something to look forward to.

By the end of the month, Bob had officially left, and Guy was leading the business that his father had spent so many years building up to be one of the most successful marketing firms in the city. It didn't take long for Guy to stamp his personality on Carter Gales once his father had officially handed over the reins. The first change he made was redecorating his father's office, removing all the light oak furniture and replacing it with a glass and chrome desk and white leather chair. Also gone was the family portrait that hung on the wall behind Bob's desk. He'd been so fond of the portrait of his two young children sitting proudly in front of their parents, but it was now replaced with a modern and expensive piece of artwork. One day Guy troubled Mattie for her opinion, and when she genuinely asked if his young niece had painted it, he was less than amused. But with smug satisfaction, he challenged her knowledge of the art world, and in doing so, professed his superiority and intelligence. *What a*

To Whom It May Concern – *The Book of Letters*

moron, thought Mattie, brushing away the jibe, as Guy proudly strutted around the office showing off the painting and telling Mattie of its origins.

Then there were the white vertical blinds that Guy angled so that he could look out of the office at her, but she could not see directly inside. Even though it made her feel uneasy, Mattie assumed that Guy preferred more privacy, unlike his father, who'd been happy to have his office visible to the entire staff.

If it wasn't expensive unknown pieces of art he was buying through the business, it was a red Ferrari, a penthouse, and fancy holidays. He even put in expense claims for his designer suits, which no one seemed to question. When the accounts department saw receipts from a local strip bar, it only sent a giggle around the office. The finance manager still did not challenge him about a single inappropriate expense claim.

Soon it became evident that Guy was not as grounded as his father, albeit he was intelligent and knew the business inside out. They didn't even seem to look alike. Guy was much taller, extremely handsome, and as observed from the family portrait, obviously resembled his mother. However, Mattie decided that a heart-warming personality must have bypassed him at birth, for he was smarmy and self-indulgent. As he gained knowledge and experience while working his way through other major offices, the gossip at Carter Gales suggested that he had worked his way through a number of women there, too. He then arrived in London with a supersized reputation and an ego to match his supersized pay.

The first to oblige him was Cynthia.

It didn't take Guy long to notice the extra button undone on the mature woman's blouse, allowing him the pleasure of viewing her 36DD cleavage or the tops of her stockings and suspenders

To Whom It May Concern – *The Book of Letters*

when she hitched up her skirt as she sat on the new white leather chair in his office. The glass-topped desk gave Guy a clear view of what he fancied and much more. If nothing else, Mattie admired Cynthia's persistence, because considering she was much older, she knew all the right buttons to press where Guy was concerned. And any opportunity Cynthia had to go into his office to put herself forward as the next Mrs Gales, she took. *Did she not realise that he simply wanted sex?* Mattie observed the side-show and knew all too well that it would not last, but while Cynthia was now focusing her attentions on the new boss, she was no longer focussing them on the handsome New York director, much to Mattie's joy.

It didn't last long. Cynthia stepped into the shoes of many women before her and straight into Guy's bed. One minute she was swooning all over him in the office, the next she was packing up her belongings and leaving in a hurry with mascara-streaked tears down her face. It did not take a genius to know what had gone on, and the gossip spread through the office quicker than Cynthia could exit the building.

Soon enough, Guy started living up to his reputation. He liked to use women, and although Cynthia became his first London office casualty, there were still many female members of staff queuing up and willing to oblige him. Even Gavin from the post room fancied his chances, having heard rumours that Guy swung both ways. Janice thought Guy was pleasant within reason, and Derek added that he had a good sense of humour. When they told Mattie this, she said they were delusional, wondering what everyone saw in him. The only credit she could throw his way was that he had thorough knowledge of the business and the market. He was good with clients, although overworking his charm at times. But there was something about Guy that Mattie just didn't like – the way he behaved when she was near him, the way he looked at her when no one else was around, that smile of his...

Regardless of what people said behind his back, within the month Guy settled into his role in the company easily. But Mattie was determined to keep her distance and not become a notch on his bedpost no matter how rich, good-looking, or charming he was. She yearned to see Mr Blonds' handsome, rugged face and desired to hold him close, but none of that was going to happen by a coffee vending machine or photocopier. Also, recent conversations with him had been stilted, but on his following visit, he brought a glimmer of hope.

One afternoon he ran into her, and said, "I'm sorry to hear about your mother, Mattie."

The sincerity in his condolence made her tearful, but over his shoulder, she caught the prying eye of Guy who swooped in before she had chance to respond, cutting short the conversation.

"I was just passing on my condolences to Mattie," Mr Blond said.

Guy looked blankly at the pair.

"Her mother?"

"Oh yes, that. Very sad indeed, but we need to talk now," Guy said casually, dismissing the incident of Mattie's mother's death.

Affronted at his lack of sympathy, Mr Blond turned on him sharply. "I'll be there in a minute. Whatever it is can wait!"

Guy walked back into this office, but Mattie observed him keeping a close watch on the two of them.

Turning back with a sympathetic smile, Mr Blond asked her, "You'll be at the Christmas party?"

Mattie shrugged her shoulders.

"I'd like it if you were. I was thinking that maybe I could take you for a drink? There's this great new place that has happened up not far from here."

Guy was still watching, and while her heart wanted to flip with joy, the glares he sent her way left her feeling awkward. Mattie replied, "Yes, that would be great."

"It's a date then!" With that he headed in the direction of Guy's office and closed the door.

The few weeks that followed dragged slowly, but Mattie had not forgotten Mr Blonds' parting statement. 'It's a date' he'd said, and she hoped to see him at the staff Christmas party too.

At the party, with fingers wrapped tightly around a champagne glass, Mattie waited anxiously for Mr Blond to arrive. It was her second drink, and the fizz had gone straight to her head. Tonight Mattie was determined to enjoy a long uninterrupted conversation with the man of her dreams – after all, he'd personally requested her presence. He'd also said that the two of them could go for a drink. He'd personally told her they were going on a date! *I wonder where? A cosy place for two,* she assumed. The words were all planned in her head. It was going to be her night to learn more about the mysterious man that darted effortlessly in and out of Carter Gales. Maybe she could fulfil some of those dreamy thoughts she had of him. So when he said it was definite that he'd be in the UK for Christmas visiting his family, Mattie figured that if she made the right moves, then he just may realise how much she fancied him.

There was plenty of posh food and the alcohol flowed in abundance –all free and courtesy of the company, which Guy made no bones about when making a Christmas toast. Mattie waited in anticipation as Derek sidled over to her desk breaking her gaze. "Here you go, lovely. This will cheer you up," he said, refilling her glass before a small pork pie disappeared in to his mouth in one bite.

She sipped slowly on the cool champagne feeling each bubble fizz and pop in her mouth before letting it slip gently down her throat. *I really need to eat some food*, she thought, and popped in her mouth a crisp from Derek's plate.

"Are you joining the rest of the group at the wine bar later?" Derek asked Mattie.

Just then, the lift doors pinged open and Mattie's eyes averted Derek's and the mince pie he was now devouring as if he hadn't eaten for a week, at the same time telling her that his wife would kill him if she knew what he was eating. He patted his tummy in mock laughter, but she was more focused on the lift. *Oh, it's just the caterers with more wine.* She observed feeling disillusioned.

"Earth calling Mattie, come in Mattie," Derek said in an attempt to bring her back to the conversation.

She looked back at Derek in bewilderment. "Sorry Derek, what were you saying?"

Then before he bit a chunk off a second mince pie he said, "I was asking if you're coming to the wine bar later?"

"I don't think so," Mattie replied, still tilting her head around him to watch the lift.

"Why? Do you have a better offer?"

She rolled her eyes at him.

"Well, Janice will be there, plus Kristie from accounts and the receptionists. I think Gavin is coming along too with a new chap from one of the other offices, I can't remember his name – Jacob, I think, or something like that. All I know is that he fancies…"

Mattie was not quite taking in Derek's persuasive argument about why she should join the staff that preferred to abandon Carter Gales' Christmas party in preference to a wine bar, nor the detail about Gavin's love life. She sipped the sweet champagne. If nothing else, the fizzy alcohol and Derek's patter was distracting while he perched on the edge of her desk, littering his shirt with pastry crumbs.

"...but I've got to be home by midnight. Wife's orders," Derek continued.

The lift doors pinged open again and with a sideways glance, she recognised that pose and watched the man who cut a dashing figure in a black dinner suit with the bow-tie intentionally left loose around his neck stride precisely, as if he knew where every step in life would take him. Her heart pumped fiercely. He'd arrived just as he said he would. But behind him was a beautiful blonde woman.

"I see he takes your fancy?" Derek nudged Mattie.

"What! Who me, no... I don't... I think he's..." But Mattie's red-hot cheeks said otherwise.

"You don't need to defend yourself, Mattie," Derek commented in between bites of a third mince pie. "I've noticed the way he looks at you. Everyone has! He's a nice bloke."

"Everyone?" She let out a heavy sigh.

"You see, you do like him!"

"It's hard not to. But that's between you and me and not *everyone* else. Anyway, who's that lady with him?"

"Haven't got a clue, never seen her before."

"Well I guess it looks like he's taken. She's very beautiful," Mattie said to Derek with a heavy sigh, noting how striking the woman was in the red shift dress and black faux fur shawl. They made a beautiful couple and stood out from the rest of the staff, some of who were still in their navy and black office suits.

Mattie casually strode over to the buffet table and placed a few small items of food on a plate. Noticing Mr Blond looking

To Whom It May Concern – *The Book of Letters*

towards her made her feel hotter, but her view of him was blocked by Guy when he went over to them, leaving Julie, the latest office recruit who he'd been chatting to for the past half hour, alone. Mattie momentarily pitied Julie, questioning whether she thought Guy was worth it. The young woman knew of his reputation and looked more than willing to oblige him for the night, so while Guy was leering at junior staff members, at least he wasn't leering at Mattie, which was a habit he'd quickly adopted following Cynthia's quick departure.

Guy shook hands with Mr Blond and then placed his hands gently on the arms of the beautiful woman, leaned in, and gave her a kiss on the cheek. She accepted his greeting by tilting her face then casually stepped back, leaving some space between them. The lady's guarded mannerisms made Mattie wonder whether she too had once been one of Guy's conquests, or whether she merely knew of his reputation and disliked the man for the same reasons Mattie disliked him. *I could like her for that even if she is dating Mr Blond*, noted Mattie.

She threw back more champagne and some morsels of food from her plate while observing the attractive couple. Mr Blond kept looking her way, and made at least a few attempts to come over, each of which was thwarted by Guy blocking his path. Mattie forced the food down reluctantly while noting Guy leering at the New York director's date, his actions irritating Julie, who was now drinking red wine straight from the bottle.

Guy had tried on several occasions to make his intentions known to Mattie, but it gave her the creeps. He was persistent, giving her work at the last minute in the knowledge she'd have to stay late to complete it, and in the hope that he'd have her alone in the office. But when Mattie realised Guy's intentions, she and Derek came up with a plan to exit the building together every evening because the last place she wanted to be alone at night was on the eighth floor of a multi-storey office block with the slimy toad.

The Christmas party was as lively as an office party could get, and people were starting to make their way to Jerries Wine Bar, where they could abuse Carter Gales' hospitality by buying the most expensive drinks and putting them on the company tab. Mattie noticed the woman Mr Blond had brought with him take a phone call from Guy's office.

"Mattie, I'm glad you're here. I wanted to tell you something," said Mr Blond, but he never got chance to finish the sentence as the woman accompanying him returned seconds later and whispered something to him. "Well... Merry Christmas and I'm sorry for the short visit, maybe next time..." The woman looked concerned but gave Mattie a cordial smile as the two left.

But what about that drink you promised? That date? Mattie had missed her chance and now he was going. Guy sat leaning against his desk looking out of his office door at Mattie. He stared with a smug grin, sending a shudder down her spine.

I have to get out of here.

"Mattie!" She saw Derek grab his coat and make his way towards the lift as he shouted, "Can't stay. Wife just called and she's throwing up, so I need to go home now."

"Have a great Christmas!" she managed to reply. Derek stepped into the lift along with Janice and one of the secretaries who were heading to Jerries Wine Bar.

Suddenly feeling alone even though she was surrounded by staff still knocking back alcohol and working their way through the vast selection of canapés, Mattie decided it was time to go. After all Mr Blond had already exited the building and she didn't see the point in staying longer than necessary. She kept a close watch on Guy, seeing a drunken Julie sidle back to him. With him distracted, Mattie got her belongings and headed for the restroom.

As Mattie stepped out of the cubicle, she was shocked to see Guy leaning against the doorframe of the ladies restroom. "Mr Carter, what are you doing in here?" Her cheeks flushed with embarrassment as she considered how long he'd been there?

"I would prefer it if you called me Guy, like everyone else. But you insist on calling me Mr Carter, which sounds *so* formal. Don't you agree?"

Mattie refused to answer and started washing her hands, looking straight ahead in the mirror and avoiding his intense stare.

"Getting ready to leave so early, Mattie?"

"Yes, Guy."

"Now that we are officially on first-name terms, I'll ask you again if you are leaving now. Is there somewhere else you'd rather be?"

"Meeting friends," she lied.

Every word he spoke was condescending. There was nothing nice about the man who was blocking the doorway to the ladies' restroom with his arm, and whatever the reason he was standing there, it irritated Mattie immensely.

"Perhaps I could interest you in sharing a drink with me, just the two of us. I know this lovely private place where we won't be disturbed."

His partially slurred words gave her the creeps. *A drink is not the only thing you want to share*, she thought.

The smell of whisky on Guy's breath was evident as he leaned further into the restroom. *You stupid drunk bastard*, she was tempted to shout at him, but stayed at the washbasin, taking her time in meticulously washing and then drying her hands in the hope that someone would soon enter the restroom, or that he would tire of her and move on. But he wouldn't go, and taking more time to think of how to squeeze past him without making bodily contact, she started applying some lipstick.

"That colour suits you."

Still wishing for someone to come to her rescue, Mattie permitted a faint smile to appease him, nodding at his comments while she brushed her hair.

"That's where you are!" Julie grabbed Guy's arm, pulling him back and holding some plastic mistletoe above their heads as she fell into him for a kiss.

Mattie was relieved to see the silly young woman and quickly pushed past.

"Maybe next time," he called.

"Not if I've anything to do with it," Mattie muttered under her breath as she hurried to exit the building.

She flew out of the main building doors onto the pavement and caught sight of Mr Blond and his female companion getting into a black cab. He turned. Looking her way he knew something was wrong. Mattie pulled her coat tight to abate the shivers from the cold and the fury that was brewing inside her, and looked away, feeling deflated because her plans had not come to fruition. And now she had to watch her dream man leave with a beautiful woman.

"Mattie, are you alright?" Mattie turned to see Mr Blond striding towards her, and when he reached her and put his hand upon her arm, she felt warmth spread through her veins like fire. *How can you have such an effect on me?*

"Yes, everything is fine," she answered, miffed. It was all she could manage through pursed lips, thinking that she'd been dumped for another woman.

To Whom It May Concern – *The Book of Letters*

He leaned in and gave Mattie a kiss on the lips. "I'm sorry the evening didn't go to plan, it's just that... well no time to explain. If you're sure you are all right. Happy Christmas."

The woman called out to Mr Blond from the taxi.

"You better go," she told him sadly.

By the time Mattie climbed into a cab, she was still in a state of shock but wasn't sure if it was because of the fiasco with Guy or the fact that Mr Blond had kissed her, leaving her confused, while the other woman had looked on.

The most part of that Christmas and New Year were spent in a drunken state with Claire and Frankie, partly to forget about Mr Blond as they went from one party to another. The last twelve months had been difficult to say the least, and she thought constantly about a certain handsome New York director, and now that kiss. It consumed her thoughts, wondering where this would lead. The butterflies hit her stomach each time she spared him a moment in her thoughts, sending a warm feeling through her body. But as far as Mattie was concerned, he now belonged to someone else.

When Mattie returned to work in the New Year, she expected Guy to have forgotten about the staff Christmas party, but within an hour of being back, she was summoned to his office. He shouted to her loudly from his desk as he often did, unlike his father who used to walk over to her. She pushed her chair back and puffed in disgust when he bellowed her name for the second time within moments. Picking up a notepad and pen, she marched into his office. He signalled for her to close the door and sit in the uncomfortable modern white chair.

"Mattie," he spoke softly, "Did you have a good Christmas?"

"Err, yes, thank you, Mr Carter. I mean Guy," she quickly amended. To be cordial, she asked him the same question in return.

"Yes, I did in fact. Had a marvellous time in the Seychelles with Victoria..."

Victoria? I've not heard of her before, but hey, maybe you do actually have a girlfriend.

"...she loved the new speed boat her father recently purchased. Did I tell you her parents have a beautiful home in the Seychelles? Not that we stayed there. I prefer my own space," he droned on. Mattie smiled, nodded, and pretended to show some interest when in fact, she was pressed for time as she was in the middle of a report that had to be distributed within the next ten minutes, "...the hotel was beautiful, first class, perhaps the best I've stayed in. It was absolutely wonderful, and so is Victoria. She's the most beautiful woman I've ever seen."

Mattie wondered whether Victoria, whoever she was, knew about Julie. Guy, however, carried on about how they ate fresh-caught lobster and at having intimate dinners on the beach in the moonlight. She tried to glance at her watch, conscious of the minutes ticking by, knowing how urgent the report that she was preparing was. It had only been handed to her that morning by Jackson with sincere apologies for the rush, but could she work her magic and get it sorted in time? Finally warming to the bright young rising executive, Mattie assured Jackson she would sort it out.

"Though it didn't start off that well," Guy's tone had changed, became harsher – precise and to the point. "In fact, I would go as far as saying that the Christmas holidays started off extremely badly."

Bemused, Mattie figured something bad must have happened to him. Maybe his father was ill. She looked at Guy for clarification.

To Whom It May Concern – *The Book of Letters*

"A certain member of staff left the Staff Christmas Party early and was rather rude to me. A party, that my company goes to great effort and great expense putting on. Do you know who that was, Mattie?"

The remark grated on her nerves. *Oh shit!* She looked at him speechless.

"You can get that look off your face. You know I'm talking about you and what you did. I heard what you said as you left muttering under your breath thinking I wouldn't hear. I could get you sacked for that. I've sacked people for far less," he hissed.

"But I didn't do anything."

"Really? Even Julie wanted to know what your problem was. 'Bad attitude' is what I think she said. 'Not a team player,' I also recall her adding. She told me you don't like to mix with the other members of staff, preferring to lunch alone and refusing to go to social events even when I pay for them. I could always get her to give a statement. Perhaps Janice in HR would be interested in my version of events. Who would they believe, Mattie? Me, the boss - or you?"

She tried to avert his eyes by looking down at the floor, saying she was sorry and that it wouldn't happen again.

"You're damn right it won't happen again!" he bellowed back.

Guy took her by surprise, and unable to defend the verbal torrent, Mattie remained seated, being berated like a naughty child, his words ringing in her ears about what he would say to others. As he chastised Mattie, she was taken back to her early childhood days, to a time when she'd been told off by a teacher for something that she hadn't done and had stared at the polished wooden floor on that day - and countless times since in other similar situations.

Then his tone softened again, "Mattie, you are working in a

demanding environment, and if you don't want to work here and learn to get on with everyone, then there are plenty of people who do." He walked to the back of her chair and rested his hands on the backrest. She could feel his breath on her hair as he continued to lecture, "You know, the working agreement you made with my father can always be revoked."

You can't do that to me!

She gasped.

"Don't act so shocked. I'm not my father. I am the boss of this company now, and if I want to, I can change the rules. So when you go back to your desk perhaps you will think differently about the response you'll give to your boss *if* and *when* he asks you for something."

With that, he flung a pile of papers onto her lap demanding that those reports be finished by the end of that day.

Back at her desk, Mattie slumped into her chair, throwing the papers down.

"Monday morning blues?" asked Derek on his way to fix the photocopier for the second time that day. "Or are you still recovering from too much indulgence over Christmas?"

"You could say that," Mattie replied and gave him a faint smile. She momentarily revisited the fiasco in the restroom in her mind to clarify what had happened and question whether she could've handled him differently. The answer was no, but the outburst from Guy was unexpected, and when Julie waltzed past her desk in a fit of giggles, she surmised that the girl had given Guy exactly want he wanted that night. "Stupid girl!" Mattie muttered under her breath, wondering what had happened about the woman he took to the Seychelles? Victoria, the one with the rich parents? She also bet that Victoria had no idea what Guy was getting up to behind her back.

To Whom It May Concern – *The Book of Letters*

For the rest of that week, Mattie kept her head down and out of Guy's way. Derek heard rumours along the grapevine that she'd been disciplined, and one night as they headed out of the building together, he asked Mattie what actually happened. She brushed him off saying that she'd made an error on some reports and left it at that.

For the time being Guy had the upper hand and he saw how his verbal attack on Mattie made her vulnerable. He'd found a weakness by bringing her down emotionally, and he'd enjoyed doing it.

A few weeks later, Janice walked past Mattie's desk and gave her a quick nod for her to go into the meeting room. It was already five minutes past 9 AM and Guy didn't like to be kept waiting. The photocopier machine had first run out of coloured ink, then on the final print run the paper jammed, bringing Mattie's perfected production technique to a grinding halt. Mattie indicated she'd be there in a moment. Then conscious of the seconds ticking by and giving up trying to bind the report, she grabbed the stapler, punched a few papers, and then walked into the meeting room with the pile of documents she'd been preparing since 8 AM that morning.

"Sorry everyone!" Full of apologies she held up the incomplete reports, stating that the photocopier had once again let her down and couldn't wait for the new one to be installed. She was about ready to hand out what she could.

"It's nice that you can join us, Mattie," Guy joked. One of the high-ranking account managers snorted at his comment.

"The photocopier broke," Janice interjected, giving Mattie a sympathetic smile, "And Derek wasn't here to fix it."

"Then maybe I should be reprimanding Derek, or maybe Mattie should do the reports in the evening rather than leave it to the last minute."

"But you only gave me the figures..." She knew to stop and quickly retreated when he held up his hand to silence her. "Yes Guy, I'll make sure they are ready on time in future."

"Good girl, Mattie," he said and turned to face Janice and added, "The problem is not mine. I pay staff to get this right for me. Deal with Derek or I will. Someone has to pay for making mistakes and wasting my time. I've a busy schedule today and time wasted is money wasted - money that pays *your* wages!" His eyes pinpointed at Mattie.

She sighed inwardly and knew that this meeting was going to be long and difficult. It was the third one she'd attended that week and so far had left each of them feeling like she'd been belittled and humiliated by her boss. It was as if Guy didn't care how he treated her in the presence of others. In fact, he didn't seem to give a damn about how he treated anyone. The tension already prevailed around the table. Janice winced at Guy's sharp words and a few other heads dropped in embarrassment. Jackson was first to run through his report and Guy gloated about how the newest recruit to the team had exceeded way above his targets. He slapped him on the back in praise.

"You'll make a prime candidate for sales director if you continue at this level of performance." Guy's comment seemed to annoy some of the other account managers who'd been with the company far longer and who brought in more revenue. In turns, each manager talked through their targets until eventually it was Mattie's turn.

Two hours had passed. Her lips were parched and throat was dry. She'd read their statistics, listened to them gloat about their own achievements and surpassing their targets, plus she was still seething from Guy's earlier reprimand. But the moment was upon

To Whom It May Concern – *The Book of Letters*

Mattie to talk about hers. They were small accounts, yet she considered them equally as important as the larger ones, just as Guy's father Bob had taught her. She knew that no matter what she said and how much she gloated like the others, it would not be good enough. Half expecting Guy to pass a derogatory remark, she hesitated.

"What are we waiting for Mattie?" He looked down at his watch then tapped on the table with his pen, making Mattie more nervous.

She was only a few minutes into her account update when Guy slammed his pen down hard on the table, bringing her to a surprised halt. Even Janice was shocked by his actions.

"Mattie, Mattie, Mattie... did my father teach you anything about how to handle the accounts? You can't ride on the coat-tails of the other account managers." He rolled his eyes then continued to criticise her efforts, doing his best to ridicule her work.

She tensed up and held back the temptation to tell him to fuck off. She'd had enough of him putting her down, of ridiculing her in front of the rest of the team, but she bit her lip hard and kept quiet.

Then he said it. "I wanted to have a go at someone, so it may as well have been you."

The insult hit hard. Janice gasped in horror and Jackson almost spat the mouthful of water he'd just taken, but Mattie remained composed, still biting down on her lips to prevent herself from saying what was on the tip of her tongue. The meeting ended. Mattie bolted from her chair and ran to the restroom where she locked the cubicle door, dropped to the floor, and sobbed in anger that once again, she'd not stood up to Guy.

There was a gentle knock on the door. It was Janice. "I told him that was totally unfair and cruel, and that he had no right in saying those things to you."

Mattie unlocked the door.

"Look at the state of you. Go home, Mattie. Don't worry about Guy, I'll deal with him."

"Are you sure?"

"I've dealt with far worse than that over the years. Go on, go home."

Mattie's heart is racing at the verbal bullshit she put up with as a young woman. She pulls page after page from the book, glancing over the many situations she'd written about – words written in bold, firmly etched into other pages, expletives crossed out then re-written because it sounded better to write that he was "an evil fuck" over and over again, making her feel good to curse him with every bad word she knew.

~~**~~

... Why did you do that to me? What did I ever do to you to deserve such treatment? ...

... I Fucking Hate You! I Fucking Hate You! ...

... WHY ME GUY? WHY ME? You've no idea how horrible you are. You're a narcissistic wanker! ...

~~**~~

She curses at him again – even though he's not there to take the lashing – while she flicks through more pages detailing events that she cannot forgive him for, for making her feel like a fool - for making her feel inferior - for treating her so unkindly - for the physical pain she ultimately suffered. Events that took place while working at Carter Gales and at a time when she allowed people like Guy to punish her because they thought they could get away with it.

The questions to Guy etched firmly on the pages remain unanswered. She never understood why he wanted her so badly, why he went to such lengths to have her. He was a bastard, Mattie is certain of that, and she still doesn't comprehend his actions nor understand why she let him get away with it – until one particular day months later. The revenge was sweet, and with that thought, a smile spreads across her face and alleviates some of the tension that is gripping her body.

To Whom It May Concern – *The Book of Letters*

Eighteen

THE horrible and petty little tricks that Guy tried to pull on Mattie are clear. They swirl in her mind, and while she knows that she's got to get past these events to see how far she's come from the stressed and angry young woman that she was to the caring wife and mother that she now is, Mattie still cannot stand to think about *that* bastard. Yet his face is vivid, like he's standing in front of her. The memories are clear – each word he ever spoke is still in her mind, not forgotten and still hurting. *I have to go on...*she says and closes her eyes in fear.

The lecherous man started giving Mattie twice as much work as any other employee after that particular meeting, when he'd humiliated her in front of her colleagues by admitting he wanted to have a go at someone, so it may as well have been her. Then getting her to work on reports over the weekend and always adding the underlying threat of what he could do to her career if she disappointed him – as if the humiliation wasn't enough. The stress was unbearable as he consumed her every moment with extra work and unrealistic deadlines and expectations, and used every method possible to grind her physically and emotionally.

But Guy's moods swung like an enormous pendulum from one extreme to the other. On some occasions, he would come over and pass polite conversation, giving the impression he was a caring and wonderful boss. Then at other times, he'd be flippant with her, condescending in front of others, always with that vulgar smile of his.

He observed Mattie's every move at work. Yet she couldn't

To Whom It May Concern – *The Book of Letters*

comprehend how other female colleagues looked at him with star-struck and dopey eyes when she saw something completely different. He was manipulative and sly, he knew how to play the game, and he played it so well that she was careful not to underestimate his yo-yo behaviour. But the longer she stayed working at Carter Gales – even though Claire had many times told her to quit – the deeper Mattie got caught up in Guy's stupid devious games and found herself powerless to change.

She had two choices – either leave, or play the game. In a moment of madness, she opted for the latter.

Upon hearing of Guy's treatment of Mattie and noticing the gradual change in her behaviour over the past year, Claire offered her friend some advice. "Keep a log of anything Guy says to you and how he says it. And you'd be as well to take copies of all correspondence. Anything he says, you write it down. And if that wanker sits on the edge of your desk again, then write that down too. That's after you've told him to piss off. Under your breath of course," Claire added as a warning of caution. She was adamant of what Mattie should do, adding further, "It's the only way to protect yourself, Mattie. That man needs to be taught a lesson, and while you might not think collecting this information means much now, it just may be useful later on. Trust me."

February and another winter came and went, and Mr Blond didn't make his usual monthly appearance. His parting words that night of the Christmas party were that he'd see her very soon and they'd talk. Maybe go for a drink he'd offered, if that was what she wanted. Although his visits in the last twelve months had been less frequent, she still waited each month in the hope that he would walk into Carter Gales and glance at her. She missed him, but she also presumed that he was spending his time with the beautiful lady he brought to the party. Then another month passed, and as the end of March was approaching, she'd still not seen or heard from Mr Blond.

Meanwhile, the logbook was getting thicker by the day from all the entries – details of sarcastic comments Guy passed, lists of unrealistic demands, copies of memos and handwritten notes he used to leave on her desk, especially the ones marked with an 'X' - those ones made her skin crawl. In addition to that, Mattie took to recording some of the meetings on a dicta-phone without his knowledge, even though the thought crossed her mind that if Guy discovered this he would have an apoplectic fit.

It proved difficult to capture evidence of his constant leering, the proximity of his body to hers when out of sight of others, and the leaning in to whisper in her ear. Then the times he would perch at the end of Mattie's desk and lean forward, trying to look down her blouse while taking strands of her hair and twisting them around his fingers. Whatever he did, regardless of how insignificant, she made sure to make a note of it.

Claire took the occasional look through the notes, horrified at the things Guy said and more so that he was getting away with it. She told Mattie it was good information and to keep doing it no matter what.

Mattie hated Guy as much as she hated Sadie for all those years of torment, but what he was doing was at a whole new level – a game he liked to play that Mattie inadvertently was caught up in. She considered writing to his father Bob, but telling him that his son was a total and utter bastard wouldn't bode well. She even contacted employment agencies after deciding that she should leave Carter Gales after all, but without a reference and in her mind not a great deal of experience behind her, Mattie felt trapped.

To Whom It May Concern – *The Book of Letters*

People who'd left the office crying, like Cynthia, and other young women whose employment at Carter Gales came to an abrupt and tearful end, Mattie thought lucky to have escaped. Even Julie was sent marching out of the building soon after Christmas. For them it was over and done with within a matter of weeks, whereas she continued to endure Guy's ludicrous and extreme behaviour for months. She wondered how many people he'd slept with and discarded like trash. Gavin fancied his chances and sent Guy an email. It caused an outcry that someone thought he'd be bisexual, and needless to say, Gavin was given his marching orders too.

Mattie cared not to throw compliments in Guy's direction, yet she had to admit that he was good-looking, and being rich and intelligent gave him the advantage over many men. He had the pick of any woman he wanted. After all, he had Victoria, who according to Guy was the most beautiful woman in the world and came from a wealthy family. But he treated people disrespectfully. Whatever his strategy was he was dragging Mattie deeper in to it, trying to get closer to her, invading her personal life when she hadn't properly mourned her mother. How she despised the man, for behind that façade was a cold heart that made her angry.

Then came a glimmer of hope – the elusive Mr Blond made an unannounced visit to the office. It was April and the striking man stormed into Guy's office and slammed the door. His face was filled with rage and from her desk Mattie could see Mr Blond present Guy with a large envelope. He threw it at him. Guy stood behind his glass and chrome desk and opened it, swiftly flicking through the pages. The dismissive look on Guy's face said he didn't care about what he'd seen – whatever the documents were? Mattie was intrigued.

To Whom It May Concern – *The Book of Letters*

The lack of response infuriated Mr Blond, who proceeded to stomp around Guy's office running his hands through his hair in desperation. But the loud slam of the door had attracted the staff's attention and they soon gathered around Mattie's desk to listen to the raised voices. They watched on as Mr Blond eventually took a seat and spread the documents across the desk, and then motioned for Guy to sit down. Standing on tip toes she could see that some of the documents were photographs and others were typed documents, some looked like invoices although it was merely a guess.

Guy refused the order of the man who was in fact his employee, regardless of whether he was a director of the company – Guy turned away.

The chair that Mr Blond was sitting on was knocked over as he quickly rose to his feet, the two men now facing each other.

"Go on, thump him," Mattie muttered. "I'd pay to see you put Guy on his ass."

A new receptionist, who seemed to be in adoration of Guy, glared over her shoulder towards Mattie.

It all happened so quickly. Guy laughed in Mr Blonds' face, then walked away and pointed to the door to order him out. He wasn't ready to leave, and after following him around the office and waving the documents in his face, Mr Blond turned on his heels and marched out of the office. Before Mattie could reach the lift, he was gone.

No! She screamed in her head. *Don't go!*

That was the last time she saw the man she'd been admiring since her interview – storming out of Guy's office leaving the documents strewn across the floor, and he didn't even stop to look back at her as she rushed forward calling out to him.

To Whom It May Concern – *The Book of Letters*

Mattie is brought back to reality, dragged quickly from her memories, when a fox shoots in front of her. It halts on the lawn to stare back and wonder why someone else is in its territory at this time of night. She isn't supposed to be there. Its big bright eyes shine in the darkness, and while it remains steadfast – its tail dropped in submission of the human intrusion it's not accustomed to – the fox's inherent slyness only serves to remind her of Guy. Then it disappears hastily through the hedge once it decides that Mattie is too big a prey to tackle, and her thoughts turn back to Carter Gales and the letters in the red book.

Another letter addressed to Guy is thrown into the fire, and even though it was many years ago, Mattie is still cross that she let Guy get away with treating her so badly for so long. She mutters, "I should've walked out of the office, I should've told him to shove his job where the sun doesn't shine. I should've told him to fuck off. I should have done a lot of things... But I did nothing."

Soon after the premature departure of the New York–based director, Mattie was invited into Guy's office and surprisingly given two of Mr Blonds' key accounts to take over. She was still reeling from the email that had been circulated the day after that argument. It informed everyone in a very brief note that Mr Blond had resigned. Mattie thought how unkind her colleagues were in gossiping about reasons as to why the lovely man they were content to swoon over had left Carter Gales in such haste. "Whatever happened must have been really bad...," one secretary remarked, "...Directors don't leave for nothing." Then Derek had been heard saying, "I wonder how much it will cost the company to get rid of him. It won't be cheap. This supposed *garden leave* will cost them a fortune."

To Whom It May Concern – *The Book of Letters*

Mattie didn't care for their pathetic reasoning and let the verbal assault float over her in disregard. All she cared for was the fact that she'd never see him again. No longer would she look into his sexy blue eyes and have those dreamy thoughts. There would be no more looking at the curls at the nape of his neck and wishing she could grab hold of them and tug at his loose tie, pulling him into a passionate yet dirty embrace and...

"I want you to take over... Are you paying attention Mattie?"

"Err, sorry Guy. You were saying?"

"I was saying that I want you to take over the Blanches of Mayfair and Highland High Society accounts." Guy passed her two folders, each one clearly labelled with the names of two top accounts. "These belonged to..." he could not bring himself to speak his name. In fact, he even sent out a memo after their argument saying that everyone was forbidden to mention him, and if they did, then they would face disciplinary action. "Well, you know who they belonged to."

Janice laughed hysterically when she discovered Guy had sent the memo without her knowledge. "He's such a child." Further adding, much to Mattie's amusement, "He needs to grow a pair of balls and man up."

Mattie flicked through the folders and noted the neat handwritten comments made in the margins. This was as close as she was going to get to Mr Blond, for he no longer worked at the New York office. For now, it was better than nothing. He'd disappeared and no one had any idea of his whereabouts. And if they knew, they weren't telling.

"I'm sure you'll be able to handle them. It's not as if they actually need much managing. I would've given them to Jackson but he's enough on his plate clearing up after that prick!"

Was that a backhanded compliment? It was probably the best she could expect from Guy however she didn't like his derogatory reference to Mr Blond.

"Fuck it up and you know what to expect." His response was blunt and true to his nature.

Mattie was under no illusion that should she make the slightest of mistakes, it would not only be the accounts that she lost, but her job, too. It was time to prove her worth again, and although Guy pissed her off, she was thrilled to be given the extra responsibility. *Maybe if I show him that I can handle this he'll show me some respect and back off.* An unlikely thought which crossed her mind.

Guy piled on more work for Mattie, as if she hadn't enough already. The two accounts were only the start of it all, but somehow she managed the workload by spending less time at home and with Claire, who'd forged a life with Frankie. Apart from seeing Claire when she popped into the apartment to pay rent and change clothes, Mattie came accustomed to returning to an empty place.

In the meantime, Mattie sold the house that belonged to her mother. It was advertised as 'requiring some modernisation', which was an understatement. Each time she arrived there and put the key in the lock, its deplorable interiors depressed her and she couldn't handle being there for longer than necessary. Stepping over its threshold brought all the misery and despair back to Mattie. Then eventually, the trips to collect unsolicited mail or give the house an airing and dusting for potential viewers came to an end. She wanted to shake the hands of the new owners and wish them luck with scraping off the woodchip wallpaper and tell them how glad she was that the house was no longer a part of her life.

Mattie decided to retain a few possessions that belonged to her

To Whom It May Concern – *The Book of Letters*

mother and grandmother. The house clearing people would've taken all of them, but only for the little money they were prepared to give in return. So she took all the clothes to a charity shop, including some musty-smelling items that belonged to her grandmother, which should've been cleared when she died - along with some porcelain ornaments. All that was important to Mattie was her mother's jewellery box, and apart from the china dinner service, some old but sturdy baking equipment, and a few keepsakes, the rest was cleared out. In addition to that and for reasons Mattie could not fathom, she also kept a number of photo albums and the framed photographs that once adorned the sideboard, placing them in a large brown cardboard box for safekeeping along with a handful of certificates – mainly death certificates. Within a week, the house was completely empty, and it didn't take long to reorganise the kitchen cupboards in the apartment and find space for the newly acquired items.

The day Mattie handed the keys over to the estate agent she took one last look at the empty rooms. She noticed the blackened edges of the green carpet that her mother never got around to replacing. Dark patches adorned the walls where paintings had hung over the years, and she suddenly realised even more how dim and depressing the house had become, even though her mother had done her best to brighten up the place. Mattie closed the front door on that house for the last time, vowing never to live her life the way her mother and grandparents had, and returned to work.

Days began to roll into each other and Mattie, at an all-time low, felt trapped. The more she tried to be strong the further she was dragged down into a pit of despair, feeling angry and resentful towards manipulative and controlling people. Even cancer had manipulated her life by taking her mother, and she struggled to think clearly, when all she could see in her peripheral vision was a black shadow.

Mattie saw no way out – the more she said yes to Guy's work demands to appease him, the more visible the cracks became under the strain of it all. She fast resembled her mother's sick pallor. Even the creases in her leather satchel matched the creases of the dark circles under her eyes. Her clothes hung loose from the weight loss and her hair looked limp.

As much as Mattie knew she had to say no to Guy, she could not summon the strength, regardless of how many times Claire told her to do so. Mattie would role-play the many scenarios in her head, but the outcome was always the same – fearing how he'd react and that she would ultimately suffer the consequences of saying 'no'.

The May Day bank holiday approached and in the weeks leading up to it, Guy had started spending more time out of the office. He was secretive of his whereabouts, but Mattie cared nonetheless if he was absent or what he got up to. As long as it didn't involve her.

One morning, she arrived early to wrap up some work and clear her desk because she'd planned to leave early as she had made arrangements with Claire. But it wasn't long after her arrival that Guy arrived when she understood him to be out of the office all day. His arrival darkened her mood, but putting on a brave smile, she greeted him politely as always as he approached her.

"Make sure the report is on my desk by 9 AM Tuesday, Mattie. That's a good girl."

Good girl! Who the hell do you think you are! She gave him a sardonic grin as her temper simmered under the surface for treating her like a child when he could've sent an email instead of proving his point face to face. "But I thought you were going away for the week," said Mattie. She took the memorandum out of his hand and saw specific words highlighted in yellow, and when she placed it on her desk, he tapped on the underlined words and repeated the deadline.

"I can read," Mattie said under her breath, thankful that the phone ringing nearby drowned out the muttering, and she passed another of those sweet smiles she'd come to perfect in response to Guy. The one thing he couldn't fault her for was her impeccable manners. He couldn't quite make out that smile, but a false one was as good as the niceties were going to get for him, especially if he was demanding work to be completed – which he was that weekend, screwing up the plans she made with Claire.

"I may come back early. My father wants to see me about something. Anyway, don't look so unhappy about it. Everyone in this line of work has to prove themselves, and if that means working weekends, then they just get on with it without complaining, unlike some people I know."

Mattie cut him short, "Please send my regards to your father. I hope he is well."

She bit her lip tight wanting to scream, *I have a life too!* Mattie slipped the memo into her bag wishing she could shove it in a place where Guy would require medical assistance to remove it. Another piece of evidence to add to the folder that was quickly thickening up, she thought.

The demand, which was the standard method of work that she was accustomed to working to where Guy was concerned, didn't go down well when explained to Claire. An argument ensued between the two friends with Frankie intervening, telling them that the plans could be rearranged.

When Mattie arrived earlier than normal the day after the bank holiday, Tuesday, to hand in the report, she tossed it with contempt onto Guy's desk. It slid precariously across the sleek glass surface, only to be stopped from falling over the edge by the silver penholder.

"Let's see how you like that when you arrive, you prick!"

"What's that?"

Mattie turned, fearful that someone had heard her. "Oh, Janice, I didn't realise anyone was there!"

"Mattie, calm down. I know what Guy's like and I know how he likes everything to be neat on his desk. It's one of his peculiarities, isn't it? This neatness and cleanliness thing he's got going on. He probably sterilises himself after sex, truth be known."

Mattie let slip a giggle at the crudity and bluntness of Janice's remark, and an image of Guy sterilising his penis was now planted firmly in Mattie's mind. "Yuk! He's got more than peculiarities, Janice," she commented, shaking her head to remove the disgusting picture. "I just wish I knew what I was doing wrong. One minute he's charming, the next he's literally throwing reports at me and telling me off in front of colleagues. You've seen how he treats me."

Janice sat her down at Guy's desk and closed the door. "He won't be back for a few days. Let's talk."

"A few days?" Mattie erupted. "I don't know how much of this I can take. He told me to have this report done first thing today because he would be here. I worked on it over the weekend. I had plans with my flat-mate that I had to cancel, that we argued about because I was more concerned about getting this done for Guy. You see, this is exactly what I'm talking about. Things like this! I can't take it anymore..." she fumed and dropped her head to her chin as a sob started to rise.

To Whom It May Concern – *The Book of Letters*

"Calm down, Mattie," Janice said and pulled a clean tissue from her pocket. "Perhaps you should take some time off. These past twelve months have been difficult for you with the death of your mother and with the sale of the house. I'm sure you need a break. Take some time to think things through and when you get back, you can decide what's best."

"But what will Guy say? I'm supposed to give notice about taking holidays."

"Never mind him. I'll smooth it over."

"Are you sure? I don't want to cause any problems – you know how ruthless he can be." Mattie refrained from using the few expletives that were on the tip of her tongue.

The trip was last minute – an impulse decision – much to Guy's disgust. Mattie wasn't even sure what clothes to pack because she'd never been on a cruise. In fact, she hadn't even travelled further than Calais before, which seemed to amuse the tour operator who'd recently returned from Canada after visiting her brother for the third time in three years.

Of course, Guy tried his best to stop her from going, checking whether she was actually entitled to the leave. He even passed an idle threat informing her someone else would be sitting at her desk by the time she returned, but Mattie had gone past the point of no return and no longer cared about what he said he could or would do. *Maybe that is what I should do, not return at all!* She didn't have to worry about earning money for quite a long time. In the meantime, she settled for getting away as far as possible – even if it was only for a week – from London, from Carter Gales, and particularly from Guy, who was emotionally suffocating her.

When Mattie told Claire of her holiday, showing her the brochure and pictures of the cruise liner that was in effect a

To Whom It May Concern – *The Book of Letters*

floating hotel, Claire thought it to be a fantastic idea.

"I wish I could go with you but I can't leave Frankie at the moment. He's stressing out about the new restaurant and I said I would help out." Claire cussed again for not being able to go, telling Mattie that if she'd asked just only a few weeks earlier, the answer would most definitely have been yes. "We would have had a great time together."

"You'd make a great translator, are you certain you can't squeeze a week away from him?"

Claire shook her head.

After a moment's reflection, Mattie admitted, "Maybe it's for the best I take this trip alone. I need some time to think and reassess my life and I won't be able to do that if I'm drunk most of the time which is probably what will happen if you come with me." She further added making light-hearted of the conversation.

The cruise ship docked at Livorno, and following a day spent in Pisa taking a tour of the historic Leaning Tower before the start of a five-day cruise around Tuscany, Mattie was excited to be staying on the floating hotel and looking forward to soaking up the sunshine and the gorgeous sights. The weather was glorious, even though it wasn't quite the height of summer, and instantly, Mattie felt refreshed, having been transported away from her London lifestyle and into the beautiful Italian surroundings.

Early that evening as the ship slowly cruised out of the port, she stood on the top deck to watch the sunset. Mattie marvelled at the view, leaning against the balustrade and watching the lights of Livorno get smaller as they sailed further out to sea. All alone but content, she allowed herself one romantic indulgence and thought of Mr Blonds' arms enveloping her. But that notion had to remain as such once she'd learnt of his resignation, and her dreams

To Whom It May Concern – *The Book of Letters*

started to slip away.

The warm evening breeze brushed over Mattie's skin – a wonderful sensation that sent tingles all over her body. She lifted out her arms, dropped back her head slightly and let the sea breeze blow back her hair and the blue satin scarf that was resting across her shoulders. There was a sense of freedom for the first time in her life as the warm air brushed by – no one to repress her emotions or to tell her what she could or could not do. No slimy Guy to leer and make lascivious passes. No wannabe entrepreneurs climbing over one another at work trying to make their mark in life while leaving size ten footprints up each other's backs. And no noisy London traffic congestion. It was only her along with the dreams in her head and a few thousand other people sailing around Italy.

By the time it was day three of the cruise, Mattie was hitting the footpaths of Rome. Impressed with Vatican City, she vowed to come back one day and spend a long weekend just in that place, and in particular, to take another tour of St.Peter's Basilica, as this one had been rushed. Trying to see Rome and all its splendour in an eight-hour window proved difficult yet not impossible. Mattie could have easily spent that amount of time sampling the restaurants and good food. Yet during the one day that was allocated to this historical and romantic Roman city, she managed to fit in a tour of the Coliseum, an open-top bus tour around Rome, and spaghetti and wine in a quaint little restaurant down one of the side streets. For the first time in her life she felt full of life, sitting at the rickety wooden table outside the whitewashed rustic restaurant, admiring the throngs of people busy clicking their cameras and taking in the delights that were on offer.

But the five days passed all too soon. It was hard to believe that it was all over as they sailed back into Livorno, followed by one last night in Pisa before the homeward-bound flight to London. Mattie had the most wonderful of times and met some very charming and charismatic people. Some of the older gentlemen enjoyed swirling her around the dance floor while saying they wished they were thirty years younger, much to the amusement of their wives, and other than the odd glance from a young waiter, there were no unwanted suggestive remarks she had to defend herself from.

On the last day of the cruise, Mattie promised herself that she would take charge of her life and not let people like Guy control it. She'd met inspirational people during the holiday and wanted to be happy like them. It meant she had to stand up to Guy and anyone else who trampled all over her emotions. Guy was simply another hurdle for her to jump over, and the sooner she dealt with him the better. How she was going to do that was another matter. Meanwhile, she was going to get a grip of life and stop being so miserable.

During the week of Italian sunshine, Mattie gained a few pounds, which according to Claire she needed to because she looked all skin and bones. Her complexion glowed from the Mediterranean tan, and for all the walking and sightseeing she'd done, she was surprised that she didn't feel weary, but in fact the complete opposite, buzzing from the new and invigorating energy. However, during the short flight back to London, the depressing feelings began to creep back. But she pushed these feelings to one side, adamant not to tarnish the last few hours of her vacation.

The rush through the morning traffic was soon upon her, and on a normal Monday morning, she was once again pushing open the glass doors that led into Carter Gales' offices on the eighth

To Whom It May Concern – *The Book of Letters*

floor. With determined confidence in her step, Mattie strode down the corridor towards her desk. All eyes were upon her for a change. She'd left her hair loose in a new, shorter style and ditched the formal navy suit for casual beige trousers and a matching jacket. The court shoes were also gone, replaced by a chic pair of ballet pumps, and instead of the creased leather satchel that was normally hung across her shoulders, Mattie carried a brown leather Gucci bag – a treat from Rome – which was far too small and posh to stuff manila folders into. Another promise she'd made was that she would no longer take work home.

With an extra touch of lip gloss and liberal spray of perfume, Mattie not only looked amazing but she felt amazing.

Derek was the first to approach her.

"Welcome back," he greeted her and patted her on the back in the typical Derek manner. "We've missed you."

The small welcoming committee made Mattie smile. "I've only been gone a week."

"A week is a long time in this business," Derek replied.

You're telling me! Then he commented on how different she looked but wasn't quite sure in what way, so Mattie simply accepted the compliment. As Derek filled her in on a week's worth of missed office gossip, she spied Guy over his shoulder. As usual, he was talking on his mobile phone and pacing his office, engaged in what looked like an irate conversation. Then she saw his jaw drop slightly as he watched her settle at her desk. *Put your tongue back in your mouth, Guy*, she thought assuming he was leering at her over her makeover.

The adrenalin started to kick in – it didn't take long for that to happen when Guy was nearby. Mattie reminded herself over and over that she'd be just fine, that this was the first day of a new

To Whom It May Concern – *The Book of Letters*

era. It seemed to work. Derek moved on to install a new computer for yet another young woman who'd started during her absence. Mattie sat down and prepared to tackle a mountain of work that normally greeted her at the start of the week. Failing to notice the pen and notepad resting by the keyboard on her desk, she looked around and realised her paper trays were in fact empty.

It took a few moments to recall Guy's last words as she departed for Italy. When she looked back at him, he shot her a derogatory glance, his lips then curled. Then Janice quickly scuttled over and handed her a letter.

The words 'conduct' and 'behaviour' leaped at her. "A meeting in thirty minutes? What's all this about?" Mattie asked, puzzled, as she scanned the rest of the letter.

"Mattie, Guy was annoyed that you went on holiday without giving much notice. I tried to calm him down and get him to see sense quoting as much legislation as possible in your favour."

"Yes, but I was stressed... and..."

"Don't worry about it. There's nothing he can do. He's playing games, just like you said." Then Janice went on to say how bad she felt for putting Mattie in this position in the first place. "If it wasn't for me suggesting it..."

Mattie told Janice it was okay, not to worry, and that she could handle him.

Janice continued, "I'm beginning to realise the lengths he will go to get his own way. Look, my best advice to you at this moment is to say nothing to him. Just sit and let him get it out of his system, and if he calls me in, then I'll back you up one-hundred percent. You were entitled to take the holiday leave and he knows that." She cocked her head to one side and gave Mattie another apologetic but sympathetic look. "Would you prefer it if I went in with you from the start?" she asked kindly. "You are entitled to be represented."

Mattie had read the company policy handbook word for word many times over. She knew exactly what to expect of the forthcoming meeting, and within reason, Guy had the right to sack her. "No, I'll be fine," Mattie replied. "As you say, I'll say nothing." She paused and then said, "Well that's a great welcome back – not quite what I was expecting."

"You know what he's like. Even I was threatened to be sacked," said Janice. Then she added light-heartedly, "Me, get sacked? I'm their Human Resource Manager!"

Janice quickly showed Mattie to her new desk tucked away at the back of the office, out of sight.

"Well at least he can't leer at me here. Maybe I should go away more often," Mattie mumbled to herself.

Twenty minutes remained until the meeting. Mattie had to think fast about how to handle Guy, adamant that she would not allow herself to be belittled. Then Mattie remembered the dictaphone she had left in the drawer of her old desk and scrambled through the relocated items in search of the small old-fashioned yet reliable tape-recorder – another item of good use bestowed upon her by Claire that time she told an extremely stressed Mattie to start logging anything and everything Guy said or did to her.

As the time of the meeting at 9:30 AM approached, with a few deep breaths to steady her nerves, Mattie walked calmly into Guy's office. He gestured for her to sit in the white leather chair then returned to stare out of the office window, eventually he turned to gaze upon her.

"Good morning, Mattie. You look radiant. I trust you had a delightful holiday?" He casually stepped away from the huge pane of tinted glass and sauntered around the office – hands in his pockets, his crisp white shirt unbuttoned at the top, and the

To Whom It May Concern – *The Book of Letters*

colourful tie he normally wore thrown on the back of his chair. Mattie assumed he must have had a bad morning so far, but he was portraying a relaxing mood as he moved behind her making her twist in her seat and crane her neck to keep him in view. She didn't trust this man standing behind her, and this added to the stress that waiting to be berated yet again was causing.

Guy's pleasantries were unnerving but Mattie listened and attentively watched his movements.

"You were greatly missed, Mattie." The words were spoken softly as he made his way casually to close the vertical blinds along with the door that Mattie had purposely left open for Janice, who was sitting nearby out of sight. "I, in particular, missed you. You know I value you as an employee."

"Perhaps you should value me as a person," she replied petulantly under her breath, only to have her first attempt at standing up against him being drowned out by the office phone ringing.

"Pardon?"

"Nothing," she responded and shot a look towards the phone, suggesting he answer it.

While he held a brief conversation with Jackson, who'd been sent to New York on urgent business and was now working between the London and New York office, Mattie indulged in a dream about Mr Blond. She was soon snapped out of it when Guy barked some orders and slammed down the phone.

"Where was I?" he asked, composing himself.

"You were telling me how much I'd been missed."

"Yes, well, you know how I like having you around. I haven't been able to look at your beautiful face from my office. I have to admit, you are looking extra radiant this morning, positively beautiful. Perhaps the Italian sunshine suits you."

To Whom It May Concern – *The Book of Letters*

"You like having me around?" she hissed. "Normally you are making a fool of me in front of my colleagues." Mattie had taken another step at standing up to Guy. This time she was more vocal and direct. Her heart beat fast having plucked up the courage to challenge his remark. It had to be done, but challenging him still made her shake on the inside. She waited to be rebuked.

Instead, Guy moved to perch on the edge of the desk in front of Mattie and leaned in. "Your fragrance is very refreshing. Is it new?"

She smiled, holding back contempt for the man whose proximity was far greater than her liking. Guy leaned in closer and took a few strands of Mattie's hair, twisting them around his finger, but she moved back from his powerful aftershave that was catching in the back of her throat. "Please don't twist my hair, Guy." Another effort made on her part to stand up to the things she detested about him.

"Playing hard to get, Mattie? Well I like games as much as the next person. Perhaps the two of us could play some, if you know what I mean?"

Once again, she was sucked into another of his stupid games where he was toying with her emotions. And now that Janice could not hear the conversation because the door was closed, Mattie had to think hard about her actions. She paused for a moment then made an impulsive yet irrational decision - to goad him, to push him to a point of no return.

"If you like having me sat near your office so that you can see me then move me back," she nodded towards her old desk. "That way you'll get to look at me in the way you like to. But you have to be nice." Mattie dropped her chin slightly and looked up with enlarged eyes. "You have to learn to ask nicely. If you know what I mean," using his own words seductively to draw him in.

To Whom It May Concern – *The Book of Letters*

Guy gave her that smile she detested so much. She'd seen it so many times, not only intended for her but any other unsuspecting female that he wanted to jump into bed with. He liked the suggestion and certainly this new side to Mattie that he'd never experienced before, adding that the dominatrix kind of woman was very sexy and appealing to him. Then he said to her provocatively that she'd been moved because she'd been naughty.

The hairs on her body stood on end at the insinuation, and that single word 'naughty' pulled her back to a place she no longer wanted to be, but she took a breath to let the comment wash over her as she stayed in the game.

Stuck in a situation she had unwittingly put herself in, she wanted to push him further – take him to the edge then throw the insinuation right back at him, as he so often did to her. She got up from the chair to walk around the office, needing to think on her feet and quickly. *I've got to get the bastard to say something that'll bring him down.* She stopped at the window he'd been looking out of and wondered if the busy people below had to endure what she did. Partially tempted to bang on the glass and scream to get their attention, not that they would have heard her from eight floors above, her inner voice said to hold tight. A few more minutes and it would all be over.

"I guess I should let you go on holiday more often, Mattie, if it's going to have this kind of effect on you. I like the new look and I like the new attitude. You have no idea how you make me feel."

"I'm glad you like the new me, Guy."

He moved closer and pressed into her back. He'd hardened and pushed up against her so she could feel him. Her insides twisted, making her feel sick that this ludicrous situation had

To Whom It May Concern – *The Book of Letters*

turned him on.

Mattie swallowed hard and stared out of the window, thinking carefully of her next move, planning strategically what to say, how to say it, perhaps what not to say, if saying nothing was the best option, pulling Guy into *her* game – the one she was trying to take control of.

"I've had a lot to think about this last week. Let's say I've evaluated what is important to me," Mattie said finally.

"You and I would make a good team, Mattie," Guy said and brushed her hair to one side exposing her neck. Then he leaned in and every breath of his sent shivers of repulsion and loathing down her spine.

"What type of team?" she asked, holding on to the last bit of sanity she could muster.

"That's the spirit, Mattie. But I think we both know what I'm talking about."

With a few more deep breaths to quell the rising tension, she asked him seductively to be specific. She needed to know exactly what he wanted from her. Guy simply nuzzled into her hair and again told her how wonderful she smelt and how soft her skin was – gentle to the touch.

Go on, Guy, say more. I want to hear it. But she pulled away slightly in disgust – just enough for him to want her more.

"Hmm, a woman who likes to play hard to get, you're such a tease Martha Barton. I like that." His own words were turning him on and he hardened more, pushing it into her back. Mattie felt the bile rise within her. "There's so much I can show you, do to you. All you have to do is ask."

She had put herself in this position and there was no turning back no matter how sick she felt. *I'll never forgive you for this, Guy!* He was pushing her to say what he'd always wanted her to say, and with great reluctance, she asked him, "What would you like to do to me Guy?" Her own words made her shudder.

"First of all I want to fuck you hard on that desk – that would be such a thrill, and I know you'd love the coldness of the glass on your ass. Cynthia did."

Her throat burned from the rising acidic bile she was biting back, and even though her legs felt like jelly, she stood firm and encouraged him to carry on.

"This position looks inviting too," he said pushing his leg between Mattie's, parting them and placing his hands on the window either side of her head, trapping her against it. "Is this how you like to be fucked, Mattie, from behind?"

Mattie said nothing other than tilt her head back enough to suggest she approved. Even when he mentioned a threesome with his current girlfriend Victoria would be sexually gratifying and entertaining. She listened as his breath quickened with the sexual intimation, surprised that he didn't ejaculate there and then even when he went on to tell her that after spending a week being fucked by him she'd definitely have no more pent up anger.

Each word sickened her to the core as he detailed some of the things he'd done to other women. Yet she remained still, holding back the rising sickness.

I've got you at last!

Unsure if Guy was going to move and still trapped in the nightmare of this game, Mattie swallowed hard and asked softly, "Surely Victoria wouldn't agree to this? I can't imagine her wanting to share you with anyone else." Struggling to hold back the bile, she had to find a way to get out of the office.

"Victoria, Victoria... she's not an issue. Tell me what I want to hear and she'll be gone quicker than you can imagine."

"I want what's best for me. Anyway I thought you two were

To Whom It May Concern – *The Book of Letters*

an item and that she'd soon be Mrs Guy Carter." *Perhaps Victoria would be interested in hearing this too*, Mattie secretly wished.

He kissed Mattie on the neck, biting gently on her ear lobe. Then he turned her around to face him. "You are far more interesting than Victoria. There's something about you, Mattie, that makes me want to do... well I've already said enough," and he ran a finger down her cheek.

She returned that undetected sardonic smile and his reaction was one of joy.

"God, you are a sexy bitch. I want to take you right here, now!"

I can't do this anymore! Her instinct was to run out of the office and get as far away as possible from the despicable creature, but she was also close to ending this saga. "The office is full of people, and what about Victoria. Shouldn't you at least end your relationship with her first? Then we'll talk about it."

"You're so formal, Mattie. I'm surprised how much that actually turns me on. You are so different from other girls I've dated. They just fuck me for money, especially Victoria. Pass me the phone and I'll deal with her right now if that is what it takes. She was never a good fuck anyway."

Guy let go of his hold on Mattie to stride towards his desk. She shivered with despair and watched him tap a number on the phone. Every bone in her body trembled with fear as she walked painstakingly towards the door. She pulled it open slightly and held onto the handle for support, her legs still shaking, her palms sweating from the tight grasp on metal. Mattie turned to face Guy as the phone dialled through to Victoria's, and she smiled back at him the way she always did.

"That's such a shame, Guy," Mattie's voice started to rise.

To Whom It May Concern – *The Book of Letters*

"Never in a million years are you ever, EVER going to touch me or do any of the things that you've just said," she screamed at him. The delight fell from his face. It turned puce with anger when he realised what she was up to. Then another hit of adrenalin rushed through Mattie's bloodstream while she screamed at him again, "I will NEVER, EVER let you near me. If you so much as breathe on my hair or even in my direction one more time, then I'll... I'll..."

"You spiteful bitch!" he spat back, "What fucking game are you playing? Have you any idea who I am? I'll get you sacked for this!" He banged his fist on the table, sending the silver stationery items scattering to the floor. And with a firm yank of the telephone cord, he snapped it from its socket just as the dial tone connected to Victoria and hurled it at Mattie. It hit the door hard, the resounding thud and shouting forcing Janice to scurry into the office.

"What the hell is going on in here?" she shouted in Guy's direction.

"Get that bitch out of my sight!"

Mattie ran to the toilet and threw up the little bit of toast she'd eaten that morning – her stomach wrenching from his words ringing in her ears and from the disgusting smell of that aftershave he often wore, which clung to her clothes. Combined with the acidity in her throat, the spiralling thoughts made her heave even more until her stomach ached from being empty. *Why me?* She cried. *Why me?* And she wrenched some more.

Janice followed soon after and placed a comforting hand on Mattie's back as she rinsed her mouth with water. "Look at me!" Mattie sobbed and looked back at the dull face in the mirror staring back at her. "I can't stand him! He's such a bastard!"

"What happened in there?" Janice asked. "Everything seemed

okay and then you started shouting at him. What did you say to him to make him so angry?"

"You've no idea what he's like, the things he's just said and what he wants..." more bile forced its way up at the thought of Guy's sexual fantasies.

"I don't know what's going on between you two, but don't let him see you like this. If he does, then he knows he's won. Believe it or not, I'm on your side," Janice assured Mattie. "I don't like the way he does things, but to date he hasn't made a mistake legally, or at least been caught making one."

Mattie told Janice there was nothing going on between the two of them, that there never has been and never will be. She was partly tempted to share the fact that she'd been making notes and recording conversations, but Mattie wasn't yet convinced that Janice was on her side. The HR manager was a nice woman but Carter Gales paid her wages too, and with two kids to support and a lazy husband who refused to work since his redundancy three years earlier, the last thing Janice needed was to lose her job. So Mattie decided it wasn't fair to drag her into her own mess, deciding only she could sort it out.

"If it makes you feel any better, then there is light at the end of the tunnel," Janice said.

Mattie shot Janice a quizzical look.

"I shouldn't divulge this information, Mattie, so what I'm about to tell you could get me sacked if you tell the wrong person."

"Go on."

"Guy has a chequered past. Let's say that Daddy has already bailed him out of a few sticky situations. Selling drugs in school for one, and I've also heard he assaulted a woman in Italy."

"This is what I've been trying to tell you," said Mattie. "Isn't it obvious to everyone that he's an evil, manipulative bastard? Am I the only one in this firm that can see right through him for the horrible man that he truly is?"

"Believe me, Mattie, more people than you think know about his reputation and they don't like it. I just think they are too afraid of saying anything. Do you think the other directors would allow Bob to let Guy take over the business if he was allowed to do whatever he wanted?"

Mattie shrugged her shoulders.

"He's on a tight leash with his father *and* the directors. Perhaps if his father was to discover something incriminating about him then who knows what would happen. One foot wrong and he's out."

"From what I can see, Janice, he's been doing what he wants and *has* been getting away with it since he took charge of the company! What happened back there is just..." Mattie stopped herself from saying anymore knowing it would infuriate her further.

"There are things about Guy that I can't tell you," Janice stated. "It's more than my job's worth. All I can say at this moment in time is stand up for yourself. You're better than this. Whatever you said to him back there has certainly put him in his place. He even told me to make sure you were alright after he'd calmed down."

Mattie was confused with his quick change in attitude, but one thing she knew was that she *was* better than him and had to find a way of dealing with his erratic behaviour and sexual advances. She decided that she was going to catch that curve ball and hurl it right back at him. No matter what it took, then she'd be the one wiping the smile off of his face. She just wasn't sure how.

The confidence that Mattie had walking back into work an

To Whom It May Concern – *The Book of Letters*

hour ago had gone and she was left a quivering wreck, shocked at his behaviour and more so at her own approach. She found it all too much to handle. She touched up her makeup and clipped back her hair. Janice had left, and Mattie returned to one of the cubicles. "Ouch," she silently hissed pulling the cello-tape from her inner thigh to remove the dicta-phone before dropping it into her new bag.

A few stiff coffees later, she was thankful for sitting out of Guy's sight but couldn't concentrate on the mounting work and missed client calls. Janice occasionally checked in on Mattie. Later when she was standing by the water dispenser, she spotted Guy appear at Mattie's side. He leaned casually against the desk.

"You know it doesn't have to be like this, Mattie." Was this the same man who a few hours earlier was shouting and banging his fist on the desk and hurling phones across the office? "If you change your perception of me then I think we could have a very good relationship."

Mattie thought the man was insane.

He pressed his leg up against hers and inched closer, the smell of his aftershave floated past once again, and the sickly feeling came back. Tears began pricking her eyes, as he took strands of her hair and twisted them. Mattie lifted her face and glared back at him, prompting and reminding him of her earlier warning.

"Perhaps I can take you out for a drink after work to show my true appreciation and to say sorry for my earlier behaviour? You may actually discover how enjoyable I am. I can show you so much, Mattie," he added perversely.

Not this again, I can't take anymore! She buried her head in her hands, clutching her hair out of despair. Enough was enough. Mattie stood up pushing her chair back and faced him. "I've got evidence of what happened earlier and if you so much as touch my hair or speak to me the way you did this morning then I'll take it to the police. Is that clear?"

At that moment Janice suddenly appeared at Mattie's desk.

"Oh, Janice, can I help?" Guy asked, quickly moving away from Mattie.

"I've left a report on your desk," Janice said to him then further asked, "Is everything okay here?"

"Fine. Perfectly fine," Mattie told her, leaving Guy speechless. Then he was gone.

The afternoon passed slower than ever, but as soon as it was 5 PM, Mattie rushed out of the office, not even waiting to tell Derek of her early departure. The journey home was long and tedious. A diversion on the underground due to maintenance repairs meant Mattie had to navigate up and down long escalators traversing to another line. Finally, she stepped into her apartment wearily, feeling sickly hot and still seething with fury as she flopped lifelessly on her bed, sobbing with frustration. The sobs stopped for a brief moment when Mattie turned to look at a framed photograph of her mother on a nearby dressing table. And the overwhelming feeling of loss and self-pity swamped her again as she buried her face and more tears streamed into the pillow.

The next morning, Claire finally breezed into the house like a lone leaf on a gust of wind. Mattie had made vain attempts to contact her last night but she had been unsuccessful, assuming that she was either working or most likely in bed with Frankie. It was where Claire spent most of her time these days. Feeling alone and dejected, Mattie resented Claire's light-hearted patter when she wished her a good morning.

"What are you doing off work?"

Mattie grunted back, unwilling to pass polite conversation, but then asked the same of her, to which Claire replied that she'd

To Whom It May Concern – *The Book of Letters*

taken the day off to do some work for the new restaurant.

"There's too much Italian in the Luigi house at the moment and it's driving me mad. They're all highly strung and stressing about the new place so I thought it best to get out of there. Frankie seems to be the only one who knows how to handle his father. His mother was crying when I left – something to do with the wrong tiles being shipped from Italy which has further delayed the opening." Claire flung her arms in the air in true tempestuous style, harrumphing at the Mediterranean arguments that formed part of her adopted Italian life.

Mattie watched her part-time roommate noisily stomp around the apartment, in and out of her own bedroom, as she quickly changed into some casual clothes and then went back into the kitchen in search of food. Mattie noted Claire's assured movement, how she exuded strength and determination, singing some ditto as she checked the contents of the fridge, moving freely about the small kitchen area making toast. She thought how Claire never complained about anything, never seemed afraid to tackle what was put to her, and while she gazed upon her happy friend, she wondered where she'd gone wrong in her own life – nothing ever went right anymore. Now even their relationship had become fragile over the past few months.

Working harder to produce good results at work didn't seem to matter anymore, and having tried to prove to Guy she was good at her job proved fruitless. Plus she was tired of hearing her own voice creating doubt in her mind or that of her grandfather saying, 'Mattie, you can't do that. It's rude to answer back. Those who ask don't get.' The words that formed a daily part of growing up in the Barton household still rang strong, and while her mother once told her that Grandfather Barton only said those things out of love, Mattie knew now that it had more far-reaching

To Whom It May Concern – *The Book of Letters*

consequences. And Guy? He'd systematically chipped away at the last little bit of self-esteem she had.

Feeling lonely and in danger of losing her friendship, she permitted a smile while Claire munched on toast and tended to a pile of post that had been sitting on the table for days. Mattie sat curled up on the sofa wrapped in a fluffy dressing gown. It had been a difficult night drifting in and out of sleep between bouts of crying. The bottle of red wine hadn't helped to dull the pain much either. It only made her throat dry and added to the throbbing headache.

"You look a bit frazzled, Mattie. Too much partying last night?"

"I wish!" Mattie retorted, sharply cutting Claire mid-sentence.

"Oh, I guess by that tone you're not in a great mood."

"What would you know?" snapped Mattie, and she took a swig of cold tea from the mug she'd been holding onto for the past half hour to stop herself from saying something she'd later regret.

Claire slammed a cupboard door. "For God's sake, Mattie, when are you going to deal with this?" she barked, then grabbed the kettle to fill it. "I'm so tired of hearing the same old story. Poor me, poor me." Then she opened the fridge to retrieve a bottle of milk, slamming that door too, making its contents shake.

Gripping the mug tighter, Mattie looked on wide-eyed and in shock at her friend's sudden outburst.

"Here, drink this," Claire almost yelled and pushed a fresh mug of steaming coffee into Mattie's hand. "You need to eat something, too," and within seconds, a plate of biscuits was kept in front of Mattie.

"You need help, Mattie. I mean *real* help. No matter what I say to you, you don't listen." Claire flopped into the chair in front of Mattie, tucked her feet under her bottom and proceeded to munch on one of the chocolate biscuits. In between mouthfuls, she continued her rant, "I know you've had to deal with a lot of bereavement, more than the average person for Christ sake's, but you can't keep living your life like this. You told me just the other day that you were going to change, that you'd processed a lot while on holiday – but look at you, sitting moping around again. Look at your state!"

The berated friend dropped her head in shame.

"You're making yourself ill and... and I cannot cope with listening to you whine anymore about what you don't like, who's upset you, and that boss of yours! My God, that boss of yours is probably one of the cruellest people I've come across yet you still work there. Why?"

Mattie looked up as the tears stung her eyes.

"Plus, I'm afraid that..." Claire stammered.

"Afraid of what?" Mattie shouted back, "Afraid of what?"

"That you'll do something really stupid!" Claire eventually spluttered.

"What's that supposed to mean?"

"I don't know!" Claire said, and when she saw the tears trickle down Mattie's face, she stopped the tirade. More composed now, she swallowed the remains of the biscuit and continued calmly. "Mattie, you're too depressing and miserable to be around. I've been telling you for ages to tell your boss to fuck off!" She got up and went over to one of the cupboards. "How many times have I been supportive and tried to help you? We've talked for hours on end and still you do nothing about it. You always agree with me and for maybe a few days, you are great to be with, but these last twelve months you flip at the slightest of things. I know your mother's death was really hard to handle – Christ I don't know what I'd do if my mother died, but you've got to change. Find a way to deal with it. Go to bereavement counselling or something? Something – just do something about it please? I cannot give you the confidence you need and I certainly can't go into your office and kick Guy in the balls, even though I'd love to. Maybe I should. Here!" Claire threw a telephone directory at Mattie, narrowly missing the plate of biscuits.

Stunned at her reaction and truthfulness, Mattie burst into tears again and proceeded to ramble on about what Guy had done. "You've no idea what happened yesterday, he... he..." she struggled to speak coherently through the blubbering.

Claire swiftly moved towards her and pulled her close as Mattie recounted yesterday's events.

"You see, this is exactly what I mean! Why did you do that you stupid girl? You're playing with fire and you need to leave that firm before it gets any worse!" Claire then went on to say she thought Guy was a vindictive person, and from what she was being told, it appeared he wouldn't stop until he got what he wanted. "He's the boss for Christ's sake! Isn't there someone you can report him to? What about the police? Make a complaint about harassment. Do something before it is too late, Mattie! In fact don't go back, there's nothing they can do. So what if they sack you, that's the worst thing that can happen, and it's not as if you need the money," Claire went on, trying to comfort Mattie. She further reminded her that she was an intelligent person and she'd easily get another job, probably a better one.

When the crying had finally subsided, Claire told Mattie sternly that if she did nothing else about Guy's advances then at the least she needed professional help. She held her shoulders firmly and gave out the solid advice looking her straight in the eye, "You've not even grieved properly for your Mum for crying out loud! At least consider dealing with that."

To Whom It May Concern – *The Book of Letters*

Mattie nodded in agreement. "I know, I know. I just thought that if I kept busy at work then it would take my mind off things and everything would be okay."

"Guy's a tosser!" The words rolled freely off Claire's tongue, like she was used to referring to Guy in that manner. "I don't know why you've put up with his emotional blackmail for so long. Here, take this," she rooted around her handbag and pulled out a business card. "I was given this the other day at one of those local business conferences - it might come in handy." Before reaching for a third biscuit Claire added, "Didn't you say he had a girlfriend?"

"Yes. Victoria."

"Kick him where it hurts and tell her – a cheap shot but quick, it may work." But when Mattie told her that Guy was actually dialling his girlfriend's number in front of her, Claire thought otherwise. "Look, I know life has dealt you a raw deal so far but only you can change that. Not me. I will always be here for you, but you've got to dump the crap stored in your head because you're driving yourself and me crazy."

Mattie thought she'd feel numb from the heart-to-heart chat, but instead, she was relieved. For the first time someone had shown her some direction, albeit in an unusual way. Perhaps not the method she would have chosen, but it worked. She needed to hear the truth, which Claire harshly delivered, and a few hours and several cups of coffee later, her friend watched over Mattie while she made that important call.

After booking her first session with a therapist, Mattie followed company policy and sent Guy a memo.

The following week she was back at work, and with Janice by her side, they sat patiently in Guy's office waiting for him to

To Whom It May Concern – *The Book of Letters*

arrive. Five minutes late, Mattie had noticed, and told Janice that if it was the other way around, if she was late, then she'd have been berated. Janice had to agree.

Guy walked into the room looking apprehensive, seeing the two women together in an official capacity. The word 'stress' was mentioned, at which Guy snorted in derision, but he said very little while Mattie told him she was taking time off because she was suffering from it.

"It will just be for a few days while I get some perspective on a few things," was how she put it. "Then once a week until I don't need to go. I'll even use my holiday allowance to attend the appointments," she added mindful of not abusing the company absence policy.

This didn't please Guy. His hands were clasped with his chin resting on his index fingers as he listened earnestly to Mattie's explanation. Then he did what she expected him to do. He mocked her. "Stress, is that what you're calling it?"

"Guy, it's not necessary to speak to Mattie like..." interjected Janice but Guy held up his hand as he often did when he wanted to silence someone.

"I don't believe that work makes people stressed and those who like to throw this word around casually are weak-minded and not fit for the job. But if that's what it takes to make you better Mattie then so be it."

"I'm not ill Guy. I just need to get my head clear. Sort a few things out. But there are other ways of dealing with this," she replied, a subtle reminder of the evidence she would use against him should it be necessary.

Not five minutes after Mattie and Janice left Guy's office he stepped out in to the reception area, shouted for everyone's attention and said, "Stress. There is no such thing as stress in the workplace and if anyone thinks that working here is too stressful then find another job." With that he marched back into his office and slammed the door.

The remark raised a few eyebrows, but as usual, no one dared challenge him. Guy was fast building a reputation of getting rid of anyone who stood in his way or for any other minor inconvenience to him. He even once sacked someone because of their accent, thinking it was too broad and too northern for his refined-marketing company.

Mattie had jumped the first hurdle where her boss was concerned. Now she had to attend the therapy sessions. She cared not if work colleagues knew where she was going. It was obvious that others too were struggling under the helm of Guy Carter, so she pinned the therapist's business card on the office notice board and secretly hoped others would see it. At least it would piss Guy off, if nothing else.

To Whom It May Concern – *The Book of Letters*

Nineteen

The wind is getting stronger and making a mass of leaves swirl around the garden. Mattie can hear them rustle along with random brittle ones that the wind is stripping from the trees. Jake already swept the pile in to the corner of the garden this morning, and with good intention, wanted to relocate them to the compost heap. However, by the time he cut up the logs while keeping a watchful eye on their youngest, Nathan, then prepared the chimenea and ferried the boxes outside, it was soon forgotten. Tomorrow perhaps, Mattie thinks, and further thinking about her husband again, she wishes she were snuggling up in bed with him, because the cold has set in, in spite of the heat from the log burner, the thick blanket, woollen accessories, and expensive sheepskin boots.

Mattie has lost track of time but is certain it's past midnight, if not much later, for she is weary. She looks at her watch, which confirms it's nearly two in the morning. The kindling still smoulders, but all evidence of burnt letters is reduced to ash with some tiny fragments of blackened paper still glowing with a tinge of orange. A few chunky pieces of wood that have become damp with the cold air are tossed in but all they do is smoke, sending plumes of it through the stop of the wood burner. Mattie coughs on a cloud of it and wafts her hands around trying to make the smoke go in the opposite direction. It takes a few minutes until the wood dries, eventually they spark with flames, which she hopes is for the last time, and once again, the wood crackles and spits from the heat.

The flickering flame draws Mattie to reflect on the letters she's read so far. The ridiculous ones she wrote bring a smile to her face, for she realises how far she has come in life and how much she's changed. However, a handful remain, and the tortuous journey is not over yet. But before she goes back there, to what happened next and how she dealt with *him*, she holds onto the smile and takes a moment to fill up on happy memories to ease the discomfort that is still to come.

Mattie squeezes her eyes shut and lets the happy images flash by one by one. A wedding ceremony – how handsome her husband looked when he watched his wife-to-be walk down the aisle - her children's christenings - their first days at school. Then when she thinks of Nathan playing a shepherd in last year's nativity play and trying to hook his staff around another child's neck, a snort creeps out and soon she's laughing out loud. The onset of fatigue makes her laugh heartily, but filled with overwhelming emotion, the laughter turns to tears until she is crying uncontrollably.

I have to get to the end of this red book and read that last letter, she says before wiping away the tears.

Mattie looks down at the next letter. It was long like some of the others, but this one she'd contemplated giving to Guy. It wouldn't have made a difference though. He'd probably have torn it into shreds and thrown it in her face as he mocked her over and over again.

Guy was on a mission to somehow manipulate Mattie into getting into his bed. A few letters addressed to her boss weren't going to change his behaviour or stop his voracious desire for her. He was too self-absorbed and conceited to allow a letter from an employee to change the way he behaved, and it would have most likely fuelled his stupid charade. Mattie knew that whatever she did to stop Guy Carter would take a lot more than a piece of

To Whom It May Concern – *The Book of Letters*

paper and a few choice words.

~~**~~

Dear Guy, You are a bastard. Correction! DEAR GUY YOU ARE A FUCKING BASTARD. A MANIPULATIVE, EVIL, CONCEITED BASTARD!

I feel better already for writing that.

You've made my life a misery, a living HELL!!!! And for one reason alone – because I will not sleep with you!

Your contempt for women is as vile as YOU. You think you are so handsome and sexy but what lies beneath your skin is a black heart. You want women to fall at your feet and shower you with love and respect yet you choose not to give any in return. You're a first prize dick!

All women see is a man in a smart suit with money, and for some women that works. But I can assure you that it does not work for me! You seem to have the pick of any woman you like so I don't understand this consistent pursuit and harassment of me. I've made it very clear that I have NO interest in you physically or romantically. You are my boss and that is as far as it goes.

Even though I knew you had a bad reputation I never imagined it would be as bad this. I tried to respect you

To Whom It May Concern – *The Book of Letters*

when you joined the company because I wanted to give you the benefit of the doubt and I actually thought you would be as kind as your father. How wrong you proved to be. Bob did not need to demand respect from his staff the way you do. He earned it. Maybe you should take a lesson or two from him? Isn't there some sort of academy you could go to in order to learn how to be a gentleman?

I worked so hard for your father and continue to do the same for you. And it sickens me that a person who has no integrity is in charge of the company and really does not give a shit about how hard I work. You waltzed into the London office without a care in the world other than for yourself. But it didn't take long for me to see right through you for the person that you really are, an animal. **An evil bastard in fact. Yes, that sums you up perfectly.**

You are obsessed with the way you look, with money and with power. I'm amazed that your head can fit through the door because it is so egotistically large! You possess a horrible combination of traits and one day it will be the ruin of you and I hope that I have a front row seat to see it when your world comes crashing down.

Your clothes are expensive, no doubt you purchase your suits from Savile Row but on a personal note I can tell you that the cologne you wear is disgusting. I can always tell when you have been near my desk when I am away from it because the odour lingers in the air

To Whom It May Concern – *The Book of Letters*

too long for my liking. Because you hide behind an expensive lifestyle does not make you a kind person. It's all a façade.

~~**~~

Wow, I really did get the claws out for this one! He deserved it! Mattie reminds herself as if to explicate the foul letter.

~~**~~

…The horrible treatment you inflict upon staff and me in particular makes me want to rant with rage. Look what you did to Anika, you destroyed her career as it was getting started. She was a sweet charming young woman and it didn't take long for you to draw her into your world. How long did that romance last, two weeks? You reduced her to a quivering wreck, sacked her from her job which you knew you could do because she had only been there a few months. Was she crap in bed? Did she not perform the way you expected her to? Did she say 'No' to you? Is that what you do when someone stands up to you. You sack them? Cynthia too, not that I liked her much.

Another employee, another name, another woman for you to use and abuse emotionally then throw away like you were tossing paper into the bin. I wonder, did you employ pretty women so that you could sleep with them then sack after a few weeks? It probably would have been cheaper to use a prostitute. And you knew they

To Whom It May Concern – *The Book of Letters*

could do nothing about their jobs because they'd not been there long enough and had no rights. I am still amazed Cynthia never brought you to task over the way you dismissed her seeing as she was one of your senior sales people. But perhaps that was part of the game, to make good women feel worthless by humiliating them? I wonder what happened to you as a child when you were at boarding school. Were you humiliated too? I reckon you were. Oh Poor you. Poor Guy.

But this letter is not about the likes of Anika, Cynthia and the Julies of this world, or whoever else you may have harmed. It's about me. How you have systematically over the last eight months harassed and bullied me into having a relationship with you. And when I've not conceded you have reverted to intimidation and humiliation in the hope that I would succumb to your offer.

I have been working at Carter Gales for nearly two years. Your father was an amazing boss and I work extremely hard for this company. I actually enjoy my work and I know that I'm very good at it. I have built up good relationships with my clients and I continue to bring in the high revenue that the previous account manager achieved. In fact, my targets often exceed those of your most favoured client managers when you compare them on a percentage basis. I always act in a professional manner and I have built up a healthy working relationship with staff regardless of whether you think I'm a 'team player' or not!

To Whom It May Concern – *The Book of Letters*

You know this to be true and as a result you cannot pick fault with my work or my behaviour. Carter Gales is not going to sack me because I am an excellent employee so the only tactic you can use is to intimidate me emotionally and try and undermine everything that I do.

Relocating me to another desk because I went on holiday is one of your petty ways of getting at me but I'm not going to let you win. I'm glad you moved me! Then that little trick you pulled a few weeks ago by circulating a memo regarding a staff meeting after work then secretly phoning the others on the last minute to say it was cancelled backfired on you. And you did that all in the hope to once again get me on my own. You have obviously discovered that Derek and I have an agreement when I work late so that I'm not left alone in the office with you. And I have to admit, you were rather clever to plan this on the one day that Derek was sick and - it nearly worked. But I need you to know that I too made alternative arrangements and right on cue my friend Claire swung by the office. I could feel the tension in the lift as the three of us rode down together. She was extremely charming to you, did you like that? How she leaned very close to you. I watched your skin prickle because you were not in control. It was interesting to see how vulnerable you looked while someone was trying to take advantage of you.

To Whom It May Concern – *The Book of Letters*

You have no heart and soul Guy, and if you had an ounce of integrity you would stop this extreme behaviour and let me get on with the job that I'm employed to do. But we both know that this has gone too far, too far for you to back down and most definitely too far for me to forgive you.

I have but one choice, to jump or be pushed. But this game is not over yet Guy, because as of today I am taking control. Control of my life and control of the way you treat me. I have turned the tables and it is now time for me to show you what I am capable of. There are lessons to be learnt Guy, and this will be one lesson that you will never forget. Be prepared as this game is going to get very interesting.

Yours truly,

Miss M Barton
An extremely disgruntled employee!

~~**~~

Mattie pulls the letter triumphantly from the book, and as she wanted to do to him so many years ago but in his face, she tears it into tiny pieces and throws it into the fire before turning to recall another of her many therapy sessions with Joan.

"Interesting letter," Joan reflected. "And a very long one. How did it make you feel after you wrote it?"

To Whom It May Concern – *The Book of Letters*

"I know it's only a letter but I actually felt less... stressed. It is a simple exercise but it actually works. Well at least I think it does."

"I'm pleased you are taking positive steps towards being in control of your life. The negative thoughts are controlling the way you feel but now you are becoming consciously aware of your thoughts and how they trigger your feelings and behaviour."

Mattie agreed, "I understand. After I wrote it I felt relieved – it's a powerful process dumping thoughts onto paper. When I went into work the next day I pushed that particular event to the back of my mind and focused on blocking Guy out of my thoughts. It was hard but I reckon the meditation CD I listened to that night helped me relax too. In the lift I even practised the breathing techniques you showed me because I could feel my blood pressure rising as the lift went up and I was determined to be in control and not let him get to me like he normally does."

"Good," Joan commented. "Everything you have experienced is represented here," and Joan laid her hand on her solar plexus. "Even when we are not consciously aware of it, the mind and body are connected, and when something happens to one part the other part will respond."

Not quite sure of what she was talking about, Mattie asked her to explain. Joan told her that when she thought of something bad or sad, then the body would respond in a way to exhibit those thoughts. "Your breathing may increase rapidly making you further agitated or nervous, perhaps making you feel sick or giving you a headache. Some people suffer from ringing in their ears," Joan explained.

Mattie thought how recently when her head hit the pillow her ears had buzzed, much to her annoyance, and all she'd done was bury her head further in the pillow to muffle the noise.

To Whom It May Concern – *The Book of Letters*

"Some people bite their nails or simply tap their feet to rid their body of the nervous energy. It's the body's way of responding to the thoughts in your head. Likewise, when you have happy thoughts, your body will respond differently. But..." Joan went on while Mattie paid attention to her advice, "Once the body exhibits the feelings then your mind focuses on it even more and it becomes a cycle of thoughts and associated feelings."

"So I have to change the way I think in order to change the way I feel and behave? Think more happy thoughts or at least not think bad thoughts?"

"Exactly," she replied. "Negative energy attracts negative energy and likewise for positive energy. For such a long time you've been unconsciously aware that your bad memories have been controlling your behaviour. What happened in the past is fact but in order for you to continue to move forward, you have to stop letting those negative thoughts take over you. It is your choice whether to be happy or sad."

"But Guy's not in the past," retorted Mattie.

"Of course. But once you have learnt to control the negative thoughts and replace them with positive ones, you'll be able to see and think more clearly about the way you can deal with Guy and people like him." Joan carried on, "You've made great progress, Mattie. However, it is necessary to understand and become consciously aware of the physical effects this is having on you so that you can continue to rid yourself of the negative feelings that are holding you back."

Mattie nodded, understanding and accepting Joan's advice, and realised that she had serious choices to make about her current lifestyle.

The red leather-bound book that Joan was holding on to and still opened at that letter to Guy unnerved her and even though

To Whom It May Concern – *The Book of Letters*

she was pleased with Mattie's progress, she was concerned with the latter part of the letter and the underlying message about exacting revenge.

"You should have read the first one I wrote to him about my so-called 'disciplinary meeting'. I was so angry about what he said to me, the way he touched me, and what he wanted to do." Mattie buried her head in her hands. "He was disgusting and anything and everything that came into my head about that encounter I put into words. When I read it back, I was mortified at the number of expletives I'd used. Far more than *that* letter! In fact I felt ashamed. I hardly ever swear, but Guy has managed to bring me down to this level. So I threw it straight in the bin and started again."

"Yes, I see where you have torn the pages from the book. Mattie, the purpose of this exercise is to write what is on your mind," Joan asserted. "Let the feelings out through the words and write whatever you like. Only you will read it and only I will, if that is what you wish and if it helps you. I can assure that I will not be offended by anything you write, I have seen far worse."

Then she stopped for a moment to consider how to ask the next question. "Mattie, regarding this particular letter, do you feel you need to get back at your boss or are they just words?"

She didn't know how to respond but Joan had touched on something that was a possibility – revenge. Mattie looked blankly at her, but as far as considering a master plan, she hadn't thought it through.

"I'm not sure. I don't know if they are idle threats or whether it's something that needs to be done. Something has to change to make him stop harassing me and others. I can't ignore it anymore. Trying to mentally block him out is only a quick fix and will not last forever. I still want to puke when he leans over me. He still passes sexual innuendos and tries to get close when people are not watching and there's only so much I can take." Mattie's voice began to quiver as she tried to answer the concerning question put to her by her therapist. She inhaled deeply and reached for a tissue as the tears quickly came back. "Eventually I'll crack, I know I will. Perhaps he needs a taste of his own medicine," she added briskly, stemming the flow of tears. "Plus he needs to take responsibility for his own actions and suffer those consequences. If it isn't me then someone else will do it."

"What's stopping you from leaving your job?" Joan asked frankly.

"Claire asks me the same thing almost weekly. She says I should kick him in the bollocks," Mattie blushed from her choice of words and swiftly made an apology. "Guy's playing a game and I have no intention of letting him win. I'm slowly but surely coming to terms with events that life has dealt me. All that control by my grandfather, the grief – I've accepted what happened but this, this is damn cruel." The tears eventually fell freely while Mattie described the way Guy made her feel. "He's an evil person, plus I've worked so hard for that company I'm not prepared to let him take it away from me. If I leave then he's won, so when I do leave it will be on my terms and not his."

"And what if those terms are detrimental to your well-being?" asked Joan.

Although adamant that she was determined to stay at Carter Gales until she found the opportune moment to leave, Mattie hadn't thought of how far she was prepared to go to stop Guy or indeed anyone else from controlling her life. "I'm afraid that if I don't stand up to him and confront this problem head on then I will never be strong enough to face anything. Can it possibly get any worse than it already is?"

Her therapist spoke frankly, concerned for her client. She admired Mattie's determination, telling her how much she had improved since those early sessions, but she couldn't quite agree with her possible intentions, warning her to be careful and to not put herself in danger. That day they'd talked differently than at any previous session and Joan's warning echoed in the weeks that followed. She was concerned that Mattie would do something that put her in danger, as Guy sounded like a man who'd stop at nothing until he got what he wanted.

Mattie felt at home sitting in the large, comfy chair in Joan's lilac-themed room. Just the two talking about whatever Mattie wanted – no judgements made, no criticism or negative words to badly impact upon her. Over time, she became stronger both emotionally and mentally. It was as if a physical weight had been lifted from her shoulders – a burden she'd carried for years, and the only person that could not see that burden was Mattie. Writing letters allowed her to make sense of life and view it from a different perspective when she read them back. She realised sometimes how futile some events were and others were just idiotic, but she wrote about them nevertheless.

Claire also commented on Mattie's vast improvement and no longer did they feel alienated from each other, as Mattie learnt to talk about Guy without bursting into tears and without Claire rolling her eyes in despair or hurtling books across the room at her friend.

Armed with self-help books, relaxation CDs, and other methods Joan had suggested she try, Mattie began to change her way of thinking and dealing with the torment in her head. Even praying seemed to help. Herbal teas replaced the copious amounts of caffeine she'd survived off since joining the company, and for

To Whom It May Concern – *The Book of Letters*

further relaxation, she started yoga lessons, even though it was something else for Guy to mock when she left work on time. Then when Claire finally moved into her own place with Frankie, Mattie set about transforming the spare bedroom into a place to relax in, adding soft, mellow lighting and scented candles.

By the time Mattie was nearing the end of the therapy sessions, she was giving Joan huge hugs in thanks for the work she'd done, telling her that without the help she would have found it difficult to hold her head high each day she stepped foot into Carter Gales. With that new projected inner confidence, Mattie received compliments from work colleagues who'd rarely given her a second glance. In the main she was cordial to Guy, and when it was appropriate, she engaged in some light, humorous conversation with him, which merely left him perplexed and unable to decipher the change in her. But Guy's attempts at being 'nice' were short-lived and he soon resorted to his futile attempts at disrespecting Mattie in front of others. When he did, she held her nerve and let his petty comments float by – it was the only way to deal with him.

For the time being, Mattie had the upper hand in this stupid game they played while still gathering information, which was mounting up fast, and writing a letter to him each night, followed by an hour of relaxation in the spare room, all in the hope to keep her mind clear and fresh for the next day.

Mattie looks on at the shredded letters, burning and flaking in the fire. There is a sense of pride from the realisation that at that stage of her life, she had started to take control. *If only I'd done it sooner,* she wished. The anger was in the words and no longer within Mattie, as all she felt was contempt for the vile person.

She skims through more letters written to Guy so long ago,

To Whom It May Concern – *The Book of Letters*

and without the energy to read them in full, she throws them into the fire catching glimpses of text as they burn.

~~**~~

... so you think it was clever to tell my clients that I was leaking information to a competitor ...

... why did you do that to Derek knowing his wife was sick and he had to pick his son up from school? Can't you show any empathy at all? ...

... I hate you with such a passion and I hate myself for allowing you to consume so much of my energy. You can no longer live rent free in my brain ...

... just fuck off from my life Guy ...

~~**~~

More pages are scrunched tightly in her hands. Letter after letter addressed to Guy Carter is thrown into the pit of the fire.

~~**~~

... stop leaning close to me at my desk. You need to have some awareness of personal space ...

... One of these days Derek is going to punch you if you make any more jibes about his family. I'm amazed he's put up with your crap too for this long ...

To Whom It May Concern – *The Book of Letters*

... deducting my wages because I arrived at work ten minutes late does not bother me. I've put in an overtime sheet that more than compensates for this you fool ...

~~**~~

The last snippet she glances at makes her smile, but the memories that have been clearly etched in ink make her feel stupid, having been drawn back to that time she hated so much. *Why am I doing this?* A question she's asked so many times since she began this torturous trip down memory lane. The letter about time keeping burns, and then her guts are grabbed in a sudden twist when she looks down at the thinning red leather book to see what happened next. It's clear as day and she doesn't need to see written words to remind her of it, but a mere glance at the next letter swamps Mattie with terrible feelings of dread. The sense of pride she felt earlier for standing up to Guy is crushed by the memory.

She continues taking deep breaths to control the rising heartbeat and the ache in her guts that she swore she'd never let anyone ever make her feel. And she prepares to process the next letter.

To Whom It May Concern – *The Book of Letters*

Twenty

ALTHOUGH she had arrived at the conclusion that it was a dangerous one to be caught up in, Mattie was embroiled too deeply in Guy's game. But presently, she was the one in control, deciding each move and giving Guy little leeway to take charge. Besides, she had something over him – evidence of that disciplinary meeting. All games came to an end, of that Mattie was certain. She was determined to stick with hers, possibly propelled by sheer stubbornness, until she found a better solution. *As long as I can keep him at arm's length I'll be okay,* she kept saying to herself. Enough people had told her to leave Carter Gales, to which she occasionally indicated she would, but on her own terms – not Guy's. They didn't understand that her objective was to get even with him, which was now a matter of when, not how.

However, the little Catholic girl in her kept popping up and waving the guilt flag because she knew whatever happened inevitably would bring shame to Bob Carter. That was a hard pill to swallow. He'd done her no harm – in fact the complete opposite – but Mattie could not see any other option, and if people got hurt along the way, including Bob, then so be it.

Summer drew to an end – almost a year since her mother's untimely death. Even though Mattie was only beginning to come to terms with that and despite Guy's continuing petty games, she felt the best she'd felt in a long time. Applying for jobs busied her, and while she received positive feedback, she was under no illusion of the likelihood of getting a job like the one she already had – she was prepared to start at the bottom if necessary. Her only stipulation was that the company and people be reputable and not hiding sleazebags like Guy Carter.

The weekly therapy sessions with Joan continued. She'd not only taught Mattie how to control her thoughts and feelings about negative situations, but to learn to be more realistic. This meant that she had to stop living in the romantic dream about Mr Blond, although occasionally, Mattie allowed the odd thought to slip through her mind about what he was doing and where he was. Office gossip about his sudden departure had subsided. One day, Mattie plucked up the courage to ask the one person that might know something.

"I'm not at liberty to say."

"That means you know something. I'm right, yes?" Mattie quizzed her. "You must know something, Janice. Not even a little snippet of information?"

The HR manager closed the door ensuring there was no one within earshot. She had come to like the university student who'd survived longer than her predecessors and knew she could entrust her with the information she was about to part with. Guy was out on one of his long lunch breaks – not that his staff knew where he went most of the times. When she looked at Mattie's pleading eyes for even a morsel of information, Janice swore her to secrecy.

"How foolish of him to leave such private and confidential information lying around like that," Janice said. "If that had been anyone else they would've been fired immediately. It also explains those rumoured late night meetings the director's have been attending."

"What information? What meetings?" Mattie urged.

"From what I saw, Carter Gales is merging with another

To Whom It May Concern – *The Book of Letters*

company – from American."

So he was taking his father's hard-earned money and leaving.

Janice divulged the top-secret information but told Mattie to keep her mouth shut until the merger was officially announced. The news was euphoric, but what of Mr Blond, information Mattie eagerly pressed for.

"I saw his name on one of the documents. I think he moved over to the American company."

"What?"

Aware of Mattie's liking for the director from New York more than she cared to admit, Janice told her to calm down when she saw hope on her face and a sudden flush of rosy cheeks. "Look, I don't know much. I think he's been moved sideways, just until the merger has gone through. I've got some good connections with the New York office but what I'm telling is still just hearsay so do not mention a word."

"Is that all?" Mattie probed.

Janice told Mattie that even though she was head of the company's human resource department, which recently dealt mainly with only sacking people or at least wiping up after Guy's pathetic attempts at doing the same, that she was merely a lowly manager. She went on further to say that there was more secrecy than ever amongst the board of directors since Bob left, and she hardly got to know anything these days that was worth mentioning.

Later that day, Guy asked Mattie why she was so happy, but she simply lied, smiling sweetly from the newfound knowledge and keeping her promise to Janice. He walked away confused at the woman whose display of happiness was bewildering to him – after all, he went to such great efforts to quash it.

Within a few weeks of Janice telling Mattie about the merger,

To Whom It May Concern – *The Book of Letters*

Guy called an impromptu staff meeting, after lunch on a Friday. As they bundled in to the boardroom, Janice raised her eyebrows. That was all the confirmation Mattie needed. The low murmur of staff voices increased as they apprehensively looked towards the two smartly dressed men that flanked Guy and then towards the table that on which some bottles of champagne and glasses were kept. Surely this had to be the announcement. Mattie looked on, elated at the prospect of Guy leaving.

"Good afternoon, everyone, and please extend a warm welcome to David Cole and Brian Jeffrey of Dynamic Global Marketing," Guy began. Everyone applauded for the two men they'd never met. "I have an important announcement to make."

This is it then! Mattie smiled in Janice's direction. *He's going at last.*

Guy continued, "As you are aware, we are market leaders within our business. But nothing is safe and secure in life and business, and to maintain this position of leadership and the future of Carter Gales, we have to look at other options – options which are to the benefit of the company and the staff alike," he emphasised.

Jackson had positioned himself close to Guy and the DGM men when they had entered the boardroom, obviously privy to the information beforehand. He seemed pleased with the news being made official, but the rest of the staff took a tentative step back in apprehension while they listened to Guy's monologue about company changes and the importance of getting smarter to beat the competitor because there was always someone else out there ready to take the business from under their nose. "It's a dog-eat-dog world," Guy went on. "...and I'm pleased to announce the merger between Carter Gales and Dynamic Global Marketing of New York."

To Whom It May Concern – *The Book of Letters*

Staff erupted into applause once Guy confirmed jobs at the London Office were secure, and within a few minutes, he was popping champagne corks in celebration, laughing and joking with his entourage of key account managers.

Janice sidled up to Mattie and said, "You don't have to keep it a secret anymore."

To this, Mattie said thank God as she'd wanted to shout it from the rooftops on many an occasion.

Guy walked towards the two ladies, handing them a glass each filled with the fizzy drink. They returned cordial smiles, Mattie's was more ecstatic – if this was the way Guy was leaving then at least it didn't involve any wrongdoing on her part. So she congratulated him on the turn of events and wished him well for the future.

"He makes my skin crawl," Mattie muttered under her breath at Janice as he walked away. "Thank God he'll be gone soon." She raised the glass of champagne in his direction, giving him one more perfected sardonic smile. "He's such a creep, and that's putting it mildly."

"He never actually said he was leaving, Mattie," Janice countered. "But I suppose he did mention that someone else would be heading this office. I presume that would be Jackson, seeing as he's his favourite."

"Money and women – that's all that interests him. I'll be surprised if he intends to work once he's sold his shares. He'll be worth a small fortune no doubt," Mattie added.

Janice was right. Guy hadn't been specific, only glossing over the details of the merger. Everyone joined in the celebrations, thanking their wonderful boss for letting them leave early. Mattie on the other hand kept a watchful eye on him while she pondered his next move.

To Whom It May Concern – *The Book of Letters*

It was nearly three o'clock, and already the office looked like the Mary Celeste as staff quickly left before Guy changed his mind. Derek stuck his head around the corner to announce he was going and that she should too.

"Ten minutes, then I'll be gone," Mattie assured Derek.

"Certain?"

"Yeah, you go home while you have the chance. I'll be fine." She thanked Derek for the offer of waiting and told him to enjoy the extra time with his wife and family, only for him to say that his wife was going to a school meeting.

Mattie stood by the photocopier watching multiple coloured reports print, preparing them for the weekly Monday morning sales meeting, and noticed the last few members of staff grab their belongings and leave. The sound of the machine spewing out the paper drowned out the laughing and joking between Guy and the Dynamic Global executives. She observed Janice popping in and out of his office with various documents, and Jackson seemed to be the only account manager who'd stayed behind to join the group of high-spirited men.

With the sweet taste of champagne still lingering on her lips, Mattie lost track of time. She'd miscalculated how long the report would take to finish as extra copies had been requested. Another hour passed when Mattie became acutely aware of the silence and semi-darkness while she continued her battle with the binding machine. All of a sudden, the quietness sent her heart racing. All she had to do was place the reports on Guy's desk, and she could go. *Surely he must've gone by now*. She berated herself for staying late, wishing she'd taken Derek's advice.

A few minutes later, she took a tentative step into his office. The blinds had been closed all day and the light was turned off. She scanned the dark room checking it was empty and placed the

To Whom It May Concern – *The Book of Letters*

neatly bound stack of reports on Guy's desk. She then grabbed her jacket and bag and headed for the lift, eager to get of the building. *Hurry up!* she cursed, punching the lift buttons several times for it to descend from the tenth floor.

It took a few unnecessary seconds for the lift to register that its presence was required two floors lower and eventually the neon numbers changed indicating its descent. Mattie looked around at the dimly lit reception area. It looked eerie, and when she heard a door bang at the far end of the corridor she looked back apprehensively, but saw no one.

Assuming it must be the cleaners Mattie stepped into the lift and pressed the button for the ground floor. She leant back against the cold metal interior and shut her eyes in relief as the doors slowly closed.

Suddenly, with a slip of his hand, Guy forced open the lift doors.

"Guy! I... I thought you'd gone home," Mattie stuttered, stunned.

As the lift doors closed behind him and the lift started descending, Guy glared at Mattie. Then a smirk spread across his face. He slammed his hand against the emergency button, bringing the lift to a screeching halt, the shudder sending Mattie off balance. In a flash, Guy lurched towards her, pinned her against the wall, and pressed hard with the weight of his body.

The lunge almost seized Mattie's breath and she screamed at him, "You're hurting me. Let go!" But he kept a firm hold, and his free hand started to hitch up her skirt, tearing the fabric along the tight seam. "Guy, stop!" She spluttered again, trying to free herself from his tight grip but to no avail. He was too strong.

He let go momentarily and stepped back, as if to contemplate his wrongdoing. He paced the small lift as they remained stuck on the sixth floor with the alarm ringing. Running his hands through his hair, he mumbled something about her being too good for him. Then he banged his fist hard against the wall.

"Guy you're scaring me! Let me out!" Mattie pleaded.

"Pretty Mattie Barton who thinks she's better than everyone else," Guy began, quietly. "Little Miss Perfect! If you think you're getting rid of me you've another thing coming," he hissed angrily. Still pacing within the tiny lift, shaking his head in despair, he looked up, his breathing further intensified. "I'm not going anywhere. No one gets rid of Guy Carter without a fight." He lurched at Mattie again, pressing his lips firmly against hers and forcing his tongue into her mouth.

She could taste whiskey as she thrashed her head side to side, but his tongue left her speechless and gasping for air as he held her steady. Reaching out with one hand, Mattie fumbled for the lift buttons. She hit one and the lift jerked back into action and started ascending – to which level she didn't know.

Eventually he loosened his grip, and with a sharp intake of breath, she cursed him. "You bastard," she spat and tried to hit him, but he caught her hand and grabbed her hair, pulling back her head, and kissed harder. With all the strength Mattie could muster, she twisted free from his tight grip. When she saw the blackness in his eyes, she feared the worst and pushed him away.

Guy reacted quickly. "You bitch!" Bringing up his hand and slapping her hard across the face. "You made me do this!"

The sheer force knocked Mattie sideways and she fell to the floor banging her head. The pain seared through her and she yelped. Stunned at what he'd done and dazed at the same time, she asked "Why did you do that?"

But he simply towered over her.

"You're crazy!" she blurted.

To Whom It May Concern – *The Book of Letters*

Once again, the lift came to a halt, back to the eighth floor and to Carter Gales' offices – the last place Mattie wanted to be right now. Her face still stung from the hard slap and Guy's breaths quickened with sweat pouring profusely from his forehead. Had this been his intention all along? If he could not have her willingly, would he try to take her at all costs?

He grabbed a terrified Mattie by the front of her jacket, pulling her swiftly to her feet, her bag swinging freely across her arm. And with another swift move, he turned her around, and started to hitch up the torn skirt, with one hand pressing her neck firmly against the lift wall. Mattie could see his reflection in the mirrored wall and the sheer evil in his eyes.

"Remember how I said I would like to have you?"

Mattie screamed as loud as she could when she saw the doors closing again, in the hope that someone, anyone would hear her. Then managing to slide her hands in front of her, with a firm push, she thrust him backwards. Then with all her might, she caught him in the ribs with her elbow.

Guy buckled and coughed at the pain. She turned on him and without a second thought, brought up her knee, slamming it hard into his groin. "Take that you bastard!" she yelled.

He recoiled with the pain and staggered back into the lift as Mattie made a dash through the tiny space left between the closing doors and headed down the dimly lit corridor. She could run now or never, while he was doubled over, coughing and spluttering at the ache between his legs.

Mattie prepared to dash towards the emergency staircase, the strap of her bag dangling and swinging around her neck.

Guy managed to make it out of the lift. He yanked her bag, pulling her down onto the carpeted floor. "You know it could've been so much easier, Mattie," he said breathlessly, still

To Whom It May Concern – *The Book of Letters*

recovering from the pain she'd inflicted upon him but now towering over her again. "You and me, we could've been a great team. I promised you the world. I promised you love. Many great things..." he spluttered through staggered breaths and gasps of pain that still seared through him. "Why don't you show me this evidence you said you've got. Have you been taping our meetings, Mattie? Didn't anyone ever tell you that it is rude to do that? Didn't anyone explain that you could get sacked for that?" He hissed each word at her.

Mattie attempted to stand up in vain, and each time she tried, he pushed her back down while dragging her towards his office by the strap of the bag that was now caught around her neck and shoulder. She held tight to the leather strap to stop him from strangling her, but was unable to break free, and the more he dragged her, the more the nylon carpet burnt through her sheer stockings into the skin of her knees.

They were within feet of his private office and Mattie realised that once he got her in there, she'd be a victim. "Let me go, Guy! You're fucking crazy! Let me go!"

Through jumbled mutterings of how good their life could have been, he ignored Mattie's exasperated screams as she writhed in pain and jerked at her bag to free herself from his grip.

You're not doing this to me!

Out of the corner of her eye, she spotted something red next to a waste bin. It had been moved from its original place, and as he dragged her past, Mattie reached out with a free hand and grabbed it. *Take that!* With all her effort, Mattie swung the fire extinguisher and caught him in the leg.

Guy screamed in pain and fell on the floor at the contact of the metal cylinder on bone. "Arrgh!" He recoiled, clutching his shin.

It was now or never. Without a moment's hesitation, Mattie

To Whom It May Concern – *The Book of Letters*

ran towards the emergency exit, pushing open the heavy doors and smashing the fire alarm panel that set off a high-pitched ring throughout the office block, and started running down the stairs, taking two steps at a time, sometimes three as her legs tumbled down. She frantically raced down the eight floors holding tight on to the handrail so as not to career downwards uncontrollably. *I've got to get out of here*, she repeated over and over again with her feet hardly touching the ground and her bag still swinging around her neck until she reached the lower levels. Emergency exits flung open from other office suites as people filed out and made their way out of the building at this unexpected disruption. Mattie slowed down, and keeping her head lowered exited the building unnoticed along with everyone else.

An hour later, she was sitting on the steps of her therapist's house, entirely drained from the running and the crying. Her body ached all over and still shook from the adrenalin that was pumping furiously through her veins, while she held her mobile phone tightly, and through blurry eyes, desperately hit the speed dial button to speak to Joan. *Please be there!*

Seconds passed and Joan's strong arms wrapped upon Mattie's shaking shoulders, lifting her to her feet to lead her into familiar surroundings where the therapy sessions took place. Then those same strong arms and firm hands seated her in a comfortable chair that she rocked back and forth in, letting out the tears, racking her body. Joan wrapped a blanket around a distraught Mattie, and thrust a cup of hot sweet tea into her hands, forcing her to drink it.

Mattie tried to talk but nothing of what she said was making sense.

"Take your time Mattie. Slow down and take some deep breaths."

To Whom It May Concern – *The Book of Letters*

After some time, the shaking and crying subsided enough for her to recount what happened.

"He has to be reported. Look what he's done to you," Joan insisted.

"No, I can't go to the police," Mattie sobbed, convinced that it wouldn't be worth it, thinking it futile when all she had to show were some bruises. "I'm so confused, Joan, I don't know what to do," Mattie cried more.

"Well I can't force you and I respect your wishes, but I think you should take some photos of the bruises, and as soon as you're thinking straight, write down exactly what happened, so if you do decide to go to the police then you can give them an accurate statement."

For all that Joan was giving sound advice, the words buzzed around Mattie's head. She nodded then sobbed all the more as Joan took some photographs. When Mattie saw them uploaded on the computer sometime later, the realisation of what Guy had attempted to do, the harm he'd inflicted, and how he'd defiled her was all too frightening. The thought of what would have happened if she'd not fought back was too much to bear. All she could think of was what if? What if she couldn't have fought back? What if? The more she looked at the photos of the bruise across her cheek, and those on her neck and shoulders, the more she cried, horrified at what he'd done. There were pictures of bruises on her face and across her neck mirroring where the strap of her handbag had wrapped around her - pictures of torn stockings and carpet burns, the rip up the seam of her pencil skirt - and the broken heel of the left shoe that she could not even recall breaking. Perhaps it was when she was running down the stairs, or from being dragged across the carpet. It was all too much to comprehend right now.

To Whom It May Concern – *The Book of Letters*

The therapist Mattie had come to trust and lean on for support in more ways than one took her home that night. She made sure she felt safe in her apartment and waited with Mattie until Claire and Frankie arrived.

"Are you sure you don't want me to contact the police?" Joan urged again before leaving.

Mattie assured her that she would think about it and that she'd be fine. When she finally sank into a steaming hot bath, she continued to cry more and sobbed through the aches and pains until she could cry no more. Claire was heartbroken and Frankie wanted to break Guy's legs. They insisted on spending the night with her, concerned that Guy may show up, but still filled with fear, Mattie slipped in and out of a vivid nightmare that night of what could have occurred had she not been able to get free.

Apart from getting disturbed bouts of sleep over that weekend, Mattie tried to analyse the attack on her, to find a reason why he targeted her that way and what made Guy behave like that – to which she found no answers. *Was he not happy with the beautiful Victoria he was dating or the many other women he had affairs with? He could have anyone, so why me?* Mattie questioned over and over and there still remained no reasoning for his disturbing and brutal behaviour.

By the time Sunday evening arrived, the bruises appeared in full. They were dark and blue, so Mattie took more photographs, just in case. Mattie knew she had become the victim of a repulsive crime and stomped around the apartment ranting while Claire listened that enough was enough.

"Then go to the police!" Claire said, exasperated.

"No! I've got a better idea."

Mattie had come up with a plan to bring Guy down.

She kept the letter simple and to the point.

To Whom It May Concern – *The Book of Letters*

~~**~~

Dear Directors and Members of staff at Carter Gales,

I would like to inform you of an incident that occurred on the afternoon of Friday, 28th September, the afternoon that Mr Guy Carter, the Managing Director of Carter Gales, announced the business merger between Carter Gales and Dynamic Global Marketing.

I am not sure whether you are aware of his behaviour and intentions towards me since he took over from his father. He has consistently sexually harassed me and taken any opportunity to undermine my work with clients and colleagues. I have substantial documented evidence that supports my accusations, including taped conversations.

After the staff enjoyed celebrating the announcement of the merger, I inadvertently found myself to be alone in the office with Mr Carter. When I entered the lift to leave the building, he followed me into it, pinned me to the wall, slapped me across the face, and put his hand up my skirt, amongst other things. Guy Carter sexually and physically assaulted me, evidence of which can be found in the photographs I am sending you.

I can honestly say that I feared for my life, but thankfully, I was able to break free and escape via the emergency exit.

To Whom It May Concern – *The Book of Letters*

We all know that he is not a nice man. I know what I am going to do with this evidence, but what are you going to do about him?

Yours truly,

Miss Martha Barton
A truly grieved employee

c.c Dynamic Global Marketing

~~**~~

Colleagues didn't need to know all the specifics because the photographs were evidence enough of his actions. That Monday morning, contrary to the advice given by Claire, Frankie and Joan, Mattie went to work, arriving earlier than usual. Guy never arrived before half past nine on a Monday morning, and this gave her plenty of time to put her plan into action.

Mattie printed multiple copies of the letter along with photos that depicted the bruises on her body, friction burns on her legs, and her torn clothes – especially the photograph of her face showing smudged lipstick that he'd rubbed up her cheek when he forced his mouth onto hers along with the streaks of mascara from the crying. She had to work quickly. Armed with tubes of super glue and a roll of tape, she stuck the copies all over the glass partition wall in Guy's office on both sides for everyone to see. Then as quickly as she'd done that, Mattie glued more onto his glass-topped table.

"Let's see how this pisses you off," she said as she rubbed a final piece onto the glass. The glue hardened fast and adhered

To Whom It May Concern – *The Book of Letters*

firmly to the surface. "Now that's a perfect place to stick more," she added with a hint of sarcasm to her voice when she looked up at the expensive piece of art work on his office wall. "How much did he say it cost?"

Minutes later it was covered in multiple copies of the letter and she laughed all the more at the outburst Guy was soon to have.

She had to work fast, noting the time and that colleagues would soon be entering the building. Copy upon copy was taped to every computer screen, on the inside of the toilet cubicles in both the ladies' and gents' toilets, by the coffee machine, near the photocopier and printers, on all the notice boards, along the corridor and in the lift, all over the walls so staff from other companies that occupied the rest of the building would see what Guy Carter had done. She wanted to shock them all. And wherever staff went, she glued or taped a photo and the letter in that place.

In line with her plan, Mattie had but five minutes left to put the final part into action. She quickly logged on to her computer and with a few simple clicks of the key-board she emailed the same to all members of staff, including the directors of Carter Gales, and more importantly, to the directors at Dynamic Global Marketing.

It was eight thirty in the morning. Mattie threw the empty glue packets and tape into the waste bin and dropped a letter of resignation on Guy's defiled desk, then flicked his silver stationery accessories onto the floor just to piss him off even more, leaving a scattering of coloured paperclips across the carpet. She then ripped his gold leaf business cards into tiny pieces too. Her heart was racing at what she'd done and at the reactions she was going to get from people she liked, but she wanted them all to know what Guy was really like, and if this was the only way to send out that message, then so be it, she decided. Still racked with humiliation, she swiftly left the building via the emergency exit for the second time in as many days.

"When can I expect them to receive it?" she asked the leather-clad motorcyclist waiting around the corner shortly after.

"Noon," he replied.

Mattie gulped hard – she was about to inflict pain on a person she admired. But it had to be done because Guy was not going to stop unless the people that cared for him most realised what he was truly like. She watched the courier speed off into the distance on his way to deliver documents to Bob Carter and Victoria. The deed was done. There was no turning back.

Later that morning, Mattie sat in front of her newly appointed solicitor handing him a large box file. She slid it across the table towards Mr Pilling, feeling relieved to finally hand over the information she'd been collecting these past months – a diary, memorandums, recorded conversations, post-it notes. It was all there. Mattie contemplated going to the police, and depending on what Mr Pilling would say, she left that option open.

Meanwhile she glanced at her watch, it was exactly nine thirty, and she wondered whether Guy had arrived at the office and what his reactions were. Her mobile phone sat on top of her bag, and she could easily see that there were missed calls and certainly voicemails. And the phone tinkled every time a text message came through.

The offices of Kirk Mayfield and Sons were not as she expected. Instead of dark oak-panelled walls and perhaps a shrivelled neglected yucca plant sitting lifelessly in the corner, the room was light and airy. A professional arrangement of fresh flowers sat in a square glass vase and the sun streaming through the window made her feel warm and relaxed. Mr Pilling coughed occasionally at some of the notes he was reading, at times looking up and raising his eyebrows in shock at her ill treatment.

It was never her intention, but a spur-of-the-moment and unconscious decision brought her to this office. It was only as she sifted through her purse after defacing Guy's office that she came across the business card Claire had thrust into her hand not that long ago. Mr Pilling passed brief comments about the information he now referred to as 'evidence' and Mattie listened without comment. However, the company she had just resigned from was all too familiar to the solicitor.

"Please excuse me for one moment Miss Barton."

Mattie nodded and Mr Pilling closed the file, picked it up, and left the room. The few minutes that lapsed seemed like forever, and she put her head in her hands with dreadful thought about what she'd done. Here mobile phone silently jittered in her bag from another call coming from Carter Gales. She recognised the number.

Mr Pilling returned. "Miss Barton, let me introduce you to Mr Kirk."

She stood up and shook the hand of the grave-looking associate of the firm, "Pleased to meet you, Mr Kirk."

"My colleague Mr Pilling has briefly informed me of your situation," Mr Kirk explained. "Firstly, let me say how sorry we are that this has happened." Mattie thanked them both for their kindness. "We are very interested in dealing with this case. That is if it meets with your agreement and pro bono, of course."

Mattie looked on, slightly confused. Mr Kirk went on to explain. "I have a meeting with someone else connected to this business in a few minutes. Of course I can't say any more than that due to confidentiality, but all will come clear shortly." He made his apologies and left.

No names were mentioned and no other details were divulged. They would get back to her in due course. Mattie wondered who else from Carter Gales had made a complaint. By the time she was ready to leave, her head throbbed with a headache having hardly slept since the attack. She'd eaten nothing that morning either.

"Here goes then." She was standing in the foyer and had plucked up the courage to listen to what perhaps was a barrage of abusive voicemails from Guy. Mattie also decided that if they were then it would be more evidence to give to the solicitor.

"Janice? She's congratulating me?" Surprised at the first message, she went on to listen to the others. Derek told her how wonderful she was and thankful for doing what she did. He then went on to say he owed her a decent cup of coffee. Mattie listened to the many messages of support from colleagues and was surprised that Jackson wanted to meet up for a private chat as soon as possible. She hit the speed dial button and called Janice.

"I don't know what happened but he limped into the office." Mattie recalled hitting Guy hard on the shin with the small red fire extinguisher. "He was absolutely fuming, and you should've seen him tearing around the office pulling down the pictures. He was apoplectic and ranted and raged around the place. Was that superglue you used?" Janice thought it amusing as she described how putrid red he looked in the face and about ready to explode.

"I think everyone here needs to congratulate you Mattie. You've done something that possibly most of us have only dreamt of. You stood up to Guy Carter."

"It was never my intention Janice. After what he did," and Mattie went into more detail of Guy's attempted sexual assault in the lift, "I sort of flipped and came up with that ludicrous plan."

To Whom It May Concern – *The Book of Letters*

"I'm horrified and sticking some pieces of paper on the walls is nothing compared to what he's done to you. I hope he burns in hell for that Mattie. I'm sorry you had to go through this and..."

Mattie stopped her, "I think we all underestimated him, Janice, but what's done is done and I don't think I'll be coming back to Carter Gales."

By the time Mattie had finished relaying the horrors of that night, she felt sick. Even when Janice said it was rumoured Guy was stealing from the company it didn't make Mattie feel any better, but she agreed to meet up with her later that week. In the meantime, she had solicitor's appointments to attend to and a lot of spare time to think about what she was going to do with the rest of her life.

As she listened to the final voice message, none of which to her surprise were from Guy, she made her way through the revolving doors and exited the solicitor's building. On the way out, she caught a glimpse of a man in a dark suit entering through the other side, but took little notice. They simply passed each other. Mattie, now standing on the pavement, checked the time, read the last of the text messages, and then slipped the phone back into her bag.

Her senses told her that the man she'd passed through the revolving doors was watching her, so she turned to look at him. *It can't be, can it?* She'd almost forgotten how beautiful he was and how he made her tingle all over when they briefly met. *It is you, it really is you.*

Many months had passed during which she'd tried to hang on to the occasional dreamy thoughts of him, and now he was standing there, in the flesh, and those wonderful feelings flooded her again. The blood rushed through her veins and Mattie looked into the sexy blue eyes of Mr Blond.

To Whom It May Concern – *The Book of Letters*

A few seconds later, he stood in front of her. The butterflies started flipping in her stomach instantaneously and a lump formed in her throat that was still raw from all the crying. Finally, she whispered, "Hello Jake."

"Hello Mattie." His eyes scanned her face, and it didn't take long for him to notice the bruises hiding under layers of makeup. Then with concern he said, "He hurt you, didn't he?"

Those few kind words unleashed a torrent of unexpected tears, and Mattie dropped her head and began to sob. Thinking she was all out of crying, the tears rose up and flowed freely down her face, smearing the carefully applied foundation cream that disguised the truth. With a gentle hand, he lifted her chin, stepped forward, and wrapped his arms around her shaking body. And in that moment of rubbing makeup into the shoulder of his smart grey suit, she knew where she belonged. It had simply been a long, arduous journey to get there.

To Whom It May Concern – *The Book of Letters*

Twenty-One

The memory of looking into those sexy eyes brings a genuine smile to Mattie's face and a warm feeling spreads throughout her body for the first time since she dared to read these letters. That encounter would forever be etched in her mind. As the book rests on her lap for the last remaining letter waiting to be burnt, she indulges in the thoughts of Mr Blond – Jake Hudson, her husband – and that turning point in her life.

Meeting Jake at the solicitor's office turned into coffee later that morning. She rambled on and blubbered about Carter Gales and Guy, about the horrible school years tortured at the hands of Sadie, and more so about what she thought of the Catholic Church because of the way it made her feel. To her surprise, Jake listened intently while she ranted about her grandfather.

The floodgates opened and she blurted out a lifetime of misery over a steaming hot cappuccino.

Jake said to her, "I saw first-hand the way he treated you, and others," and he went on to tell her that he tried to put a stop to it.

"That day you had an argument. Was that because of me?" Mattie asked.

"I'd been sent over to confront him," he answered and carried on, "I presented him with a signed statement from a previous employee but it didn't seem to bother him. I didn't realise how badly he was treating you though. If I'd known I would've done something."

She wanted to know the name of the person who'd made a formal complaint but refrained from asking. Time would eventually tell. It could have been any woman that Guy had slept with and then sacked. Thanking Jake for wanting to be chivalrous on that day, she told him to carry on.

"Guy laughed at me. Then I said that we were on to him about fraudulent transactions too, that we were building up the evidence, and he would be forced out of the company."

"So what did Guy say to that?"

"A few choice words. We both lost our tempers that day. In fact he even called security to try and stop me from entering the building because he knew why I was on my way, so by the time I reached his office, I was cross. I should've been more professional but I couldn't stomach him anymore. The company just couldn't prove what he was up to at that time." Jake looked at Mattie apologetically. "I'm sorry I never said goodbye or contacted you. Apart from being angry with Guy, I was under contract with a new company and prohibited from speaking with any one at Carter Gales." He gave her a reassuring smile. "I wanted to punch him. Believe me it was hard to walk out of that place without doing so. But I hear you got him where it hurts."

"How do you know about that? I only sent the email this morning," Mattie asked.

Jake held up his phone, tapped in a few commands, and showed her the email she'd sent to the directors at Dynamic Global Marketing. "I work for them, Mattie. I'm one of their directors."

"Oh, Janice mentioned something about you going to work for them but with what's gone on I totally forgot."

"The merger had been on the table since Bob was running the company. He gave it his full support, but we had our suspicions about Guy and knew that the merger couldn't go ahead with him at the helm. They moved me sideways rather than lose me because I told them that if Guy didn't go then I would.

Meanwhile, Jackson was on our side collecting evidence about him," Jake explained.

"But I thought Jackson was one of Guy's protégées, he was always sucking up to him and... Ah, I guess Jackson's behaviour explains a lot. Now I know why he wants to meet up with me this week. Another one who's got some explaining to do, I suppose."

"We needed someone on the inside to get close to Guy. He's good at his job and we trust him."

"But when Guy attacked me..." Mattie swallowed hard, struggling to talk about it again, then eventually found the courage to continue, "...During the attack he said he wasn't leaving. He was adamant about that!"

"We had to let Guy think that, but Dynamic had no intentions of keeping him in the business. Also, Jackson had at last provided us with damning evidence. I had to come to London to sign some documents and meet in private with Bob, and it just so happens that it's today that we planned to dismiss him. In fact, his father was going to deliver the bad news which you can imagine he was not looking forward to. Having to sack your own son? Then this happened to you, and well, he'll be gone by the end of the day, that's for certain. If he's got any sense he should be gone already."

"And that's why you couldn't contact me," Mattie finally understood. "It's all falling into place, why no one seemed to know anything about your departure. Not a single word, and I found it really hard..." She wanted to tell Jake how she truly felt about him and that this wasn't some sort of silly office romance. But when the conversation continued over yet another coffee and piece of carrot cake, the feelings they had for each other became evident.

That evening, Mattie slept for a solid twelve hours without

being disturbed by the sound of rush hour traffic going past the bedroom window or having to wake up to the sound of an alarm clock reminding her it was six thirty in the morning and that she had a gruelling journey and day at the office ahead. The nightmare she'd been trapped in had come to an abrupt end, and when she finally bounced out of bed, the future looked wonderful. There was no master plan now that she'd left Carter Gales, but seeing Jake Hudson and spending a few hours chatting about anything and everything had suddenly made her whole life seem a great deal brighter.

Jake spent that week in London clearing up Guy's mess, and before he headed back to New York, he took Mattie out for dinner. He laughed at how shy she acted during those brief office visits, knowing all the time that she liked him more than she cared to admit.

Then within a month, Jake had moved back to London to head the newly merged business.

Everything fit nicely in to place by the time he'd settled back into his city apartment, and soon after, he took Mattie to meet his parents in the village he grew up in. She learnt about his much younger sister Alice currently backpacking across Australia with some friends and of the black Labrador dog that for some obscure reason was known as Doodle. While they shared their life stories and the contrasts in their childhood, Mattie fast fell in love with the smart, good-looking, yet down to earth man.

On one occasion, Mattie plucked up the courage to ask about the beautiful blond lady he had brought to the Christmas party at Carter Gales.

"Bethany?" he mused. "I suppose she is beautiful, but I don't think of her in that way. She's a colleague's wife."

"Oh... I assumed that..."

To Whom It May Concern – *The Book of Letters*

"She was my date?" He finished the sentence for her. "No, nothing of the sort," and took another swig of red wine looking amused at the implied comment. "Marcus and Bethany came over for the weekend to visit her family, but Marcus fell ill. We should've been going out for dinner but he was throwing up all over the place and Bethany was all dressed up to go out. I was going to ask you to join us, but the plans had to change when Marcus phoned saying he needed to go to hospital. In fact, he ended up having his appendix out and was laid up in hospital for a while. That's why we left early."

"Can I ask, does Bethany not like Guy?"

Jake gave her a quizzical look.

"Well, she seemed to back off when he kissed her on the cheek, and I was wondering what had happened between them."

Though Mattie detested Guy as much as she did, Jake didn't hold back in providing her with the information she so desired. He snuggled up close to her as they sat in the nook of the small village pub in his hometown. He put his arm around her shoulders and pulled her close. "Guy wasn't a nice man and often made passes at inappropriate times, and to the wrong people. Let's say Marcus gave him a black eye that lasted a good few days when he was inappropriate towards Bethany one time."

"The night of the Christmas party, Guy made a pass at me in the office restroom of all places. Luckily Julie came to the rescue with a piece of mistletoe. I'm glad you were still outside even though you were with Bethany."

"You looked upset," he said and planted a soft kiss on her lips for reassurance. "I couldn't walk away knowing that something was wrong."

The immediate months that followed her unusual exit from

To Whom It May Concern – *The Book of Letters*

Carter Gales were exciting, although at times stressful when dealing with the aftermath of her departure. Bob had phoned as soon as he received the letter and Mattie agreed to meet him and his wife, contrary to what her solicitor advised. Mattie owed it to Bob, to look him straight in the eye and tell him what type of person his son was.

She kept up with the weekly therapy sessions, but as far as Joan was concerned, Mattie had drawn a line in the sand and was taking huge leaps of confidence. Prior to the meeting with Mr and Mrs Bob Carter, the therapist offered some advice. She asked Mattie to think about the consequences of her actions. Although the intentions were coming from the goodness of her heart, they may not be well received. Just because Bob was a kind boss it didn't mean that he would take Mattie's side and undermine his own son, she'd told Mattie. As for Mrs Carter, Mattie had no idea how she would react.

The knock-on effect of Guy's actions was devastating for him, Mattie realised this when she saw the sadness in Bob's eyes while she relayed all that he'd done since his retirement. She did not hold back and neither did she cry, finally finding the strength to be honest and relate all the facts calmly.

"His mother is appalled by all of this, the doctor has put her on sedatives," Bob told Mattie. "She wanted to meet with you and personally apologise but she can't stop crying."

Mattie said she knew how that felt.

"We didn't bring him up to treat people like this," Bob continued. "And I know he hasn't always behaved nicely, but I cannot believe he's done this to you. I thought that incident in Italy was a one-off after a drunken brawl, but I now realise that wasn't the case." He buried his head in his hands and begged for Mattie's forgiveness.

To Whom It May Concern – *The Book of Letters*

All that she could offer was a sympathetic hug when they parted.

Bob also met separately with Jake and the directors of Dynamic Global, not only to complete the merger, but so that Jake could present him with information on how Guy had set up offshore satellite companies and used those companies to create bogus accounts and transactions so that small amounts of money could be charged and transferred between them. This resulted in excess of a million pounds being taken from the company in the short time that Guy has been in charge.

Guy was the cause of his demise at Carter Gales and was soon disinherited by his father. The board of directors also took him to task over the fraud. Meanwhile, Mattie and a number of ex-employees had taken legal action against him for sexual harassment, and to Mattie's surprise, Cynthia was one of them.

Based on the gossip that spread around the office, Victoria, in a fit of rage, smashed up the apartment she shared with him. Mattie had underestimated Victoria's rage. She'd heard that Guy's fiancée had slashed the priceless pieces of artwork that hung in the penthouse and destroyed the contents of his designer wardrobe, shredding his Armani suits amongst other things. Then she took a knife and etched the words SEXUAL PREDATOR across the leather upholstered interior of his yellow Ferrari before pouring acid across the bonnet. According to Bob, Victoria had added insult to injury by taking a sledgehammer to the emerald and diamond engagement ring – a family heirloom – leaving it beyond repair. Victoria also sent Mattie a short letter of thanks saying that she'd saved her from a costly wedding and ultimately a costly divorce, and that her family had severed all connections with the Carters.

Mattie had managed to hit Guy where it hurt most – his

money, his prized possessions, and his reputation. She felt nothing for this person who'd put her through hell. He was despicable and she surmised that he was getting what he deserved from the people he treated so badly. But the bittersweet punishment was when Guy discovered that Jake was being brought back to head the London office.

From the day Mattie left Carter Gales and walked into the arms of Jake Hudson, her life changed for the better. What she once viewed as a great career opportunity had turned out to be her worst nightmare, but rather than blame her dead grandfather, Mattie accepted that the choices so far made in her adult life had ultimately been of her own doing. She had to admit that had she not gone to work at Carter Gales then maybe she would not have met Jake. With each therapy session, she was one step closer to discovering the real Mattie Barton, and she decided that working in an office was not to be her destiny after all.

With plenty of time on her hands, Mattie dug out her grandmother's recipe book and started baking again – happy to be back in the kitchen, up to her elbows in flour and icing sugar, creaming butters, and watching sponges rise in the oven. Mattie experimented with various recipes, making subtle changes to some, and respecting the rest of her grandmother's recipes, as they were perfect just the same. Now more content with life, and stronger to tackle whatever lay ahead with each passing day, she began to bake cakes for the local community centre as her grandmother had done. She felt proud in giving something back, even delivering a dozen cupcakes and saying thank you to the priest who months earlier had heard her confession.

"Oh, Jake, you startled me. I thought you'd gone to bed," Mattie says, jolted out of her reverie.

To Whom It May Concern – *The Book of Letters*

Jake pulls the stool close, sits down, then wraps his arms around his wife's shoulders and brushes his lips softly across her cheek until they find her lips.

"Mmm, just what I needed," she says and tells him one more letter remains to be read.

He looks down at the book titled *To Whom It May Concern*. "You know it's very late?" He nibbles on her ear, "The kids have been asleep for hours and..." his lips brush against her face as he speaks softly, sending goose-bumps up and down her back and her arms.

"I promise I won't be long. Anyway," she adds more seriously and with that air of tenacity he knows so well. "I want to convert the garage." Jake continues brushing his face softly against hers, nuzzling into her neck, then twisting strands of hair that have fallen loose from the woollen hat. The feeling is wondrous and she tingles all over with delight.

*It could be so easy to make love to you right now...*Mattie thinks. Instead she says to him, "You're not listening," and pulls away giving him a serious look.

"Yes I am. You said you want to convert the garage."

"Okay, you are listening. I've decided I want to set up my own cake business and publish my grandmother's recipes. So I need the space. It's about time I put my inheritance to good use."

"What took you so long Mrs Hudson," Jake mutters, trying his best to caress her neck, and though he's making good efforts at distracting her, the remark still pulls her up sharp.

"What do you mean?"

He repeats it and looks deep into his wife's eyes, as if to say, '*I know you so well Mattie.*'

Admonishing his look, she hastens to inform her husband that she only recently found the recipe book and even though it has

To Whom It May Concern – *The Book of Letters*

been a lifelong dream to do something like this, she felt that until now, it simply wasn't the right time.

Jake holds her hands. He slowly peels off the gloves and the bitter air bites her skin, but they soon warm up against his hot hands. He brings them up to his lips and kisses her finger tips ever so gently, making the blood rush even more through her veins, every nerve ending is reacting to his gentleness. "The recipes were all in your head. You have been making them for years."

"But I lost them and..."

"That's just an excuse. Only you have stopped yourself from doing this, but..." Jake pauses then lowers her hands, "I understand and I think it's a great idea." Then he stands up and starts to walk back to the house, holding up his hand to indicate she has five more minutes. When he gets to the kitchen door, he turns and says, "By the way, I like your new boots."

To Whom It May Concern – *The Book of Letters*

Twenty-Two

Damn him! Mattie feels hot and flustered by the little intimate disruption, and slightly indignant that Jake has noticed the new boots too. He knows what makes her tick. And as much as she wants to be by his side in their bed, there remains one letter to read.

Before she can read it, she lets go of the last of the tears she was holding back before Jake came outside, and they stream down her face breaking her heart.

Get a grip, Mattie! You've come so far. To ease the pain, she takes one last moment to reflect on the night's events – the book, now devoid of pages other than one more letter to remind her of the pain and suffering. *Time is a great healer*, Mattie understands, and realises how far her confidence has grown over the years, and as much as the letters have made her cry with emotions running high, she is aware that she's not that young person anymore and has no intentions of ever being like that again, regardless of what life throws her way.

It was early in her relationship with Jake that Mattie was introduced to his parents in the small village they eventually came to live in.

"Help yourself, Mattie, we don't stand on ceremony in this house." Mattie heeded Gail's instructions and took a dollop of mash from the serving terrine, followed by a spoonful of carrots. "Tell me about your family," Gail said.

Mattie had just filled her mouth with food and clearly had not thought this through prior to making the one-hour journey to meet

To Whom It May Concern – *The Book of Letters*

Jake's parents for the first time. What could she tell them about her dead mother, and then there was the matter of her father, her being illegitimate and all of that. However, she didn't want their pity. Swallowing her food she went on to say how her mother used to be a wonderful cook but a quiet and reserved person. Jake squeezed her hand under the table, helping her to relax. She knew at some point they'd ask, and eager to jump this particular hurdle and land on both feet, she briefly brushed over the details about her upbringing including the story of her Uncle Patrick who died tragically when he was a young man. Then with respect for her father, she said, "To be honest, I don't know anything about him."

"That's very sad, dear" said Gail.

But this time, Mattie didn't feel sad. She'd spent long enough being sad, and while she knew it would take a long time to deal with the fact that her grandfather had been responsible for her never knowing her own father, she decided not to leave her last remark so bluntly. "My father doesn't know I exist, so Jake and I have talked about it, and I think maybe now's the time I start looking for him." He gave her hand another firm squeeze. "I don't have much information to go on, but I'm going to give it a go."

"All Mattie has is his name and possibly where he lived," Jake said, adding that it wouldn't be an easy task, but it was an avenue they were prepared to investigate.

Ted raised his glass of wine, "Here's to finding your father, Mattie, and welcome to our family."

Mattie holds the red-leather-bound book in front of her with the last letter remaining. Ten years have passed and she's still no closer to finding him. Every avenue had been explored and each time she thought she was one step closer she ended up at a dead-end and taking two steps back. But Mattie had not given up hope.

The simmering wood in the chimenea glows just enough to shed light in the darkness so she can clearly read the letter. It is the one letter she actually wants to go through - word for word. To remind her of this bit of pain that she cannot let go of because of the terrifying thought that should she ever do that it would mean she's stopped looking for him.

~~**~~

To Whom It May Concern

Dear Dad,

Allow me to introduce myself, I am your daughter, Mattie.

Other than your name, I do not know anything about you. I don't even know where you are, but perhaps one day we will have the pleasure of meeting and I can tell you all about me and my life.

When my mother discovered she was pregnant she had to make a choice that would affect the rest of her life, as well as mine. It was a very difficult time for her. When I was a few years old she sent you a letter and a photograph and told you all about me. I don't know whether you received it. I'd like to think that you didn't and in that way I will not feel rejected because you never replied.

To Whom It May Concern – *The Book of Letters*

The only connection I have to you is the wooden jewellery box you handcrafted, along with the engagement ring that you gave to my mother when you proposed.

This is about as much as my mother would tell me before she died, but she never referred to me as a mistake, she never once wished that spending that night with you should not have happened. I know this to be true because her eyes lit up when she finally talked about you. I truly believe you loved each other very much.

I wish I could find you, and I wish I could tell you how much I have missed knowing you. I am certain that one day we will meet but for as long as I have the ring and the jewellery box, I will always have a piece of you in my life.

In the meantime, always believe that there is a place in my heart for you. You have and always will be my father.

With fondest love,
Your daughter Mattie

~~**~~

Mattie gently pulls the last letter from the red book, folds it neatly, places it in her pocket, and chucks the binder into the fire.

To Whom It May Concern – *The Book of Letters*

The chunks of wood already in the wood-burner have broken down under the intense heat and smoulder at the bottom but the last piece of fuel makes it flare up one final time. As she gets up from the chair and walks back to the house leaving her past behind, she listens to the remnants of the red leather-bound book crackle within the flames - a final reminder that she's left the past behind.

THE END

To Whom It May Concern – *The Book of Letters*

About The Author

This is the first book by Lou Conboye Taylor although there are many more being penned.

She lives in the elegant town of Lytham St.Annes with her husband, their youngest son (because he's too young to leave home) and their two dogs. Their eldest son has finally flown the nest but still costs them a fortune - as do most children.

Lou spent twenty years working full time for a textile firm then a further three years running a shoe shop while raising her family. When she finally realised that there was more to life than being stressed and running around like a headless chicken, she gave up work to be a full-time and less stressed stay-at-home mum.

Now she has the time to do what she has always dreamed of – to write.

For further information about the author – go to:-

www.louconboyetaylor.com

To Whom It May Concern – *The Book of Letters*

Copyright ©

2016 Lou Conboye Taylor

Lou Conboye Taylor has asserted her right under the Copyright, Designs and Patents Act 1988 to be identified as the author of this work.

Apart from use permitted under UK copyright law, this publication may not be reproduced, stored or transmitted, in any form, or by any means, without prior permission in writing from both the publisher and author. Unauthorised reproduction of any part of this work is illegal and is punishable by law.

ISBN-13: 978-1519668431
ISBN-10: 1519668430
BISAC: Fiction/Contemporary Women

This book is a work of fiction and all characters in this publication are fictitious. Any resemblance to actual persons, living or dead, is purely coincidental.